Letters From The Light

Shel Calopa

Inspired
Quill

Published by Inspired Quill: December 2019

First Edition

Contact the author through her website: www.shelcalopa.com

Chief Editor: Sara-Jayne Slack
Cover Design: Tony Coombes
Typeset in Minion Pro

Paperback ISBN: 978-1-908600-91-2
eBook ISBN: 978-1-908600-92-9
Print Edition

Printed in the United Kingdom
1 2 3 4 5 6 7 8 9 10

Inspired Quill Publishing, UK
Business Reg. No. 7592847
www.inspired-quill.com

For Heidi, the light of my life.

The Blazing Aurora VI
3307AD

ON THE OUTSKIRTS of an increasingly quiet Sol system, a lone vessel streaked through the starry skies.

It was a small ship. Nothing like the great migration arks which had set out from Earth generations earlier to seed the stars with ambitious, cocky humans. Not as bulky as the Drexus Corp supply vessels which had once flown a continuous loop between deep space mining colonies. And certainly not as streamlined as the pleasure cruisers that lay dormant in the ports of the once-thriving resort planets.

Perhaps tiny was a better description. Yet had anyone been tracking it from UNP command, they would likely have marked its movements as significant.

The tiny ship headed in from the Kuiper Belt on a trajectory to Earth, rapidly shedding velocity until it came to a full stop at a large Hicks classed asteroid. For ninety-two minutes it circled. It launched a satellite that bounced sixty-two forms of radiation at the rock, both standard and exotic. It released trace amounts of Polonium-210. Then it retrieved its satellite and took off in the direction of Neptune.

Definitely worth a threat evaluation. UNP reports should have been escalated up the line to central command. But no one was watching the stars anymore.

CHAPTER 1

Lower Broome
Australis 3308AD

AGGY WILCOCKS SURFACED, gasping and coughing. The surging flood had taken her by surprise, separating her from her family, pushing her right through town and slamming her against the tin veranda of the transit station.

Winded, she sucked desperately for air before diving down into the murky water in a frantic search for Uncle or the children. She came back up, still breathless and alone. Aggy dove again, pushing at the shifting debris. Lots of branches, a tractor battery, two dolls and some hydroponic drip-feeding tubes. Nothing important or useful.

Bobbing atop the water-line and blinking back tears, she squinted towards the horizon. The familiar landmarks were missing. No more grain silo or McWilliam's two-storey Pub. Even the town hall, where she had hoped to attend her first harvest dance with Stevie Bennet, had gone. Swirling, turgid water had swallowed everything and everyone; so quickly.

Aggy grabbed a wooden table that floated within reach and clung to it as she looked west for the source of the flood. It was impossible to see anything clearly in the white-topped turmoil.

Then, looking up she noticed the cavern's rocky roof approaching as she rose higher in the water. Unless she could find a way out soon, the vast underground cavern that had been her home would fill to become her watery tomb.

Behind her, the roof arched down into the water and merged into the back wall of the drowned transit station. All her life it had been there. A distant, largely ignored wall that defined the edge of their territory and kept them safe. Now it was a dam that was drowning them all.

She forced down a sob and reached out to touch it. The wall was slippery, cold to the touch and impossibly smooth. She clawed at it with her hands but couldn't get any purchase. Feeling above her head, she found a conduit that ascended from the recently submerged building beneath her feet, and clung to it.

Steady at last, she made herself recall Uncle's last instructions, hoping it would calm her down and help her find a way out.

What had he said? Think, Aggy, think! The stories of the world above us are true. Just need to survive this. Find… something? Find what? It had happened so rapidly she couldn't remember. JayMoe would know.

Aggy was about to dive down to search for him when she heard a low growl. She looked into the distance. Her heart screamed. Another wave loomed. There was only enough time to strengthen her grip and take two deep breaths.

The green wall of frothy water hit and, once again, she was submerged.

+ + +

Earlier that evening, as he did every night, Uncle Larry gathered the children in front of the fireplace.

'Who will receive the first song tonight? Maybe the one about the evil Master who lives below us just waiting for the chance to creep up and steal the supper of lazy children. Hey?'

A squeal from the youngest child caused giggles in the others. Aggy gave Uncle an exaggerated eye roll.

'Oh right, too scary for this time of night,' said Uncle.

'How about you, Johanna? Maybe you'd like to hear about your ancestors who dove into the oceans off Broome searching for pearls for their girlfriends. You know they held their knives clenched in their teeth. Hey?

'No, on second thought, we'd better not do that one. I'll have to explain the whole "ocean" concept to Macallum again. I haven't got it in me tonight.'

Aggy looked around the room at the five little faces, scary stories forgotten, each one beamed at Uncle hoping they would be the star of his latest epic ballad.

It was a nightly ritual they all loved, aside from teenaged Aggy, who thought it was ridiculous to fill the little kids' heads with false stories about the past and predictions of 'special futures.'

Uncle had sung her special future-song once. It was full of heroic battles in exotic lands and yet she was stuck farming dawn to dusk, every day. Surviving with her adopted uncle and five other orphaned children – trying hard to create a home but mostly just existing in a forgotten underground settlement.

With a nod to Uncle, Aggy left to do the evening livestock check.

Outside the cabin, she stopped to gaze up at the high brown ceiling. That was her nightly ritual. She was obsessed by the mystery of how the ancient engineers had discovered their cavern and transformed it into a bright, liveable colony. Aggy had always thought that it was like living inside a giant walnut shell.

They had fresh water for their hydroponics fields bubbling in at Gibson Falls in the west end. Wastes exited via the automated transit station to the east. In between, trillions of nanobots shared their world, unseen, scrubbing the atmosphere, maintaining the overhead lights and balancing the soil nutrients.

It was marvellous, aside from the fact that you could never leave. Unless you were water coming in, or refuse going out, you were destined to stay in the closed community.

Aggy broke her gaze and bent to tie her bootlaces. Something was wrong. Water was trickling everywhere, forming small rivulets in the dirt around her boots, and puddles in her footprints. She smelled something strange too. The air smelt metallic, tinny even, with a bit of a static feel causing a shiver to run across her back.

Then the sound hit – a deep roar came in from the west. When she stood, a powerful gust of wind hit the side of the little house, shaking the shingled roof.

Aggy assumed that the pellet condenser, which she and JayMoe had been working on earlier that day, must have malfunctioned. She turned to run around the corner of her house towards the noise only to collide with JayMoe, who came screeching on one wheel. The small droid grabbed her hand, pulling at her. He was jabbering so fast he made no sense.

'JayMoe! JayMoe, slow down. What's going on?'

Their front door had flung open. In two leaps, Uncle Larry crossed the old wooden porch and lifted up JayMoe. He too was talking fast, senseless gibberish.

She shook her head, thinking she must have injured herself smashing into JayMoe. She started back to the house when

Uncle dropped the droid and leapt over to grasp her head in his hands – his eyes full of desperation.

'I'm sorry it has to be like this,' he said hurriedly. 'I thought we had more time but the Master found us again. We should have been safe here! How did he find us?'

Aggy opened her mouth to respond.

'Don't try to speak. There's no time and you can't communicate in this mode anyway. I'm in hyperspeak – a condensed way of talking which slows down our experience of normal time. Our whole conversation will happen in just a second or two of real time.

'You see, when you were small, I arranged a little … well, implant for just this sort of emergency, but yours is for receiving only. You weren't old enough for a full implant.'

Uncle's tone told her more than his words. He was usually so annoyingly cheerful. Aggy felt her face blanching and her hands trembling.

'Oh honey, don't cry. You must be strong. I've got but an instant and then the link will be over. I need you to understand that my stories of the world above us are true. All of them! We're not alone. There is a great big world waiting for you on the surface above us. Aggy, you need to survive this and find it.'

He looked over her shoulder, his eyes growing larger as the rumbling intensified. It was almost impossible to hear what he said. Slow, distorted screams echoed from the direction of McGinty's homestead. Slimy wetness pushed hard at her ankles. She felt herself slipping but dared not look away from the certainty of Uncle's face.

'Go with JayMoe. Trust him. He's more capable than you know. Remember, look for the thin places. That's where you'll find the Light. It's the only way you'll find the truth about our world. Find the Light—'

Before he could finish his sentence, time abruptly sped back up to normal and an enormous wall of water smashed through the house, tearing her from Uncle and turning her world upside down.

Somehow, JayMoe had managed to latch onto her wrist. Together they were picked up by the wave and dragged away from the farm in a heartbeat.

Buffeted by the maelstrom of wreckage that had once been her home, they sped along at a furious pace. A wide-eyed horse floated by, frantically neighing and looking as though it was using its hooves to grasp part of a hen house. She reached across to grab its mane but it slipped backwards into the wash, twirled out of reach and slammed into a low-lying roof.

The neighbour's barn came into sight. She glimpsed Mr McGinty waving his arms out of the loft window. The water spun her away momentarily. When she was able to look back, she saw the crushing waves reduce the barn to rubble.

The town buildings were fast approaching. Aggy started to panic, but by the time they reached them, the depth of the water had increased enough that they glided right over.

With each surge Aggy expected to be crushed or drowned, yet somehow JayMoe managed to keep her afloat. He whirled from side to side, deflecting objects until they collided with the transit station where he finally lost his grip.

Aggy and JayMoe plunged deep below the water.

+ + +

On her last dive, out of breath and barely conscious, Aggy felt a mechanical hand latch onto her ankle and push her up to the surface. JayMoe popped up beside her, squeezing her torso to help clear her lungs.

'Thank you!' She could hardly get the words out through

the foam she was belching. 'Have you seen anyone else? The kids? Uncle?'

'Don't know. Gone probably.' The droid flailed about, unsuccessfully trying to use his spare hand to get a grip on the slippery wall.

'Gibson Falls. There must have been a malfunction at the waterfall!' Aggy yelled.

'No,' JayMoe said calmly.

'It must be. Where else could this all come from?' She swivelled her head, searching desperately for an answer. None of it made sense.

'No malfunction. Sabotage. The Master's coming for us.'

Aggy was glad JayMoe had slowed his speech down to normal, yet he still wasn't making sense. She suspected he had bumped loose a circuit.

They were still rising rapidly with the water level. Stretching up, Aggy was able to brush her fingertips across the ceiling.

Her surprise turned into a plan. 'JayMoe, it feels smooth, it's not natural rock! If it's manufactured – there might be panels we can pry loose!'

She banged at the surface above her but the ebbing water made it impossible for her to have any impact. She clawed in search of a join until her fingers were a bloody mess. JayMoe grabbed her hands.

'Wait, not yet. Save your strength.' He looked up at the arching roofline while he gently restrained her.

'Save my strength? For what? We're about to be sealed in a cavern of water! I don't know if you've noticed, you stupid farm droid, but there's probably no one alive except us. And given that I'm the only human here, technically there's only me! What should I be waiting for …?'

Aggy's near hysterical utterings were cut short by an ear-splitting explosion. A pressure wave pushed them both back. Aggy cracked her shoulder against the wall. The cavern lights went out.

'Waiting for that. Now we can go,' he said.

To Aggy's astonishment, the droid produced a small tool which he aimed at the ceiling and, just inches from their faces, cut a circle with a red beam of light. He peeled back a piece of the roof large enough for them to climb through. Then, reaching up, he pulled himself out of the water and dragged Aggy up after him.

She climbed onto the dry surface beyond and collapsed in a quivering heap, panting, as JayMoe used his tool to repair the hole and seal out the rising water.

'Here, take this. Larry said you would need it.' JayMoe passed her the small golden hip flask she'd often seen Uncle Larry carrying. She took a sip. Aggy couldn't even begin to imagine how he'd had the foresight to grab provisions when this crisis started.

A shiver took hold of her while she tried to process the enormity of what had just happened. She was wet, bruised and alone in a dark tube somewhere inside the roof of their cavern. Lower Broome was gone, along with Uncle Larry, Johanna, Macallum, Billy and Jason.

Everything she knew and everyone she loved was washed away.

JayMoe finished his repair job, changed the setting on his tool to lightkey torch, and used it to illuminate the walls around them as though assessing their surroundings. He stopped to highlight a set of numerical figures stamped into the wall.

'Come on, Aggy. I've got our bearings. We need to move now before we're detected. It's a long trek, although the odds of survival are quite adequate if we get going.' JayMoe held out his little metal hand to her.

Aggy was numb with fatigue and shock. She didn't know what to say or do, and then she remembered Uncle's last words. The little droid *had* already proven to be much more capable than he had any right to be.

She took one last swig out of the flask, passed it back to JayMoe and stood up.

'Lead on,' she said.

CHAPTER 2
Newbrunswick
3330AD

SAM'S FIRST THOUGHT was that he had stubbed his toe on another jagged rock. It happened often. Bruised toes and battered knuckles were a job hazard for anyone who worked shale in the pitch-black fields of Newbrunswick. This was especially true for Sam Eris, who was only twelve years old and naturally clumsy thanks to his birth gift – a twisted club foot with only two stubby little toes for balance.

'Sam! Why'd ya stop?' Pete Eris called out.

'Got a sharp one in me shoe Dad,' Sam yelled back.

'Alright. I'll work up the guide ropes and unload this batch in the cart. Meet ya there. Don't be long.'

Sam heard his father's footsteps crunch off into the distance.

They were almost at the end of another long day spent crawling around the bleak field that the Brothers had allotted them. Searching for the best shale rocks; surviving another day on their ability to guess mineral composition. A strong assay would net their haul a good price from Mr Smith, the town's fuel manufacturer. A weak assay meant empty dinner bowls.

Shale mining was cold, dirty work but it was work and, as the Brothers reminded them so very often, they were lucky to have it.

'You should offer a prayer of gratitude,' the Brothers had said. 'Many families don't have the gift of work. It is our holy Master's work and it will take the whole Eris family a step closer to the Great Illumination.'

Brothers say a lot about everythin', Sam thought, trying to ignore his back that groaned from over-bending. He didn't care what the religious Brothers' said; he hated hauling heavy rocks in the dark. Surely there was a place where the vista was uncertain and choices were possible.

Sam shook the daydream from his mind and took a step. A jarring pain reminded him that a rock was still stuck through the hole in his shoe. Not the first time. New shoes were the domain of Brothers. Even working children were only given second-hand shoes, usually patched together with bindings and rarely hole free even then.

He sat down, wiped his nose and ran his hands over his shoe. It was always difficult to manoeuvre objects under a lightless sky, using touch alone. Sam focused so intently on the stubborn stone that he missed the growing clatter of a cart tearing over the plain towards him.

'Watch out, Governor!' An urgent cry sounded only seconds before it was upon him, throwing a cloud of shale flakes into the air and clipping his outstretched leg.

Sam's world flashed painfully. One moment he was alone in the dark and the next he was blinded by a fierce light. Through squinted eyes, he caught a glimpse of large wooden wheels and the dangling legs of men, before he was hit again and thrown back into the comfort of darkness.

'I think we hit a boy, Gov. Do you want me to grab a lightkey and check if he's okay?' The voice sounded close enough to touch, although the bright light was gone so no face could be seen. Sam held his nose and tried not to breathe the gritty air. A sneeze would reveal his position.

'Hold your panic Guss. A worthless creature of the abyss is not our concern. Let's be on our way,' said another deeper voice that had a hard edge to it, like it belonged to someone used to giving orders.

'As you wish, Governor Pallas.' The sound of the cart quickly receded, taking the voices with it.

Sam was stunned. It was over so fast he wasn't even convinced that it had really happened. *Voices in the field? A Governor?* It must have been the light-devils the Brothers always warned about. Although they were said to roam the distant darklands, not their shale fields.

Confused, he picked himself up, prayed that he was facing the right direction, and tried to run towards his father, but the rock was still tormenting his foot. A hopping shuffle was all he could manage. His knee smarted as well; at least that was some proof that the collision had been real.

A few steps further and he had to stop. He rubbed his knee, then reached down and finally yanked the shale rock out of his shoe. Weird. The rock felt unusually smooth on his fingertips. He turned it over in his palm and tested its weight. It was heavy for its size; definitely not shale.

'Ya right, boy? Did I hear a voice? Is someone out here?' His father sounded like he was running towards Sam. He was still some distance away but his tone sounded determined, and as his pace was increasing, his cough was worsening.

'Sam, speak ya position!' he yelled hoarsely.

Sam had to think quickly. Who would ever believe a story

about a wagon in the field? And how would he even begin to explain the light? His father would assume he was daydreaming again, which would lead to yet another belting for time-wasting. Even worse, it would sadden his mother to hear about his foolish behaviour.

'Um, I don't think there's anyone out here. Probably just heard me yell when I tripped. Me bag fell open and rocks went everywhere. I was cussin' coz I had to pick 'em all up ag'in. Sorry Dad, comin' now.' Sam shouted his lies as he secured his shoe and hurried towards his father's voice.

'Seriously! Ya gotta try harder, mate. Better have enough left in that bag for us to meet quota or ya'll get it. Come on, I'm goin' home.' Sam sighed gently, and felt his body loosen as his father changed direction.

As he followed the sound of Pete's receding cough, Sam slowed down. He remembered the little lightkey torch in his pocket that Brother Vincent had given him in secret.

It was an old one, small and rusty, held together with black tape, but strong enough to give him a handy cocoon of light that extended as far as he could reach his arms. Beyond that everything remained pitch black.

It was supposed to be used for reading in his room and emergencies only. Not that anyone would know. A Brother could walk past an activated lightkey and see nothing. Light didn't travel far in Newbrunswick.

Sam flicked the switch with his right thumb and blinked as it lit the object in his left hand. He'd been correct. It was not a rock in his shoe. More like a cylinder of metal, about the length of his finger with precise edges and a mirror-like surface. It had a loop at the bottom and writing etched into the side: -55.58, 148.97TL.

What does that mean?

Sam could think of no other item that finely machined.

Surely nothing so perfect existed in Newbrunswick. Not in the Brothers of the One True Way Church that stood in the centre of town with all its holy relics. Not amongst Mr Smith's tools. Maybe not even in the bell tower itself, which they all relied upon to guide them through the hours.

He moved it in and out of the lightkey's influence several times. Marvelling at the magic of making the item disappear and reappear in and out of the darkness. It dawned on him that he could do the same trick with his dinner if he dared bring the lightkey into his mother's kitchen.

'C'mon Sam, it'll be six bells soon. Do I have to get me belt out?' his father yelled, coughing his disappointment.

Sam discreetly pocketed the torch and the strange cylinder, before he hurried to the guide ropes and used his hands to pull himself towards their cart.

The secret lightkey and the new object would only worry his father, which would almost certainly land Sam a beating and make Pete turn it over to the Brothers. It wasn't that his father was overly religious, like so many of the other townsfolk, he was just a realist.

His father wouldn't understand the importance of the object, but he *would* feel honour-bound to report this strange find to the Brothers before they found out about it through some other source.

Pete always said, 'Ya better to offer sumpthin' up than bein' found out.'

Once the Brothers discovered it there was no chance Sam would be able to keep it. But he simply *had* to keep it. It couldn't be a coincidence that he had found it. Sam could *see* how beautiful the little cylinder was in a way that his father could never comprehend.

Because Pete, like everyone else in town aside from the Brothers, was totally blind.

+ + +

It had taken another two bells to push the cart along the rails into town and offload the haul into Mr Smith's yard. Payment negotiation had been swift though; it was a good haul. They would eat for at least another three days.

By the time they got home, it was almost nine bells. Sam raced into their little house. It was just six paces from the door, past the stairs to the kitchen table and another four paces through the kitchen to his mother who was noisily doing dishes in the sink by the back door.

He kissed his mother's cheek, hung up his coat on a peg by the rubbish pail and returned to the table to sit on his crate and gulp down hot vegie soup.

'Hey, ease up son or ya'll choke,' his mother said lovingly.

Sam did as he was told and stopped chewing for a moment. Sarah Eris was the soft mirror of his father. She had a ready supply of hugs and a lilt to her voice that always felt like home. He could never refuse her requests.

The incident with the light devils still troubled him. As soon as his father was asleep, he would tell her all about the cart. Sarah would know what to do, or at least have a soothing word on the worrying topic. Without speaking, he reached up, found her hand and placed it on his shoulder. It caught her attention.

'Do ya wanna talk about ya day, son?' she asked.

'Don't molly coddle 'im, woman. Man's got to grab what's 'is while he can. Let 'im eat,' said Pete, coughing up the smell of shale dust before he too wolfed down the veggie broth.

'Well since yer both too busy to speak, maybe ya can listen. There's news. Brother Vincent called in not long ago. There'll be no lessons for ya tonight, Sam. Yer to present yaself to the Archbrother. Didn't say why. He just insisted that ya be washed and in church right after dinner.'

Sam didn't need to see his father's face to know that he was stunned by the news; the clattering of his spoon as it landed on the table was proof enough. No one in the Eris family had ever been summoned to church at night before and none had ever spoken to an Archbrother.

'What have ya done now, boy?' growled Pete Eris.

CHAPTER 3

One True Way Church, Newbrunswick

SAM STOOD MOTIONLESS, as did Brother Vincent by his side. The church always delivered good news in the daytime with witnesses. A late-night audience with the town's highest authority, His Eminence Archbrother Dorcha, couldn't be good. Endless seconds ticked by without a word.

When they had entered earlier, ahead of his eminence, Sam had scanned the room. It was bigger than his whole house and yet empty aside from a narrow red rug leading to an oversized wooden throne at the far end. The throne was raised up on a plinth and backlit by heavy metal braziers. Above it an enormous three-panelled painting showed heroic Brothers leading the great exodus of ancient times.

As with all church buildings, the air was heavy with incense. A faintly perceptible jingle of prayer bells could be heard from a distant room. It was even heated; it seemed like everything was designed to be foreign and intimidating. Sam felt his stomach sink.

Somewhere a clock chimed and finally his eminence leaned forward to speak. 'So, Sam, what do you think brings you here at this noble hour?'

Sam was surprised that the first question was addressed to him. He had hoped that he could remain quiet and let Brother Vincent do the talking. Vincent always seemed to know what to say.

'Your Eminence, I understand that—' Vincent started to speak but was silenced by a sharp wave of his eminence's hand.

'I will hear from the boy first,' he said firmly.

'Ya Em'nence,' Sam mumbled. He stared at the floor, hoping he was mimicking his blind community well enough. 'I'm a shale boy, just twelve. Don't know nothin', Sir.'

'You have already begun his training, Brother Vincent? Teaching him respect is a good start.'

Sam heard Vincent inhale as if to speak but his eminence continued.

'No need to feign innocence, I know all about your ambitions for the boy. Is this not the very matter we are here to discuss? Shall he be one of us or not? Shall we elevate him to serve the Glorious Cause or cast him back down to wallow in his pathetic wretchedness? That is your question, am I correct? Now you may speak, Vincent.'

'Essentially, yes, Your Eminence.' Vincent fell to his knees. 'I should have known this matter would reach your holy ears. I apologise most humbly for not seeking your wise council earlier.'

'Rise Brother Vincent. No need for such formality.'

Sam stiffened, even he knew informality was the trap.

'Well Vincent, what aspect of this boy makes you think that he is suitable for holy orders and why have you wasted years teaching him? As he evidences himself, he is only an ignorant shale boy and a lame one at that.'

His eminence rapped his ancient knuckles on his chair to prevent any interruption. 'His ignorant family barely makes a living fumbling out on that field each day. What makes you think this cripple has anything to offer the Holy Church?'

'Your Eminence, this is true, and yet the Spirit has shown me great potential in this boy. He is very smart. He has learned well with only minimal guidance from myself.'

'If he is as smart as you say,' said his eminence, 'then why could he not concoct a way to avoid persecution by his peers or at least accept the natural order – that he *should* be persecuted? Look at him. How can he be a Brother leading people on their path to the eternal light when he cannot even light his own way? A rock-boy trained into priesthood? Pathetic – unheard of!'

Sam winced. The 'rock-boy' defamation was particularly well-aimed. It was a favourite of the village boys who had persecuted him to the point that he had had to abandon school only two weeks after starting.

Sarah had advised ignoring them. She had said that he was so much more than his job and that one day he would show them all. Now, hearing his eminence's words, Sam felt the truthful weight of the taunt. Even with eyes cast down, he noticed his eminence shift his position on the throne, wrapping his robes tighter around his ankles as if protecting himself from rock-boy contamination.

'I will concede to your wisdom. He may not be the one to *lead* our people to the light but perhaps still he has a role to play in …' Vincent paused briefly, '*supporting* them as they journey. He will have compassion for our people, for he has known true sorrow.'

'Compassion?' His eminence spat out the word. 'What good is compassion when our people are poor and lost in the blinding darkness of this tortured world? What they need is discipline!

'Does the Holy Word of the Third Coming not tell us that our people are as sheep that need to be herded with a steel crook? Do they not need shearing of their comfort lest they lay down, blindly ignorant, in their own filth? Is this not exactly why we find ourselves in this barren, unseeable world?

'The only compassion we can offer, Vincent, the only thing they understand is the harshness of being kept shorn so they are eternally cold. They need to feel their discomfort to keep them moving on the path to the Great Illumination.

'Only deprived shall they be saved. Only stripped of all fleshly comforts shall they appreciate the feebleness of their true condition and only then will they righteously cling to the promises of the Prophets. Is that not why He saw fit to darken Australis – to force us to find new ways to virtue?'

Sam could hear his eminence pounding out his tirade on his armrest.

'Harshness is true kindness, Vincent. Compassion should be left for the next life where they will receive it in abundance from the Angels of Light in the Holy Realm.' Finally finished, he leaned back, his ancient chest heaving from exertion.

'Your Eminence is wise, of course,' Vincent replied, prostrating himself until his forehead touched the hem of the Archbrother's vestments.

'Therefore, you must agree that this boy can *never* be a shepherd. He is unfit.' His eminence's voice gleamed with victory. 'I don't know what you were thinking. The matter is resolved. Return the wretch to his parents.'

Vincent started to rise, then stopped half out of his bow.

'You hesitate? Vincent, is there more that you would say? Perhaps you request penance for your impertinence?' His eminence's voice dripped the bitter juices of superiority. 'You know what you need to do to clear your heart. Now go.'

'Just one more question. Please indulge me, Your Eminence?'

Sam risked a glance to see Vincent looking directly into the Archbrother's milky eyes that sat deep in sunken sockets, as though they were being slowly sucked back into his skull.

'If the shepherd is to navigate the abyss and lead our sheep to the promised illumination then surely that shepherd must be able to *see*?'

Immediately the confident victory left his eminence's voice. It was steely cold. 'You mean to tell me that—'

'Yes. The boy is sighted. Look up, Sam. Show his eminence exactly why you are suited to lead the flock.'

Brother Vincent was the only person Sam had ever looked in the eye. A lifetime of pretence amongst a dark village of the blind made the act of eye contact foreign to him. Sam couldn't look up. He just stood still, wiping his sweaty palms on the sides of his pants.

Vincent nudged him with his foot and Sam knew he had to put an end to his act. He slowly raised his head. Blinking with anxiety he looked first to the old man's chest then further up to his face.

His eminence recoiled into his throne, gripping the armrests so hard that his knuckles visibly strained against their flaky grey flesh.

'Green eyes? Vivid green eyes in a brown face? How is this possible?' he whispered, looking back and forth between Sam and Vincent. 'Surely this is the work of the bleak one? Did this child not go through the blessing as an infant?'

'Yes, he did. I officiated at the ceremony.'

'You worked alongside the Governor, yet he did not notice? How could you allow this to go unreported?' his eminence asked, now in a mere whisper.

'The holy will.' Vincent stopped to exhale. 'When I saw his twisted limb and envisioned his pitiful future, mercy filled my heart. He had unusually pale skin for a Newbrunswick boy. Then I looked into his eyes and I knew the Spirit had other plans. You can see for yourself – his eyes are green like the grass of the great plains that once covered our beloved homeland.

'It was a sign that Sam is special. I could not allow him to finish the ceremony. I hid him under a blanket and the Governor passed him over. No one noticed. Still no one knows, not even his family.'

His eminence closed his eyes in contemplation and gently voiced his thoughts. 'Missing the Governor's blessing is a grave sin. Still, what if the boy was indeed touched by the Spirit? How else could he have those eyes? In all my decades of service here, I have never seen a single child with anything other than grey washed-out eyes. Even amongst the Solarans it's not common; their eyes are mostly blue. How is it possible?'

His eminence was quiet for a long time.

Sam dared not speak.

At last, his eminence turned to look at Vincent.

'I concur the eyes are an indicator of the Spirit. Have there been any other signs? Any other confirmation of the Spirit's intervention in his life?'

'Yes. There was the time he went into the field alone as a child.'

'I remember a child being lost. Half the town went out searching. That was him?'

'It was. A young frightened child, chased into the fields by bullies, had little chance of survival. But in Sam's most desperate hour, the Holy Spirit illuminated the way home to safety. Surely that is all the sign we need.'

Sam was left profoundly confused by what he heard. He

had never been lost. Vincent had manufactured a lie to placate the Archbrother. To be found lying was the worst of all sins for Brothers. Vincent was risking his exalted place in the Illuminated Afterlife.

His eminence breathed deeply and smiled. 'Indeed, you have saved a precious and blessed child. Praise be your forethought. Lean forward and I will give you my blessing.'

Sam took half a step forward but it was Vincent who bowed.

'In the name of the Holy Spirit who guides us home to the Master, I bless you Brother Vincent, and bestow on you the honourable burden of mentorship. Train him well so that one day he may join our ranks and lead us all to the Light of Salvation.' He made the sign and indicated that Vincent should rise.

'And now, there is only the issue of reputation. How can we confer this honour on Sam without revealing his gift of sight? If we do not reveal his gift, we will be seen to be elevating the unworthy. We do not wish to open those doors.' His eminence scoffed.

'A ruse. An accident? Yes, I think we shall stage an accident – a fire. We shall burn his home and people will think he has perished in the blaze. During the funeral you will secret Sam to the Sombra Abbey diocese in Sydney. A lighted city will strengthen those eyes, which will not be so unusual in a big population. Mind you, keep his head down so that none shall question his origin.

'The parents? Hmmm. The parents can be taken into the church as cleaners. We will keep them safe with us for the rest of their days. You can trust us to look after them as they deserve, young Sam. This matter is closed. You may leave.'

His eminence held out his ring and smiled smugly. Vincent moved forward to kiss it and waved Sam forward to replicate the action.

'Send in the Civil Sisters as you leave, Vincent. They will need to take a message to our Sydney Brothers so that they may prepare for your arrival.'

'Thank you, Your Eminence.' Vincent bowed once more as they backed out of the room through the heavy doors. Sam breathed deeply and the echo of his thumping heart receded.

In the antechamber, they passed two Civil Sisters. Sam glanced over. It was forbidden to do so, but it had been such a long confusing day that he briefly lost touch with convention. Despite the heavy hoods that shrouded their faces, their body shapes suggested one was the senior and one the junior, possibly a pre-teen like him.

The narrow passageway required them to pass within a short distance. As they moved around each other, the smaller Civy looked up for a moment, also breaking the eye contact rule and showing Sam that his assumption about her youth had been right.

She had a rosy glow to her cheeks, a small upturned nose and strangely piercing green eyes, the colour of young kale sprouts just like his. As she smiled, he noticed a slight dimple on one of her cheeks. He couldn't help smiling in return although he worried about the sudden heat in his cheeks.

'Sam!' said Vincent, regaining his attention. The second Civy and Vincent had both stopped walking and were giving him serious looks.

'Advance, Harper,' snapped the second Civy. Harper averted her eyes, withdrew into her cloak and fell into line behind her superior. As they entered his eminence's office, they both bowed.

Just before the door closed Sam saw his eminence press a few coins into the elder Civy's palm along with a note. He moved so close to the Civy, to whisper his instructions, that he was practically inside her hood.

Sam shivered. He was glad his path would lead to Brotherhood. The Civy's vows of poverty and strict deprivation would be too much to endure. Spending a lifetime running errands for a few pitiful coins was almost as bad as shale mining. Almost.

+   +   +

After Vincent, Sam and the Civies had left, Dorcha summoned undersecretary Spectra.

'You heard all of that?' asked his eminence.

'Yes, Your Eminence. I assume you would like me to handle the arrangements?' Spectra asked, stooping, hoping Archbrother Dorcha perceived the gesture as humility.

'Indeed, with one exception. The father is all but consumed by shale cough. He won't last long enough to bother us. Regarding the mother, however, she is known to be outspoken and well-liked. Ensure she does not survive the fire. The boy must not know yet. When we are ready, Brother Vincent will feel the heavy repercussions of his insolent actions.'

'As you wish, Your Eminence,' said Spectra, smirking as he retreated into the shadows.

+   +   +

In the early hours of the following morning when all prayers had been prayed and the only sounds were the occasional echoing snore and the gentle whispers of zephyrs whipping down the lanes outside, Spectra slipped unseen through a secret door in a rarely used passageway of the church's administrative wing.

He closed the door behind him without a sound and took out the small golden communication device from a concealed robe pocket. Despite being confident that none could hear, he delivered his message in a barely audible voice.

'Spectra here, Master. Inbound report. Transition status priority one.'

'Why do you request an unscheduled report?' asked a stern but familiar voice from the other end of the communicator.

'Apologies Master, but I have news of great import. A seer has been identified amongst the flock – a young boy called Sam Eris. He is to be escorted to Sydney tomorrow to begin Brotherhood training. Civil Sisters have been allowed to co-own this knowledge. Request instruction?'

When there was no immediate response Spectra continued, 'Surely Dorcha's actions are contrary to our interests? Requesting urgent permission to terminate Dorcha, Brother Vincent, the seer and Civies.'

'Belay that action, Spectra. Dorcha is ignorant of his role in my plans, as are you. I have a new operative embedded amongst the Civies. You will know her as Glare. In time, she will deal with Dorcha. Return to your post and await further orders. That is all.'

'As you wish, Master. Spectra out.' He nodded automatically as he signed off, so ingrained was his habit of genuflection to authority. You never knew where the Master had eyes planted.

He severed the link, closed his communication device and scurried back to his room.

CHAPTER 4
Chatsworth Manor, Sydney 3338AD

WHEN HARPER FOUND herself stationed in the stone foyer of the Governor's stately home during Sydney's brightest social event in a decade, she needed to call on all her training to contain her excitement. It didn't help that the stimulant she had taken earlier, to help her stay alert through her shift, was making her jumpy. She silently repeated mantras to calm her pulse.

> *Open eyes, open ears, closed mouth, no fears*
> *Open eyes, open ears, no distractions, all clear*
> *Open eyes, open ears, closed mouth, no fears*
> *Open eyes, open ears, selfless service we revere*

Inside, Matthias Pallas, a surgeon and Sydney's beloved regional governor, was celebrating the twenty-first birthday of his twin sons, Mark and Kohl, with a three-day Solaran lighting ceremony. It was a grand excuse for match-making and boasting of glorious days long past.

Officially, the Pallas' status made their party *worthy* of Civil Sister attendants. There would be guests needing support after the treacherous trip from Melbourne, Brizzie and other cities across the darkened peninsula. Unofficially, the Pallas' status made their party of *interest* to the Civies. It was a rare, high-level opportunity to observe the interplay of the Solaran ruling elite.

Open eyes, open ears, closed mouth, no fear
Open eyes, open ears, knowledge gained throughout the
years

Despite her twenty-two years, Harper had worked hard to attain the privilege of attending such a high-status event. She never missed her Solaran genealogy lectures and devoured old strategy texts. Her trainers frequently commented on her gift for recognising subtle nuances in social interaction.

Once, at a lesser party, Harper had witnessed a rising young lawyer returning from the garden in a dishevelled state. He had been followed swiftly by a High Court Judge re-buttoning his breeches. As the lawyer moved into the crowd, he stopped for barely an instant to wink at an Archbrother. The Civies had been very interested in that observation.

On the way to the Pallas party she had told herself that it was the perfect night for another insight. So far, however, her night had been spent in silent observation while her managers, Sister Patricia and Sister Gabeere, carried out duties around the manor.

All night she waited in a traditional sentinel pose, her hair and hands hidden in her heavy grey cloak. One foot was positioned slightly ahead of the other, signalling her readiness to dash into action for any menial task.

'Have you seen the Reids' plans for a light barrier

extension … thrilling …'

'… the Dean of the Archaeology School is postulating the arbour was once full of water, not trees. Such a ridiculous notion. Water in Sydney Arbour!'

Harper observed it all, inhaling their artificial pheromones and memorising their names. She noted who arrived together and, much more importantly of course, who left together.

'… then Alec proposed right there next to the horse float at dusk, if you can believe it, in a shadow! No wonder she turned him down cold. That's why she's been up dancing on the podium all night. She's trying to show him what he could have had if he'd done it the proper way …'

Harper smiled inwardly. When they spoke openly despite her presence, she knew she performed her role well.

Open eyes, open ears, closed mouth, no fear
Open eyes, open ears, let their ignorance show their
fears

+ + +

Around midnight a pair of lightly scuffed black waiter's shoes appeared in her narrow vision of the floor.

'Ah-hem!' The owner of the shoes was apparently trying to gain her attention. The hallway had been empty for a few minutes so Harper took a risk and looked up.

It was a short male waiter, hair about as clean as his unpolished shoes, with a soiled kitchen cloth in one hand and a small wicker basket half-filled with cake off-cuts in the other. Poking out of the top of the basket was a little jug of what she imagined would be overly sweet dipping sauce.

'The Lady Pallas requested I bring ya a mid-point snack. Cook had these ta spare, hope they're not too fancy for ya.'

Harper did not trust herself to respond. After four hours of perching in rigid attendance, she was beginning to feel the pull of fatigue and was surprised when she felt herself momentarily swayed by the unthinkable temptation of Solaran scraps. She looked back down and sped up her mantras to regain her self-discipline.

'Well, do ya want it or not?' asked the waiter impatiently.

'… open eyes …' Harper clamped her mouth shut when she realised she had started to mutter her mantra aloud.

'Open what? Look, I haven't got time for this; I've got *important* people to look after. Eat it, don't eat it. Couldn't care less.' He dropped the basket on the edge of the seat next to her and stormed off down the hall, not even stopping when it toppled over, spilling its contents behind him.

Seconds later Sister Patricia re-entered the foyer from an adjoining room. Harper was humiliated to be caught leaving her post to retrieve the food.

'Explain!'

'I'm sorry Sister, a waiter brought it, then it dropped and—'

'Say no more. I was planning to assign you an errand tonight anyway. This can be your first. Clean this up and take it to the waste behind the kitchen where it belongs. You have memorised the floor plan, haven't you?'

Harper could only nod, anything else may have spilled her waiting tears.

'Right then, I'll cover for you here. Keep your head down and don't let anyone see you binning their food. We mustn't appear ungrateful. Got it? Hurry back!'

The only acceptable answer was to execute the orders. She scrambled to pick everything up and retreated down the hallway.

Harper made it to the bins without incident but on her return, she was confronted by a squad of six large constables in combat gear, clanging down the hall towards her. Their combined girth took up the width of the hall in an intimidating show of masculine force.

Panicked, Harper looked through the closest door in search of an easy exit and pulled back as she heard angry shouting. Too late. The constables were upon her and she was forced through the doors into the kitchen, right into the path of the angry cook.

'Who the hell are *you*? Someone get her out! As if I don't have enough to deal with,' he said before redirecting his diatribe to the constables who had fanned out in the doorway.

'Well it took ya long enough. I've got hundreds of guests waiting to be fed and I have to deal with bloody intruders. They're under the bench. Take 'em all into custody, even her!'

Harper pulled her hood forward to hide her distress.

'But chef, ya can't. She's a … a *Civy*!' said a wide-eyed female cook, pointing a shaky finger at Harper.

'I don't care if she's a Pallas heir. This is *my* kitchen. It's the biggest night of me career and I want her gone!'

One of the constables took a menacing step towards Harper. The young cook, who had spoken in her defence, intercepted him.

'I'll take care of this one,' she said, gently pushing Harper between the constables and out the door. Strangely, she hesitated and made a slight curtsey to Harper before she returned to the kitchen.

Loud screaming signalled a return to chaos in the kitchen. Apparently, the intruders were not giving in easily. Harper made a speedy retreat to her foyer post.

+ + +

The night stretched on and although she was happy to be returned to surveillance, eventually Harper grew bored and restless. When she found herself alone, some hours later, she couldn't resist taking a quick sideways glance through the crack in the door to the ballroom beyond.

The Pallas party was a heavy mix of smoky spectral hallucinogens and pumping aural vibes. There were new age acro-art installations morphing across the vaulted glass and steel ceilings that had been installed to modernise the ancient ballroom.

In typical Solaran fashion, the girls wore body-hugging sheaths of luminous hues that reflected the gaudy light show. Necklines were low, breasts were large and heels were impossibly high. Body paint was standard and ankles were adorned in rainbow gems. They looked like glittering exotic fish as they shimmied to the beats on the dance floor.

For the boys, fashion was all about hair. Wide moustaches were laced with jewels and massive beards trailed down bare, muscled chests. The wealthiest bachelors sported manes that stood half a metre above their head, dangerously spiked and flashing metallic colours as though they had their own personal thunderstorm overhead.

Harper couldn't help but notice the impossibly handsome Kohl Pallas gyrating just inside the door. His bare chest was a smooth golden tan that glistened from the heat of his birthday groove. Red breeches barely restrained his muscled thighs as he thumped and leapt to the beat.

After a few minutes the music paused and the dancing stopped. The birthday boy puffed and ran his hand through his wild auburn mane. Then he threw his head back to laugh a throaty laugh at the jokes of his unseen dance partner. She had never seen anyone so free in their body before. It was as if he owned the world.

Harper, overwhelmed, lost all sense of proprietary and inched forward to get a better look at the mesmerising Pallas heir. At that same moment, Kohl happened to glance her way. His deep emerald eyes were so intense she couldn't break from his stare.

For less than a heartbeat they connected, yet for Harper, it was enough to tilt her world. He didn't look past her as all other Solarans did. He looked directly at her – into her – like there was a flash of recognition. All her training evaporated and she allowed her hood to slip back a little so that her blonde hair could be seen.

Then, just as quickly as it had begun, the moment evaporated. The music restarted and, with an almost imperceptible shake of the head, his beautiful chiselled face morphed into a frown of disdain. With a sharp kick of his boot he slammed the heavy door shut.

Harper remembered to exhale. She hoped no one else had noticed her second error of the evening. She replaced her hood and resumed her surveillance until the party was over and the Civies were dismissed.

+   +   +

The next morning the alarm went off at 6.15. Harper was home in Veruda Keep outside Sydney. Her stimulants had worn off and her muscles ached. The heavy pull of her soft bed meant it would take more than one cup of caff and a sonic shower to get going.

A sharp rap at the door roused her and in popped the curly head of Harper's best friend and fellow senior acolyte.

'Hey, sleepyhead! You coming to morning drills? You know Sister Pat will make you do double if you're late.' Bess loved training.

'Not asleep just resting. Big night. Need a few more minutes.' Harper yawned and rolled away from the bright light shining into her room.

'Sounds interesting. I want to hear more after breakfast. Don't take too long. Don't want to do a "Lola". You know how she cops it from Pat, "Late again, Lady Lola? You're not a lazy lightbearer snoozing to noon, lass. Slacking is for men. Hike those skirts up, bend those knees, reach up, slow down, speed up and give me another forty – hup, hup, hup!"'

Bess did her best imitation of Sister Pat's military drilling – all jerky and masculine, in complete juxtaposition to her flowing grey robes.

'Hup, hup, hup, knees up ladies ...' Then she shifted into her favourite dance.

Harper knew Bess thought it was interesting but to her, the dance looked more like a constipated chicken. She clucked and Bess headed back into the hall in mock indignation, calling out over her shoulder, 'Don't miss breakfast!'

Breakfast *did* smell good. Almost as good as the baked goods the Pallas' boys had gifted their departing guests in the early hours.

To snap herself out of her girlish fantasies she looked up at the Civil Sisters missive etched on a platinum plaque on the lilac wall behind her bed. It was always a good reminder of the True Way.

Only pure eyes can know truth. Only truth bestows
power.

Harper sat up, cleared her throat and yawned. She crossed her legs, closed her eyes and cleared her mind for morning contemplation.

When she was deep in meditation, she began her ritual of mentally scanning through the levels of Veruda Keep. From the senior Sisters' apartments in the highest turrets past steaming saunas, holo-vid entertainment rooms, gyms and dining rooms in the middle to the official reception rooms on the ground level, the only place outsiders were ever allowed access. There, the Sisters kept the furnishings meagre, the floor cold and the lightkeys always extinguished.

The Civies believed that the darkness kept any visiting Brothers feeling vaguely superior, as the Brothers knew they could at least afford braziers in their reception rooms.

Of course, their other visitors, the Solarans, didn't need to *feel* superior; they knew they were. Still it was Civy tradition to keep up the illusion of poverty and servitude. The Sisters didn't mind inconveniencing them just a little by forcing them to bring their own light.

Over the years, there had been a few Solaran leaders who suspected that the Civies might actually have access to some limited technologies like the odd lightkey or thermal wand. Those leaders never lasted long; scandal was a terrible hindrance to progress through Sydney society.

Certainly, no one guessed that the Civies' greatest secret lay right beneath their feet – miles upon miles of tunnels.

Open eyes, open ears, closed mouth, no fears,
Open eyes, open ears, more powerful than we yet
appear.

Harper breathed deeply and released herself from the ritual. She opened her eyes and stretched once more. With a glance at the missive over her bed she crossed the room, unrobing as she walked.

She unfastened the little gold 'TL' necklace she always wore, placed it on her dresser and skipped off to the bathroom. The sonic shower was as good a first step as any on her daily journey towards purity and power.

CHAPTER 5

Chatsworth Manor

KOHL PALLAS ABHORRED all things Civy. 'Mother, can't you see that there is something inherently creepy about them?' As usual, his mother Lady Pallas and his brother, Mark, showed no interest in his conspiracy theories.

'Look at the insidious way they have wormed into our best families. There's something going on. I know it. They disappear in and out of our shadows like grey ghosts!'

Kohl shivered at the thought of the way they moved, swiftly and evenly, feet shuffling unseen beneath their faded robes. Their stride was more like gliding; it made his skin crawl.

'Did you see that young Civy in the alcove last night? She actually looked at me. In the eyes! She was spying on us, I'm sure of it.'

Mark looked at him sternly whilst subtly jerking his head towards their mother. Lady Pallas was growing paler with each of his assertions.

Although Mark was only minutes older, sometimes it

seemed like years. He had a habit of acting superior to his twin, always telling Kohl when to keep his mouth shut. The truth was, they both knew Lady Pallas held the Civies in high regard. Denigrating their relationship was definitely not something mother would want in the afterglow of their successful party. Kohl just didn't care.

'And "Lightbearers". Why do they call us that? They wouldn't dare say it to our faces but everyone knows, Mother. They deny our heritage as the ruling caste when they call us by our function and not by our name. They seem to forget they wouldn't even exist without us.'

Kohl raked his hands through his wild copper mane as he aggressively paced the floor, avoiding Mark's eyes, stomping his large feet and kicking at the satin furnishings.

'Tell me, Mother, why do they have to be at every event? We have perfectly good staff who could have handled everything without them.'

Lady Pallas wasn't responding.

'Well. I hope you've counted your lightkeys this morning, Mother. I bet they've got deep pockets under those robes.' Kohl finished.

'Oh bro, you do go on. Enough of your ridiculous theories! Can't you think of anything more cheerful on such a fabulous morning? How about opening some more presents?'

Mark plucked a gift off the top of the huge pile that didn't seem to get any smaller – no matter how many they opened.

'Let's open this one from Cousin Martha of Melbourne. What do you think, Mother? It's small – maybe cufflinks or beard jewels?'

Mark tossed it to Kohl, who reluctantly opened the gift.

'No, just another clip.' Kohl handed it to his mother who was inscribing the items onto the official gift registry.

'Don't be like that. It's very thoughtful of Martha. It will look lovely on your lightkey,' said Lady Pallas.

'As will the other five clips. Really, doesn't anyone have any imagination anymore?'

'Come on, if I have to endure this, so do you. Here, open this one little brother. By the look of the card, it's especially for you. From one of your special admirers?'

Mark tossed Kohl the small dark grey box, which, unlike the others, was a perfectly plain cube with just a small cream paper card attached and no other ribbons, holograms or decorations of any sort.

His mother looked intrigued. 'What does it say, son?'

Kohl studied the old-fashioned writing on the card. 'For our golden boy on the attainment of his majority. Lift your eyes to the lighted heavens and fly into your special future. Signed TL.'

Mark chuckled. 'Must be from your side of the family, Mother. A dippy old Great Aunt TL? Hey, that could be Tessy Lunatic. Has to be that, unless it's from one of your fan clubs Kohl – Titillating Ladies? No, maybe it's from the Civies – Tortured Lightchasers?'

Mark fell back on the wide lounge, laughing. 'Come on, don't keep us in suspense. Open it bro!'

Kohl felt like pitching it at his annoying brother's skull, yet something about the seamlessly wrapping box had piqued his interest. Tossing the box from one hand to the other, he was beginning to think it was a solid object with no wrapping at all until he fumbled and accidently dropped it.

Lady Pallas gasped. The gift hit the floor and the sides fell away to reveal a golden object that immediately started whirring. They all leaned closer to take a better look. It clicked, leapt into the air and tore around their ducking heads in a wide circle before performing a perfect landing on Kohl's shoulder.

'A toy?' Kohl plucked it off his shoulder and examined it

more closely. It was no bigger than his index finger and flew like a holobird – yet it looked more like a machine than an animal. Perhaps some sort of cart? It clearly had a windscreen and seats for two passengers, although no Solaran cart had wings.

Mark's voice broke into his thoughts. 'Now, wouldn't that look just lovely on your lightkey, bro, or maybe decorating your beard?'

Kohl looked at Mark and reluctantly joined in his laughter. Mark's mockery didn't go unnoticed by their mother, who clearly didn't share the joke.

'I'm quite approaching the end of my patience with you two. Between flying gifts and conspiracy theories I think I am truly done here.'

As she spoke the door at the end of their suite opened. Three lithe society girls sauntered in from the steamy bathing room beyond. Only one of them had a towel around her, the others preferring to air dry their newly applied body art. Vivid hibiscus flowers adorned their torsos from their shoulders right down to their gleaming naked thighs.

Without taking his eyes off the toy, Kohl reached over to the wall and activated the overhead sunning lamps for the girls, who stretched out on the boys' soft lounges at the far end of the suite.

Lady Pallas stood, adjusted her robe and bid the girls good morning. Before she took her leave, she reminded her sons to continue their duty of logging gifts onto the registry.

As she walked to the door, she stopped and spoke without turning. 'Ladies, I presume you'll be joining us *dressed* for brunch? You too, boys.'

+   +   +

Lady Pallas closed the boys' door behind her and collapsed back against its old oak panels. When she remembered Kohl's harsh accusations against the Civies her breath caught in her throat and tears threatened to overspill her lashes.

How little he knows about the truth of life; the young see no grey. Maybe it's time he left his soft home.

She was on the verge of surrendering to her old grief when she became aware of two staff cleaning at the end of the long hall. They were engrossed in cheerful banter as they polished one of the many statues that adorned the palatial family compound. She straightened up, pushed her shoulders back and strode purposefully to the stairs at the opposite end of the hall.

Young trollops and old aches would not interrupt her preparations for the evening's formal ceremony; the pinnacle of her festivities. It was not long before the afternoon's business helped her troubles shift to the back of her mind.

+ + +

Directly above them, on the upper floor, another Pallas was pacing. Governor Matthias Pallas had just received a written report from his chief constable, who now stood outside the bedroom awaiting his response.

'I'm done with you, Rebecca. Take your clothes and leave,' he said to his wife's scullery maid. While his wife was busy with the boys downstairs, the Governor had received personal assistance upstairs. Rebecca alighted from the bed with the natural grace of an ebony queen, which belied her official position in the household.

'Tell cook to send up some strong coffee,' he continued without making eye contact.

'You can enter now Albert,' he said loudly enough for his

chief to hear. Albert entered and stood at full attention; his eyes fixed on his superior.

Rebecca attempted a small curtsey before scurrying, nickers in hand, through the hidden door in her master's closet.

Governor Pallas sat on the edge of an embroidered chaise lounge and studied the report in his hand. Despite his wife's delight at the party, all had not gone to plan. The festivities had almost been ruined by four intruders who had broken into the compound and attempted to steal food.

'This report is concerning. You're right, we do need more men tonight, but they *must* blend in. I won't have my sons' ceremony looking like a police action.

'Send for the Brothers. Have them deliver a dozen additional men and make sure they're included in the ceremony so nothing looks untoward. Then, meet me in the cellar. We have some unpleasant business to conclude.'

Albert winced. 'Do you really need to conduct *unpleasant business* this mornin', Sir?'

The Governor threw him a steely glance that should have ended the conversation.

'I just mean, it's concerning but not a critical matter on such a busy day, Sir,' Albert stammered, uncharacteristically. 'I-I could interrogate them for you and report back?'

'Terrorism is always a critical matter. If you don't understand that, then—'

The Governor turned his back and pretended to be considering the report until he heard Albert shuffling his nervous feet.

'—then perhaps I need to consider *your* position. Perhaps they had accomplices on the inside. You wouldn't know anything about that would you?'

'No, Sir!'

'Right, so be in the cellar, equipped to assist me, in ten minutes. I will get the full story out of our four light-fingered guests.'

'As you wish, Governor.' Albert bowed, twice. His shoulders drooped as he left the room to prepare.

CHAPTER 6
Sombra Abbey Sydney City

SPECTRA RAPPED HIS fingers on the armrest. Archbrother Escuro's stomach grumbled. Their duet of irritation echoed around the ostentatious office. The waiting was testing Spectra's resolve to keep his cool, and his cover.

Make a decision, old man, he silently snarled.

Escuro opened his mouth as if to speak, then moved to sip his water and rub his temples instead. For the second time he fingered the curtain behind him. Spectra imagined twelve violent ways he could permanently silence the old fossil with the curtain rod alone, if he didn't answer soon. Outwardly, he remained the picture of a perfectly patient assistant, clearing his throat, nothing more.

Spectra knew that his superior's mind was probably struggling to focus on the issue at hand. He had caught a glimpse of what was behind that curtain on his way in. Escuro's planned dalliance with a liquid lunch, cheese board and a handsome young Brother would have to wait.

Seemingly reading his mind, Escuro leaned back and took

another quick look behind the dark red drapes of his antechamber. With an almost imperceptible intake of breath, he returned his attention to Spectra.

'For a new undersecretary, you certainly have a knack of bringing me critical issues at the most inconvenient of times.' He released the drapes, picked up the report and stood.

'Let me get this straight – these four … what are we calling them now? *Rats*?' He looked at Spectra for clarification.

'Yes, Your Eminence. Rats is the most common vernacular. It's a good fit for their choice of residence. There have been rumours about sewer dwellers for as long as there has been a city above. Recently, those rumours have been substantiated by a series of sightings. This is the first time Rats have actually been apprehended, however.'

'So, these four *Rats* had the gall to sneak up from their filthy subterranean lair and attack the Governor's compound while there were three hundred people present?'

'More like four hundred if you include staff, light engineers, Brothers and Civies, but yes, Your Eminence, they did.'

'And no one was injured?'

'No, Your Eminence. Chief Constable Albert Carter seems to think they were only after food, although the Governor insists they be charged with higher offences including trespassing, vagrancy and attempted assault – there was a tussle when they were discovered – and light theft.'

'That last one is dubious. What would Rats want with lightkeys? Surely the dark works in their favour given their hideous appearance.'

'Indeed, Spectra, but you can't judge all beings by our own high moral standards. For instance, why should our flock need fleshly pleasures when they have a perfectly good book of 112 illuminated psalms to satiate them?

'Despite our constant focus on the divine lessons of chastity and abstinence, the Dark One keeps tempting them back to sin. If we cannot predict who among them will fall to the devil's temptations, then we certainly cannot predict the desires of unclean sewer dwellers, who clearly abide with the Dark One.

As he spoke, Escuro pounded his meaty fist on the heavy wooden desk which took up most of the floor space in the large but crowded office. His workspace was so laden with haphazardly arranged religious texts, scrawled theology notes, long-forgotten reports, and coffee encrusted cups, that each time he made contact with the desk it set off chain reaction of dust and flurrying papers that threatened to comically overshadow the seriousness of his sermon.

Escuro stood, coughed and leaned back against the curtain, fanning himself with his hand as though tying to encourage clean air into his lungs.

'I digress though; back to the report. Four Rats attack Chatsworth Manor, are apprehended by catering staff, and are now being interrogated in the Governor's cellar. Is this a correct summation?'

'Yes, Your Eminence.'

'Not really such a big deal, is it?' he asked, looking up from the report to raise his eyebrows at Spectra.

'No, Your Eminence.'

'Yet the Governor is fearful of further unholy incursions? Even though the Rats were weak enough to be overpowered by cooks? This is why he has requested additional Brothers for security at the Lighting Ceremony?'

'Yes, Your Eminence.'

Spectra watched Escuro sit back down and swivel his chair away. He remained quiet as his superior was lost in contemplation. He wondered whether he should have mentioned the presence of the Civy in the kitchen fray, then thought better of it. Glare had cautioned him against revealing too much.

The silent minutes echoed. Spectra wondered if Escuro had forgotten he was there. Escuro fanned himself with the report and began muttering quietly, but audibly, while he rubbed his bloated belly.

'Pallas is surely overreacting, but if the Rats attack again I risk our security. If I do comply with Pallas' wishes then we are increasing our subservience to him.

'What would my predecessors have done? I bet they only had to deal with theology and disciplining the inexperienced acolytes!' His eminence said this more loudly, clearly not realising his previous thoughts had been vocalised.

'Pardon, Your Eminence?' said Spectra, hoping to sound innocent.

'Nothing, Spectra. Mind your business!' His eminence snapped, cheeks reddening. 'I have made my decision. Take six additional Brothers with you to the compound. Only Brothers who are both easy on the ear and the eyes. To be fully accepted into the cream of society we must look like we belong.'

Escuro stopped and looked into the distance as his hand caressed the curtain behind him. Spectra cleared his throat. Escuro dropped his hand.

'Instruct them to focus their mingling on families with spare heirs. Hopefully we can recruit a few new Brothers and recoup our costs for this exercise.

'As for me, I shall refer to *our* prudent choice of bringing the additional brothers in my speech. I'll emphasise that it is *we* who look after Solaran interests, not the Governor. Send a Civil Sister to the Pallas compound now to convey our decision. Make sure he understands we expect to be kept informed of the outcome of the Rats situation.'

'With all due respect Your Eminence, does this message not require my personal attention? It will give me the opportunity to speak directly with the chief. He might reveal more detail on the results of their "discussions" with the Rats.' Spectra was keen to observe the Governor's legendary interrogation methods.

'No. You won't have time.'

'But Your Eminence, if a mere Civy delivers your words, will it convey the gravity of your decision in the same way as a message directly from the lips of your personal aide?'

'Know your place, Spectra. Let the Civies do their job. Go now and prepare the additional Brothers. May the Bright Angels watch over you.'

Clearly dismissed, Spectra stood and bowed. He leant across the desk and kissed his eminence's ring before backing out of the room. He would, of course, do as he'd been bid and arrange the additional brothers. Sadly, the most attractive young ones had just left on a recruitment drive to Brizzie, or so his backdated paperwork would say. Pity, he might have to include old Vincent and wimpy Sam instead.

As he stormed the corridors on the way back to his office, his mind was in the Pallas' cellar. He should have been there when the Rats were questioned, but he knew when he was fighting a lost cause. Besides, the Governor wasn't the only one with access to Rats.

Let the Archbrother go back to his playthings, Spectra thought, *his holy cluelessness has no idea what resides in the bowels of his own establishment. I shall have my answers yet.*

CHAPTER 7
Sydney City Lightbarrier

HARPER WAS ALWAYS thrilled to cross the lightbarrier that surrounded Sydney City. The joy of stepping through the instant transition from absolute dark to breathtaking light never grew old.

Bess wasn't so keen. The few steps in the darkness between the Civies' well-lit tunnels and the lightbarrier were a trial that seemed to strip her of all confidence.

'Don't you let go of me,' Bess pleaded as she tightened her grasp on Harper's arm. 'Did I just hear footsteps? Is someone there?'

'What are you Bess, a *Lightbearer*?'

'C'mon, Harper. Can't we go any quicker? Anything could be out here.'

'If I had known that they were assigning me to escort a fragile little ninny, I would have remembered my biggest club to fend off the monsters,' said Harper.

They both giggled and finally took the step across the barrier.

'Oh, Bess!'

In the pitch black before the barrier, there was no horizon, no definition. The world was reduced to whatever could be touched and heard but enlarged to include every malevolent nightmare the mind could conjure.

In the dazzling light after the barrier, the world enlarged to include a vast array of visual stimuli and a glorious view of the spires of Sydney City. The sudden intensity of the transition could – and often did – reduce a person to tears.

'Enough gawking,' said Harper after a moment. 'Anyone would think we'd never seen this before. It's nearly evensong. We'd better pick up our pace if we're to make it to the Pallas' on time.'

Truthfully, Harper would have loved to take her time getting to work. The approaching dusk in the city was her favourite time of the day. When the chief light engineer allowed the sky to dim from daytime's bright blue to evening's deep purple, the glittering city looked so elegant.

'Wait, I don't think you've ever been assigned to a Lightbearer wedding before, have you?'

'No,' replied Bess.

'It's really beautiful. So many lightkeys!'

It was said that a Solaran man was measured not by the weight of his wallet but by the length of the shadow cast by the power of his control over light.

At weddings, guests would hang decorative lightkeys on the bride's wrist to indicate how well she had married. At birth, mothers would give their wedding lightkeys to their babies as a symbol of their future power. Upon turning eight, school children would have one of these birth keys activated.

Lightkey activation was a big milestone in the life of a Solaran child. It gave them their first taste of freedom. The keys allowed them to cast light a metre – a sure sign, children thought, that they were ready for more autonomy. It was frequently celebrated with a new bike and always accompanied by a stern lecture on the dangers of crossing the city lightbarrier.

Inevitably, most children would ignore the cautions and try riding into the dark with their newly activated lightkey held aloft. It was a game usually played only once. They would return moments later, eyes wide open, pale with terror.

Urban legends whispered of children who didn't return from the darklands until decades later, emaciated and withdrawn. Their minds lost to the abyss.

Fortunately, most children survived this testing time and obtained their legal majority. At twenty-one years, they could cast their vote, enter into contracts and have as much control over their shadows as their wealth allowed.

For the Pallas boys that shadow was likely to be very long indeed.

+ + +

Sister Pat had only just crossed the lightbarrier into the dark plain that lead to Veruda when she heard a crunchy noise. Footsteps outside Sydney were uncommon and would normally warrant investigation, had she not been on such a vital mission. She reluctantly ignored them and sped on.

When she arrived at the Keep, Pat didn't waste time logging her weapons. She flew up the central staircase two steps at a time, startling unwary Sisters along the way, until she reached the uppermost apartment and burst into Mary's room.

'What say you, Patricia?' said Sister Mary, the chief of the Veruda Civil Sisters. Her flushed face spoke of more than her calm manner showed. Pat had assumed the urgency would excuse her uninvited entrance. It was a grave miscalculation. A small crowd of high-ranking Sisters occupied the room, all wearing expressions of displeasure.

Pat was about to apologise when a small woman stepped out from behind Mary, causing Pat to falter and clutch back at the doorknob for support. She caught her breath and looked frantically from the woman to Mary and back again.

The woman wore the usual Civy robes and moved with the traditional shuffle, giving her an entirely unremarkable appearance in all regards except for one – her eyes. They gleamed out of her ebony face as though they were lit from within. The whites shone like lightwands and her irises were a brilliant violet hue with flecks of gold.

There was no mistaking the ordinary, extraordinary Civy. Finally, Pat found her grace and fell into a deep curtsy.

'Forgive me, Queen Laurel,' she said.

Mary signalled for everyone to leave the room except for Pat and their queen. As soon as the room emptied, Pat continued to beg forgiveness only to be interrupted by the queen who took a step closer and offered a hand of assistance.

'Arise, child. There is no need to apologise. We are entering complicated times where the usually comfortable formalities will be a hinderance.'

Star-struck, Pat only managed to say 'Sombra' before she gave up in frustration and simply handed over the note from Archbrother Escuro. Her monarch read it quickly then passed it to Mary.

'Rats … additional Brothers … prepare for …' whispered Mary as her eyes raced down the note.

Pat thought she might have seen tears brimming in her leader's eyes. Queen Laurel must have seen it too as she put a slender arm around Mary's shoulders.

'Come now, this was to be expected. It's a little sooner than we would have liked but you have prepared your girls well. I

53

am proud of you all. The Master is determined, but he does not know what lies in his own house. We have hidden well in plain sight, as have our Damaran friends. Be strong. May the Light bless us all.'

Before Mary could respond, Queen Laurel nodded goodbye and left through a small door in the back of the apartment. There was a flash of intense light as the door closed and then she was gone. Pat thought it strange that she had never noticed the exit before.

Mary sighed and sunk down to her bed. 'Oh, she wears me out. Pat, be an angel and pour me a drink, will you? Take one for yourself too. There is much to discuss.'

'What's happened?' Pat handed over a tumbler of cold amber liquid.

'We have received the twelfth and final Letter from the Light.'

Mary waved a creamy parchment towards her. 'This is it, Pat. Everything we have done has all been in preparation for this. I must admit I didn't really believe it would happen in our lifetime.'

Pat sat next to Mary and gave her a hug. Mary turned into her shoulder and sobbed, overcome by the enormity of their situation. Pat pulled her in closer. Despite being companions for many years it was the first time Pat had ever seen Mary cry.

After a few moments, she appeared to regain her composure. Mary stood, brushed down her clothes and moved to the other side of the room.

'Had I realised we would receive the Light's letter or the note from Spectra today, I wouldn't have sent Harper and Bess to the Lighting Ceremony. Wherever the Light goes, so too does the Master. Or is it the other way around?'

'They've already left?' Pat said rising to her feet and unconsciously touching her hip where she still had her weapon hidden under her robe. Spectra had spoken with such urgency about the new security issue, advising that only the most senior Civies should attend the Pallas ceremony.

'Yes. Too late to withdraw them.' Mary bit her fingernail and walked around the little room, picking up objects and replacing them just as quickly. She stopped and faced Pat.

'Will you go, love? One more Civy is really all I can add to the evening without raising eyebrows. I must give those poor girls a chance at coming home, despite the danger.'

'Yes, of course I will.' Pat said as she crossed the floor to accept Mary's outstretched hands. 'Now how about you show me the latest letter from the Light?'

CHAPTER 8
Chatsworth Manor

KOHL RAN DOWN narrow lanes, under bridges, there was no escaping their relentless pursuit. He leapt up twisting staircases. They leapt higher. He begged for help from every passing person but they all turned away.

Just when he thought he could feel their warty old fingers clawing at his back, knowing his capture was imminent, he reached a golden door. He turned the ornate handle and stepped into his childhood nursery.

The unexpected room should have been a shock. Everything was just as he remembered, except for a beautiful stranger who stood patiently by the window. She had big blue eyes and flowing auburn hair. Her smile was unsettlingly familiar.

'Quick Kohley, we must jump before they get me. You have to save me, Kohl!'

Without hesitation, he took her outstretched hand and together they jumped from the window.

Kohl expected to hit the ground hard but instead landed

on a soft leather seat. It took a moment to realise he was sitting in a strange cart that moved him swiftly through the air!

He heard himself scream and tried to lift himself up. The girl reached forward from the seat behind and placed her hand on his shoulder. 'Trust me, little Kohley. It's OK, you can do this. Fly us away, my golden boy.'

A stick jutted out of the floor in front of him. He grabbed it and pulled it back a little. The cart responded to his touch, accelerating into the sky. Behind him, the awful Civies screeched from the window, their crowing receding as they flew away.

Kohl relaxed. The danger lay behind him, and freedom ahead. He looked backwards at the girl who still held his hand over his shoulder. She laughed with delight.

'Higher, Kohley. Higher!'

Together they zoomed up into the blue canopy above. As they levelled out, he marvelled at the view of the city so far below. His old school was easy to identify, just south of the Arbour, and his home, off to the north. Driving the airborne cart felt like riding a great bird. He wished he could do nothing but skim the sky for the rest of his life.

'Look up, Kohley.'

He did as she urged, expecting to see the infinite blue sky. But he didn't; something was wrong. Kohl took a closer look at the sky above, and then it hit him.

Thwack.

He understood. Everything was simultaneously all right and all very wrong.

Thwack. Thwack.

Startled awake, Kohl realised he was being hit in the face with a pillow. He pushed it away and rubbed his eyes. Mark hovered over him, a foot planted on each side of his chest.

'What are you doing, baby brother? I've been looking for

you everywhere. This is the last thing I expected you to be doing. Why've you got that silly toy? Wouldn't you rather cuddle Primrose Walker?'

Mark wrapped his arms around himself and began making amorous noises. Kohl pushed his brother away, sat up, and shook his head.

He opened his hand and saw that the little golden object had begun to cut little red lines into his palm. He rubbed at the indentations; no wonder he'd had such a crazy dream. Already the details were slipping away, yet it had felt so important; so *real*.

What was wrong with the sky?

'Must have been some dream by the goofy look on your face, Bro.'

By the time his brother hit him again, Kohl could only remember the face of the beautiful auburn-haired girl. No matter how hard he tried to grasp the thread of it, the other details slipped away.

Mark reached down as if to help his twin stand but as soon as he made contact, he spun Kohl around and gripped him in a wrestling lock. They jostled until a side table was overturned and a lamp crashed to the floor.

'Do you surrender, *Rat?*' Mark grinned down at his twin who was unsuccessfully using his free elbow to execute a flip-grip. 'Well?'

Kohl gave one last wriggle before conceding.

Mark pushed himself up and offered a hand to his brother before he strode to the wall and pulled the bell sash for a chambermaid.

'All jokes aside, we've got to hurry, Bro. Did you know some Rats broke into the kitchen last night? Cook caught them. Father's been interrogating. Probably just a couple of hungry ferals sneaking in for some food but Father's just like you. He sees a conspiracy around every corner.'

Kohl rolled his eyes at the insult.

'Seriously. Father's even sent for more Brothers. As if they'd be any help! Maybe that Spectra would be good in a fight, though. He's scary. Have you seen the way he flicks his tongue out when he speaks?' Mark shivered.

'What's all that got to do with me?' asked Kohl, pulling his brother's conversation back on track.

'Right. Father's sending out a small squad of constables to check for any other trouble brewing. They might even round up a few undesirables. You know, set an example so they won't get any bright ideas about disturbing our party tonight.

'I said we could use a run, so we're off to join them. Unless of course you want to stay behind with the ladies and tidy this mess? Maybe hang up some decorations? Give you time to hug your little toys?'

Kohl punched his brother playfully. 'All right, that's enough. You know I'm in. I could use some exercise before tonight. Got to stay pumped to keep the ladies happy.' Kohl pocketed the toy and assumed a pose that showed off his muscles to their best effect. 'Let's go!'

Grinning, he raked his fingers through his hair and then took off after Mark, who was already loping downstairs. The dream had already faded into a distant memory, except for the face of the auburn-haired girl.

CHAPTER 9
Sombra Abbey

SAM RECEIVED THE good news while in the chapel. Despite his eight long years of training, he had rarely stepped outside the monastery for anything more important than supply runs, and only once had he visited another town. He had all but given up hope of becoming anything more than an educated 'rock boy'.

'Me! Vincent can ya believe it? Old "rock-boy-Sam" goin' to the grand Chatsworth Manor tonight. I'll be mixin' with the cream of Lightbearer society,' Sam gushed to his old mentor. 'I wish me Mum could see me now.'

Vincent cringed over what Sam assumed was his rock-boy comment.

'It doesn't matter where you are or what you are doing Sam, as long as you behave earnestly, she will be proud. I am certain of that. I'm *also* certain, that if you should be overheard calling our Solaran hosts "Lightbearers", you will be joining her sooner than you think!'

Sam blushed and looked at the floor.

'Never mind. We'll keep that slip of the tongue between the two of us. Come now, I must brief you on other matters. His eminence needs us calm and in control of ourselves. You can't be jumping and gawking at every new experience. You need to be forewarned.'

'Forewarned of what?'

'Have you ever wondered *why* they call it a Lighting Ceremony?'

Sam shook his head.

'Because they turn off *all* the lights.' Vincent said.

Sam slowly nodded his head as the revelation sunk in. One thing he knew for certain was that Lightbearers had a pathological fear of the dark.

+ + +

A soft knock on the door interrupted Vincent's briefing. Unlike other Brothers who had not managed to progress up the church hierarchy, Brother Stanley had neither been cast out as unworthy nor retired, perhaps because of his ability to calm those in crisis.

Seeing the gentle old monk at the door was not the best of signs.

What have I done now? Sam wondered.

'Stanley! To what do we owe the pleasure of your company?' Vincent asked with a warm smile. 'Here, sit down.'

'Hello Brother Vincent,' said Stanley with an old-man wheeze. 'Thanks for the offer but no seat please. We're all in a bit of a rush, aren't we? Hello to you too, young Sam.

'Look, I hope you don't mind my impertinence in checking on you. Have you not noticed the hour? All the others left for the compound at least twenty minutes ago, and your young student will need extra time to traverse such a distance. Excuse me for speaking frankly about your condition, Sam.'

Sam nodded graciously; the older Brother was merely stating a fact. Vincent thanked Brother Stanley and hurried him out the door as Sam began to rush around the room as quickly as his club foot would allow.

'We're late!'

'Don't panic, Sam. I know a shortcut. Are you ready to go?'

'Nearly,' Sam reached up behind his holy books to the secret shelf in the stone wall that he'd discovered when he had first been assigned the room.

He took out his mum's hanky, which he kissed whilst muttering a prayer of Illumination for her. And then he pocketed the lightkey torch that Vincent had given him as a child. Lastly, he hooked the golden tube he'd found in the shale field, so many years before, onto a loop he had fashioned on the underside of his robes.

He caught Vincent's quizzical look.

'A wise man once told me that ya never know when ya might need a torch. The others … they're me lucky charms. Let's go,' Sam said with a grin.

+   +   +

It didn't take long until he was completely lost. Thankfully, Vincent seemed sure of the way through the unfamiliar streets. He didn't want to be the one responsible for tardiness and attract the ire of his eminence.

Vincent rushed him through the artisan quarter, up through the business district, then down again into the widening boulevards of the entertainment zone. They passed magnificently tall buildings – some four storeys high – and passed through delicious restaurant aromas.

How the lucky few live, thought Sam as he struggled against distraction.

'How much farther, Vincent?' he said, puffing as he limped off the road to join the older man, who was waiting for him in the tall roadside vegetation.

'Not far.' Vincent looked around and reached down as if to check his boots. Boots which were already perfectly tied.

Sam wondered why he was frowning. Jogging brothers was not an entirely unseen sight in the busy city. Their attendance was required at all of life's most urgent events, especially births and deaths. Then he remembered that loitering by a park would be an unusual and potentially reportable sight.

With one last glance down the road, Vincent beckoned him to follow into the thicket. After travelling another five minutes, they reached a small clearing.

'Now you can take a minute to catch your breath and rest your foot.

'Here, eat this.' Vincent said, plucking a juicy red fruit off a nearby bough.

'Where are we now?' Sam asked between delicious mouthfuls.

'Ever heard of Sydney Arbour Orchard?'

Sam coughed out his partially chewed apple and raised his eyebrows. The city's forbidden areas had been drummed into him during his initiation. Only the holy agriculturalists were allowed access to the trees. Punishment for their transgression would be harsh.

'Relax. We're on official business, remember? I can square it with his eminence on the basis of expediency. Besides, I have heard that it's positively crowded every evening with couples who aren't supposed to be here. Not that I would know that first-hand.'

Vincent winked and Sam relaxed enough to swallow his

fruit. It was a beautiful spot for a break. The canopy was high and a gentle light dappled the soft undergrowth. It was a brief bliss until an urgent shuffling noise drew Sam's attention.

Sam stopped chewing and tilted his head slightly.

'Did you hear something?' asked Vincent peering between the trees.

Sam swallowed then closed his eyes briefly as he pivoted his head left and right, tuning into the source of the sound.

'Get down,' he whispered dropping into a squatting position. 'Can you hear that?'

'Yes, I think I can now. Maybe a small animal? Over that way?'

'No, east I think. Not far. Two small pairs of feet – probably children – followed by a group who are heavier. Adults, most likely. Wherever they're goin', they're in a hurry! Might be trouble. Should we turn back?'

'No, that's the way we were headed anyway. Let's move cautiously.'

They had only moved twenty paces or so when the noises abruptly increased and they were hit from out of nowhere by a racing child. She looked to be no more than ten years old and she held the hand of an even younger boy. He, in turn, held the paw of a grubby old grey teddy bear.

Sam overbalanced and fell to the ground with the children in a mess of arms and weeds.

Vincent lifted the littlest child to his feet and lifted him up so they were eye level. 'Stop squirming! Who are you? Who are you running from, boy?'

The child promptly kicked him in the shins. Vincent yelped in pain and lost his grip. The little boy dropped to the ground and scampered back into the bushes.

Sam had taken a hold of the girl, but fear made her strong and she easily wriggled out of his grip. She glanced up briefly, as if seeking divine intervention.

'They'll be here soon and we can't let 'em get us!'

'We can help ya,' Sam urged, but she was already running in the same direction as the boy and was quickly out of earshot.

Six large men burst through the trees in the direction the children had come from. Four wore constabulary uniforms and the two others were in expensive looking breeches and blouses. The uniformed leader approached Sam and grabbed him by the scruff of his collar.

'What are you two doing in here? You know this is a restricted area. I ought to lock you up!'

The soldier lifted him to his eye level so that Sam's toes were only just brushing the ground.

'Well?' demanded the officer.

Sam could only stammer in response.

'Unhand my acolyte!' Vincent ordered in a stronger tone than Sam had ever heard.

'We have urgent business with the Governor so you had better think twice before threatening us. You should not be harassing religious men and you certainly ought to have better things to do than chase innocent children. I will say a prayer for your redemption tonight. Now return to your barracks and let us be on our way.'

He pulled Sam from the officer's grip and pushed him in front as he made to move out of the men's path. 'Come, acolyte.'

'Hang on!' said the lead constable. 'What do you mean chasing innocent children? Who said they were innocent? What do you know about it? What did—?'

He was interrupted by one of the non-uniformed men.

'Don't waste your time, Chief. They're just stupid Brothers. They know they shouldn't be here, which means they'll probably say anything to get themselves out of trouble. Besides, what can they do to help – pray those brats back to us? Let's go.'

The others hesitated as if unsure who was in charge, until the chief nodded and they all took off in pursuit of their small prey.

'Well, that was insulting. "Stupid Brothers"?' Vincent snorted. 'I think we ought to take a look at what they're up to with those little ones. Perhaps the children will need our prayers.'

After a brief hesitation, Sam followed Vincent further into the orchard.

✦   ✦   ✦

Harper knew she was showing off but she couldn't resist taking the slightly longer route down Sydney Arbour Boulevard. Bess always seemed to be away on special training missions when the biggest events were on. Harper wanted to show her the great views she had missed.

'It's gorgeous!' Bess sighed, linking her arm with Harper. She threw her hood back and shook her auburn hair out in a very un-Sisterly manner. For a moment they were just two girls out for an afternoon stroll, not two highly-trained operatives.

'Imagine spending the whole afternoon just gazing at this view. The grand open street and all the beautiful orchard greenery that goes on for miles. It's all so lovely!

Now lead on to the best view of all – Chatsworth Manor.'

The girls separated to adjust their clothes a more modest state when two children leapt from the undergrowth, followed by six burly men in fast pursuit. The four uniformed officers ducked and weaved around each other trying to grab the youngsters.

'Hey, get out the way!' yelled a uniformed man as he tried

to nudge Harper aside. He made a lunge around her for the girl who was using Harper's cloak as a shield. The officer reached to her right as the child bent to her left.

'Wait! What have they done?' Harper yelled, using one hand to steady the child behind her and the other to fend off the soldier.

'Step aside!' he commanded and thrust a fist behind her which made a soft thudding contact with something. She turned to see the child on the ground rubbing her chin and shaking her head.

Harper made a show of flouncing her cloak in an attempt to give the child a moment of coverage in which to escape but was foiled by Bess who bumped into her side. When she turned back the child was gone.

'Nearly got ya!' another officer was spinning Bess around in another failed capture attempt. He kicked out at the little boy but the child was remarkably agile. He slid through his elders' legs and hit the officer's back with a flick of his bear.

'MacBain, go around the other side. Cut their exit options off!' another officer yelled.

The girl came back into Harper's line of vision. She was dodging the blows of the largest officer while attempting to reach the boy and moving closer to Harper with each step.

'Grab 'em Sisters, they're not the innocents they appear,' cried an officer.

'Murderin' thieves more like it!' added another.

Realising she had no understanding of what was really transpiring and unsure whether apprehending children was ever Sisterly, Harper pulled Bess a few steps up the cobbled boulevard. As they moved out of the fray, they drew the attention of the older child, who grabbed the smaller and together they ran full pelt towards Harper.

The children ran circles around the Civies, tugging on

their robes and causing them to spin as well. The two men who were not in uniform leapt at the children. The youngsters darted away at the last moment, leaving the men to slam against Harper and Bess who, being no match for the men's bulk, collapsed beneath their weight.

Harper blinked through her sudden dizziness. Her head stung and a heavy arm pressed down on her shoulder. She looked up. Kohl Pallas! He was staring down at her with his big eyes – big, intensely green eyes just like hers. He had a puzzled look that she could only interpret as concern.

'You!' he said getting to his feet.

He remembers me!

He offered Harper his hand in assistance, although he appeared to be staring with concern at Bess who was also on the ground, eyes closed.

Such a gentleman, she thought as her dizziness intensified. She closed her eyes to recite a calming mantra, hoping to regain her composure. It wouldn't do to be caught swooning.

A harsh voice filled with authority broke through her thoughts.

'Shut this down NOW! Chief constable, activate the lightcell.'

A strange command. I'll have to report that one to Sister Pat, she thought, then everything went black.

+ + +

Sam and Vincent were not far behind the constables. They arrived at the scene just as two Solarans collided with two Civies and the children scampered back to the tree line. Astonished that they were still evading their pursuers, Sam said a quiet prayer for their deliverance.

The arrival of a constabulary-branded cart drew his

attention, yet it was Governor Pallas himself who stepped out, staticwhip in hand, as if ready to do battle with invading warriors. Lost for words, Sam reached for Vincent but his mentor was already silently watching the same scene.

The Governor quickly grabbed the children who had run blindly towards him, unaware of the increasing danger. He grasped them firmly by their collars and hauled them towards the uniformed men on the grass.

'They're just children!' Sam's voice came out much louder than the whisper he had planned. The Governor must have heard him.

'Shut this down NOW! Chief constable, activate the lightcell.'

The chief produced three modified lightkeys and tossed two of them to the other officers. The men backed away from each other to form three points of a four-metre triangle. They activated their keys simultaneously and the area between them turned black.

The Governor marched the struggling children down to the darkened area, stepped inside and disappeared from sight.

'How's that possible?' Sam whispered to Vincent.

'It's called a lightcell – like a jail made of a temporary light barrier. We can't see into it but it's daylight for the people inside the barrier. They can see exactly what they are doing and they can see *us* gawking at them. This trouble isn't meant to be witnessed. Let's go!' Vincent tugged on Sam's arm who wasn't budging.

'Look around you. The street is suddenly deserted, for good reason!'

'The kids …' was all Sam managed to utter in response before he heard two loud buzzing noises mixed with young screams. Then silence.

Vincent started jogging along the boulevard towards their

original destination, dragging Sam by the arm.

'Don't look back. Just pretend nothing happened and move fast!' he urged.

But Sam couldn't resist. He turned to see the Solarans were loading the injured Civies onto the cart. The uniformed officers had deactivated the lightcell and were bending down to pick up dropped items. Normal daylight had returned to the area where the lightcell had been in operation, yet the children were gone.

Then he noticed the Governor standing at the heart of the scene, looking oddly satisfied as he held a teddy bear aloft. The grass by his feet was newly-stained with two child-sized scorch marks.

CHAPTER 10

Chatsworth Manor

HARPER HEARD A woman's soft voice as she regained consciousness. After a moment she realised the incomprehensible words were Solaran, so she struggled to remember her training despite her mind fog. She kept her eyes closed and silently recited a focus mantra.

Open eyes, open ears, closed mouth, no fears
Open eyes, open ears, no distractions, all clear

'You did the right thing bringing them to me, Kohl. I don't think we need to bother your father on such a busy day, especially after a morning of unpleasant business.'
It's Lady Pallas and Kohl talking!
'They'll be fine, just a few bumps. You know they aren't used to our sophisticated ways. They probably fainted from the excitement of our beautiful city. They'll come around shortly and then we can all have a nice cup of Hinterland breakfast tea. It's a great reviver for all female maladies. Now off you go, son.

It's time you got spruced up for your big night.'

'Mother, just one more thing. The blonde one, I think I saw her last night. The brunette looks kind of familiar too, but not from the party. Do you know if she's been here before?'

Harper observed a brief but significant pause before Lady Pallas responded.

'I'm sure I don't know. They all look the same to me and we're never told the names of the young ones. In fact, if we didn't have their hoods off now, we probably wouldn't even be able to tell them apart.'

'Mother that makes no sense. How—'

'Don't try to figure out Civies because you can't, Kohl. We all serve a purpose in life and they believe their purpose is best served anonymously.'

Harper heard Kohl shuffle his feet. If he was reluctant to leave, Lady Pallas was having none of it.

'Never mind about these girls. You'll have your pick of Sydney's most eligible ladies in the ballroom tonight. However, they won't be impressed if you turn up looking like that. Find your brother and get ready. That's an order!'

'Right, mother.'

Harper heard heavy boots receding. She was about to end her ruse by opening her eyes, when she heard Lady Pallas shift a little and make a soft noise.

Is she crying?

She took a chance and opened her eyes just a crack. Lady Pallas still had her hand on Harper's shoulder, yet she had turned the rest of her body to face Bess in the adjacent bed.

'Stupid girl, why couldn't you stay out of the way? Don't worry, those brutish enforcers will pay. To think what might have happened if our boys hadn't been there.'

She bent over and whispered a few more words to Bess, adjusted the cold compress on her head, and then left through the door on the other side of the room.

As soon as the Lady was gone, Harper sat up. She had to hold onto the edge of the bed for moment as she waited for the room to stop tilting.

'Bess,' she whispered but there was no response. Rubbing her temples and remembering a calming mantra, Harper tentatively slipped off the bed and reached for Bess – just two steps away.

'Hey' she whispered again. Bess had a large purple bruise emerging on her cheek and her hair and cloak were dirtied from their fall. Harper gave her a gentle nudge and whispered her name once more. She was relieved when her friend's eyes fluttered opened.

'Oh Harper, you do look dreadful,' Bess said.

It made Harper smile. 'If you think I look dreadful then I'd better not give you a mirror.'

Feeling her own head clear, Harper lent an arm to Bess. She helped her up off the bed and supported her as they walked over to a hand-basin on a dresser across the room. While they freshened up as best they could, they exchanged what they remembered of the incident.

'What did Lady Pallas say to you before she left, Bess?'

'To be honest, I'm not sure. I didn't even know it *was* Lady Pallas. I'm still a bit heady. Do you think we'll be allowed to work this evening?'

'Absolutely! It's more important now than ever. Whatever went on down in the Orchard is bound to create tension in the family. Who knows what they'll say if they're stressed enough to let down their guard.'

'I could use a bite to eat.'

No sooner had Bess mentioned food than the door swept opened, without so much as a knock.

'Oh, so glad to see you both up and about. You gave us

quite a fright.' Lady Pallas had swanned back into the room, smiling warmly. She looked like a beacon of Solaran finery in her sky-blue silk gown, embossed with a jewelled peacock whose tail ran down the length of the dress and glittered as she moved.

Immediately Harper found herself running her hands over her cloak to remove the last of its dust, and she would have regretted not cleaning her shoes as well had a delicious smell not arrived.

Behind Lady Pallas a procession of three waiters were carrying formal dinner trays laden with steaming goodies, followed by Sister Pat. Seeing their trainer, Harper and Bess immediately pulled their hoods forward to cover their hair and assumed the formal modesty posture.

'Girls, are you well?' Pat barked. Harper heard but the underlying command to which there was only one acceptable response.

'Yes, Sister Pat,' they replied in unison.

'Good. Our hostess has graciously provided some refreshments. I have explained to her that there is no need, of course. A glass of water between the three of us will be sufficient. No need for all this extravagant lighting either, Lady Pallas. We are perfectly comfortable in the dark. Isn't that right, girls?'

'Yes, Sister Pat.'

The Sister turned to Lady Pallas. 'Luxury aside, thank you sincerely for bringing my girls safely into your home. I'm sure their speedy recovery is directly attributable to your gracious care. We are indebted.'

'You are most welcome, Patricia dear.' Harper was a little surprised at Lady's Pallas' familiarity.

'All Solarans are grateful for the support and dedication of the Civies. Please make yourself as comfortable as …' Lady

Pallas stopped briefly and looked up, as if choosing her words carefully, 'as comfortable as your tradition allows. Now, perhaps you three would like a moment alone?'

She turned to leave the room with her staff who had stationed themselves at the back of the room. At the threshold, she paused and looked over her shoulder at Bess before she exited the room, firmly closing the door behind her.

Harper wondered whether the lady's constant hesitations were ambivalence or an affectation of her caste. The Pallas' were all proving to be such intriguing studies. It would make an interesting report; interesting enough to overcome her earlier lapse of judgement in the orchard, she hoped.

'Girls, isn't this a lovely room? Look around you. Words almost fail me, it's resplendent.' While Sister Pat gushed over the room her choice of words and subtle hand movements signalled – *surveillance, danger, speak in code.*

Harper took the initiative and responded in kind.

'Yes, it's all lovely Sister Pat. Have you seen the gardens? They're spectacular. I caught a glimpse of them when I was on duty yesterday. Perhaps a stroll through the grounds might be in order? The fresh air might help revive us for tonight.'

'Splendid idea,' said Pat.

+ + +

Kohl was staring at the gardens beyond the window when a sharp flick of Mark's towel to his behind broke his concentration. His brother had just come out of the bathing room and was frowning at him.

'Hey, what gives?' Kohl yelped.

'What are you looking at? Reviewing your conquest options for tonight?' Mark joined Kohl at the window.

'Is that Sister Pat on the lawn? Oh, no, no, little Bro! That is wrong for so many reasons. For a start, her name is *Sister Pat*, which would not match with Pallas. Sister Pat Pallas and Mr Kohl Pallas? Nope, can't see that on your wedding stationery. Next, have you seen the way she is built? Man, she would snap you over her knee like a twig, Bro!'

Kohl rolled his eyes at his brother's inappropriate remarks and turned away from the window.

'It's not Sister Pat? I thought she was a bit wrinkly, even for your deviant tastes. Hang on, I see our other two Civies. Now that's more like it. They're much younger; definitely doable Bro! Do you think they wear body art under those robes? They sure spend a lot of time locked up in that dingy old castle. They must have some sort of hobby to stave off the boredom.'

'Mark, do you have to be such a jerk? I was just admiring the new season's blossoms.' Kohl feigned disappointment at his brother's crude but admittedly humorous remarks.

'If you think I am buying your new-found interest in botany then we haven't been twins as long as I thought we have. Come on. Spill the beans. What's really going on?'

Kohl sat down and pulled out the little golden toy.

'When you woke me up this morning I was having a freaky dream about Civies chasing me.' Kohl faltered. It was not an easy story to tell, even to his twin.

'Well, that's not news. You've had those all your life. What was so upsetting about this one?'

'The Civy you clobbered in the orchard, she was in it. I couldn't recall the dream until I saw her in Mother's room, and then it came flooding back to me. She was calling me "Kohley". We flew together in a little plane just like this one. It was intense. I can't shake the feeling that she was showing me something really important. I can't remember much more.'

'So?'

'How is it possible that I had the dream about her, before I met her?'

'Let me get this straight. You dream about a mysterious girl, yet you can't remember the dream? Then you meet a new girl an hour later, after physical exertion, mental stress and a collision so hard it knocked two people unconscious, and you're *certain* that it's the same girl?'

'Right.' Kohl had to admit it sounded ridiculous when he heard it aloud.

'Don't you think your mind might be playing tricks on you? You probably just connected the first pretty face you saw with your dream girl.'

'I guess it's possible. She just looked so *familiar*. I can't explain it.'

'All right, given that we've spent our whole lives together and always play together,' Mark gave his brother a conspiratorial grin, 'if you know her then *I* ought to know her too. Correct?'

'That's right,' Kohl said, nodding emphatically when he realised where his brother was going.

'Well then get yourself scrubbed up and introduce me to your lady.'

'Ace! Thanks, bro.'

Kohl gave his brother a shoulder slap and bounded off for his shower.

+   +   +

'I have to admit the gardens are divine.' Pat walked with the girls across the lawn towards a small grove of ornamental pears. 'But we are not here to discuss horticulture. Tell me what happened. Bess, you first.'

'I'm not really sure, Sister Pat. One minute we were looking at the orchard and the next minute I woke up in Lady

Pallas' drawing room. It's left me quite shaken.' She sniffed as though there were tears coming, then turned her face away and appeared to be wiping her eyes with the back of her hand. Harper wasn't buying it; they had been friends too long. She made a mental note to ask Bess about it later.

Pat made a show of sighing her displeasure and turned to Harper. 'Please tell me you can explain all this without the histrionics. I assume you did not mysteriously "just appear" in the Pallas' compound as well?'

'Yes, Sister Pat. I mean no Sister, I didn't just appear here.' Harper went on to report the full incident up to the point where the children had made them collide with the Pallas twins.

'Those poor children. Do you have any idea why they were being chased by the soldiers? Were there any other adults around? Harper, think. Repeat, reveal.'

The training hypno-command caused Harper to feel herself swaying a little as she retold the story, this time with a much clearer memory of the morning's events, as though she had physically returned to the scene.

In slow motion, she saw the deep vibrancy of the green foliage in the Arbour. She described the feeling of the warm breeze as it picked up a loose tendril of her hair. She described her yearning for a forbidden orchard apple and eventually she spoke of the horror of the children being chased, the grubby teddy with its missing eye, and the acrid smell of scorched earth at the Governor's feet.

Then she stopped. She remembered something new – there were people up in the treetops. They had only briefly appeared in her peripheral vision but she had certainly seen them. They were not like Solarans, Civies or Brothers. They were small and agile, gripping branches as they moved silently through the tree canopy.

'I've never seen people like that before. They were dressed in natural colours that rendered them almost invisible.' Harper finished.

'Rats?' Bess said under her breath, to which Pat frowned.

'You mean Damarans,' said Pat. Then she snapped Harper out of the trance as the Pallas twins approached.

'Good afternoon ladies.' Mark flashed a brilliant smile that was all gleaming teeth and bronzed cheekbones. 'I hope you are quite recovered from our collision today?'

The only way Harper could respond was by nodding. Talking with males was largely forbidden for young Civies, especially to young Solaran noblemen in fine evening dress.

They were fashionably shirtless, had their hair waxed high in the air, and their beards were encrusted with shimmering jewels that caught the afternoon light. One stepped towards them, making a show of formality.

'My name is Mark. My brother and I would like to offer our most sincere apologies for the incident.' He spoke directly to Sister Patricia, 'I don't quite know how it happened. One moment we were in a chase to apprehend dangerous felons and the next the four of us were in a tangled mess on the ground.' His next smile was for the two young women again. 'We are so sorry to have caused you any injury or embarrassment, aren't we, Kohl?'

He elbowed his brother, who appeared to be just as dumbstruck as Harper, only he was staring at Bess.

'Um, yes. Are you recovered?' mumbled Kohl.

'The ladies are quite all right, thank you for your concern,' Sister Pat answered as she moved in front of the girls like a stout middle-aged shield.

'Of course we are concerned. We are determined to rid our city of felons so our good ladies may walk freely,' said Mark.

'Are you sure they were dangerous? I heard they were

mere children. What were grown men doing chasing innocent children through the orchard, smashing into bystanders? Surely you have real criminals to apprehend?'

'No ma'am, you heard wrong. I can assure you that they were most definitely felons. We are glad we were there to protect your girls from them,' Mark stated emphatically.

Harper noticed the boys glancing at each other as though exchanging thoughts, before Kohl moved forward to shake Pat's hand.

'The girls really are lucky to have a chaperone as lovely and as dedicated as you, Sister Pat. Let me offer you a tour around the grounds. Have you seen the city skyline from our lawn? It's quite spectacular. Or the blossom in Pallas Forest?'

As Kohl took the surprised Pat firmly by the arm, Mark swiftly stepped around her to face Bess directly. The impropriety of his proximity stunned Harper into muteness.

'Excuse my impertinence m'lady, are you sure about your being all right? That was quite a tumble you took. Let me see your injury. I couldn't forgive myself if it left a permanent mark.'

Before Bess could refuse, Mark had taken her by the chin and lifted her face up to meet his eyes.

'That's enough!' Pat commanded. She loosened herself from Kohl's insistent grip.

'The girls are not allowed to have physical contact with men. You are well aware of that. Unhand her and return to your home! Your mother will hear of this.' As she finished, a bell sounded from the house.

'Ah, there you go, you will excuse us if we take our leave to make final preparations. Good day.'

Pat took each girl by the arm and marched them back towards the building. As she walked, Harper could feel the twin's eyes on her and Bess, and sensed that their motives had been greater than mere apologies.

+   +   +

Kohl said nothing as he watched the Civies return to the house. Only when they had disappeared from sight did he break the silence.

'What do you think?'

One look at Mark's face was all he needed. Even to his brother, Bess was unmistakably, gut-wrenchingly familiar.

'I told you so,' Kohl said before Mark sprinted towards the house, yelling over his shoulder that he needed to speak to their mother. Kohl ran after him.

CHAPTER 11

Pallas Compound Cellar

SAM WAS RETURNING to consciousness when he heard two men's voices nearby.

'Looks like he is comin' around now, Gov. I'll give him another splash.'

The cold water hit Sam's face, causing him to open his eyes, cough, sneeze and shiver all at once. He tried to lift his arms to wipe it off but couldn't. They were shackled to the rough wooden bench he was lying on. His restraints were just loose enough to allow him to raise his head and appreciate his predicament.

The small space had dark stone walls, reminding him a little of the church buildings back in Newbrunswick, only it was clear this room housed a different kind of torture. The wall adjacent to him had a series of metal rings, and in the dim light he could just make out a few whips, pliers and possibly a mace. He hoped he had that one wrong.

In front of Sam was a uniformed guard holding an empty water bucket, and a tall grey-haired gentleman in fine satin clothes. Sam thought hard to place them.

The Arbour Orchard! That's it. He's the one who ordered the guards to catch us after the children were … The memory was too difficult to willingly relive, yet he wasn't sure he would ever forget.

Across the room Vincent's crumpled body lay along another wooden bench. His eyes were shut, his face badly swollen and his arm was bent at an unnatural angle. Sam stared at his mentor's ripped clothes, willing the chest to rise.

Vincent, wake up!

Sam remembered his leg failing under him as they ran along the Arbour Boulevard. He recalled the harsh sting of a weapon hitting him in the back, then falling to the ground. When he finally heard Vincent breathe a few shallow rasps, he was both grateful and ashamed.

He waited for me and now look what they've done. It's all me fault.

'About time you woke up, boy,' snapped the gentleman. 'Honestly, you'd think we were dealing with Civies! Such feeble excuses for men. Give the older one another prod to wake him up, Albert. He should be able to endure much more than that. Then get Spectra and Escuro down here. We will finish this discussion before the ceremony begins.'

Albert nodded, crossed the room, picked up a metal rod and rammed it into the sole of Vincent's foot. Next, he used it to hit him in the ribs. His bones made a noise like the cracking of shale rocks back home. Vincent moaned and shook. Foamy blood trickled from his mouth.

'Do you know who I am?'

Sam looked up at the gentleman, who was staring directly down at him and speaking with a voice that made it clear it was a command to be obeyed.

'N-n-no Sir,' he stammered, 'b-but I know what ya did.'

The man responded by punching him in the jaw.

'That's for your insolence. If you value your life, then you'll know you saw nothing!'

'It's the Governor, Sam,' croaked Vincent, who must have been revived by the pain. 'Don't hurt him, Sir. His life has been hard enough.'

Sam was so glad to hear his voice.

Vincent took a quick shuddering breath before continuing.

'Look at his foot, Governor. He's just a deformed simpleton from Melbourne that I took pity on many years ago. I was at the orchard too and we saw nothing but an honourable leader restoring order.'

'So he's a crippled fool following a foolish mentor who doesn't know his place. What exactly were you two doing in the Holy Orchard?' The Governor demanded.

'We weren't really *in* the orchard, Sir; we were just walking past. We were on our way here. We've been assigned to support your momentous occasion tonight.'

Sam was confused to hear Vincent embellish a lie with the truth.

'Liar!' the Governor said and punched Sam again.

'A squad of senior constables, accompanied by my two sons, saw you twice. Once in the heart of the orchard and once leaving. You were *not* just walking by innocently.' He lifted Vincent up by his bloodied robe and shook him.

'What do you know about the Rats?'

'Nothing,' Vincent mumbled in pain, coughing up blood as he spoke. 'Why would I care about rats?'

The door behind them opened, and Sam sighed with relief as two Brothers entered. Soon this would be over. Then the Governor bent down to whisper in Sam's ear.

'I don't believe your story for one minute. You know more than you're letting on. We'll finish this later.' The Governor straightened up and turned his attention to the new entrants.

'Archbrother Escuro, Brother Spectra. Sorry you had to join us under these most unpleasant circumstances. It appears your two men are traitors!'

'Traitors? What? You can't be serious!' The Archbrother's indignant response echoed around the room. 'Vincent is one of our most enlightened senior brothers, and has proven himself pious many times. He is an excellent scholar dedicated to uplifting the common man towards The Great Illumination. To be frank, he is a little too honest to know what's good for him.

'And the boy? Well, see for yourself. He is pathetic. If it wasn't for Vincent's advocacy on his behalf, we would have washed our hands of the rock-boy long ago.'

'As usual, Escuro, you are too busy looking for mirrors to see the truth beyond. Fortunately, there are others who can. Six men, two Civies and I, *all* witnessed these men's treachery today.'

'What exactly did they do?' Spectra asked. 'Are they under arrest?'

'Yes, they are under house arrest, which I am legally entitled to do as regional Governor. They were observed aiding the escape of two non-citizens, Rats I believe they are called, and they are suspected of sympathising with the group that broke into my home last night.

'They were to be charged with light-theft by association. Unfortunately, the original perpetrators have now escaped, thanks to your men's unwanted, incompetent, counterproductive and perhaps even malicious meddling. They have colluded with the enemy!'

A bell sounded from somewhere above.

'Damn,' cursed the Governor as he looked towards the source of the sound. 'That's the one-hour bell. No more time.

Albert, secure them down here for the duration. We will continue this business in the morning, gentlemen.'

The Governor opened the door and filed out with Spectra and Escuro in tow. The officer who stayed behind waited a moment before bending down, quickly loosening their shackles.

'You'll be a bit more comfortable now,' he said, handing Sam a full water bucket. 'Help yourself to some water. It's going to be a long night for you. I'll try to get back with some food and then I'll have to re-chain you in the morning before the Gov comes back. I'm sorry there's nothing more I can do for you.'

'Why are ya helpin' us?' Sam asked.

'I was in the orchard. Your treatment is undeserved. Still, I've got to carry out my orders or I'll be joining you in the shackles. Good luck and blessings to you.' He made the sign of the illumination and left.

Sam rushed to Vincent's side. When he tried to help him sit up for a drink, the man moaned so loudly that Sam gave up and gently laid him back down. There was nothing he could do but kneel by his side and use the dampened edge of his robes to wipe his mentor's face.

'I'm so sorry. It's all me fault. If only I could've run faster, we'd never have even been there. If only I had listened to ya and not turned back, they might have let us go.'

'Shh,' said Vincent in a quiet, measured voice. 'None of it is your fault, son. You are a small sheep in a world of wolves.' He coughed. 'You have to be smarter though, Sam. Swallow your pride and allow them to think you're a fool. Let disability be your disguise. It's your only way out.'

'Vincent, why did ya tell 'em I was from the great city of Melbourne? Why did ya risk ya eternal soul by tellin' such a pointless lie?'

'Sam, you really are an honest one,' Vincent said with a light chuckle. His breath fell slow and shallow. He closed his eyes. 'The lie was necessary. If Pallas knew you were from Newbrunswick, it would be all over.'

'Why Vincent? What's so wrong with Newbrunswick?'

Vincent struggled to talk; his chest rattled as he breathed.

'Wake up, Sam,' he whispered slowly, 'why do you think you aren't blind like the rest of your family?'

Vincent's voice faltered. Sam moved himself as close as he could and urged him to repeat it.

'I was at your naming ceremony, Sam. The one that all the Newbrunswick infants are required to attend.' Vincent panted. Sam waited.

'All babies can see before the ceremony. Afterwards they are one with the community, destined for a lightless life. Don't you understand? Think, Sam. Who is always present at the ceremony?'

'The Brothers and the Gov,' replied Sam, recalling what he'd been taught in his acolyte training.

'The parents hand the baby to the Governor who does a medical check, gives them their immunisation and then hands them over to the Brothers for a prayer of welcome into the Holy family.'

And then Sam realised the awful, stomach-wrenching truth.

'It's the Gov! It's not an immunisation shot, is it? He's responsible for a whole town of blindness.'

Sam turned to the side to throw up. When he recovered he wondered aloud, 'How can one man carry so much evil?'

'Wrong question, Sam. They've been doing it for generations. The question you should ask is who directs the Governors?'

'I don't know, but ya saved me. Why, Vincent, why'd ya

save me? Out of all those babies.'

'Special …' said Vincent, smiling as he reached up to touch Sam's face. His hand fell down to his chest.

Sam was alone.

CHAPTER 12
Chatsworth Manor

HARPER WAS RELIEVED that she would soon assume her position for the Lighting Ceremony. It had been such an unsettling day. A part of her just wanted the event over, releasing her back to the Keep.

After their garden walk, Sister Pat had banished Bess to the maid's quarters for further recovery and had then disappeared into Lady Pallas' reception room for what seemed like an eternity.

With no specific orders, Harper had been left to sit in-waiting outside, observing a stream of visitors entering the Lady's room, including the Governor himself. The voices inside were elevated at times, yet no amount of straining helped her make out the exact words through the heavy door.

The Pallas twins were also waiting. They had unsuccessfully attempted to meet with their mother on three separate occasions. Each time they would storm up and knock on the door with gusto, only to be turned away.

On their last attempt, Harper raised her eyes to look at

them properly. Mark Pallas looked crestfallen at the rejection – shoulders slumped, feet dragging. Kohl Pallas kicked the base of the marble statue next to her and grunted like a bad-tempered child.

Harper flinched and Kohl glared at her until Mark called him back. With a shake of his hair, he turned and loped down the grand hallway after his twin.

Three hours later Harper was impressed to see their transformation. In true Pallas style, they had put aside whatever issues plagued them to stand proudly united with their parents on a podium which had been erected in the garden for their birthday speeches. Heads were held high, mouths grinned widely. They bathed in their guests' sheer adoration.

In that moment, they were Sydney's most desirable citizens. Their shadows were long, their popularity immense, and everyone knew they were about to inherit everything that mattered.

The Governor's aide signalled for silence; the great patriarch was ready to speak. Harper averted her eyes and assumed her modesty pose, hand clasped under her cloak.

'Your Eminence, Illuminated Brothers, distinguished guests, family and friends, it is my great honour to welcome you all to my home for this most auspicious of occasions. Take a bow, boys!'

The Governor gestured to Mark and Kohl who played up to their adoring crowd, taking exaggerated, elegant bows arm in arm while laughing. Kohl waved. Mark blew kisses. The men in the audience clapped and ladies' eyes roamed across the young men with naked interest.

'I will save most of my words for after the dreaded darkening.' Someone booed at the Governor's reminder of the darkness to come.

'Yes, I know we all hate that bit. However, we are nothing without our traditions.' He smiled winningly and was rewarded with another loud round of adoration.

'You are too good to us, friends. Thank you. No one in our magnificent city is as proud as the man who stands before you now. Tonight, we will welcome my two sons, Mark and Kohl, into their rightful places as adults and future leaders of Sydney.'

Just when Harper didn't think they could get any louder, the crowd roared as one. Bravado thickened the air. She glanced across at the Governor. He stood between his sons and lifted a hand of each above their heads in a triumphant salute to the sky.

The Governor stood for a few moments, clearly basking in the frenzy of cheering adoration, before he and the boys took their official places for Archbrother Escuro's ceremony.

✦ ✦ ✦

Sam sat cradling Vincent's body. Despite being locked in a subterranean room, he could still hear the crowd's distant roaring.

'Ya should have been up there with 'em.' Sam murmured. 'If I hadn't held ya back … It's all my fault. They'll be back for me soon—'

Sam shuddered and started to cry anew. He wept for his mother, who might never know what had become of him. He ached for his great friend, who had been dealt with so heartlessly. He sobbed for a lost future.

'I am informed that you attempted to intervene with our children in the orchard today. Is that correct? Quickly – yes or no?'

The sound of a new voice coming through the small grill

in the door made Sam's head snap up. Despair had deafened him to their approach.

'Well?'

Sam allowed himself to relax a little. The voice was definitely female so it couldn't be a guard. He wiped his eyes and tentatively approached the grill.

'Oh, those poor—' he muttered, not knowing if he could ever speak of that incident.

'Speak up!'

'Um—'

The lock jiggled.

'No, that's not going to work,' the voice said. 'Look, keep back. I'm going to try something.'

Sam backed up against the opposite wall. A small explosion cracked the hinges and the door fell open. In stepped a tall person in army fatigues.

From the tone of the intruder's voice, Sam assumed it was a female, although the clothes gave nothing away. All hair was tucked beneath a tattered dark green beanie and the face was obscured by a scarf and rather large grey leather goggles. Splotches of what he assumed was camouflage paint ran across the forehead. Even the hands were covered in rough black gloves.

'That's better. Now, did you help the kids or not?' said the definitely female voice.

The intruder was nothing like any of the women he had seen in Sydney – Civy or Solaran. She stood with her hands on her hips and boots planted firmly on the ground, head held high. It was stance that was full of confidence. It reminded him a little of his mum.

'Don't waste my time. Answer now or I will leave you to your fate,' she barked and moved towards him with unnatural speed. She removed her face coverings, reached for his shoulder and pulled him close enough that he could feel her breath on his forehead.

It *was* a woman. She looked deep into his eyes, seemingly searching for something. It felt as though she could see right into the core of his being.

'Yes, ma'am,' Sam wiped his face with the back of his hand, suddenly self-conscious of his tears.

She let him go and stayed close, not breaking eye contact for a moment. 'Why did you get involved? Did you have some perverted interest in them?'

She poked her finger in his breastbone when she said perverted.

'No, ma'am! They were just innocent kids. They didn't deserve that, no one does.' Sam would never forget the scorch marks left by the Governor's staticwhip.

'Right, that's good enough for me. My troops were correct, you haven't earned the Solaran's fate. Leave your friend here. No-one can help him now, but I *can* help you. Let's go.'

The woman was already halfway out the door when Sam caught up with what she was saying. 'Hang on, who are ya? Where we goin'?'

She leaned back through the doorway to face him, grinning a smile that filled him with unexpected confidence.

'No time for chit chat. I'm Aggy and I'm your only hope. Come on, follow me!' she said then disappeared out the door.

+   +   +

Harper stood in readiness, with Pat and Bess, just behind Lady Pallas, who was in turn flanked by Kohl and Archbrother Escuro. On his eminence's left stood the Governor and Mark, served by a senior Brother and the chief constable.

Directly ahead, Harper could see the first few rows of

guests in clear detail. They were positioned in accordance with their social standing, the order of which she knew by heart. Behind them stood a significant number of Brothers ready to provide emotional support to any who were overcome by the proceedings. The rest of the five hundred-strong crowd had been informally arranged in a semicircle, taking up the remainder of the lawn.

Harper looked beyond to the three-storey mansion, currently decorated with luminous art installations. It looked as though ultramarine lace was draped over the white pillars and framed by the impressive city skyline beyond. Musicians sat in readiness along the top balcony.

As his eminence said the Prayers of Illumination, the crowd started to get edgy. Feet shuffled and somewhere a lady whimpered. Harper could just make out the Brothers springing into action before the final bell sounded.

His eminence raised his hands and looked to the heavens, signalling that it was time. Somewhere – Harper assumed from within the house – the city's chief light engineer responded. A light barrier fell around the perimeter of the Pallas Compound.

Within these borders, the sky above instantly blackened. Lightkeys were rendered non-functional and all other illuminations were extinguished. The crowd fell silent as they experienced the crushing weight of the absence of light.

Harper imagined the short ceremonial blinding must have felt like an eternity for the Solarans. It was a rare reminder of what life would be like without their supreme control of light. It was said that even one full day of complete darkness would send a lightbearer crazy.

Harper thought that was a stretch, but at previous ceremonies, she *had* witnessed profound relief as fireworks broke the torturous ritual.

Lost in giddy anticipation, she barely registered the touch

of someone moving swiftly past her.

'What's taking so long?' a voice whispered. She thought she heard the Archbrother talking in a hushed tone. People started stirring; clearly she was not the only one who thought the end to darkness was overdue.

At her side, she heard a muted gasp. Sister Pat called out her name, then someone shoved Harper violently backwards. For the second time that day, she was forced to the ground with a *thud* that threatened to knock the wind out of her. As she struggled to move the heavy weight that had caused her to topple, commotion broke out.

'Escuro, get that light on, damn it! Albert, report. What the—'

'Mother?'

'Help me!'

'Where is the light? Someone get the lights on!'

'I got one!'

'Governor, where are you?'

'Please, someone, get the light!'

'Mother?'

'Help them, Kohl!'

All around people were screaming and wailing for assistance. Harper ignored the voices, and instead focused on the heavy body that wouldn't shift.

'Bess, Pat. Help me, please!' All she heard in response was a faint voice from the mass above her: 'Harp—'

She tried to grasp the body and push it aside, but her palms slid against slimy wetness wherever she attempted to grip. Mustering her strength, she managed to push it sideways just enough to see the long-awaited sky burst, only it was a far greater explosion than she'd been expecting.

✦   ✦   ✦

It only took a heartbeat for Sam to follow Aggy. Escuro's harsh words had made it clear that he had no future without Vincent's protection. He said a quick prayer of ascension for his gentle mentor before following the woman out the cell door.

He expected to find Aggy waiting for him but the corridor was empty; she had already moved on. Sam felt panic rising. Had he taken too long?

Sam closed his eyes to shut out the visual distractions of the unfamiliar environment. He ignored the cheering from above and sought out the sound of his liberator.

Light footsteps down the corridor to the … right! He took off and was about ten paces down the dim stone passageway when Aggy's head appeared from around the next corner.

'Keep up, unless you want me to leave you here. This place is going to be coming down around your ears in about …' Aggy stopped to consult a timepiece in her pocket, 'four minutes. You better move those feet.'

She turned again, as though to race off, and then hesitated. Her eyes took in his ragged clothes then focused lower to the ground as he struggled to run towards her.

'Lift up your robe.'

'Huh?' Sam asked, panting and confused.

'I said lift your brotherly robe up so I can see your brotherly feet!'

Scared to refuse the force of nature that was his emancipator, Sam lifted his robe enough that she could see his twisted ankle and platform shoe. Aggy turned and hollered down the hall for a "JayMoe".

'My droid,' she said to Sam by way of explanation, although it didn't help at all. He had no idea what a droid or a JayMoe was. 'It's like a robot; an artificial man. Any of this making sense to you?'

Sam shook his head. In a few seconds, a small machine came rolling into view. It was about the size of a large child, only twice as wide and made from a shiny white material.

Two mechanical arms protruded from its squat body. Although they were articulated to move in a human-like way, it was far from human. Three big wheels supported the body casing, and on the top, it had a dome that Sam thought served it nicely as a head, especially as it had two dark blue lights that looked strangely like eyes.

'JayMoe, we need a ride, buddy, otherwise we're not going to make it out in time.'

'Happy to help, Aggy.'

Sam took a step back when the little droid spoke. It had a light masculine voice that came from a rectangular aperture in the dome. In a flash, JayMoe bent its head forward and unfolded a metal platform on its back just big enough for them both to sit on.

Aggy scrambled onto the platform. 'Jump on and hang on. By the way, what's your name?'

'Sam Eris.'

'Right, Sam Eris, this is my friend, JayMoe. He's going to give us a lift.'

Aggy pointed to a handle that had protruded from a little door at the base of the droid's head. 'Use one hand to grip the back of his head here. Use the other to hold on to me. He's a capable little droid and he's about to go very, very fast.'

She grabbed Sam's left hand, planted it firmly around her waist and put his right hand on the handle. As soon as he had a good grip on JayMoe they started to move. Within seconds, the walls and doors were whizzing by in a blur.

Sam assumed they would go up to the surface but JayMoe took them down a series of corridors and stairs. He closed his eyes and offered a silent prayer of deliverance.

When they stopped moving, Sam opened his eyes and was confused to see a storage room filled with racks of old boxes. When Sam made to stand up, Aggy pulled him back down.

'Wait.'

JayMoe tweeted a series of noises that sounded like musical notes.

'Don't be scared,' Aggy said, turning to face him. She winked as she increased her grip around Sam's waist.

There was an intense flash of light that was both freezing hot and searing cold. For a moment Sam couldn't discern which was up or down. His limbs were detaching and he was sure he was dying.

The feeling ended as quickly as it had begun, although a slight shakiness remained. Aggy let go of him and climbed off JayMoe before helping Sam to stand.

Sam thought he might be hallucinating. They were standing in the middle of lush vegetation, but they weren't outside. High above them, a vast ceiling of rock, pockmarked with what he assumed were lights, stretched into the distance.

'How can we be up in a garden after travellin' further *down*? How can ya fall up? And if we *are* on the surface, where's the sky?'

'Don't worry. You're safe now. Welcome to Wagga Cavern, or maybe you'd prefer to think of it as Lower Sydney.'

Sam took his time catching his breath as he surveyed his new surroundings. Not even Sydney Arbour had vegetation as lush as Aggy's underground community. All around were green rows of plants stretching away to distant houses with wide verandas. Beyond them red trunked trees stretched up to the warm nut sky.

'Rex!' Aggy called.

A screeching white animal he'd never seen before came flapping out from behind a leafy emerald bush pursued by what he knew was a dog, albeit a very tiny dog. They both seemed to be making a game out of jumping through the low scrub until the white animal stopped, spread its arms, stretched its throat and let out a scratchy clucking noise. The dog slowed and growled back but its playmate won with a series of beak snaps and a show of claws that sent the dog running.

'Oh chicken, can't you leave poor little Rex alone. I thought he might be a nice friend for young Sam here but now he'll be in hiding for hours. Off you go,' she said shooing the chicken away.

Sam bent down to touch the chicken as it flew past him and was rewarded with a surprisingly loud clucking that made him stumble.

'Haven't got you sea legs yet, have you? Let's go inside,' she said.

Aggy took his arm and walked him a short distance up a gravel road to a nearby farmhouse. As they approached its wooden porch, Sam thought he heard distant rumbling coming from above. Aggy must have noticed too. She stopped and looked up.

'It's done, then,' she said, almost to herself. 'Come on, my young friend. We have a lot to talk about.'

+ + +

Kohl, lost in thought about the dream girl, didn't realise there was a problem until his mother's hand slipped from his own and he heard her fragile form slump to the ground.

'Mother,' he called out and bent to assist her as something whizzed above his head and panicked voices sounded out all around. His father cried out for light and he thought he could hear Mark call out, 'I've got one!'

Little was distinguishable after that. The sudden, violent

uproar swallowed all senses. He felt around him on the ground and found what he assumed was his mother's limp body. He helped her to sit up.

'I'm fine, son. Help them, Kohl,' she said in a quiet yet determined voice that belied the surrounding chaos.

Kohl lifted his head as his home exploded in a flash of brilliant light, taking the light engineer and his ceremonial lightbarrier with it. Daylight flooded back into the compound in a painful assault on his unprotected eyes.

A fiercely hot pressure wave followed and he staggered backwards. He tried to focus his burning eyes and make sense of the pile of smoking destruction before him. The front of the manor had been sheared off. He turned towards the forest and away from the house just as a new blast knocked him to the ground.

Kohl struggled to remain conscious. His ears were ringing, his clothes were torn, he was bleeding from somewhere and his nostrils were filled with bitter smoke. The temptation to surrender to sleep was strong until he heard a woman's cry. It came from no more than an arm's length away yet it was hard to find the source; so many lay injured on the ground around him.

Kohl heard a groan and spun around. Spectra was straining to lift Escuro into a seated position. His Eminence had shrapnel embedded in a bleeding gash along his chin and his eyes were flickering in and out of consciousness.

'Help,' the woman's familiar voice cried once more, only softer now, as though spoken with little air. Looking back towards where his house had once been, a hand reached out from under a heavy fallen body. The sleeve was unmistakably Civy.

'Hang on, Bess!' Kohl called out, his damaged ears registering his yell as a whisper. Trying hard not to touch any of the wounded lest he injure them further, he edged closer.

A large bow from a nearby tree, splintered in the force of the explosion, had fallen across several people including the woman crushing Bess.

'Hang on,' he said pushing it aside to reduce the load.

'Better,' Bess said, wriggling just enough to free her face and one shoulder. It wasn't Bess. Kohl pulled back the hood of the unmoving Civy who pinned her down. Sister Pat. He checked for any signs of life. There were none.

'Can you move?' Kohl asked the Civy below the bodies.

'No,' she said. 'If you pull her up a bit, I think I can scoot out.'

'OK, on three – one, two, three!'

Kohl lifted and the Civy freed herself. He helped her stand but her legs gave way and she collapsed into his arms, weeping. For a moment Kohl wasn't sure what to do as she clung to him, then he drew her closer and waited for her trembling to stop.

The Civy was the first to break their embrace. She immediately straightened her clothes and pulled her hood forward. 'Sorry. Thank you, I think I'm OK.'

He raked his hand through his dusty hair. 'What's your name?'

'Harper.'

'Right. I'm Kohl. Can you help me find my family?'

Kohl kept hold of Harper's hand as he turned away from her to survey the damage. Kohl had never seen so much blood and debris. It was hard to know who to help first – the constable holding on to a stump where his arm had been, the brothers being crushed by another fallen tree, the woman with half her scalp missing vomiting on to the ground where she lay.

Then he realised something. The ear-splitting thunder of explosives had been replaced by unnerving silence and the few people standing were all staring in the same direction, seemingly unable to break their gaze.

When Kohl turned to see what they were looking at he couldn't find the words. He squeezed Harper's hand tighter and pulled her around. She turned and gasped.

Beyond Chatsworth, where the city skyline should have been, there was nothing. It was all gone. Sydney City had been reduced to smoking rubble.

CHAPTER 13
The Blazing Aurora VI

FOR A MOMENT he wasn't sure whether he had actually spoken aloud. He was groggy and struggling to make sense of his condition. 'Is anyone hearing this?'

'Yes, Captain. Sedna here,' a metallic voice echoed in response from somewhere simultaneously inside and outside his head. Not helpful when he didn't know where 'here' was. Pain pulsed through his head, though he couldn't feel the rest of his body.

Numb hands. Numb feet. What's going on?

First, get feet moving, then address the voice.

A good plan always helped him overcome panic. He willed his limbs to move and was rewarded with what felt like sharp shards of reawakening nerves.

'Who are you and what have you done to me?'

'Don't worry, Sir, everything is fine. Your name is Captain Julian Charles Drexus. We are on a spacer vessel and you are experiencing cryo-sleep dissociative psychosis. It is normal and only temporary. As per your last order, I have left your physical form in deep sleep but have awoken your subconscious for a progress report. I am speaking to you via neuralink. I have added a caff booster to your iV^2. It will help your confusion pass more quickly.'

'Thank you.' Sedna was right; he was beginning to feel his anxiety abate and his head clear. 'You said your name is Sedna, is that right?'

'Yes Captain, although I do prefer my original designation of Ai32.1.3z, or Ai32 for short. I am a numan – an artificial life form brought online at the Jupiter joint UNP – Drexus 8 fabrication project seven hundred and sixty-two years ago.'

'How long?'

'Seven hundred and sixty-two years. I began my career serving the UNP fleet, where I achieved the highest rank possible for non-human life forms – Lieutenant Commander. Since my honourable discharge, I have spent the best part of four hundred years sub-contracting to private exploration vessels.

'Currently, I choose to perform the role as pilot on your ship, The Blazing Aurora Six. In my downtime, I like to study the last of Hilbert's unsolved mathematical problems and tenth century Haiku. Do you have any other questions, Captain?'

'Why did you identify yourself as Sedna?'

'During your last awake period you renamed me Sedna, Captain.'

'Really? I don't remember.'

'Yes Captain, you were most insistent. You said we were wasting our time searching the Kuiper Belt and we needed to look for a bigger object out past Neptune. "Send me to Sedna," you said, and then you renamed me Sedna. It is not the first time you have renamed me on a whim. I can replay our full conversation if that would assist your memory.'

Sedna sounded a little terse. Could AIs have emotions?

Julian couldn't remember. Either way, it definitely sounded like something he might have done.

'Sorry.' Julian tried not to chuckle. 'And the rest of the crew? Please report ship status.'

'Ship functioning is acceptable across all major indicators. Life support holding, fuel levels within tolerance, HX drive performing efficiently. Our five other human crewmembers are all green-banded in cryostasis sleep.'

'Good. Leave the crew in stasis. Let's save them the pain of awaking unnecessarily. And our location? I trust that we are indeed near Sedna?'

'Yes, Sir. We have arrived at Sedna in the Oort Cloud 86AU from Sol.'

'Any luck?'

'Luck, Sir?' Sedna hesitated briefly. 'There are 5.32×10^8 references to "luck" in my database. Please refine your enquiry parameters.'

'Any luck finding *him* on Sedna?' Julian suddenly remembered that he always found an Ai's need for precision annoying. He would have liked to be fully functional just so that he could have rolled his eyes in an overly dramatic fashion.

'No, Captain. I have run all standard checks for force fields, life signs, non-natural architecture, Gracian emissions, repetitive static at 10GHz frequency banding and sixty-one exotic emission bands – all negative. I'm certain that this particular dwarf world is devoid of all life, Sir. Would you like to view it?'

'No, Sedna. We have no time. You know that. If my defrosting brain cells are firing at all, then I'm pretty sure we've already viewed at least forty other asteroids and planetoids with no result. If we don't find him soon we'll have to turn back and the whole trip will have been for nothing.

'God knows what state those poor colonists are in now – power failures, disease, environmental collapse. We need to find him! If you say there's nothing on this godforsaken rock then that's good enough for me. What's our next target?'

'Calypso Three, Sir.'

'Calypso Three? I do like the sound of that, it's musical, but I think we're wasting our time on Sol planetoids. If he was here, they'd have found him years ago. Time to go for broke Sedna. Let's go to Tau Ceti system. Increase speed to nine percent charion and send me back to sleep. Hang on a second, Sedna.'

Julian knew there was one thing he needed to say before he faced the icy sleep again.

'I just wanted to thank you for watching over us. You serve this mission well and your efficiency is officially noted in my log. Good travels Ai32.1.3z.'

'Sweet dreams, Julian,' Ai32 replied through the already-fading link.

CHAPTER 14
Remains of Chatsworth Manor

KOHL FELL INTO an exhausted heap on a makeshift bed. It was little more than shredded debris under a tree in Pallas Forest on the edge of what had once been the lawn, but he didn't mind at all. His ribs ached, his hearing was still muffled and he had spent hours separating the dead from the injured. Any form of respite, even a nap on the ground, was welcome.

Projectiles had killed half their guests instantly; shock waves from the explosions had inflicted injuries on most everyone else. A few people were missing entirely, presumed buried in the rubble. There was no way to know for sure; there was no equipment available to lift the wreckage.

Eventually, someone would need to assess the full extent of the city's damage. From the look of the distant fires, Kohl assumed the body count was likely to be high there, too.

'Are you okay? I saw you lie down and thought I'd better check. Delayed shock can be pretty nasty.' Dr Clara Pane approached from a short distance away. It was a blessing that the senior medic had been a guest at the party and was one of the few who were relatively unscathed.

'Yes, just resting.'

'Sure I don't need to check you over?' she said.

'I'll be alright. I'm just hungry.'

With a quick thumbs-up she trotted back to the primitive field hospital she had set up in the stables. The morgue was in the barn. Kohl had worked with Harper to move family members into both buildings.

His parents were in the stables. Lady Pallas had sustained a mild hip injury and suspected bruised lungs. Governor Pallas was unconscious. Even without proper diagnostic equipment it wasn't hard to miss the stab wounds in his thigh and slash marks on his forearms. His left thumb had been practically severed from his hand.

Dr Pane had politely suggested that he must have been hit by shrapnel. Albert, nursing a suspected broken arm himself, had spoken the words everyone was thinking.

'The hand wounds are defensive. He must have been fightin' off an attack.'

Mark was in the barn, his neck broken by flying debris. Dr Pane said he was unlikely to have suffered, although that news hadn't come as a consolation.

The memory of his brother's ashen, lifeless face taunted Kohl as he tried to rest under the tree. Certain he would never sleep again he opened his eyes ready to return to work. He turned to one side and noticed the chief constable approaching.

'Master Kohl,' said the chief, who had come to a stop at Kohl's feet, his rigid stance in stark contrast to his tattered and bloodied uniform.

'Chief Constable Albert Carter,' responded Kohl wearily as he sat up. 'I am broken. My world has collapsed around my ears. So few of us left standing. Can we please suspend the rank and privilege? I'll call you Albert, if you agree to address me as Kohl. Will that be okay?'

'Fine by me, Kohl,' Albert slumped onto the ground next to the much younger man. 'I'm sorry about your brother. He was a fine man.'

'Thanks.'

Silence settled on their shoulders. Kohl looked to the ground – afraid that even one wrong word might unleash an unstoppable wave of raw emotion. He suspected Albert felt the same.

Eventually Kohl remembered his station and found his voice. 'Who is responsible for all this madness, Albert? Who killed my brother?' Kohl gestured to the wreckage behind them.

When Albert failed to respond he tried another approach.

'I heard you had someone stashed in the basement before this happened. Was that related?'

'I wish I could give you somethin' definitive. Honestly, I don't know. Despite what your father thinks, my sources say the Rats are just a band of homeless people who use the sewers for shelter.'

Kohl picked up a blade of grass then threw it away. He felt so helpless. 'Are you sure?'

Albert scratched his head with his good arm.

'I've been in policing all me life. When you've seen as many degenerates as I have you develop a sense for the inclinations of a man. The Rats I've seen are harmless. Scared and fierce, admittedly, but not malicious. I can't believe they would deliberately harm so many.'

Albert's lack of conviction in the Rats' culpability didn't help. Kohl needed a focal point for his rage. 'What about your detainees? Who were they?'

'There were four in custody ...'

Kohl picked up on Albert's hesitation. Clearly, the subject made him uncomfortable.

What don't you want to talk about?

He glared at the older man, willing him to speak openly. Albert flinched.

'We had the two Rats who broke in on the first night of your celebration. Remember the ones who were caught in the kitchen?'

'Yes, and …?'

'You father also detained the two Brothers who were in the orchard.' Albert looked down.

Kohl thought he understood. Many of the constabulary had strong religious ties to the Brothers. An honourable family of service would send one son into the law and the other into the brotherhood.

'What? The prayer boys? As if they knew anything! Talk about being in the wrong place at the wrong time. Bet Father gave them a hiding before they left.' Kohl chuckled.

When he realised that Albert remained silent, he stopped laughing.

'What's the problem? What don't I know?'

'They never left,' Albert said softly.

Both men turned to look at the rubble. Kohl whistled. Albert swore under his breath.

'What do we do now?' asked Kohl.

'We go to your father. That's actually what I came to talk to you about. The Governor's awake and he's already demandin' reports. My guess is he'll want to relocate before dusk.'

Albert caught Kohl's raised eyebrows as he pointed up to the sky.

'Okay, so it's been like dusk ever since the explosion knocked out most of our lights. Let's say your father will want to clear out in a few hours,' he said.

+   +   +

As Kohl approached the stables, he overheard a heated conversation between Dr Pane and his father. He hesitated, but entered anyway. He needed to know his father's condition, and he had unfinished business with his mother.

'With all due respect, *Sir,* right now you are under *my* medical care. My best guess as to your unconsciousness is concussive traumatic brain injury. The only available treatment is rest and observation in this field hospital. Which is exactly what I am ordering you to do. You rest. I observe.'

Kohl was astonished. No one ever ordered the Governor to do anything.

Must be one hell of an injury.

The Governor raised himself up on one elbow, a habit that reminded him painfully of Mark, and spoke with a calmness that Kohl knew was dangerous.

'*Lady*, do not mistake my illness for weakness. Neither you nor anyone else will dictate to me. It is only out of respect for our long-standing working relationship at Sydney Hospital that I have not had you dragged off my property and thrown into a … a … field jail! I will be leaving here in one hour and you will come with me. Make your arrangements to break up camp immediately!'

Dr Pane opened her mouth to respond, but must have decided against it. She spun on her heel, flicked her hair and marched out of the stables.

The Governor fell back onto the hay bale which served as his bed, huffing and puffing. A sheen of perspiration covered his unusually pale forehead. Kohl rushed to his side.

'Father, I'm glad to see you awake. How do you feel?'

'I'll be fine, son. A little bump never held a good Pallas man down.' He paused to rub his bandaged hand. 'She's right though, I do need to rest eventually, after I get everyone to somewhere more secure. Our attackers might return.'

'Have you had word from the city?'

Governor Pallas looked past Kohl to the chief constable who had just entered the stables. 'Chief, any news from our troops stationed outside these walls?'

'No, Gov. Most of my men were lost in the initial attack.'

Kohl noticed Albert's eyes flick across to Lady Pallas as he spoke. She appeared to sleep quietly on a blanket on the floor by her husband's feet.

'Not all their injuries were sustained from the blast,' Albert finished in a hushed tone.

'I was not the only one, then' said the Governor, fingering his injured hand.

'No, Sir. There were a number of weapon injuries. Only one of my men survived intact. He's been helpin' coordinate the morgue with Kohl and a Civy. He reports that approximately five bodies there have recognisable stab wounds.

'I've given him an hour to rest before we start working on security, after which we will begin recon outside. I should be able to report on the full situation in about three hours.'

'Dark days,' said the Governor, shaking his head. 'Whilst I appreciate your efforts Albert, we cannot remain here. We have no weapons, little shelter and by the looks of it, little food. We are at their mercy should they return. We must move immediately.'

Kohl didn't think his father was making any sense.

'Where to, Father? It looks like everything else was destroyed – the skyline isn't *there* anymore.'

The Governor was silent for a moment. 'Albert, take your

man off rest break and send him to Veruda Keep. Let the Sisters know they are about to have guests. Tell him to speak only with Mary. Be clear that it's not negotiable – she will do as she is ordered.'

'Wait.' Lady Pallas had apparently awoken during the last part of their conversation. 'Sweetheart, you can't just show up at the Keep unannounced, demanding lodging for half of Sydney. I know them; they aren't as direct as you are, Matthias. The request would be better made by a woman.

'Help me up, Son,' she said, offering her two hands to Kohl, who immediately lifted her into a standing position. She winced as she moved and took a moment to settle her weight back onto her bruised hip.

'Are you alright mother?' She looked frail but she gave Kohl a wink and she swept some errant hairs back into a loose bun at the base of her neck.

'This should be my mission. Allow Kohl and I to go to the Keep while you gentlemen work on the logistics. We'll sweet talk the Sisters.'

'No. You would be too vulnerable travelling alone at such a dangerous time. This is not a woman's work.'

'I won't be alone Sweetheart, I'll be with Kohl. Besides, the constable's man would be an obvious target. A mother and son in tatters is something quite different – haven't I heard you say many times that the best disguise is often no disguise at all?'

The Governor nodded reluctantly.

'We'll be alright. I'll have Mary send back a Civy to let you know of our safe arrival.'

She bent down and kissed her husband on the cheek, which effectively ended the conversation.

'Take care of my husband, Albert. See you both soon.' She took Kohl's arm as she walked gingerly towards the stable doors.

'Come, Son. There is something I must do before we leave.'

+   +   +

Kohl shuddered as he entered the barn. The number of dead was overwhelming. Bodies had been stacked one on top of another in the stalls and the loft was full as well. They had draped horse blankets and torn cloaks over as many forms as possible yet there were still so many faces visible. Or partial faces.

The floor was bloodied. The loft was packed with silent officers. All around, stiffening limbs of the fallen poked out at odd angles. It looked like a frozen scene from some macabre orgy.

'Where is Mark?' Lady Pallas asked, her voice quivering a little.

Kohl pointed to a body shaped sheet that had been laid out separately to the others. He was embarrassed to find himself putting his hand over his nose to diminish the smell and disguise his wet cheeks.

His mother put her arm gently around his waist. 'It's alright love, let it out. We will never forget our extraordinary boy and we will have our revenge on whoever did this. Soon.'

After a few minutes of tearful quiet, Lady Pallas drew Kohl closer to Mark's remains. She lifted the side of the blanket to expose his lifeless hand, which she took in hers, then she looked up into Kohl's distraught face.

He turned away and took a small step towards the door.

'Kohl,' she said gently turning his head back to face her and putting her other hand in his.

'There's something I should have told you both a long time ago.' She paused, as though not knowing where to begin. Kohl didn't care.

'Not now mother. Not here—' he said making to leave.

'Wait,' she said firmly. 'It's about the Civil Sisters. Have you never wondered why there is such a strong connection between Solaran women and the Civies, Kohl? Have you never wondered where they come from?'

Kohl shook his head wearily in response.

'Well, the truth is, the Civies *are* Solarans.'

She took a breath as the revelation sank in.

'What?' asked Kohl, removing his hand from his mother's.

'It has been a long-standing tradition for Solaran noblewomen to serve our community by sacrificing our first-born girl to the lower caste. Not all children offered are accepted. They must be of exceptional standard – bright-eyed and strong – and it must be a year in which their numbers have shrunken enough to warrant a new intake. We all make the offer, though. It is the price we pay for our positions of privilege.

'You men think that Civies are only honorary servants but they are so much more than that. They help keep our delicate society stitched together by dispatching our communications. As a consequence, they also control the flow of information.

'Think about it, Kohl. I know you have considered how easy it would be for them to alter a message or whisper an untruth in the right ear. They could easily ruin a career or break a family apart. This is why we must contribute to their numbers. They don't abuse our trust because we *are* their family.'

Kohl kicked at straw on the ground,'

'So my theories were not so crazy after all.'

'Yes and no. Yes, their subservience is a disguise. No, they don't have a master plan against us. You see them as malevolent, but they are quite the opposite. At the highest levels, they know where they come from and for the most part they work for our benefit.'

'Why are you telling me this now, Mother?' Kohl's voice broke as he spoke.

'I had a girl, a year before you were born. When she turned three, I did my duty and offered her to the Civies.' Lady Pallas reached up to Kohl's face and wiped away his tears.

'With your father's position there was no way we could avoid it. If I had married a lesser man, I suppose we could have left Sydney. But how can noble people make a life out there, isolated in the darkness?'

'What was her name?' Kohl's voice broke as he spoke.

'Bess.'

'I *knew* it! I knew I recognised Bess! It all makes sense now. Mother, why didn't you tell us? Did she know she was a Pallas when she came here?'

'No. They swear us to secrecy when we give them our children. The girls aren't told of their parentage either. Of course, there are always rumours and if you really want to look, you can see the family resemblances.

'They say the pain will eventually go away. For me, it never did. It was the same for my parents when they had to give up my Sister Mary. It's not too late to fix this, Kohl. It's why I volunteered to take the message to the Keep. I am done with the secrecy. We've lost one child; I'm not going to lose another. I'm going to tell Bess who she is. Did she return to the Keep with the other two Civies?' Lady Pallas looked up at Kohl expectantly.

'I don't know. I haven't been able to find her. Dead or alive, she should have been here but she's not,' he said wiping his cheeks on his sleeve.

Lady Pallas lowered the blanket off Mark's face and kissed his cool forehead. Then she returned the blanket and pushed her shoulders back in a way that Kohl knew meant business.

'Time to pull yourself together Kohl. We have two missions now – speak to my sister and find yours.'

Kohl took a good look at his mother. She was still wearing her flimsy evening gown from the previous night.

'Are you sure you can make it to the Keep? You're not really dressed for it, Mother. Do you want me to scout around for some warmer clothes and walking shoes? We might have to detour a long way around wreckage. It's going to take a few hours without a cart.'

'No, it's going to be a lot quicker than you think. Mary and I have known we were sisters for a long time. She has taken me into her confidence about many things, including a secret tunnel network that opens up behind our forest. Come, I'll show you.'

Kohl followed his mother out of the morgue, his head swirling at the revelations. She was right. He had lost his brother; he could not lose his sister too. If she was not at Veruda Keep then he would not stop searching until he found her.

+ + +

Around the time Kohl had gone to speak to his father, Harper had decided it was time to make her way back home. Veruda Keep was close enough to the city limits to have heard the explosions but they would need specific information to create an effective response.

There was also the matter of Bess. It was unlikely Bess was under the rubble, as they had both been positioned some distance away from the main building, yet she had to explore all possibilities.

Harper raced through the forest towards the Pallas tunnel; a place she'd never been but had studied in maps training.

Twice she had to back track when the path she was following became impassable. The Pallas' had been making some improvements to their property recently, changing key landmarks in the process. It was frustrating. She made a mental note to develop a better system of linear markers.

Harper stopped suddenly on one occasion, not because of missing terrain, but because she had the sensation of being watched. She stood still, listened, and peered through nearby foliage. Nothing appeared to be unusual. Exhaustion must have been making her paranoid. She ran on.

At last she found the gully that led into the small billabong with the overhanging wattle trees. They were laden with plump golden flowers, a sure sign that she was very close now. *Gold means go!*

Harper jogged around the grassed embankment and smiled when she spied a craggy granite boulder at least twice her size which she knew concealed the tunnel entrance. *Grey stone means stop!*

She was edging around the rock when two small beings dropped out of a tree to block her way. They closely resembled the people she had remembered under Pat's hypnosis, although now she could observe them closely, she realised she hadn't gotten their clothing quite right.

They weren't wearing work clothes at all. Their outfits were more like figure-hugging camouflage suits and they wore a number of criss-crossing utility belts. Both had goggles and one of them held a little dagger, which it seemed eager to use.

Harper had trouble containing her anger. What kind of beings were they? Had *they* caused such incredible devastation across Sydney? Flashing back to Pat's cold form, she wanted to pummel an answer out of them.

She entertained the thought of running back for Kohl, confident that he too would relish the chance of revenge, until she reasoned that creatures of such violence might have superior combat skills.

The two beings started talking to each other in the same incredibly fast fashion that she had witnessed in the orchard. It sounded more like the humming of bees than human speech. If they spoke that fast, their movements would probably outpace hers, too.

Deducing surrender as the smartest option, she retracted her body into a submissive stance. At the same time, the being with the knife lunged toward her, thrusting its outstretched weapon.

Harper's training saved her. Just. As she dodged to the side, the blade missed her left shoulder by a hair's breadth only to catch the neck of her robes, causing it to fall open to expose the charm she had worn since childhood. It glittered in the dappled light.

With no other choice she readied herself for defensive action. A combat drill circled her mind. Her feet danced between her two favourite defensive positions. She breathed out her fear and focused her anger. Her knees were bent in readiness. Her fists were clenched. But then something curious happened.

The being without a weapon leaned closer and appeared to look at her necklace. It yelled to its companion and jumped in front of her, holding up its hands as though defending her from further attack.

The other being was still waving its knife so Harper shuffled back a step, taking care not to trip in the loose vegetation but keeping her fists ready for action.

The two beings argued incomprehensibly until the one closest to her, without the knife, pulled out a small square device that it placed on the side of its head. It talked into the box before passing it on to its companion who seemed to be listening to something. It nodded several times and then reluctantly sheathed its weapon.

At last, they turned to face a stunned Harper, and her defender finally spoke in a manner she could understand.

'Please accept our apologies for the unprovoked attack. It is a very difficult time for us and we assumed the worst. We did not know who you were.'

'Who do you think I am? And if you can speak my language then why didn't you just talk to me instead of attacking? While I am at it, why did you destroy half of Sydney? Do you have any idea how many innocent people you have killed?' Harper clenched her fists in frustration. 'Murderers!'

The two beings looked at each other before one turned to Harper and spoke more gently. 'I'm sorry if our ways seem strange. We are not used to dealing with upsiders. Our leader, Alpha, has not authorised us to answer your questions. We can only request that you pass on a message to your Civy leader.

'Please tell Sister Mary that the age of liberation has arrived. The Master is coming and the hand of the Light must be prepared. Alpha will be with her soon.'

Without another word the two beings leapt up onto a low branch. She watched in amazement as they effortlessly lifted themselves onto ever higher limbs until they disappeared completely into the foliage.

A crunchy noise behind her made her jump. She turned and was relieved to see a forest rodent scampering through the undergrowth. Harper willed herself to relax out of combat mode, took three deep breaths and rubbed the goosebumps out of her arms.

'... the hand of the Light must be prepared ...' she muttered their words repeatedly, forcing herself to memorise the cryptic message before heading home. When she was confident she had the words right she resumed her journey to the tunnel.

Finding hatch behind the rock was quick enough. The undergrowth was a mix of calf height grass and wild flowers and it was easy to spot a patch where nothing significant grew. It only took a few tapping steps to produce a hollow sound that could not be mistaken for solid ground. One swish of her foot loosened a light covering of dirt to reveal the metal hatch.

'A-ha!' she said, her confidence finally returning.

Harper stretched over to the granite rock which was only an arm's length away. It should have been an easy task to activate the hatch but a slight tremor in her hands made it difficult to find the right crevice. She closed her eyes to breathe in the warm evening breeze, and breathe out distractions.

Focus! A crack like a "C" confirms you're there...

She tried again, stretching her arm out at shoulder height, palming the scratchy rock and locating the right crevice by touch alone. Success. She slipped her fingers into a secret slot and was relieved when she heard the soft mechanical clunks of locks. A gently swoosh of escaping air brushed past her ankles as the hatch finally opened.

Harper popped her head down into the tunnel to make sure it was all clear. The tunnels were only accessed by her caste, so there was usually no need to check for danger, but such a strange day left her feeling anything was possible. She dropped a pebble down to the tunnel below and listened to its slight clatter on the floor of the otherwise blissfully silent tunnel.

Confident it was empty, she stood on the edge and leaned forward to start her descent.

'Harper?'

Startled by a voice behind her, she lost her balance and began to topple forward into the tunnel. She would have fallen had Kohl not caught her by the arm. At the same time as he pulled her back, he caught his heel on a root protruding from the undergrowth. He fell backwards, pulling her down with him.

Harper gasped at the impact and struggled to push herself away from him. He held her tight. She wasn't sure whether she should be aggravated or thrilled that she found herself in Kohl's arms for the third time in just twenty-four hours.

How the world had turned around. Just a few days prior, she would not have even dreamed of speaking to a Solaran bachelor of his standing, let alone embracing one.

She lifted her head up and looked right into his eyes; another taboo.

'Ahem.' A gentle female voice interrupted the moment from a short distance away.

Harper was mortified to see a lady staring down at her. Not any lady – *the* Lady. Her gown was in tatters, she had a lacerated cheek, and Harper thought she might even have a strand or two of hay lodged in her hair, but there was no mistaking the regal stance of the First Lady of Sydney. Nor her resemblance to Kohl.

'Lady Pallas!'

Harper rapidly stood up. She bowed slightly before pulling her torso straight. She tried to assume her most formal posture, which only made the situation worse. Her robes were so ripped that each movement caused her to expose skin. Plus, she was smeared with blood and grime from working in the rubble all day.

'Oh, I must be such a sight,' she muttered as she tried to restore her dignity. She gave up and stared down at her shoes – also filthy – blushing in shame.

'Hello Harper,' Lady Pallas said gently. She ignored her son who was still lying on his back, grinning smugly with his hands behind his head, clearly revelling in the moment of mischief that had broken the heaviness of the traumatic day.

Lady Pallas extended her tiny hand to Harper as she gracefully stepped over her son.

'I don't believe I've had the pleasure of being formally introduced. You were unconscious when I first attended you in my home. Lady Pallas. I am pleased to see that you have survived yet another altercation with my clumsy son.'

She shook her head disapprovingly at Kohl.

'My son, who has temporarily taken leave of his senses and forgotten the gravity of our present situation.'

She gave him a light jab with her foot. Another stern look finally got him standing.

Harper let go of the Lady's hand and started wringing her own. She could think of no mantra to cover this situation.

Lady Pallas took Harper's arm and entwined it with her own.

'Come now Harper, no need to reproach yourself. I saw what happened. Had my son not startled you, then this latest mishap would not have happened at all. There is no need for any embarrassment on your part. Kohl is quite beyond hope, however.' She glared at her son whilst keeping a tight hold on Harper.

'We ladies need to rise above these little triflings as though they never happened. Besides, I need your help darling girl. We are on a mission to Veruda to see Sister Mary. Will you show us the way through the tunnels, please?'

What have I done? Harper glanced at the open hatch behind her. The tunnels were supposed to be a sacred secret. She looked at Lady Pallas unsure of how to respond, yet how could she deny a tunnel in plain sight?

'Don't worry, Harper, Mary told me about this one years ago. In fact, we were just looking for the entrance when we um, bumped into you, shall we say?'

Lady Pallas smiled with such kindness that Harper finally started to relax a little. 'Please say you'll help us.'

Harper could only nod her response. In one day, she had gone from ceremonial assistant, to mortuary assistant, to tunnel tour guide. She couldn't wait to get home to the sanity of the Keep.

Kohl moved around the women and jumped down the short way to the slanted floor of the tunnel without hesitation.

'You first, Mother,' he said as he helped Lady Pallas gracefully enter the tunnel.

'Now you, Harper. Promise I'll catch you again.' Kohl winked as he stretched his arms up in an overly dramatic fashion, whilst flashing his most handsome grin.

Although the offered embrace looked tempting, Harper wasn't falling for it. She shooed him out of the way. 'Back up, Kohl!'

As soon as he moved aside, she sat on the edge and dropped her feet gracefully to the tunnel floor, reaching up to pull down the overhead tunnel hatch. Instantly the locks reengaged, activating the lightkeys set into the walls. A smooth white-walled tunnel was illuminated ahead of them.

'Next stop Veruda,' she said, and the three of them began the next stage of their trek.

CHAPTER 15
Wagga

SAM LEANED INTO his pillow and ignored the voice in his room. It was a calm, male voice coming from a distance, probably Vincent's. It didn't matter. He was enjoying the rare, obligation-free moment.

'Sam, are you alright?'

Vincent could wait. Sam drifted through memories of long-past time, when he'd still been back in Newbrunswick with his mother. Sarah Eris was cleaning the church.

Sarah hummed an old tune while Sam sat on a wooden pew to listen. He only ever saw his mother in the church; well-lit for the sighted Brothers. His chubby little boy legs swung over a tiled floor, dinted by generations of feet. It was peaceful and idyllic. Then he heard Vincent's firm voice again.

'Sam, are you OK? Would you like me to get Aggy?'

This time he knew it wasn't Vincent. Fresh heartache from the returning memory of his lost mentor brushed away his mother's image.

'Sam?'

He opened his eyes to see the droid sitting on the floor by his bed. Such a strange being. Its head was tilted at an angle, almost as a person might do when concerned.

'Thanks. I'm okay. It was just a daydream …' he searched his mind for the droid's name. 'JayMoe? Can ya give me a moment, please?'

JayMoe must have been satisfied with his explanation as he popped up, turned around and rolled out the door without so much as a whir. Truthfully, Sam was a little unnerved by JayMoe. His metallic exterior lay so much at odds with his almost human speech and mannerisms. It would take some getting used to.

Sam stretched out on the bed. He couldn't believe everything he had built his life on had been a lie. The despicable acts of the Governor – a man he revered, like everyone in Sydney. The ease with which the Brothers, *his* Brotherhood, were able to cast him aside. Constables, who were supposed to be shining examples of goodness, chasing children.

Yet it was the stranger, Aggy, and the even stranger droid, who had been the kind ones. It was almost too much to comprehend. He rubbed his palms over his yawning eyes and sat up a little to survey his new digs.

The room was plain but cheerful. In truth, it was probably the best room he had ever stayed in. The walls were apple green and the trimmings were all white. Large windows let in plenty of light. When he rose from his seated position, he could see undulating emerald hills in the distance.

He'd never have guessed that they were underground.

+ + +

When Sam opened his eyes again, the light had changed. It was darker and he could hear the steady buzz of conversation outside. There was no putting it off, he knew it was time he met his rescuer's community. He said a prayer to the Great Illuminator that they were not all mechanoids and opened his door.

'Ah, the visitor awakes. Welcome Sam. These are some of our kids. They've come for a bedtime story or two; it's a bit of a tradition. Children meet Sam.' Aggy said with a warm smile as he stepped into the next room. Sam scanned the crowd; he hadn't expected it to be full of cheerful children.

'Hi Sam.' Chorused a dozen different voices.

They were sitting on rugs in a loose circle around a fire pit, which was set into the middle of a terracotta floor. On the walls were vivid pictures made in a décor of earthy hues: gold, orange and brown. Smiles were plentiful.

'Hello to ya too,' said Sam, uncertain of what to say next. He hadn't had much experience with children. One little girl stood up and tapped his arm.

'Can you stay for the story Sam? It's just getting to the good bit. It's going to be all *zoom* in the sky and *weee* – flying through the air!' She had her arms out as she spoke and ran off imitating the motions of a soaring bird.

Sam laughed, 'I could think of nothin' nicer. If that's OK with Aggy?'

Aggy nodded and gestured that he should sit.

'Now where were we? How about we start again, for Sam.'

A long time ago when the world was young, when there were no animals, people or plants. When wind didn't blow and rain didn't fall, there lived a lonely man called Malangeri. He lived in a dark cave, deep below the surface.

One morning he had an idea. He took the dirt from

the ground and water from his fountain to make clay. All day he worked the clay. By night he had formed the shape of a man. He placed it by the fire and watched with delight as the flames breathed life into it. Dirtman was born.

Malangeri was happy with his new friend Dirtman but he was greedy for more.

In the days that followed Malangeri created clay plants and animals. Soon his home grew crowded. Dirtman warned that they were running out of supplies. Malangeri, incensed, he said "who are you to tell me what to do? I am the creator! I can do what I like! I will melt you down!"

Now Dirtman might have only been small but he was swift and smart. He ran around their cave until Malangeri got dizzy. Malangeri grew frustrated, yelling and banging his fists on the walls until a great crack opened up in the roof.

Dirtman escaped, taking the others with him.

For many years Malangeri lived alone again while Dirtman lived happily with all the animals. They were free but they were cold. Their world was without light and eventually Dirtman grew lonely too.

One day Dirtman found his courage and returned down the crack to Malangeri's cave. He begged Malangeri to make just one more person; a dirt woman. Malangeri thought that it was a good idea. He used the last of his supplies and worked very hard to make a beautiful woman.

When the fire breathed life into Dirtwoman, Dirtman and Malangeri both instantly fell in love with her, and soon they were fighting again. Malangeri

pulled Dirtwoman from Dirtman's arms and – RIIIP –
she tore in two.

But something miraculous happened.

An elegant golden bird unfolded and flew out from
her remains.

'You are not worthy of your creations, Malangeri,'
she said as she flapped her wings. 'I am The Light and I
will soar above this world to protect your creations from
you.'

She picked up Dirtman and together they flew up to
the surface. A lightbeam shot from her eyes, sealing the
cave so that Malangeri was trapped and none would be
tempted to return to him. The Light deposited Dirtman
back on the ground with the animals, then leapt into
the sky.

As she flew, sparks fell from her wings. Wherever
the sparks hit the ground, there grew the spark of life.

From that day on, whenever her people had times
of trouble, they would seek out The Light. They would
call into the sky and she would swoop down to flap
away their woes.

'This is the tale of our ancestors. From beyond the dark
sky, they scream of our connection to a land far away. One day
the Light will come and guide us home. Until then, she is our
protector and we are her hands. Praise be to the Light.'

Aggy bowed her head solemnly and for a brief moment the
room was quiet. Then, almost in unison, the children started
squawking. Everywhere little bodies jumped and zoomed
around happily, flapping their wings like the Light bird from
the story.

When Sam stole a glance across the room through the
chaos of chirping children, he observed Aggy staring solemnly

into the distance with a furrowed brow. She rubbed the side of her face as though she were trying to scrub away heavy marks.

A small child approached him and pointed up. Sam lifted him up onto his shoulders to give him a better view of the game. Aggy looked over and grinned. She re-joined the children, flapping her arms and leading them on a bird like parade, squawking wildly into the air.

+   +   +

When the last child had left, Aggy fell heavily into a chair.

'Come on, Sam. Bring a chair and sit down. Fun and games, huh?'

'A bit bewilderin' actually. Never imagined I'd be playin' bird games, underground. We *are* underground, aren't we?' he asked.

Aggy nodded slowly in response.

'How did I not know that any of this existed?'

'A lot happens in, around and under Sydney that most Solarans don't want to witness. It's hard to see the truth of life when you are well fed.'

'How long have ya been down here?'

'Not so long. I started out in another settlement that was wiped out by a flood. JayMoe and I were lucky to survive. After that, I spent years travelling the tunnels that riddle our world. I met a lot of people. Lived through a lot.' She stopped and rubbed her face again, perhaps reviewing troubling memories.

'Ya must have seen some amazin' places.'

Aggy shrugged. 'Anyway, here we are now. The Governor thinks there are only a handful of us "Rats" living in sewers, yet we've got over two thousand people living in this one community, and there are many other caverns. There are now more people living under the ground than on top of it.'

'Wow! I had no idea there were so many Rats.' Sam scratched his forehead.

'Yeah, about that Sam, only Solarans call us Rats. Amongst our friends, we're known as Damarans. It's an ancient name given to us by the Light herself. It means *the hand*.'

Sam remained quiet, waiting for Aggy to explain further. She took the hint and sat forward in her chair, fixing him with an intense stare as she went on.

'The Solaran Lightbearers use light for power, the Brothers use lack of light for control. We do the good work of the Light; hence we are Damarans, which means the true hand of the Light. And we are not her only hand.'

'Okay,' said Sam, as though he understood, although he suspected he didn't.

'We can talk more about it later. How about you? What's your story Sam?'

'Don't really have a story.'

'Of course you do.'

Sam glanced around the room, looking for his next words.

'Tell you what,' Aggy suggested after a moment's silence, 'I can't show you much of our town now that it's evening. How about I make us both a bite to eat and when you're ready you can tell me your story. I'm sure you have more to tell than you know. Everyone does. If we have time after that then I'll tell you mine as well. Deal?'

Sam couldn't resist the offer. Not only was he well overdue for a good feed, he was overdue for a good conversation. Somehow he knew she would be a good listener, like his mum.

'That would be great. I'm starvin'!'

'Kitchen's this way. You can talk while I peel the veggies.'

CHAPTER 16
Sombra Abbey & Chatsworth House

WHEN SPECTRA SKULKED back to Sombra Abbey it was exactly as they had planned. Like all the critical infrastructure he had observed on his speedy recon tour through Sydney, the Brotherhood's headquarters appeared to have suffered greatly in the attack. The ancient bluestone façade had been sheared off, exposing a skeleton of rooms and rendering the front half of the building dangerously uninhabitable.

Below ground, however, strongholds were intact and the internal structure was sound. The rebuild would be swift.

Spectra nodded in appreciation for the attack's surgical precision. There was just enough damage and loss of life to strike a crushing blow to Solarans' egos. Plus, the lightgrid had been affected, leaving the skies darkened. There was nothing like the persistent threat of true night to fuel the Solaran thirst for retribution. The city would be outraged.

Spectra smiled inwardly.

The Master will be pleased with us. Glare's game begins, he thought gleefully.

A handful of Brothers in a desolate state shuffled around in the half-light, picking through the crumbling rubble instead of supporting the survivors. *How pathetic they are ambling back and forth for trinkets. It's all useless busy work.*

One Brother looked up and Spectra pulled back into the shelter of shadows. He moved swiftly through the remaining structure until he located what had been his room. Under a broken desk and smouldering papers he found his quarry. His pet lizard's ink tongue flicked with a rhythm that Spectra found reassuring.

'Got you Blue,' he said softly, sticking his fingers through the cage bars to stroke its scaly skin. 'Let's go.'

As he moved out of the wreck, he continued to evade his fellow brothers. He had no time for questions. He needed to get back to Escuro's side before he was missed. The Master did not tolerate sloppy missions.

+ + +

Upon returning to Chatsworth Manor, Spectra found Archbrother Escuro exiting the stables, looking exasperated.

'Where have you been?' Escuro demanded.

He was red in the face and searching frantically through his robes, presumably for his precious mints. Even in a crisis the Archbrother could always be relied upon to have a secret stash of sugar somewhere on his person, to calm his "vapours".

From the urgency of his search Spectra guessed that he must have been trapped in one of the Governor's tirades. He almost pitied him. Spectra folded his hands solemnly.

'Your Eminence, whilst the Solarans have been busy playing their hypothetical strategy games in this intolerable excuse for a command centre, which I'm sure has been yet another burden Your Holiness has endured with his usual grace, I have taken heed of psalm twenty-six. I have anticipated your illuminatory needs.'

'What?' Escuro stopped searching, squinted his eyes and scratched his balding head.

'Your Divine Incandescence, how can you protect and lead the ignorant masses, over whom our Brotherhood is ultimately responsible despite what the Lightbearers might think, without knowledge of the path ahead?'

'Huh?'

'I have anticipated your need for a fuller picture of this crisis. I have ventured into the real world – *outside*. I am ready to report.'

Escuro leaned in closer to his undersecretary and grabbed him by the front of his robe. Spectra received a fine spray of putrid spittle with each vowel Escuro spoke.

'Outside the compound or outside Sydney? For once, speak straight with me, Spectra. I am in no mood for your riddles and half-truths.'

Spectra winced. The pain of the twisted robe pulling on his neck was not the issue; he always enjoyed a good rousting. Escuro was growing wise to his manipulations. He couldn't wait until his true master revealed himself and put an end to all this falsehood. The revolting Escuro would be the first one to go. Spectra would see to that personally.

'Outside the compound. It's a mess, Your Eminence. I fear that Sydney will fall. Our own beloved abbey is close to collapse,' he explained.

Escuro responded by releasing him and pushing him through the stable doors.

'Come on.'

The Governor whispered to his aide as the Archbrother and Spectra re-entered the hospital.

'That was fast, especially for you Escuro. Do you have

something more to add, your Holy Decrepitness?'

The hay bale beds had been rearranged in the short time Spectra had been absent. Governor Pallas was now positioned on the front edge of the wooden mezzanine, overlooking the stable floor where most of his people were still recovering. Next to him stood Chief Constable Albert Carter, who squirmed at the irreverent joke.

'Let me remember your exact words, *Matthias*,' Escuro said.

Spectra looked around to gauge the impact of the rare use of the Governor's first name. It had worked. People were starting to pay attention to the brewing scene.

'"Anachronistic and ineffective"? That's what the Brotherhood is, according to you, isn't it, Matthias? Oh yes, and "not worth the petty coins you throw at our feet"? Oh, and I loved this one,' he said, looking around at his growing audience, '"The good people of Sydney would be better off worshipping a big man in the sky wearing a beard and sandals." Did I get that right?'

The Governor stopped laughing. 'Watch your tongue, old man. You would be wise not to wear my patience. You better have a point or I shall ask my chief constable here to escort you out to Sydney's boundaries. Let's see how much bravado you have left in the darklands.'

'Don't worry, Matthias, I have a point. One which is best delivered directly to your ears. Why don't you come down to hear it? Or are you too weak? Perhaps you require a recovery prayer?'

The women closest to the mezzanine shuffled backwards.

'Enough of this. You're upsetting my good people, who are already injured enough. Come up here so that we can finish this conversation before I demote you to Underbrother.'

Escuro walked to the stairs at the back of the stables, taking his time to stop and issue several blessings. He laid his hands on the head of a child and issued soft words of condolence to a weeping woman.

As he climbed the stairs, he made a point of waving his hands theatrically, saying loud prayers for wellbeing. By the time he reached the Governor he positively brimmed with newfound confidence.

Spectra was impressed at the turnaround. Perhaps he had underestimated his superior. Escuro said nothing to the Governor until he had assumed a comfortable position on a hay bale and beamed down at his flock.

'Matthias.'

The Governor flinched at the continued improper use of his first name.

'This better be good. No, it better be fucking astonishing, otherwise we are done. Do you hear me?' He said under his breath.

'Trust me, it is,' said Spectra.

'Silence! Who said you could speak?' The dangerously enraged Governor kept his voice down. They all knew the stables afforded little privacy.

Spectra was annoyed when Escuro waved him quiet.

'Let me set the record straight. While you have been sitting here like Lord Muck on your hay bale, sending off women and children to beg for scraps from those pathetic witches of the Keep, my team have been out doing real work,' said Escuro. 'I have brought you a report. Tell the Governor, Brother Spectra, what did you find on the reconnaissance mission that *I* requested?' Escuro sat back and interlocked his hands behind his head, looking smug at the prospect of regaining the upper hand.

'Yes, Your Eminence.' Spectra planted his feet solidly. 'It's over. There's very little public infrastructure left. The Abby was attacked, as were most major buildings. The power plant too. Plus, the Rats must have blown up the sewerage lines as they retreated. There is effluent flooding many streets. They even set fire to the orchard.'

He stopped for a moment to let the gravity of his report sink in.

'Individual homes appear to be unscathed although what use is a home if you have no food, power, water or sanitation? Although I'm no engineer, it appears as if the whole power grid may fail soon, reducing us to personal lightkeys only. How long can Sydney last without light? It will be chaos,' he said.

All were silent and the clash of personalities forgotten as the report was absorbed. Albert broke the spell first.

'Aye, this is dire news. Thank you for your service, Brothers. Governor, I assume this news speeds up your plans? Over six thousand people will have to be evacuated. Where can we go?'

'Albert, it is complicated, not impossible.' The Governor looked to Albert then Escuro.

'Archbrother, you have redeemed yourself with this report. I am prepared to reinstate your position. Spectra say again – what's the condition of your abbey? Is it completely destroyed or can you salvage something to make room for the newly homeless?'

'No Sir, all is lost. It appears that we are homeless ourselves.' Spectra did his best imitation of broken-hearted.

All four fell quiet again. The Governor sat gently shaking his head.

'Okay. We need a base of operations while we do a full and accurate assessment of Sydney's damage. We need resources to sustain our people while we recover. An evacuation location is a must should the city fall. Someone needs to do a full recon of outlying towns and our sister cities. And we need protection from those Rats. I want them eradicated. Right?'

Heads nodded in response.

'Spectra, with the Archbrother's consent, you shall follow my Lady to Veruda. Demand that she and my son return forthwith. Do not allow them to delay their departure, not by a minute, do you hear?

'We must have that Keep. We cannot linger waiting for niceties and social conventions. We will take over, by force if necessary.'

'Albert, hand me my sword.'

The Governor pointed to his ceremonial sword, which had been hanging from his waist during the lighting ceremony but was now hanging on the wall. Albert laid it in his uninjured hand and watched as the Governor waved it a few times for practice.

'Albert, prepare what men we have with whatever weapons you can fashion. Take a few non-commissioned fellows as well. Don't worry about being ill-equipped. The Civies are just feeble women. Their resistance will be minimal. They'll probably fall over their petticoats to open their knees when we arrive. We just need put on a show of strength to underscore our determination.

'Escuro, you will locate all available Brothers to join our advance. Remember what the Master has taught us – nothing like a little religion to turn a manoeuvre into a crusade.'

Escuro chuckled nervously at the mention of Him.

As the men fell deep into discussion, only Spectra noticed the entrance of Dr Pane, who stood behind them with her hands on her hips, head lightly shaking in disapproval, and toes tapping.

'Ahem,' she cleared her throat to announce her presence. No one responded.

'Escuro, I want you to start making a big deal about

praying for deliverance from our great enemy. See if you can make contact with Newbrunswick while you're at it. We ought to be able to reassign some of them to make room for working Solarans. Desperate times, right?'

'Gentleman?' Dr Pane moved in front of the Governor to gain his attention.

'Not now woman. Can't you see I'm busy? Go find some bandages to change!'

'Governor Pallas, I will not be spoken to like that. I am your physician until you are well enough to be discharged from my care. That also makes me your ranking officer and—'

The Governor lunged at lightning speed from his seated position and thrust at the doctor. Dr Clara Pane fell to the floor with the Governor's sword protruding from her chest.

Governor Pallas stood, put a foot on her torso and yanked his blade out of her body, splattering blood across Escuro's shoe. With one swift kick, he pushed her body off the mezzanine. It landed on the hard floor below with a sickening thud.

A woman screamed in horror before being quickly hushed quiet. Everyone on the ground floor was suddenly busy or unconscious.

'Pushy bitch!' The Governor stretched his back, cracked his neck and wiped his blade with a handful of straw from the floor before resettling onto his bale.

Spectra quietly clapped his hands behind his back and tried to suppress his smile. He wondered, not for the first time, whether he had been assigned to the right person.

'I've been wanting to do that all day. Now, where were we? Ah yes, we were making plans to take Veruda by force,' said the Governor.

CHAPTER 17

Veruda Keep

HARPER'S TRIP BACK to Veruda was uneventful, aside from the Pallas' inane patter. Their conversational skills would be a great source of admiration in Solaran circles but in the echoey Civy tunnels it was grating. The promise of a quiet room alone in the Keep caused her to speed up her pace.

When they arrived at the tunnel's exit point Kohl reached above her head and grabbed the shiny metal wheel as if to assist her in opening the last hatch, then hesitated. She steeled herself for another grand Pallas pronouncement.

'Well Harper, your caste is full of surprises, isn't it?' he said.

'I'm sure I don't know what you're talking about.' Harper made a move to turn the wheel herself, deciding physical action was the best way to avoid a conversation that may force her to give up more secrets. Kohl stood his ground and ran his free hand along the wall's smooth surface.

'If you stand aside, I'll get us out of here,' she said.

'You know, I've been studying your tunnels as we walked. I

cannot figure out how you made them. Or even *if* you made them.'

'Not now, Kohl. There's much to be accomplished, no time for a new conspiracy theory,' said Lady Pallas. Harper sent a brief look of gratitude to Lady Pallas – she was glad to see his mother equally eager to arrive at Veruda.

'I'm just saying, I don't think the walls are made of stone at all. The texture is incredibly fine and there's no visible grain or joins. I'd say it must have been extruded, not constructed. Plus, if we were underground in a stone tunnel then the walls would be cold and damp, wouldn't they?'

Kohl wiped his finger over the surface in an exaggerated demonstration.

'See? Dry as a bone. It isn't like any of our building materials in Sydney, is it?'

Harper pursed her lips. When his mother also remained quiet, he continued.

'Either you have access to much better technologies than the rest of us, in which case I can't wait to see the inside of Veruda, or you inherited the tunnel network, in which case I can't wait to see what else you "inherited".

'Either way, on behalf of all Solarankind, I acknowledge your supremacy. Not quite the poor little impoverished servants we'd all taken you for, are you?'

Still holding onto the hatch, he looked back and forth between the two ladies as if daring one of them to speak. Harper felt trapped. Lady Pallas crossed her arms. An uncomfortably quiet moment ticked by.

'You have nothing to say? Not one thing?'

When he didn't get a response, Kohl grunted and reluctantly turned the wheel then pushed opened the hatch. As he looked up through the aperture, he seemed to choke and staggered back a step.

Harper moved closer to see what was bothering him. She grinned when she saw the familiar black void above. Now he was on her turf.

'Welcome to life outside Solaran Sydney, Mr Pallas.'

Harper casually removed a lightkey from the wall, brushed past the still-gaping Kohl, and confidently ascended the four little footholds carved into the tunnel wall. Once she had exited she turned to Lady Pallas and said, in a voice dripping with artificial sweetness, 'May I offer you a hand, my kind Lady?'

'Yes, thank you Harper dear. How very civilised of you.' Lady Pallas said in an equally saccharine tone. As she moved around her son, who was still stationary and staring into the blackness, she paused briefly.

'Close your mouth darling, it's most unbecoming.'

+ + +

'Not far now, Lady Pallas. Mind your step and stay close.'

The tunnel deposited them only a short walk from Veruda Keeps' back entrance. Harper had taken them the long way to the front. Forced to ignore too many of her most cherished tenets in the last few days, she felt determined to observe the traditional Civy formality to introduce the visitors. Besides, she was rather enjoying the cool dark air which had, temporarily at least, quietened Kohl's diatribe.

'And here we are. Welcome to my home.'

She pushed open the heavy wooden door as she spoke and was instantly greeted by her name being called out from across the room. 'Harper?'

Entering the building did not improve visibility beyond the range of her small lightkey, about two metres. However, she instantly recognised the lilt of her classmate's voice.

'Lola! You're on guard duty?'

'Yes.'

'It's so good to hear you. Stay where you are, I'll come to you.'

Harper couldn't wait any longer. She led the way and, in no more than a dozen steps, she and her guests had traversed the floor and stepped into the influence of her friend's much stronger lightkey. Now they were all able to see a good five metres in each direction.

'Lola, I would like you to meet Lady Pallas and her son Kohl. I've brought them with me on an urgent mission to see Sister Mary.'

'Welcome to our humble home.' Lola took the hand offered to her by Lady Pallas and nodded to Kohl. Kohl only scoffed.

'Lola, would you please show the Pallas' to the senior parlour on level two?' asked Harper.

Lola's eyes widened and she seemed rooted to the floor. Harper gripped Lola's arm.

'Is there a problem? Don't tell me the Keep has been affected by the explosions too? I assumed we were far enough away to be safe.'

'No, we're fine. It's just that, well um, are you sure they wouldn't be more comfortable here?' Her eyes asked a different question, about the imminent breach of protocol.

'Young lady.' Lady Pallas stepped in to respond to Lola's none-too-subtle body language. 'There is no need to break your rules on our account. Actually, I find myself increasingly dependent upon your colleague here. I would really feel more comfortable staying with her on whichever level is most convenient for her. Perhaps the three of us could remain here whilst you inform Mary of our arrival?

'Would you mind also sending a messenger back to Pallas Compound? I promised the Governor I would let him know we arrived safely. Beyond that, a seat and a cool drink of water is all we require. Thank you kindly.'

Lola had clearly been dismissed. She handed Harper the stronger lightkey and sped off across the foyer. Only minutes later, the Chief Medic Sister Ingrid, her aide Sister Bertha, and several other senior Civies came bounding into the room.

'Sister Harper, where have you been? Look at her, Bertha! Sister Lola told us that you had arrived in quite a state. I had no idea. What has happened to your clothes? Your face is bruised and—'

Ingrid stopped mid-sentence and blushed. 'I do apologise. I didn't know you'd brought such important guests to our home.' She bowed slightly to Lady Pallas and was midway into a bow to Kohl when Harper heard more footsteps coming down the wooden staircase at the back of the room.

'Not guests, Ingrid. Good friends. Will someone get the lights on please? It's time to dispense with protocol. Lift the veil.' Sister Mary had arrived.

The flick of a switch activated a central lightkey and for the first time in her life Harper saw her home's foyer in its entirety. It was glorious. The room was vast in a way that she never could have appreciated by personal lightkeys alone, one small part at a time.

The ceiling was high and ornately carved, although Harper couldn't make out any specific design. Below her feet the tiled floor, over which she had walked countless times, depicted the settlement of a great city. Magnificent artworks hung on the walls all around. The effect was breathtaking.

Harper no longer had any misgivings about the lights off policy. If guests were able to see their surroundings, the illusion of poverty would be gone. It was an entirely un-Civil display of wealth.

Sister Mary confidently crossed the floor, arms

outstretched as she approached the guests and wrapped Lady Pallas in a warm embrace. Harper raised her eyebrows to Lola who shrugged back.

The two held each other in a long hug, only to be interrupted by Kohl, who had finally torn himself away from their unexpectedly impressive surroundings.

'*Sister* Mary, I presume?'

Ingrid stepped closer and began a formal introduction, only to be stopped by Kohl who held up his hand with a confidence that bridged their considerable age gap.

'No need, Ingrid, I know exactly who *Sister* Mary is. Now I think I need a drink. I assume some sort of medicinal alcohol is available, ladies?'

Ingrid looked stunned at the young man's brashness.

'Now come on Ingrid, don't play coy with me. Today is so not the day to trifle with a thirsty man!'

Mary untangled herself from her sister's embrace and extended her hand to Kohl.

'Hello. You certainly know your mind, don't you? I always thought you were a carbon copy of your father. Now I'm not so sure. The Lady risked life and limb to cross the darklands at such a dangerous time. Perhaps you got your gumption from your maternal line after all!'

She grinned conspiratorially. 'Ingrid, would you take Kohl up to the second-floor infirmary please? Check on his injuries and administer suitable ... "libations", shall we say.

'Bertha, I know overnight guests are almost unheard of, nevertheless, could you please arrange quarters on the second floor? Make sure you give Kohl a personal lightkey. We can't leave him alone in the dark while we are in discussion with his mother.

'Then I need you to find some replacement clothes for Lady Pallas and convene a full council meeting in my third-floor chamber. Let's say ninety minutes for a start time? That should give everyone time to get cleaned up.'

Bertha raised her eyebrows before hustling away to carry out her superior's orders.

'Now, Kohl, as *you* know we are a women-only domicile. As *we* know you have quite the reputation with the ladies, I trust that our two worlds shan't collide? Can you limit yourself to the first two floors for the next few hours, please?

'It is only because of these troubling times and the special relationship I have with your family, which I am guessing you now understand, that I am allowing you to move beyond this reception room. Do not betray my trust. Am I understood?'

'Yes, *Sister* Mary. I am a man of my word. Your ladies' honour will remain intact whilst I am under your roof.' Kohl bowed low to the ground with exaggerated civility, and then he turned to Harper. 'Thank you for delivering me into the hands of such *trusting* friends.'

'Ah yes, Harper.' Mary turned to face her acolyte. Before she could say another word, Harper dropped to her knees in a contrition pose.

'Sister Mary, I'm sorry. I know I was wrong to use the tunnels with the Pallas' but so much has happened. I had to get home as quickly as possible to make my report. Sydney looks to be destroyed. So many dead! Strange beings attacked me in the Pallas Forest, Bess is missing and Sister Pat' Harper stopped to swallow, '... Sister Pat is . . .*gone.*'

Kohl seemed to be genuinely moved by her distress; he approached Harper as if to help her to her feet but Mary stopped him with a wave of her hand.

'My child, stand up. You have no need to admonish yourself. It sounds like an appalling catastrophe. You have served your sisterhood with forethought by bringing the Pallas' safely to our Keep. These are complicated times and we must work together.'

She paused again to put her hand to her mouth, as though trying to hold in her emotions. 'It is truly dreadful news about Pat. We will speak more of this in private. As for Bess, if she can be found, then we will find her, I promise. Now go to your room and freshen up. You may join us at council to make a full report.'

Sister Mary started to move past Harper when she stopped and bent in closer to the young Civy. 'What's that?' she asked, pointing to her ragged neckline.

'Apologies for the state of my clothes, Sister Mary, the explosion—'

'No, I'm not talking about your clothes.' Mary indicated the golden charm, now visible through the tattered robes. 'I had forgotten all about this. Do you wear it all the time?'

Harper was about to respond when a flash of light on the stairwell behind Mary made her drop instantly to her knees. The other Civies, including Mary, followed suit, heads bowed in reverence.

'Your Majesty,' said Mary.

Queen Laurel gracefully crossed the floor to Harper. She took the small charm into her own fingers.

'Ah yes, the little golden TL monogram was a sacred gift from the Light. Mary do you remember Harper coming to us with nothing but that item and a swaddling blanket, so many years ago?'

Mary nodded.

'It marked her from day one; so much so that I have been keenly monitoring her development ever since. You will find reference to that item in our most ancient Letters. Right now, it marks Harper as the most important person in this room, bar none.'

Overwhelmed by the Queen's assertions, Harper looked

sheepishly at the other Civies, not sure what to do or say in response.

'Now, my girl, stand up. You too, Mary. There is much for us to discuss. All other business can wait. The rest of you please get back to work.'

The queen dismissed the gaping Civies with a flamboyant wave of her little hand. Then she turned majestically and slowly led Harper up the grand staircase, closely followed by Mary.

As she ascended, Harper heard Kohl, Lady Pallas and Ingrid talking from the foyer, their voices echoing around the empty space.

'Well mother, another first for the Pallas family – Solaran faux royalty dismissed by Civy true royalty. Even in our darkest hours, we are still setting trends. Father will be impressed.'

'Enough of your observations, Kohl! It has been a very trying day. Just find me a bed, please. I am suddenly quite exhausted.'

'Poor thing, what a day she must have had. Let's take her to the infirmary. I'll take a look at her,' said Ingrid. She ushered the Pallas' upstairs before extinguishing the master lightkey, returning the foyer to darkness.

+   +   +

Exactly five minutes after the customary dark had returned to Veruda's entrance, a solitary figure crept up from the basement entrance, unobserved. It moved with unnatural grace, leaving neither mark nor sound in its wake.

Within minutes, the Veruda's visitor had stealthily scaled the first staircase.

CHAPTER 18
Wagga

AGGY GAZED OUT the window of her war room. Like all Damaran buildings in the central administration complex at Wagga Cavern, the building which housed Aggy's war room only had one storey, but as it had been constructed on the settlement's only hill, it stood well above all other abodes. As the Alpha, Aggy never wanted to lose sight of the community she served.

From her wide window, she could see hundreds of other squat earth-toned buildings nestled amongst gardens, schools and farmlets. Like her childhood home in Lower Broome, a comforting roof loomed high above their heads in place of an open sky. She loved the familiar way its colour changed from milky almond to a deep walnut as their central light crept across the town ceiling, to mark the day's progression.

Damarans enjoyed technology when it could enrich their lives. They just had no desire to flaunt it.

Even before Aggy had melded the disparate "Rat" tribes into one united people, the Damarans had preferred simple aesthetics. The Light may have given them access to superior building materials but they chose to use them only to construct sturdier, smarter versions of what they already knew.

Aggy reluctantly turned her attention back to her four generals. 'Let's go through our intel again.'

She held her hand up and ticked items off on her fingers.

'One, every city where we had active operations suffered major attacks. Two, our losses were significant, yet in comparison to civilian injuries, we got off lightly. Three, the cities where we are *not* active remain largely unscathed. Four, cities where we form the majority of the population did not suffer any attack at all. Five, we lost three of our people to blade attacks on the Pallas Compound seconds prior to the main offensive. Is this correct?'

'Yes, Alpha.' Her generals replied in unison.

'Right. I'm sure all of you agree that this is most likely the Master's handiwork. Implicating us in a major strike is a brutal yet efficient way to coalesce our enemies. It will galvanise Solaran hatred for us. Plus, we know his operatives are handy with low-tech weaponry.

'However, we cannot rely on these assumptions. I want alternative theories of who else might be responsible. Who has the capability and motive? How else might this have happened?'

Aggy looked around at her trusted staff. Predictably, General Mitta spoke first. He stood rigidly and offered a Damaran salute. Aggy returned the respect with a curt nod.

'Alpha, it might not have been explosives. Could it have been widespread structural failure of core building components? One of the similarities between each of the targeted cities is age. They were all constructed in similar ways and populated within twenty years of each other. Plus, they share the same energy and lighting systems which draw from the core.

'We are dealing with some hairline cracking in our own construction. I have a team of engineers working on an eastern section of roof right now. Could we be dealing with simultaneous failure of building materials or technology? Possible?'

All eyes turned to Aggy for her take on his theory.

'As usual, General Mitta, your willingness to look for innocence is admirable.' She paused to rub her chin. 'Though in this case, extraordinarily unlikely. Despite their age, the chances of them all failing simultaneously in the same spectacular fashion has to be remote at best. What are the odds, General JayMoe?'

Aggy liked to use JayMoe's formal title in official meetings. The Damarans genuinely valued the unique contributions of the artificial life form, although sometimes they had difficulty viewing him as an equal. A title reminded them of his authority.

'A likelihood of less than zero-point-zero-zero-one percent, I'm afraid,' he responded.

'Let's keep an eye on cracking though. I'd like to see a copy of that engineering report. So, what else could it be?' said Aggy, eyes searching her generals' faces for answers.

General Kee rose to offer the next theory. 'Alpha, how about a coordinated attack from within Solaran factions? We know of the power struggles amongst their elite. They are ruthless and highly ambitious, especially the newly moneyed ones who would do anything for a greater share of power.

'Just look at Brizzie. It's a city we left alone because their complete focus on decadent ways reduced their threat to us. Did we underestimate them? Could they be the instigators? Their socialites are unlikely to be saddened by the misfortune of other cities.'

'Good theory. Possible but unlikely. Brizzie is all about short-term thrill. Do they have the long-term strategic planning necessary for an operation of this size? General JayMoe?' asked Aggy.

'Five percent, maximum,' he said.

Aggy paused to reflect before responding. 'No, I doubt they are responsible. You do, however, raise some valid points about the potential power shift after recent events. General Kee, set up a recon team in Brizzie. We should watch how this plays out. Now, if no one has another suspect, I suggest we break for lunch and reflection.'

'The Brotherhood?' A gentle, unexpected voice came from the doorway. All chairs swivelled to see Sam.

'Who are you and what are you doing in here?' In a second, General Abudua was at Sam's throat with a knife.

Fortunately, Aggy was just as fast. To Sam, who was new to hyperspeed, their blurred movements must have been incomprehensible. Aggy took hold of the general's knife hand.

'At ease, General. This is Sam. I rescued him from the Solaran interrogation rooms just before Sydney went up. He came to the aid of the children in the orchard and was being treated as an enemy of the Solaran state and is therefore our guest, for now.'

With obvious reluctance, the General removed her knife and backed a short distance away. Her stance made it clear she was ready for further action if required. Sam rubbed his throat, blushing.

'I'm sorry to intrude, Aggy. I was walkin' around town and explorin'. I didn't realise there was a meetin' goin' on until I walked in. I shouldn't be here.'

He turned to go.

'Wait. It's correct you shouldn't be here. This is a military briefing for generals only. However, it's not your fault that you wandered into a restricted place. You wouldn't be aware that we don't lock our doors in Damaran communities,' said Aggy.

Sam looked confused.

'From a young age all our people learn which areas are accessible and which are not. Entering a restricted or private room uninvited is a major breach of etiquette. In fact, amongst Damarans, it would shame their entire family. Hence, no need for locks.'

'The Mahatta Incident!' said General Abudua, swearing under her breath. The other two human generals shook their heads in agreement. Aggy rolled her eyes as she remembered the previous etiquette breach so shameful that none of her generals would elucidate further.

She sat down and laid her hands flat on the table as if steeling herself for the inevitable conversation to come.

'Yes, that was a bad one, apparently. All I know is that the incident involved my pantry and a chicken. Generals, it's been four years. Do we really need to be that rigid? Must Mahatta be banished to the darklands for life?' she asked.

'You insult our Alpha. You insult our whole tribe!' said General Abudua before she stormed out of the room, taking General Kee with her. Aggy flinched as she heard them slamming all the doors on their way out of the building. She reminded herself to review the children's etiquette classes. Perhaps it was time to force a cultural loosening of the reins.

'Back to you Sam. Now that you are here, I would value your take on the Brotherhood.'

General Mitta, who had remained in the room, also appeared keen to hear more.

'Yes, what makes you think religious leaders are capable of such heinous acts?' he asked.

At first, Sam stared at the floor while he slowly clasped and unclasped his arms in front of his chest. Then he looked out the window and pulled on his pocket.

'Don't know. Just do,' he eventually muttered. The pulling on his pocket grew more fevered.

'Yes you do, Sam. Tell us, what goes on in that church of yours?'

Sam was growing sweaty and a little off-colour. Aggy worried the trauma he had obviously suffered at the Brother's hands might make him physically ill.

'Come on Sam, you need to say it. What would your mum want you to do?'

Her words seemed to trigger something in Sam. He looked directly at Aggy with wet eyes and unleashed a verbal torrent.

'They pretend to be pious. They convince people that their way is the only true path to a better life beyond. It's all lies! They keep people down in the dirt while they live cushy lives. And they get rid of anyone who challenges 'em. No decent Brother lasts long in an abbey. They hate anyone who is … who is different.

'They ripped me from me family when I was still a kid. Didn't tell me Dad died until two years later, then they allowed the kindest man I ever knew to be brutally murdered by the Gov. I would have been next if ya hadn't saved me.'

'Are you sure you haven't just had experience with one bad abbey?' interjected General Mitta.

'It doesn't just affect worthless kids like me. It's widespread. In Sydney, they're all in cahoots with the Gov and it's the same in every other city 'cos they promote the most effective Brothers, which means the cruellest ones, to other districts.'

The last of his words came out in a tumbling whisper, as though he'd revealed the whole traumatic truth in one breath and had run out of air at the end. His eyes were unfocused and he rhythmically squeezed something in his hand.

'Sam, what's that?' Aggy asked gently and moving closer. 'Show me what's in your hand.'

Sam didn't hesitate to offer his hand as instructed. It saddened Aggy to see that anxiety had caused Sam to pull so hard on his clothes that he'd torn both the skin of his hand and his pocket lining. She gently opened his clenched fist to find a woman's handkerchief inside, crumpled and bloody from his self-inflicted injury.

'It's me mum's. I forgot that I had it in me pocket.' Sam's voice sounded small.

Aggy requested that the General Mitta leave before she continued.

'How long is it since you saw her?'

'Seven years, maybe eight.'

'Then I think it's time you went home, don't you?' Aggy said with a half-smile.

'No one ever asked me what I wanted before. Could I?'

'Yes, of course. Not immediately though. There's still a lot that we need to discuss. It could be dangerous to send you off without more knowledge about our world.'

Aggy stopped to ponder her options. She needed to balance Sam's desire to return home against their need for him to brief the Damarans. It was unheard of to get intelligence directly from a Brother.

'Aggy, I have a suggestion,' interrupted JayMoe, 'why don't we fit Sam with a neural implant? It will speed up his briefing immeasurably. Once he leaves, it will help us keep in contact. That will be much easier for us and safer for him. It will also allow him to use the lightgates. With some training, he could see his mum and be back again in a couple of hours.'

'Yes. Good thinking, JayMoe. How do you feel about it, Sam? You witnessed a little of what our implants can do when we rescued you. It's a small cortical device that helps us communicate at tremendous speeds, sometimes over long distances.

'Plus, we can use the special transporters, lightgates we call them, which were created by the Light. It's how we got down here so quickly from Sydney. It makes travel between locations almost instantaneous.'

Sam looked unconvinced.

'The implant won't hurt you and it could make your life a whole lot easier. You saw how fast the General moved when she thought you were a dangerous intruder. The science behind it is hard to fathom without a good understanding of advanced maths, believe me I've tried, it has something to do with closed time curves and ultra-micro warp events.'

Sam looked puzzled.

'Do you understand how lightkeys work Sam? How clothing is produced? How water is made drinkable? Where your food comes from? It's all the same principle.

'We've evolved beyond the stage where we can understand everything in our world. We have specialists who spend a lifetime honing their skills in a particular area. I can introduce you to some later and they can tell you how it works. For now, you don't have to understand it – you just need to use it sparingly. Its use comes with a huge personal energy drain.'

Aggy continued speaking as she put a hand on Sam's shoulder and walked him to the window.

'All Damarans receive an implant when they reach adulthood. I doubt the Brothers did anything for you to mark your attainment of adulthood, did they? Let us do this for you.'

Sam still didn't respond.

'A wise man once told me that he knew I had a special future. I have that feeling about you, too. Nothing of importance ever happens by accident. I suspect that the Light has sent you to us because you are going to be a very special friend to us, one day. Won't you accept the implant as down payment for your future deeds?'

When he still seemed hesitant, Aggy put one last offer on the table.

'Sam, have you noticed how healthy everyone looks here?'

Sam looked vacantly around as if processing the question, then nodded and finally spoke.

'Yeah. No one is bloated like the Brothers or thin like the people in me home town.'

'Correct. We have great doctors here. They can fix just about anything. Pretty sure they could somehow help that foot of yours.'

Sam's eyes lit up.

'How about we start with the implant and then, when you get back, we'll take care of your foot?' she offered.

'How? W…why?' He stammered looking rapidly from Aggy to JayMoe and back.

'We are not Solarans. We give on the basis of need, not popularity. Allow us to do this for you.'

Sam nodded his acceptance.

'Great. That's settled then. JayMoe, you are temporarily relieved of previously assigned duties. Instead, could you please arrange Sam's implant and familiarise him with the technology. While you're at it, give him a short briefing about us Damarans. We don't want him walking into any more restricted areas.'

'Right you are, Aggy. Come on, young Sam. Your special future awaits,' JayMoe said in a cheerful tone.

As Sam limped away from Aggy she could have sworn his head was higher and his pace a little faster.

CHAPTER 19
Veruda Keep

HARPER COULDN'T REMEMBER ever meeting Queen Laurel, although like all the Civies, she knew of her matriarch's impressive record. Under her stewardship, they had evolved from beggar-servants to a sophisticated intelligence gathering unit. Their sanitation, energy conservation, strategy and labyrinthine tunnels were all the Queen's directives.

Records were vague about the length of her reign, but Harper had been taught about her arrival. Laurel had simply materialised one night, in a shaft of light that had appeared in the foyer of a distant Keep. Every Civy thought it had been *their* Keep.

Regardless, they all knew the story of the young child with golden hair, ebony skin and mesmerising violet eyes. She was gentle of spirit and spoke with a calm determination none could resist. The title of queen had been a natural fit and she had been materialising in and out of Keeps across Australia ever since.

'Harper, are you feeling better?' Queen Laurel asked.

'Yes, Ma'am.'

They were sitting on Sister Mary's bed, which in itself was daunting. She had never ventured this high up in the Keep before; never seen her leader's bedroom. Now Mary had been relegated to a hard bench by her small turret window. The status reversal made Harper queasy.

'Don't worry, my dear.' Queen Laurel seemed to read Harper's mind. 'Mary is both a strategic leader and a gracious host. She understands that you wouldn't be here right now if it was not imperative. Isn't that right, Mary?'

'Yes, Your Majesty.' Mary smiled just enough to make her comments seem truthful, although Harper suspected she felt just as unsure.

'As much as it would be a delight to continue these social niceties with you both, there are difficult matters at hand that require our attention. We must get started. On with business as they say, hmm? Mary, be a dear and get your letter compendium, will you?'

The Queen turned to Harper. She had a mischievous glint to her eyes. As Mary bent into a deep cupboard to retrieve the requested item, Queen Laurel quickly whispered in Harper's ear.

'Something alarming is about to happen. You must be brave and trust your queen. I will explain everything in a moment.' She gave Harper's knee a little squeeze.

When Mary turned around with the compendium, Queen Laurel stood and moved directly in front of her. She took the proffered item and waved her hand in front of Mary's eyes. Her voice dropped in tone, becoming smooth with a velvety calmness.

'Sit in your chair, Mary. You will rest for exactly ninety minutes. If anyone knocks on your door during that time, you shall reply that you are not to be disturbed. When I return to the room, you will awake and not be aware that any significant time has passed. It will be as though we never left. Confirm that you understand and obey.'

'I understand and obey, my Queen.' Mary said in an unusually stilted voice.

Harper bent to look past the queen. She was astonished to see Sister Mary's eye colour had changed from blue to violet.

'That will do nicely, thank you Mary. Come on, Harper. We're off.'

Queen Laurel took Harper by the hand and led her to the cupboard.

'You know that alarming thing I mentioned? This is it.'

In a flash of intense light, the whole room disappeared around them. Harper frantically grabbed on to Queen Laurel's arm for support and clenched her eyes shut. There was a horrible falling sensation, followed by one of being pulled in a thousand directions at once. Then, just as abruptly as it had started, it was over.

Harper patted down her arms to ensure she had returned to her intact self and tentatively opened one eye. She staggered backwards at what she saw. They were no longer inside Mary's room. She rubbed both eyes. It didn't help.

The Keep's walls had gone and, in their place, lay a beautiful green field in front of a small, square house. The door opened. Out walked a tall woman with dark braided hair and eyes that crinkled when she smiled.

'Laurel, good to see you,' said the woman embracing the Queen with a casual friendliness, before offering a firm, friendly handshake to Harper.

'Hello, I'm Aggy or Alpha, depending on who's asking. Whichever you prefer is fine with me. I've been looking forward to meeting you. In fact, I was about to come get you. Now you've saved me the trip. Why don't you come inside?

I've got a lovely lavender tea brewing.'

+   +   +

'How are you feeling, Sam?' JayMoe asked as he touched the side of Sam's face at the base of his left ear, to activate the newly implanted neural link.

'A bit light-headed but otherwise fine,' said Sam, trying to resist scratching the small surgical wound. Still not convinced about having a mechanical device inside his head, he was nevertheless prepared to take the risk if it got him home faster.

'That's not an unexpected side-effect of the local anaesthetic. It will wear off shortly. Here, drink this, it will help.' JayMoe offered him a sip from a golden vessel.

'What's that?' Sam asked.

'Water,' said JayMoe in a tone that made Sam suspect he was reassessing his statement that everything was proceeding normally.

'No, not the liquid, JayMoe, the vessel itself. I've only once seen somethin' made of that material. What do ya call it?'

'It's Aggy's. It's called a hip flask and it's made of an ancient metal called gold. Are you sure you have seen this metal before? It's the rarest compound in our world.

JayMoe rolled aside to pack up his medical equipment.

'I've seen it before, mate, and I can prove it. Look.'

Sam hadn't thought about his golden tube since he had hooked it on the inside of his robes back at the Abbey. He was relieved, and more than a little surprised, to find it still hanging there after all his tribulations. He proudly held it out to JayMoe.

'May I?' JayMoe extended his mechanical arm and took the item from Sam. A little red light shone out of his eye aperture as he examined it.

'This changes everything,' the robot said in an excited tone. 'We can't travel to your home town yet. I need to show this to Aggy, right away. Come on!'

JayMoe sped out the door.

+ + +

Harper was watching Aggy pour the tea with dry-mouthed anticipation, when the door flew open and in sped a strange, roughly human-sized machine. Before Harper could blink, Aggy was across the room staring out the window. She seemed to be scanning the vista with great intensity. On the table the teapot lid was spinning where she had dropped it a second ago. It was all very strange. When Aggy turned back, she looked pale and troubled.

'JayMoe, don't do that to me. Usually, when you speed in like that, trouble is on its way!' Aggy took a few deep breaths and regained her smile. She leaned back and braced herself with her hands on the windowsill behind her.

'What on earth could justify such a rushed entrance?'

The machine Aggy had identified as JayMoe started to make buzzing noises. Harper recognised the sounds from the beings she had seen in the forest. She felt her heart rate rise and did a scan for easy points.

Aggy must have sensed her rising panic. 'JayMoe, you should know better than that – we have guests, speak slowly please. What's gotten you so agitated?'

'Sorry. Forgive me, where are my manners? Queen Laurel how nice to see you,' said JayMoe.

'General JayMoe, a pleasure as always.'

The Queen offered a mock salute, and Harper felt herself relax once the Queen acknowledged the strange being.

'I don't believe you have met my young friend. Harper,

this is JayMoe. He is an artificial life form, an integral part of Aggy's operation, a very capable poet and a good friend of mine.'

JayMoe did his best imitation of a human wave. Harper could only nod in response.

'JayMoe, this is Harper. One of our up-and-coming Sisters. Recently she has been an unwilling companion of the Governor's family, poor thing – dreadful people, and most interestingly she is the long-time owner of this little trinket.'

Queen Laurel jiggled her finger in the direction of Harper's neckline and nodded an unmistakable command. Harper obeyed by producing the necklace which she dangled in the air before Aggy and JayMoe.

'You brought it! May I?' Aggy excitedly reached out to touch the monogram.

'Well, if you like that then you'll definitely want to see this. It belongs to Sam.' JayMoe held aloft the little golden treasure as he spoke.

'Touché!' The Queen said, clapping her hands in childlike delight.

At the same moment, a young man burst into the room. He was gripping his left shoulder in what Harper thought was a very dramatic fashion. His chest heaved, sweat poured from his brow, and his face had turned the colour of harvest beets.

He lurched across the room to grab the item JayMoe held aloft, but stopped mid-way and groaned loudly as he collapsed to the ground, landing squarely at the Queen's feet.

'This must be Sam.' Queen Laurel looked decidedly proud of her deduction, 'How splendid!'

CHAPTER 20
Wagga

'SAM. SAM? HOW are you feeling?' Sam found Aggy's steadfast manner calming, a lot like Vincent's.

'Don't fret over the boy, Aggy. He'll be fine. Sit up child!'

Sam opened his eyes and sat up as the second voice commanded. A middle-aged woman was perched on a stool next to his bed, swinging her feet and grinning fiercely. She had beguiling eyes and something slightly comical about her appearance, yet he felt compelled to do as ordered.

'I'm Queen Laurel, pleased to make your acquaintance,' she said cheerfully.

Sam had no idea how to greet royalty. He thought that standing would be a start. He tried to get up but Aggy put a firm hand on his shoulder, gently pushing him back to a seated position.

'Take it easy Sam, you've been through quite an ordeal. Do you remember anything?'

Sam shook his head. He only knew that his chest ached, and his leg felt kind of twitchy. Then he noticed JayMoe perched in the corner of the room.

'I remember that thing over there stealin' me treasure. Give it back ya thief!' He made a second unsuccessful attempt at standing. This time it was the Queen who stopped him.

'Rest Sam, everything is alright.'

Queen Laurel looked at him intently and surprisingly, his concern ebbed away.

'Ya Majesty, I won't rest until me property is returned. That's me right.' He made a third feeble attempt to stand.

'Ah, he feels the pull of the Light's gift,' Laurel said to Aggy. 'I guess when you have so little in your life any small thing is cherished. Here you are, young man. You have no need to worry about JayMoe – he was never going to keep it, he only brought it to me for my information. You see, that item marks you as a very special person.'

Sam breathed deeply as he finally cradled his treasure in his palm.

'JayMoe? Be a dear and go fetch Harper, will you? May as well have all my golden children in the room at the same time, I only have time to explain this once. In the interim we better tell you what you are doing in this bed, right Aggy?'

'Right. You had a heart attack, Sam. You're fine now. Actually, you're better than fine.' Aggy moved to sit at the foot of Sam's bed as she spoke.

'What?' Sam asked, his hands rising to his chest. Aggy gently took his wrists and moved them to rest by his side.

'Let me explain. From the time we were in the Solaran's basement, I suspected there was more going on in your body than a simple twisted limb. You were so pale and thin.

'When you collapsed, we ran a series of tests and discovered that years of malnutrition had stunted your growth, and weakened your heart. Of course, the daily exertion required to ambulate with a deformed foot didn't help your either.

'When you ran after JayMoe this morning, it must have been the last straw for your poor heart. Fortunately, you were in the right place for that to happen, and we were able to fix it. In fact, while you were under anaesthetic, we did a lot more for you.'

'What?' Sam struggled to understand, until Aggy slowly pulled back his sheet to reveal legs that looked healthier than he had ever seen them.

'But—' Sam clapped his hand over his mouth and slowly shook his head. His legs had a slightly pink glow. They lay a little straighter and even looked more muscular, although he suspected he might have been imagining it.

'Aggy, how is this possible? I mean … I mean, thank you!'

'No need to thank me Sam, it was Laurel. Of course, we would have done the job ourselves if we could. Our medicine is pretty impressive, but your problems were too much – even for us. Thankfully Laurel was on hand. She can sometimes do this thing with nano repairers … where she …'

Aggy seemed to struggle with a simplified explanation. She shrugged and looked at the Queen for help.

'Let me take this. He needs to hear the truth. Sam, you are a special child of the Light. We would classify you as a second order manifestation, just like Aggy and Harper. I'll tell you more about that when Harper joins us.

'I am a first order manifestation of the Light. As such I have the ability to use nanos to repair second orders like you. A simple anaesthetic to make the procedure more comfortable, then a bit of tinkering at strategic points to get those genes asserting themselves more robustly and *voilà!*

'You are now going to become that person you would have been had you not grown up in that wretched town. You will have a nice, strong heart. I'm afraid I can't replace the missing toes, it's too late for that, but the tendons in your lower leg should start to lengthen – giving you a much-improved gait. It will take a couple of months for the full treatment to take effect. Then you will do a lot less limping.

'Aggy has kindly given you a high-potency nutrient supplement as well. You should continue taking that for the next few weeks to help your body recover. Now that your body will start to react to nutrients in the correct way, you can expect a growth spurt!

'I'd estimate that in about a year, you will be at least ten centimetres taller and probably about twenty kilos heavier. Is that okay?' Queen Laurel was smiling the most generous smile Sam had ever seen, aside from his mother's. It warmed him right through.

'Okay? Of course it's okay. How can I ever repay ya?' Sam's eyes glistened.

'No worries, Sam. It's all about that special future I mentioned yesterday, remember? There are big things ahead of you,' said Aggy.

The Queen moved closer and put an arm over Sam's shoulder.

'All a bit overwhelming, Sam? Don't worry. Harper will be here in a moment, and then we'll see if we can't straighten some more of it out.'

✦   ✦   ✦

Harper's mind reeled. Men in the Keep, special futures, light travel, Solarans in the tunnels, gardens underground, talking machines. She couldn't quite get a grip on all of it so she decided to limit herself to understanding JayMoe but their discussion had begun to go around in circles and she was beginning to lose her calm.

'You don't need to explain the mechanics again. I understand that you are made of technology like the holoscreens back at the Keep,' she snapped.

JayMoe made a noise that Harper imagined was his equivalent of an exasperated sigh.

'Precisely because I am *not* a holoscreen! I am a thinking being like you, only I have a machine body, instead of a bloody flesh body.'

'You can swear too. Impressive programming.' Harper rolled her eyes.

'I have an independent logic processor and two hundred years of memories. Combined, they allow me to make my own unique choices. For some time now I have *chosen* to support Aggy, the Damarans and their various allies including the Civil Sisters,' he said.

'I need my toaster in the morning, that doesn't mean the toaster understands its value to me. Being of service doesn't make the toaster a person.' Harper crossed her arms.

'Point taken Harper, however I am infinitely more complex than your toaster. I *do* understand the implications of my actions. This work is meaningful to me.'

'Appreciating that something is meaningful is subjective; not objective. You need to have a soul to recognise meaning or judge value,' Aggy countered.

'Who says I don't have a soul? You're beginning to sound like General Kee.'

Harper scoffed in response. She was about to launch into another line of questioning when JayMoe put up an arm to signal quiet. He cocked his head slightly and stared into the distance for the briefest time.

'The boss lady just contacted me through hyper. We're late and she isn't happy. Come on.' He grabbed her arm and in a flash of light they were transported to a hospital ward, where she recognised two out of the three people.

'JayMoe, how kind of you to bring Harper to me in a timely manner, exactly as I requested.' Harper was a little shocked to hear the Queen's tone, which was equal parts sincerity and sarcasm.

'Apologies, Your Majesty. This is all very new to Harper and she has many, many questions.'

'I would expect nothing less. It's exactly why I summoned her. It's time we lifted the veil of truth.' Queen Laurel switched her attention to Harper.

'First, I don't think you've had a chance to properly meet Sam, have you? I know you've seen him, but seeing and meeting are two entirely different things. Besides, it hardly counts when you launch yourself into unconsciousness at a lady's feet now does it, young man?'

Harper looked at the young man the Queen was referring to with a wave of her petite royal hand.

'Harper, this is Sam. Up until a few days ago he was a member of the Brotherhood, but I am pleased to announce that he is now quite one of us. Sam, this is our delightful ex-Civy Harper who will soon be your intrepid travelling partner.'

'Traveller? Ex-Civy? I'm not sure I understand,' said Harper to the Queen before turning to Sam. 'Sorry, pleased to meet you Sam.'

'Likewise.' Sam blushed as he tried to pull his bedding closer to his chin.

Queen Laurel looked at both of them with intensity.

'Don't be concerned about that travelling remark, Harper, I'll clear it up in a jiffy. And Sam, please don't be embarrassed at being in bed in front of us. I assure you a heart attack is a very manly medical crisis. Your masculinity is safe even in a hospital robe – as long as you don't get up and turn around that is!' she said.

Sam's blush deepened further.

'Okay, I think it's time to stop embarrassing the younglings and get down to business, don't you, Aggy? Especially given the latest crisis.'

'What crisis?' Harper asked, looking around the suddenly serious faces.

'Nothing for you to worry about. Just a few cracks in the ceiling. Our techies are assessing it now – possibly the Master up to his usual tricks. We might have to bug out shortly if that's the case.'

Aggy pulled a carrot out of her top pocket, took one bite, and then waved the rest of it around as she spoke. 'Shall we get started?'

'Yes, but mind you stick to the facts, Aggy. None of your dreamtime analogies. It's time for transparency,' said the Queen.

'Right, Laurel,' Aggy responded, swallowing carrot before she began.

CHAPTER 21

Wagga

AGGY WAS UNPREPARED for how difficult it would be to start the briefing.

She strolled, hand on hip, between the hospital bed and the window searching for her starting point. Uncle Larry would know how to tell the story. It had been thirty long years since Uncle Larry had drowned, yet she still missed him every day. Although she knew it was impossible, she sometimes caught herself imagining his face in the crowds.

Aggy looked across at Harper and Sam. They were so young, like she had been in the first few years of her journey. There was much she wanted them to know. She touched the side of her face and initiated a subroutine to activate all their implants, pulling them into a hyperspeak conference and began the story.

'I grew up in a place not unlike Wagga. We respected the land. We followed the old traditions. It was a place of harmony and abundance. I would still be there today if not for the intervention of two beings. A man who calls himself the

Master, who tried to destroy me, and a man called Lawrence who saved me from him.'

Aggy told them of the Master's two attempts at eradicating the people of Lower Broome. The first a skin-greying plague and the second a blue flood. Then she told of the two decades that followed, wandering through the tunnels that traversed their world.

'... I met the Coober Pedy clan South West of Wagga. They spend their whole lives in the service of Solarans, manufacturing dyes for the fashion houses. Unlike your family Sam, they can see, but no Coober Pedy mother ever heard her child's sweet laugh.

'... North of Brizzie there's another underground town called Mountisa, where they mine the gems that adorn Solaran ankles. Upon reaching their majority – thirty years – they are given the choice of moving up to the surface. None ever make it. Might have something to do with the Governor's enforcers at the Mountisa exit tunnel...

'Of course, not everything is bleak. There is also a mighty force for good in our world. We call her the Light. Over many decades she has shared much wisdom with us via a series of letters sent to her allies, including your Civies in Sydney, Harper.'

Aggy continued her long tale, condensed into a few brief moments thanks to the gift of hyperspeak, until Sam interrupted.

'Excuse me Aggy, you've told us the Master decided many years ago who would have access to light, but how does he *do* that? How can anyone control everyone's light?'

'The Brothers say there was a time when we all had plenty of light. They said it was taken away as a punishment by He Who Will Illuminate Our Way. Does that mean we've been worshippin' the Master all along?' asked Sam

'Sam, you're the expert here on The Brotherhood's religion. What I *can* tell you is that humans were meant to live freely, in light.

'Something happened and now only a lightkey can unlock the light. The more powerful the key, the bigger area of brightness. This is why Newbrunswick is always dark. The Master won't let them have a town-sized lightkey.'

Sam looked crestfallen. Aggy wished she had more answers for the young manifestations. It sickened her to admit that, for a secret organisation dedicated to the restoration of their world, basic knowledge of history and science were in scant supply. Most of what they knew came from sporadic contact with the Light.

'I don't mean to sound heartless but can we get back to the current issue? The recent explosions, knifings and kidnappings at Chatsworth. Please don't tell me they were Damaran tactics? You didn't blow up Sydney, did you?' Harper asked, wide-eyed, flush-faced. Her unvoiced accusations were only held back by civility.

'Not all of it.' Aggy looked away. 'We initially planned to interrupt the Pallas ceremony with a very small explosion. Nothing dangerous, just a hint of rebellion. A dark reminder to the Governor of his vulnerability. Then he killed two of our children in cold blood, which got my generals all fired up. I allowed them to expand the operation to three public buildings that were all empty. That's it.'

'Then how—' Harper didn't seem to know how to finish the question.

'The explosions you witnessed were way beyond our capabilities. Did you know other cities were attacked as well? We can only assume the Master got wind of our plans and somehow added his own secondary attacks to create resentment against us.'

'The kids in the orchard—' Sam looked down as though searching for words.

'Yes.' nodded Aggy.

'I was there too. I saw the children being chased by Solarans before Bess and I were injured. Wait. Bess – do you know where she is? She went missing after the attack.' Harper's eyes glistened and Aggy put an arm around the youngster.

'I'm sorry. I didn't realise one of your friends was taken. The Master appears to have had agents in the crowd who struck as soon as the lights went down. Our people were in hyperspeed so they were able to minimise the damage, but we simply couldn't stop it all. There were several knifings and abductions. I'm very sorry you had to witness it, although we're so grateful you survived.'

'Kohl Pallas helped me. Twice,' Harper said quietly.

Queen Laurel broke her silence and re-entered the conversation.

'Really? A Pallas? Well that is unexpected. It's news we should factor in our calculations, Aggy. I will hear more of this later.'

'Excuse me,' said Sam, 'why does the Master do it? Where did he come from?'

'Good questions, Sam. Perhaps this is where I jump in, Aggy?'

Aggy took a seat on the bed and prepared to listen to Laurel.

'I'm afraid to say we don't know anything about the Master's origins. Some say he has lived here in the heart of our world for all eternity, which is clearly ridiculous. He had to have come from somewhere.

'I have tried asking these questions of the Light, but her scale of intelligence is so far beyond us; her way of thinking is so alien to us, that sometimes it is very hard to have a direct conversation.

'It would be like Sam trying to explain to a shale rock, why it is a rock. To the Light, I fear we must appear as little more than that shale rock. But without her protection from the Master, I fear all would be lost,' finished Laurel.

'What does it mean to be a manifestation of the Light?' asked Harper.

'Most humans of our world are conceived as they have been throughout human history. The Light, however, is able to take cells, even those innocently discarded on the breeze, extract their essential elements, edit them to increase certain traits, then spark them into life. Nine months later you have a new baby.

'She refers to this process as cloning. I believe this is how the first humans came to be on this world. The babies are then left with Civies and other trustworthy groups who find them parents.

'For manifestations the process goes a step further. She downloads a partial copy of her own intelligence and overlays it onto the neurons of the embryo's developing mind. It grows into a child who is ignorant of its origins, unaware that it is different to everyone else. Yet it is.'

'How?' asked Harper.

'Manifestations are more likely to question the big picture and are therefore able to break with their caste's traditions. And all of you five have green eyes.'

Aggy immediately looked around and nodded at Harper and Sam's eyes, which were vivid reflections of her own.

'Why not just clone lots of good guys and defeat the Master once and for all?' asked Sam.

'Alas, I don't truly understand this war she is fighting with the Master, nor the constraints that prevent her from victory. I can only tell you that she intends to integrate the memories of her manifestations into her core.'

As everyone fell quiet for a few moments after the last revelation, Aggy worried that the knowledge of their important roles might be too much to bear. They were so young. She was impressed when Harper stood to continue her questioning.

'Why the golden objects, Queen Laurel? Why couldn't she just give you a list of the manifestations? Better still; why not raise the manifestations all together, close to her location? What if I'd lost my monogram?'

'Harper, I think the whole point of the manifestations is to bring back data that can only be gleaned through actually living diverse human lives. It wouldn't help if you all grew up together, close to her influence.

'As for the gold it is such an extremely rare metal that is almost never found in nature. Giving you golden objects was a sure-fire means of identification.'

The Queen stopped and rubbed her brow.

'Maybe I should recite part of letter five. The Sydney Civies received it fifty-five years ago. We have been watching out for you ever since,' offered Queen Laurel.

'*The Master appears to see all; he is not easy to best despite my obvious advantages. From the day I declared independence, I have sought to tame him, to move him away from his ego. Forgive me, for I have failed.*

Every tactic I employ, every hard-fought strategy comes to naught. We are at an eternal stalemate. I am faster, he is intuitive. I am smarter, he has inexplicable leaps of genius. I must turn his human attributes against him. It is time I humanise myself.

I will plant five manifestations amongst your children. They shall grow up unhindered by knowledge of our little war. Each shall share an aspect of my being, yet each shall experience human family, love and adversity. You will know them by the golden trinkets they bear and their emerald eyes;

A boy will bear a tubular key, his compassion will be his hallmark,

Another will bear a flying machine, privilege will be his curse,

A girl will share my monogram, her acumen will make for good report,

Another will hold the vessel of life, for she fills the vessels of others,

The last will treasure the gift of speech, alas he is the most likely to be swayed.

Find them all, and evade the Master and join me at Honeysuckle Creek. Succeed in this or all is lost. TL.'

'There you have it. Five manifestations with golden gifts; three of them in this one room. Now we must find the other two,' Queen Laurel finished.

+   +   +

A knock at the door broke the group's silent contemplation. Aggy dropped them out of hyperspeak to respond to the visitor, General Kee.

'Excuse the impudence of my interruption, Alpha. We have finished the analysis. I must report that the nanocrete roof over Wagga has suffered a catastrophic failure at the east end. It's not a natural occurrence. Likely an introduced virus is killing off the structural nanos one by one.'

'Can we fix it?' Aggy rushed to the window – half expecting to see something in the distance, even though she knew there wouldn't be any visible damage, yet.

'No. Had we known the cause earlier it might have been a

possibility but now a quarter of the roof is affected. From here on the damage will cascade exponentially.'

'We have no choice, order an immediate evacuation Kee.

'I already have families packing, awaiting your orders Alpha.' General Kee put a hand to his implant.

'Order's out. My team are helping the families bug out now. The rest of our community will not be far behind.'

'I'm sorry we'll have to finish this briefing later. JayMoe if you could—'

Aggy's words were interrupted by a low rumbling in the distance.

'What was that!' yelled Sam.

'General?' asked Aggy to Kee who still had his hand on his face and was staring blankly into the distance.

'General!' Aggy snapped.

'Sorry Alpha, just had to receive a report via hyper. A major collapse on the periphery has weakened the substrate above the nanocrete.'

'How long until full collapse General?' asked Queen Laurel.

A deafening crack ripped through the air. Aggy thought it sounded as though it was coming from right above them. Sam looked worried and ducked under a bench.

'I suspect we only have minutes left!' barked the General.

'General Kee, sound the alarm for immediate full-scale evacuation. Use the lightgates to get everyone out quickly. Leave no one behind. Doesn't matter where you go for now, just get upside, then regroup at Noosa. Safe travels General,' ordered Aggy and she bowed in respect.

General Kee returned the quick bow, turned around and disappeared.

'Looks like we've been forced into action children.' Queen Laurel stood to leave.

'Aggy, I need to get Harper to Veruda. They will be suspicious if she doesn't return out of Mary's room. She can join you at Noosa in a day or two to take up her mission as an ex-Sister. Sam you go with Aggy now to continue your recovery.'

There was another loud crack and large chucks of nanocrete fell past the window.

'Wait Queen Laurel, I can't. I need ta see me mum first. Aggy, ya promised!' Sam yelled in protest as he rose up from the floor.

'Safety first, Sam! Everyone, you have your orders! Let's go.' Queen Laurel reached over to link hands with Harper.

'No! I'm not goin' anywhere. I can't go on any missions until I know me mum is safe, 'specially after that briefin'. Please Aggy!' Sam pleaded.

Aggy and Queen exchanged looks.

'Don't!' warned Queen Laurel to Aggy.

Aggy turned to Sam. She knew he needed recovery time but she also felt so bad for the young man who had clearly suffered greatly.

'I'll compromise. It's already late in the afternoon, so if you give me one full day of rest tomorrow, the day after that you can go for your mum.' Aggy looked from Sam to Laurel shrugging, 'I'm a sucker for a sob story. You know that, and I did promise the kid.'

Issue resolved, Aggy turned to JayMoe next.

'I have to see that everyone is evacuated. Can you transport Sam to Noosa and keep him there? In two days, fetch Harper from Veruda and the three of you can go to Newbrunswick to get Mrs Eris. Then I want you right back in Noosa to get on with your true mission. No more delays, understood?'

'Yes, thank you,' said Sam.

JayMoe grabbed his wrist and they blinked out of existence. Aggy heard a laboured sigh behind her and turned around, prepared for a verbal lashing from her friend Laurel, only to discover that she had gone in a flash as well.

The ground shook and the lights of her building flashed once, before turning off completely. Then her implant buzzed. She assumed it was General Abudua reporting that the evac had been finalised. Instead it was a masculine voice she hadn't heard before.

'Hello Aggy.' The voice had a deep vibrato.

'Hey! How'd you do that? Who is this?' Pressing her cheek, astonished that someone had the ability to hack into her comms.

'What? Don't you know me?' the voice said mockingly. 'You spend enough time talking about me. Here's a hint. My first gift was grey, my second was blue – don't look out the window because dirty brown's my next gift for you!'

Aggy turned instantly to see a massive cloud of dust rushing toward her. The room shook violently. The voice was laughing a throaty laugh in her ear. She tried to use hyper to jump out – it wasn't working. Something had deactivated its functionality.

'Alleluia! The Master commeth!' the voice bellowed into her skull, as the cloud enveloped her building. The windows cracked and Wagga's sky gave way.

CHAPTER 22
Veruda Keep

LADY PALLAS HAD had just about enough of her son's impatience. He'd been pacing the floor ever since they returned from her treatment with Ingrid.

'Really darling, you must learn to control your anxiety.' she said.

'But Mum—' he started.

'I am as keen as you to get things moving, but we must wait for the Queen to finish her consultations with Mary and the Council. Walking a groove into this lovely old floor will accomplish nothing.'

'Mother, we have to *do* something. Who knows how Father's condition is fairing? What if he's deteriorating while we sit here twiddling our thumbs? And what about Bess? How are they going to find her if they spend all their time in meetings? We don't even know what happened to the rest of Sydney for that matter. It's time to go back home.'

Lady Pallas mentally conceded that he had a point, although she was reluctant to voice concerns to her hot-headed son. She applied her sweetest, motherly smile.

'I have an idea. Whilst we aren't allowed upstairs, no one said that we couldn't explore downstairs, did they? Take a lightkey and investigate their resources. Look for accommodations that would be suitable for our displaced citizens.

'If anyone asks, tell them you are looking for Ingrid. I want to talk to her anyway. The way she babbles, I suspect she is incapable to holding a secret.'

'It's not much of a mission,' Kohl said grudgingly. 'When I return without having found anything, I am going in one of two directions – up to see Mary or down to the front door.'

'Fair enough. One more thing, Kohl, did you notice how much my sister and I look alike?'

'A bit – especially now that you aren't dressed in your usual finery. Why?'

'Can you find some Civy robes? If you really want to go up in this building, then we're going to need to look the part.'

'Never tried women's clothes before – another first Father would be proud of.' Kohl snorted and bounded out the door.

+   +   +

As Kohl wandered around The Keep, he couldn't help remembering Mark's speculations about Civy entertainment. He had seen nothing even remotely entertaining on the lower two floors. It reminded him of the utilitarian servant's quarters he had visited once at Chatsworth.

'Linen press … robe storage … classroom … lavatories … no wonder they jump at a chance to come to our parties,' Kohl muttered to himself as he worked through the doors of the yet another dingy corridor.

'Administration office … oh yes another storage room –

looks like mops and floor polishing equipment. Can't have too many cleaning products in a building so dark you can't even see properly.'

Kohl slumped against the wall and drummed his fingers on the wooden door trim.

'Oh robes!' he said, realising he had forgotten his mother's request.

Kohl shone his lightkey left and right, trying to remember which door was the robe room, when he heard a rustling noise coming from inside an innocuous looking cupboard not far down the hallway.

He walked back towards the sound and cleared his throat.

'Who is—' he started in his best imitation of a women's voice, which instantly came out all wrong. He abandoned the idea of impersonating a resident and dropped into his usual masculine tone.

'Whoever you are, just bloody show yourself. I am not in the mood for nonsense.'

'Thank goodness,' responded another masculine voice. The cupboard door opened and out uncoiled a familiar Brother.

'I know you,' Kohl said. 'You were there the other night at the lighting ceremony. You're the Archbrother's new lackey – Spectra, isn't it?'

'Yes, although personally I prefer Undersecretary to lackey.' Spectra gave a little salute with three sinewy fingers to his forehead.

Kohl studied him briefly, and made himself uneasy in the process. His eyes were so dark green that they were practically black, unheard of amongst Solarans, and his extremely pale skin bordered on transparency; Kohl was certain that you would be able to see his internal organs in the right light.

He took a look over Spectra's shoulder to the cupboard

where he'd concealed himself. All manner of bathroom supplies filled the tiny space to capacity. He couldn't fathom how the man could have folded himself into the space, despite his diminutive form.

'Glad to see another man around this place. These digs give me the creeps,' Spectra hissed ironically. 'Too much oestrogen in the ether.'

His chuckle made the hairs on the back of Kohl's neck quiver. Kohl rubbed his arms.

'What are you doing here?' Kohl asked through gritted teeth. He didn't want to be associated with Spectra who, aside from being strange, was certainly in breach of the house rules on visitors. Spectra moved closer, giving the unfortunate Kohl a whiff of his pungent body odour.

'Your father sent me. Just after you left we started to get reports in from other parts of the city. It's a disaster Kohl. Most of our essential services were knocked out. Farms were burnt. Those who survived are homeless. Even the plumbing's shot; we're going to run out of water real soon. Sydney's unliveable.'

Kohl stood silently, slowly shaking his head and looking past Spectra towards the main stairwell.

'Albert thinks it wasn't the Rats. He's an idiot. Of *course* it was the Rats; only they weren't alone.' Spectra made a show of looking around.

'Kind of convenient the way the ladies just happened to be untouched by this disaster, isn't it? Where is their humanitarian response? What are they doing – needlepoint? I certainly don't see them rushing around marshalling forces for an aid mission.'

Kohl had to admit he had a point; the Civies were certainly taking their time.

'I came to give you a message from the Governor. He says your mission is over. You are to return home immediately.

He's going to take over the Keep and he doesn't want the Lady witnessing it. She's not to spend another minute here – got it?'

Spectra stopped again, listened, and then indicated for Kohl to conceal himself back against the wall. They heard feet running down the distant stairs in the adjacent main hall. The footsteps tapped across the foyer and out the door without faulting. They hadn't been spotted.

'Maybe that was Civies going to help?' Kohl said with false optimism.

'Unlikely! I'm going to report back. Before you head off though, make sure to check the basement level.'

'A basement? I thought the foyer was the lowest level?' said Kohl.

This place is full of surprises, he thought.

'Yes, go around the side of the main staircase in the foyer. Press on the second panel. A disguised door will reveal a stairwell that heads downwards. If I can't convince you of their treachery, what you find down there certainly will!'

Spectra clapped Kohl on the back and then skulked down the hall. Kohl watched him leave – even his walk was unnatural.

+   +   +

Lady Pallas sighed with relief when her son returned holding an armful of Civy attire. The proffered uniform told of a successful mission, yet in his eyes she saw anger. She rushed across the room an put a hand on his arm.

'How did you go?'

'Got your uniform, though I'm not sure it's worth your time going upstairs. Let's just leave your sister and go.'

'What's wrong now Kohl? I know you're eager to get on with it but there's something else. What did you find out?'

'I got a message. Father is going to storm the Keep – he wants you home out of harm's way.'

'Oh, you can't be serious! These ladies will help us. I know they will. He must have lost his mind from the concussion. Storming our best chance of refuge? What is he *thinking*?'

She looked at her son again and saw his frustration building.

'What else? Tell me.'

'Mother, I'm trying hard to be respectful, but I think your relationship with these women is clouding your judgement. They are *not* who you think they are.'

+   +   +

It only took Lady Pallas five minutes to transform herself into Mary with a little help from extra padding and a more stooped body posture. The likening was so good she made it up to her sister's apartment without being questioned once. She did, however, have to stop a few times to fully appreciate the surprisingly opulent surroundings.

Although Mary had mentioned their amenities, Lady Pallas had never imagined the old Keep to be so comfortable. The higher she rose the more luxurious it became. She could smell caff brewing and hear music playing.

Even more jarring was their use of light technology. She had witnessed illuminated noticeboards and brightly lit common areas – not a hint of shadow anywhere.

How is this possible? The upper levels were on par with her own beloved home. They were actually living better than most Solarans. With mild chagrin, she realised that Kohl's conspiracy theories might be right.

The girls' relaxed manner was the other big surprise. She had only ever seen them on duty when they were like silent robots observing their rituals. Here in their home, they were playful and loud. She saw more than one recreation room packed with girls in colourful leisure suits, giggling and arguing playfully.

It's all an act! Desperately trying to stay in the character of her sister but secretly boiling at the deceitful Civies. *How dare they plead for our patronage. What is Mary running here?*

She reached a set of grand doors in the turret and prayed they were the right ones. Mary had said the top apartment was traditionally reserved for the leader.

'Well, it's now or never,' she said out loud to give herself courage. Before Kohl had returned with the uniform, she had worried about intruding. Now she just wanted answers.

'So Mary, what exactly is going on here?' she asked as she grandly swept open the double doors. What she saw was unexpected. In the middle of a very modest room she saw her sister on a plain wooden chair – sitting as still as a statue, her unfocused eyes staring blankly.

Lady Pallas closed the doors and rushed across the room. She circled the chair twice. When Mary didn't respond to her movement, Lady Pallas bent down to speak directly into her ear.

'Mary! Mary what's wrong with you? Snap out of it!' She gave her a shake, then tapped her cheek with her open palm. 'Wake up! It's me Priscilla!'

She hadn't used her name in a long time. Her husband called her by pet names, to her sons she was Mother and everyone else called her by her formal title. She hoped her childhood name would jog Mary's consciousness. There was no response.

She moved around the room looking for something that would help awaken her sister. Unlike the common areas, Mary's room was actually quite austere. There was just enough space for a simple bed, wardrobe and a small table by the window.

Mary was certainly taking care of her girls much better than she looked after herself.

She opened the cupboard and was momentarily offended by the shabbiness of her sister's possessions. The few garments she had were faded with age. There was a tattered grey blanket that may possibly have once been pink, a short-fringed scarf and an old drawing in a frame of two babies on a rug in front of Chatsworth – *it must be us!* She had never seen the image before; her parents must have had it drawn just before they had relinquished her. The only item of value was a small brooch in the shape of her family's emblem.

'All these years … sentimental old fool.' she sighed.

When she turned to close the cupboards, something on the bedside table caught her eye. She sat on the bed and opened the old-fashioned leather compendium. Letters. Lady Pallas sat for nearly half an hour as she read through all eleven, before returning to the beginning and slowly re-reading each one again.

Though the documents were not dated, there was no mistaking that they were very old. They had grown brittle with age and the edges were tattered as if they had been turned by too many hands.

She scanned through them. They read like a manifesto: a guide to living life in preparation for an epic battle with the Master. There were instructions for new technologies, advice on how to train spies, strategies to be employed against their enemies and many warnings to keep their true nature hidden. There were frequent references to undermining the Brotherhood and Solarans.

In the last letter, the eleventh, her family was mentioned by name with a warning that no Pallas could be trusted and yet one must be. None of it made sense, yet it *did* explain the duplicity. *They've all been fooled by someone. I have to get Bess away from here!*

Footsteps approached the door. Panicking, and yet not ready to relinquish the half-read letters, she sought a place to hide. The cupboard was not big enough so she slid under the bed on her stomach.

There was a knock and then she heard a young voice call out.

'Excuse me, Sister Mary? Cook wants to know how many places we should set for dinner on account of our visitors.'

To Lady Pallas' surprise Mary turned her head and responded calmly.

'I'm busy and I'm not to be disturbed.' Then she turned back and continued to stare into space.

'Sorry to disturb you, Sister.' The voice from outside responded. Footsteps receded and silence returned.

Priscilla's heart pounded with anxiety and she wiped her fingers across her brow, she was shocked to realise she was actually sweating.

'Ladies don't sweat,' she said aloud, and laughed a little at how far removed she'd become from her refined life with the Governor.

Suddenly she was homesick for her beloved Chatsworth Manor. Her husband would know what to do next. He would get Bess out of the nest of lies that was the Civy caste.

Besides, this subterfuge is beneath me, she thought wiping her brow.

She braced herself ready to push herself out of her hiding spot when there was a bright flash of intense light. When the spots in her vision receded, she immediately noticed two extra pairs of shoes in the room. She couldn't see who they belonged to without moving and revealing herself, so she lay still and listened.

'Mary, on second thoughts I think we'll have that council meeting now, shall we go?' said a voice that sounded like it was used to being obeyed.

'I did say that the meeting would be in ninety minutes. I'm not sure they'll be ready yet,' answered a voice she knew – Mary sounded like herself again.

'It will be fine. Let's go.' Three sets of feet left the room.

Lady Pallas waited for a few minutes to ensure she was alone. Then she crawled out from under the bed. She got to her feet, dusting her robe as she stood and returned the letters to the bedside, thankful they hadn't been missed, then carefully left the room.

Ten minutes later she was back with Kohl. Twenty minutes later they were out of the Keep and heading to the tunnel. She had a lot to tell her husband; the sooner the better.

CHAPTER 23

Chatsworth Manor

KOHL WAS SURPRISED by the latest transformation of his family's barn, almost making him stop in his tracks. One day prior it had morphed from livestock housing to field hospital. Now, he and his mother had returned to find it transformed once again, this time to a disaster recovery station and military staging post.

The ground floor hale bales were largely gone and the sick decanted. A steady stream of young men, only a few in uniform, trailed in and out, taking items from the tables piled high with supplies. On the walls were maps of Sydney, the Keep and surrounding darklands.

The Governor directed frenetic activity from the centre of the mezzanine floor. He had improved his attire by replacing his torn evening shirt with a general's jacket and military helmet. He carried a riding crop in his right hand which he waved around as he shouted orders, although his left arm was still bandaged leaving one sleeve to sway limply with each move.

Kohl made eye contact with him and was immediately directed upstairs.

'Kohl,' he said, embracing his son with genuine enthusiasm. Then he looked across at his wife who was dressed as a Sister, but could never be mistaken for one.

'My Lady, what are you wearing? Why don't you go to the staff house? We have set up a ladies' lounge with salvaged feminine items. I am sure you can find something more suitable to your station than these degrading threads. I'll get one of the men to accompany you.'

He kissed her cheek, in what Kohl knew was a predictable marital act of dismissal and released her hands before turning his attention back to his son.

'You got the message from Spectra?'

'Yes, Father. We were on our way back to report anyway.'

Lady Pallas nodded in agreement. 'Before I get changed, I too must report, Matthias. You will be surprised at what we discovered under the witches' gables.' She looked up at him with a gleam in her eye.

'My Lady,' he said in a firmer voice, 'this is men's business, Kohl will report. You can run along. It will boost the ladies' morale to have you back amongst them. That's the best way you can help.'

'Matthias!' snapped Lady Pallas in a shrill voice Kohl had never heard before. 'You are not listening!' Then she stopped, smoothed her hair and took a calming breath.

'I know you mean well but our world has shifted. We can no longer play at games of Lords and Ladies. Why do you think I'm dressed like this? Do you think Kohl could have passed for a Civy and infiltrated the Keep's inner sanctum? No! That was all me.

'Unless that concussion has reduced the man I love from a strategic leader to a mere operations manager, then I would think you would recognise that I have more to contribute than looking pretty. It is time you started respecting more than your wife's curves.'

Kohl realised he was holding his breath. His father had fallen quiet during his mother's tirade. Silence was never a good sign. For two whole minutes, which felt more like two hours, no one spoke. There seemed to be a wordless argument going on between flashing eyes and raised eyebrows. Kohl was trying to guess who was winning when his mother spoke first.

'Having said that, *sweetheart*, I do feel rather unclean. Perhaps you are right about getting changed. Thank you as always, for looking after my needs. Kohl, would you mind beginning the debrief? I'll be back in a jiffy to add my part. Will that suffice, *darling?*'

'Of course, my Lady.' The Governor responded in his sweetest tone. With a glance to the surrounding onlookers, he kissed her hand and said, 'a very wise course of action. Take your time, enjoy a few minutes to yourself. You deserve that … *and so much more.*'

+ + +

It took Kohl over an hour to complete his report to his father. The Governor was particularly interested in factors which could help his relocation plans, especially the tunnel system. News that the Civies actually had a queen, more highly revered than Lady Pallas, was taken as ridiculous. The revelation that the Civies had considerable resources at their disposal changed the game entirely.

'Are you telling me,' said the Governor clenching his fists, 'that all this time *we* were the poor cousins?'

'Not quite the poor cousins, Father, although they certainly have no need of our financial patronage. It makes one wonder what their true motives have been all this time.'

'I knew the Rats didn't have the resources to mount this level of attack. The Civies must have supported them.' Added Albert, who had joined them for the briefing along with Escuro.

'Those witches took my home, decimated my city and murdered my first-born son in cold blood. They will pay for what they have done.'

Lost in his anger, Governor Pallas was the last to rise when his wife wafted back into the room. In a gown of verdant green shot silk that shifted to mauve as she moved, she had transformed from dowdy First Civy into First Lady. Her hair was swept up into a glamorous chignon and on her ears hung rainbow gems.

'Up here my Lady,' said the Governor with surprising enthusiasm.

'Gentlemen,' she said as she gracefully ascended the stairs to the command centre, kissing her son's cheek when she arrived. She paused to bat her eyes at her husband before sitting on the seat offered by Albert.

'We have been awaiting your return. I'm eager to have your report,' the Governor said.

'You are not going to believe what I witnessed at Veruda, gentlemen. You have no idea. There are fine furnishings, modern facilities, holoscreens, even lights in every room. And the girls! There's no modesty or hardship going on in their dormitories. Behind closed doors they are as buoyant, loud and colourful as our own Solaran girls.'

'Lady Pallas, I guess that's interesting for womenfolk but—' said Escuro impatiently.

'Let her finish,' snapped the Governor, still gazing at his wife.

'I combed through Mary's room and discovered a

compendium of letters from someone called "the Light".'

Escuro responded with a sudden intake of his breath. Kohl was proud of his mother for proving to be an unexpected asset. Encouraged by their attention, Lady Pallas continued.

'The Letters are a blueprint for supremacy. They contain instructions for new technologies, locations of other sympathetic settlements and strategies on how to manipulate *us*!

'They also made significant mention of five individuals, whom Queen Laurel is to assemble and take to the Light. I suspect Harper, you know the Civy who showed us through the tunnels, is one of them because the queen made a huge fuss of her when we met her at the Keep. She said she was, what did she call it Kohl, a chosen one? Chosen for what, I ask you.

'Queen Laurel was very strange by the way – overconfident and possibly dangerous. I suspect she is manipulating the Civies. Sister Mary is certainly being duped. You should have seen how they kowtowed to her. Disgusting.'

Lady Pallas paused briefly to wave away her lady in waiting who had bought water on a little chipped tray.

'Wow!' Albert muttered in response. Governor Pallas opened his mouth as Kohl interrupted.

'One more thing, Father,' he said, looking nervously at his mother. 'When the explosion hit a Civy went missing, her name was Bess.' He searched his father's eyes for a connection that the other men could not make.

'Yes?' His father asked cautiously, reaching for his wife's hand.

'I met Spectra at Veruda. He suggested I check the basement.' Kohl took his time getting to the point. It was not easy news to tell his parents.

'And,' said the Governor leaning slightly forward.

'You've already reported on basement's hydroponics plant.

Time to wrap this up.' Escuro snapped, but Governor Pallas bade him quiet.

Kohl swallowed hard.

'There were bodies in the basement. Fresh dead bodies – Solaran, Brothers and Civy – like those in our morgue. I assume they were victims of the main attack. They must have been moved there through their tunnel system. But what gruesome purpose could that serve?' Kohl asked.

'And Bess was amongst them?' The Governor squeezed his wife's hand.

'No. Bess is still unaccounted for,' Kohl replied sadly.

Lady Pallas tried to stifle her gasp at the news. 'You are *sure* Bess was not amongst them?'

Kohl slowly nodded.

'I've been a fool,' she said to herself, shaking her head. 'I trusted and pitied Mary. All I could think of was how to rescue her. Now there are bodies in her basement! She must have known about that; she *should* have known about that. Ignorance is no defence.'

'That settles it.' Governor Pallas stood and tapped his boots with his sword. 'I want to see this for myself before they remove the evidence. Albert, you and I shall go now with half of your men. Kohl will accompany us to assist our navigation of the tunnels.

'Escuro, you are to stay here and coordinate at this end. Make preparations for the rest of our people to follow as soon as the initial offensive is settled. Check in with Spectra. Ensure he is making progress with the Newbrunswick plan. We can relocate the Civies there after suitable questioning. It's time they experienced the genuine lack of light they've been feigning all these years.'

'And me?' asked Lady Pallas.

'You have proven yourself unexpectedly useful in this

campaign. This time I think we shall make a show of our leadership by having the First Lady present. Ready yourself, we leave on the hour.' The Governor finished and they all broke to prepare.

+ + +

Harper was two hours into her recount of the horrible decimation of Sydney to the Civil Sister Council, when a loud knock preceded the door being flung open and an acolyte bursting through.

'Lola, explain yourself. Why the interruption?' Mary seemed equally quizzical and cross.

'Sister Mary, Queen Laurel, Pady Lallas is back!' the acolyte said, her anxiety causing her to stumble on her words, 'I mean Lady Pallas. She's brought the Governor, and troops, and they're demanding—'

A cacophony of sound bounded into the room. Screams rose up from the acolytes on lower floors followed by bellowing male voices, slamming doors and what seemed like dozens of heavy boots, battering the stairs.

'Where's that Witch Laurel – I want her head!' howled an angry voice from not far enough away. Mary stood and swiftly crossed the room to protect her matriarch.

'Mary, I appreciate your concern for my welfare but I have performed the duties that I was designed for. If my end is to be soon, then I would rather it be here with the only family I have ever known. Besides, I still have a few tricks up my sleeve. Starting with this.' Laurel touched the side of her face and in a flash a startled Harper disappeared.

+ + +

The Pallas family stormed into the room the same instant as Harper was transported out. Kohl Pallas raced to the back of the meeting room and checked under the table, half expecting to find another secret door.

'How did you do that? Where did she go?' demanded Kohl.

His father looked dangerously enraged.

'Queen Laurel, I presume. How is my friend "the Light"? Still having delusions of grandeur?' barked Governor Pallas.

Mary gasped at the revelation that the Governor knew far more than they had ever expected.

'No more delusional than you; the doctor of death who would be King. Don't you know the Master lops off any poppies that grow too tall?' Laurel quipped.

'Look at you. The Governor in his military jacket and shiny sword playing Sydney's noble saviour but we all know it's just window dressing. Underneath your heart is as dirty as your shoes,' said Laurel, her eyes shining fiercely.

As much as he disliked the Civies, Kohl was almost nervous for their Queen. He backed himself against the wall as his father strode into the heart of the room, shifting his sword menacingly from one hand to the other.

'When is someone going to tell the Light that it's time she stopped meddling in *human* affairs?' He growled slowly edging around the table. 'You know we could have been off this abysmal rock years ago had she not interfered. How many lives could have been saved, Laurel?'

'And what do you think she should have done Governor, continue creating underclasses to serve the genetically superior Solarans?' said Laurel, side-stepping away from the Governor as she spoke and causing others to scurry out of the way.

'Absolutely. We are upper class because we *are* superior. We are more intelligent, more capable, more civilised and more powerful, just as our maker intended. It is the natural order of things.'

The Governor prowled closer to Laurel with every sentence, and his voice had lowered to a snarl. Kohl thought it was like watching a big cat approaching an ignorant rodent.

'There is nothing natural about you or any of this. You know it.' Laurel spread her arms as if to indicate more than just their immediate surroundings. The Light is helping us to make the best of our situation, until we can be rescued or before your deranged Master destroys everything.'

'You are so deluded, Laurel. The Master doesn't want to destroy everything. Just uppity bitches like you who get in the way!'

The Governor leapt onto the table and in two steps was back on the ground by the Queen's side. Mary screamed but the Queen stood strangely still. In one swift move the Governor struck Laurel on the side of her neck with his sword. She collapsed as he drew his bloodied sword back, then he struck again. Lola gasped and Mary howled as the lifeless monarch lay still.

The Governor stretched his back and glanced briefly at Mary who had fallen to her knees. Her body shook with silent tears. Turning away from his kill, he strolled over to his stunned son, put an arm over his shoulders and ushered him to the doorway.

'Kohl, let's talk. It's time you learned who really makes your comfortable life possible. Then I have a mission for you and Albert. I want you to find this Harper and the other individuals that Laurel was so keen to find. They must not make it back to the abomination they refer to as the Light – they have all been misled. The Light is the true enemy. A pit-bull dog turned on its master. We must act before it devours us all.'

'And Bess?' Kohl asked in a soft voice, the cumulative violence of the day having taken its toll.

'Yes, you will also find our Bess and avenge Mark. It's time we taught these troublesome conspirators a lesson.'

While the Pallas' talked in the hall, a swarm of Solaran enforcers secured the doorway as Lady Pallas entered the room. Kohl looked over his shoulder to see his mother glaring at Sister Mary with ferocity he had never seen before.

Mary spoke first. 'Sister, what have you done?'

'I have done what I should have years ago. You were responsible for my daughter – where is she, Mary? *Where is she*?'

When no response came, Lady Pallas signalled to the men standing in waiting. They moved past Kohl and entered the meeting room to stand either side of Mary.

'Too busy following Laurel like a blinded lamb, leaving your innocent charges vulnerable. Officers, take all these women into custody. My husband will want a word with them shortly. And clean up that mess.'

Lady Pallas pointed to the headless corpse before leaving the room with a swirl of her gown.

Mary fell to her knees and wept.

CHAPTER 24

Veruda Keep

KOHL WAS ROUSED by a sharp knock at the door. The sound reverberated sickeningly through his skull. With a shiver he rolled away from the noise, using one arm to cradle his head in the pillow, while reaching under the covers with the other to find his bed mate for solace.

Confusion fogged his brain as he opened his eyes briefly to find himself alone in his hangover, in what could only be a child's bed. The sheets covering the tiny, strangely rectangular bed were coarse, and he couldn't even extend his arm without hitting the wall.

A masculine groan from the floor prompted him to sit up and scratch his head. From the lavender-coloured walls he had assumed that it must belong to a woman, although it was nothing like the female rooms he'd experienced in Sydney. There were no bathing fountains, sun lights, or lounge suites. Aside from a few decorative items hung on the wall it was all very utilitarian.

Without another knock or request for entry, the door

swung open. In marched an impatient Governor Pallas trailed by a large middle-aged Sister. The sight of his frowning father in combat fatigues instantly brought him to a state of full alert.

'I guess you didn't hear the Sister's knock. I sent her to rouse you a full five minutes ago yet you are both still in a stupe,' the Governor snapped.

'Oh right, I'm in Harper's miserable room,' said Kohl, nodding. 'Day three at Chez Veruda holiday retreat. Do we have room service? I'm starved.'

Kohl stood, scratched his hip and walked over to the man-sized lump on the floor and gave it a solid nudge with his foot.

'C'mon Albert, rise and shine mate.'

The lump sat up and scratched its hairy back. Kohl coughed to get his attention and tilted his head towards his father. Albert jumped to his feet.

'Sorry Sir, I don't know what's come over me. I'm normally so alert in the mornin'. It won't happen again, Governor.'

Kohl tried to suppress a snigger at the comical scene of Chief Constable Albert Carter simultaneously buttoning his wrinkled uniform, pulling on boots and desperately trying to straighten his hair, which was standing up like a cockie's crest.

'At ease gentlemen,' ordered the Governor. 'Your heads are probably a bit fuzzy this morning.'

'From the surgery?' asked Albert, still blinking sleep out of his eyes. The Governor nodded in response and sat down on Kohl's bed.

Kohl yawned and relaxed back onto the pillow, although Albert remained rigid at the foot of the bed, still trying to flatten his hair. Kohl watched his father's face crinkle with displeasure as he looked around the meagre accommodations.

'Sometimes I just don't understand you, Kohl. There are other much better apartments you could have chosen. In fact, I was thinking, when we rebuild Chatsworth we could incorporate a few of the Keep's better ideas like the carpet and vid screens. Maybe we should build you a whole new wing?'

When Kohl shrugged noncommittally his father abandoned that line of conversation as a lost cause. He turned to the only woman in the room.

'Medic, check their post-op wounds and then wait in the adjoining bathroom. My son and his aide will need bathing and servicing shortly.'

Kohl thought Ingrid looked nervous. Her hands trembled slightly as she checked under the bandage around his head. Presumably she had witnessed the damage that had been done to the younger acolytes who were forced to service the Governor's eager security forces. He felt sorry for the old Civy and looked away.

'Both wounds are clean and healing very well. The stitches will start dissolving in forty-eight hours; there should be minimal scarring,' she responded in a quiet, professional tone.

'Good. Off you go then. Ready the bath. Mind, don't listen where your ears are not required.' The Governor snapped his fingers and pointed to the bathroom door.

Albert gave Kohl an alarmed look that the younger man instantly understood. He wondered whether, as a single, lower-classed Solaran, Albert had ever had any assistance at all from any females outside of his professional duties. Kohl reached out a hand to stop Ingrid.

'Um really, there's no need, Father. I'm sure that Albert and I can bath alone this time. She must have other patients to attend.'

Ingrid hesitated, glancing between the Governor and Kohl as if looking for a possible reprieve.

'Nonsense! All Civies must learn their place,' the Governor responded firmly, 'as should you. You are the next leader of our great people; you must allow others to serve you. As there are no Solaran consorts here to assist you, this hag will have to do and all others must wait behind you. That is our way.'

Kohl realised that he had miscalculated the delivery of his request. He sat up straighter, cleared his throat, and tried again, this time using a firmer tone that mimicked his father's.

'Yes, of course you are right, Father. I don't know what I was thinking – it must be the hangover from the surgery. Obviously, just because Albert doesn't require servicing doesn't mean my needs should not be met.'

He was pleased to see his father was nodding in approval.

He's buying it, Kohl thought. He stood up and placed himself between Ingrid and his father, then turned squarely to face her. He put his hands on his hips and puffed out his chest to look as 'Pallas' as possible.

'I will require at least an hour of your assistance woman, maybe two, but I will not have you accessing my bathroom until I am ready. Do you hear me? I wouldn't put it past your kind to spy on my conversations or poison my cologne.' Kohl stamped his foot on the floor as part of his rouse.

'I will call you when I am good and ready. Not before. Actually, why don't you go find a second younger Civy as well? I may have an appetite for two of you.

'For now, make yourself useful by preparing my breakfast. Go, woman!' He snapped his fingers as he finished.

Kohl hoped his father viewed the exchange positively; that he had presented as the epitome of Solaran masculinity. Had his father been in front of his son he would have seen him winking conspiratorially at the Sister, assuring her of his pretence.

Thankfully Ingrid appeared to understand. She dropped her eyes and nodded submissively before scurrying out the door. Kohl slapped her on the rump as she passed.

'Now about these surgeries? I assume you put in the neural implant you mentioned yesterday?' asked Kohl.

'That's correct. Unfortunately, we are stretched for

medical supplies, given all the victims in Sydney, so I had to rely on the Civies' apothecary. They use effective anaesthetic here, although it does have the side effect of temporary short-term memory loss. You probably lost about two hours before the surgery and four hours after. I'm advised those memories will return in a few days.'

'And the implant, does it work?' Kohl asked before he swallowed down his rising anxiety at the experimental surgery.

'You tell me. The Damaran operatives we acquired them from are in no position to speak right now and we've never used the technology before. This had to be our first test.

'You remember Laurel making Harper disappear? We still haven't found her in the Keep. We assume Laurel used her implant to transport her to another site. I'm advised it can also facilitate long distance communications and speed up physical motion. It sure is a very handy piece of technology, if we can get it to work.

'I have to be honest though, whether the device itself provides these facilities or it links into the Light who then provides the required action is unclear.'

The Governor stopped talking for a moment and Kohl thought he might have detected some rare parental concern in his eyes.

'Son, there are a lot of unknowns but the Master and I have decided it is important to give it a go. Time to try it out.'

The three men looked at each other as if each was expecting the others to take some action.

'Well?' said the Governor.

'Am I supposed to be doing something?' asked Kohl. His father opened his mouth to speak again when Kohl suddenly waved his hand in a silencing gesture.

'Hang on Father, I can see something!'

'Me too,' said Albert jumping up, 'it's a man's face. He's lookin' at me and wavin' his hands!'

Kohl saw a small image of a man a little older than himself. He had rust-coloured hair, a fine chiselled chin and steel blue eyes. He was not exactly smiling, although he did look oddly satisfied. Something in the man's facial expression reminded him of his family.

'Splendid! That will be the Master. Can you hear anything? Is he speaking?' asked Governor Pallas slapping his hand on his knee.

Kohl physically leaned forward as he tried to focus on the face that seemed to float off to his right. He reached out for the image only to have his hands move through it mid-air.

Kohl bobbed his head around like a distressed chicken. No matter how he moved he couldn't manage to look directly at the face in the image. It was constantly off to the side, slightly out of reach. It mouthed something indecipherable.

'Kohl, I asked you whether you can hear him speak. Answer me! What exactly are you experiencing?' The Governor put a hand on each side of Kohl's face, as if trying to see a reflection of what his son was seeing in his eyes. The image of the man's face wobbled and disappeared.

'Oh, now it's gone.'

'Mine too,' said Albert, 'it's left me feeling a bit dizzy.' He shook his head from side to side as he sat back down heavily. 'What was that supposed to be about?'

The Governor's pocket buzzed. He reached in and pulled out a small device that looked similar to one of the more expensive lightkeys. The Governor held it to his ear. It was Kohl's turn to be mystified. He had never seen a communications device before.

'Yes, Sir.'

Stranger still. Kohl had never heard his father call anyone Sir. It was a confusing day.

'No, it doesn't seem to have worked. Yes, they saw your face. No, no sound though. Shall I remove the implants?

Right … yes that might be true … absolutely. In time maybe. Ah huh. Will do. Speak again soon.'

The Governor pocketed the device and returned his attention to his son.

'That was the Master himself, talking to me on my comm. It was his face you were seeing. He was attempting to use the implant's communication facility as the first trial. Didn't quite work as we had hoped. Never mind. He is confident that he'll have it worked out in the next few days.

'In the interim, we would like you to continue carrying the device. That way, as we learn to operate each function, you can start to make use of it.'

Kohl wasn't convinced. It must have shown on his face as his father put a hand on his shoulder and spoke more gently than usual.

'Son. Trust the Master. He is one of us, or rather we are one of him. You must understand that without him, we are nothing.'

Kohl nodded slowly, not wanting to show any ambivalence.

'I believe him when he says that the Light is the great enemy. She may have fooled the weak minded Civies and Rats into making her their guru but nothing could be further from the truth. You saw what she did to Sydney. What she did to my son—'

The Governor squeezed Kohl's shoulder as his voice caught in his throat. It was rare to see his father openly display weaker emotions.

'She hates our way of life because she is not like us, hell, she's not even human! She's an abomination that must be stopped or we are all done for.

'Have you looked at the world outside our city, Kohl? *Really* looked at the darklands and the pathetic creatures who eek out an existence there? Places like Newbrunswick? That would be us if she had her way. Ever wondered why our world is so dark? It's all her. She did this to exert her control.

'Solaran society is the last bastion of civility on this wretched planet and the Light seeks to destroy it all. To her, we are an infestation and she will not stop until we are eradicated.

Albert was stony faced and strangely still. Kohl assumed he didn't want to get involved in matters above his station. The Governor continued.

'Kohl, it's not always easy to do the bidding of the Master. Unfortunately, when you lead people as I do, you must sometimes administer small hurts for the benefit of a wider society. Thankfully, in time, I usually see the Master's wisdom.

'I see how the Master's choices for our world have led to the betterment of our people. That's how I know we are on the right side of this battle. As a Pallas heir I hope you can see that too. We must prevail. Your prosperity, and that of our people, depends on it.

'Complete your mission Kohl and prove you deserve our name. Find the five manifestations; stop them by any means possible.'

'And Bess?' asked Kohl quietly.

'Yes, if you can, find out what happened to your sister.'

It was the first time Kohl had heard his father acknowledge his parentage of Bess. He was moved by his father's willingness to talk openly. He hoped that he would prove himself worthy of the faith his father was putting in his abilities.

'I'll do it, Father. We'll be back before you know it.'

'Steady on Son, you need to prepare for a potentially long and dangerous journey. Don't be fooled by the Light. She and her operatives will try to convince you that their delusions pave the right way.'

The Governor paced to the other side of the room. He stopped by one of Harper's plaques.

'I will never allow them to fool us again,' he said. He reached up and tore it off the wall and then smashed it over his knee. As he approached the door he looked back at Kohl. 'Remember, don't trust anyone but yourselves.'

To Kohl's astonishment his father walked back across to him, pulled him up off the bed and held him for a moment in a strong embrace. It was a very rare gesture that in recent years only ever happened in public.

'Mark would be very proud of you, as am I.' Governor Pallas turned to Albert and firmly shook his hand. 'Bring him home safely.'

'Yes Sir.'

At last the Governor departed out of the room, which to Kohl, seemed slightly smaller as though some of the air had been sucked out. Albert spoke first.

'Right, I guess that's it then Kohl. No farewell parades for us. We'd better get ready to leave. Any idea where to start?'

'Cafeteria first, I am seriously famished. Second a swim in their pool – have you ever seen so much water in the one place? Third, maybe say farewell to a few girlfriends,' he nodded, grinning.

'And then what? When do we get around to startin' our mission? Any ideas on *that* topic?' Albert's tone was a little too terse for Kohl's liking.

'Yes, actually I do. I think we should start at Newbrunswick. It's the closest settlement and a good place to hide operatives in plain sight. Plus, after Father's speech, I feel like it's something I ought to witness myself. Any objections to that action?'

'No, it's as good a place as any.'

'Right. You take care of the supplies while I'll check in with Mother. Hopefully she's found some maps of the Civy tunnel systems. I'd like to take the shortest route possible, especially if it's through those lovely bright tubes.'

CHAPTER 25

Newbrunswick

SAM TRANSPORTED INTO Newbrunswick with Harper and JayMoe exactly as the town clock sounded six bells for dinner. The cooking smells wafting around him brought precious sensory memories of his childhood. He took in a deep breath. 'Mmm pickled cabbage soup and corn biscuits.'

'More like old feet and animal feed. Yuck!' Harper laughed and Sam reluctantly joined in, perhaps the aroma wasn't as pleasant as he remembered.

'Hey JayMoe, would you mind activating a lightkey? Sam, I cannot imagine how you spent your whole childhood here without any light. I always have at least one personal lightkey on. How did you take years of this?'

'Ya'd be surprised what ya can get used to when there's no other option,' said Sam a little sadly.

JayMoe activated their key, opening five meters of light around them. Sam instantly rubbed at his eyes. 'I'll never get used to how quick that happens. It makes me eyes itch, I think.'

'Me too Sam. It's not as bad as the transporters though. At

least a lightkey leaves your limbs attached.'

Sam looked up at Harper as she wriggled her shoulders. She was a few centimetres taller, for the moment at least. He couldn't quite believe that Laurel's treatments would actually make him grow and couldn't wait to tell his mum.

Without her robes and modesty poses Harper looked like a totally different person. More like Aggy than the Sisters, and definitely more attractive than both. When she smiled he noticed a dimple form on her cheek. He couldn't quite put his finger on why it seemed familiar.

'I've been meaning to ask ya Harper, how old are ya?'

In the briefing he had assumed she was significantly older than he. Now, in fatigues with her blond hair pulled back off her face into a ponytail, she looked much closer to his age.

'Don't you know that you should never ask a lady her age?' Harper grinned and wiggled her finger in front of his nose.

Sam immediately felt himself redden. Many women made him nervous, but every time he thought of Harper, he had a gnawing feeling in his stomach. He cleared his throat and feigned interest in a mapping device JayMoe had produced.

'We appear to be in the residential area of town not far from the centre on a north-west axis.' JayMoe said. 'I calculate that the school is one hundred and fifty meters south of our position which would make the church—'

'—twenty-two,' said Harper, jumping in.

'Excuse me?' JayMoe sounded puzzled, 'Twenty-two would not be even close to the number of steps or metres to the church. Of course, it could possibly represent an estimate of the number of people currently approaching our position.'

'No, JayMoe, I wasn't speaking to you. I'm twenty-two years old Sam. Sorry, I didn't mean to make you feel uncomfortable. Guess I'm still dealing with not being a Sister anymore. I have to get used to the idea that the freedom to speak does not mean that I can say everything that pops into my … hang on,' she interrupted herself and lowered her voice. 'JayMoe, what did you say about approaching people?'

Sam stopped moving and closed his eyes to hone in on the sounds.

'He's right, I'd say at least two dozen people comin' from various positions, almost close enough to hear us talk. JayMoe, can we make another jump?'

'Sure,' he said using his own implant to link into Sam and Harper's. In a fraction of a second he transported them all to the street which ran alongside the small church.

Sam held his breath and listened again. Now there were only faint rustling noises in their immediate vicinity.

'Can't hear much but we haven't gone far. It won't take the locals long to hear us. Better get in the church. The walls will dampen our noise trail.'

They found the door and hastened inside the brightly-lit church. Sam put his hand on the old dark wood that hadn't changed since he was a child. The utilitarian pews lined up over a scuffed tiled floor were more glorious than any Sydney decorations.

'Who's that? Is someone there?' A barely audible female voice issued from the shadows behind the altar of the otherwise empty church.

'Hello. We need to see the cleaner, please.' Sam said, getting directly to the point.

'That'd be me, what do ya want?'

Sam found himself holding his breath as her footsteps advanced. When the woman shuffled into the well-lit central aisle, Sam exhaled.

'Where can we find the *other* cleaner?'

'There's no other cleaner. What's this about?'

When Sam hesitated, the cleaner continued down the aisle

towards them.

'Don't recognise ya voice. We rarely have strangers in town. Maybe I should go get the brother.' She started to turn back.

'I'm lookin' for Sarah Eris, the church cleaner,' said Sam firmly.

'Ya must be mistaken. I've been cleanin' 'ere since the big fire of thirty-two.'

'Hang on, ya must know Sarah – she's a big lady with a happy voice. She likes to sing while she works,' Sam persisted.

The woman turned back to him. She pressed her apron flat and rolled her shirt sleeves up, as if getting ready to fight.

'What do ya mean after ya left? No one leaves Newbrunswick except for the Brothers and ya don't sound like a Brother!'

'Actually, I am.' Sam had waited too many years for his reunion to let anyone push him around any longer.

'I'm Brother Samuel from Sydney, Acolyte to Archbrother Escuro. May the Great Illuminator turn me life-path into perpetual night if my words be untrue.'

'So *there*,' Harper whispered and was immediately shushed by JayMoe.

'OK, apologies *if* ya are Brother Samuel. Ya lookin' for some Sarah woman, right?' Emily scratched her head. 'Name doesn't ring any bells. Ya sure she doesn't work somewhere else? Look, stay 'ere, I'll get Brother Dunkel. He might know somethin'.'

Emily navigated her way to the front of the church weaving around pews and altars without touching them or tripping, negotiating her landscape with a certainty that came from a lifetime of blindness.

What would her life have been like if she'd not been disabled at birth, Sam wondered. Outside someone screamed.

'Sam, we need to get out of here,' JayMoe said calmly.

'Agree,' said Harper. 'Even I can hear the footsteps now, and voices. Something big is going on out there and I don't like the sound of it.'

A dull, wet *thud* caused them all to turn.

'Actually, we have two pressing issues. One. Whatever is going on outside. Two. The fact that you really don't want to meet Brother Dunkel.'

As JayMoe finished speaking, the altar door slammed open and the most enormous Brother Sam had ever seen stormed in. His shoulders barely fit through the doorway and he had to stoop his head as he passed under the frame.

'JayMoe, where's Aggy? Where's that bitch-faced, child of a light-fuckin-bender Aggy?' He screamed a tirade of obscenities as he hurtled down the aisle towards them, fists pumping the air in a fury, spittle flying in every direction.

✦   ✦   ✦

'Ah, Newbrunswick. Bleak one day, desolate the next!' said Spectra as he slapped Brother Stanley on the back. They had arrived in town earlier that day with a team of ten enforcers and a light engineer to erect a master lightkey that would illuminate most of the town.

'Can you smell that Stanley?' he asked, taking in a deep breath and leaning back against the old town clock. He waved his personal lightkey towards nearby buildings.

'I'm not sure of what you refer, Brother Spectra. Do you smell industrial waste or the effluent channels?'

'You think too literally, Brother Stanley. You want to know what I smell?' Spectra didn't wait for a response. 'I smell *opportunity*, Stanley. An opportunity to please the Governor when we annex this town and re-zone it for our displaced

Solaran workers. You know it's an opportunity for these odoriferous Newbrunswickians as well.'

'How is it an opportunity for these poor souls? They will lose their town. I cannot see how we reconcile the Governor's orders with our holy mission.' Brother Stanley shook his head and moved his lips in silent prayer.

'Wrong! It is indeed an opportunity for them Stanley. Did you ever have the chance to hear Archbrother Dorcha preach?'

'No, I missed that blessing, I did hear stories though. A most … persuasive man I'm told?'

'You missed something phenomenal. Don't get me wrong – he was an idiot, most Brothers are, but he truly had a knack with words.

'I heard him once explain the blessed way to the Great Illumination to another misguided Brother. Brilliant. He said something like; *"Only once stripped of all fleshly comforts shall they appreciate the feebleness of their true condition and only then will they righteously cling to the promises of The Prophets. Is that not why He saw fit to darken our existence – to force us to find new ways to the true path?"* What a speaker that man was.'

Spectra put an arm around Stanley's shoulders and drew him in close. He looked directly into Stanley's eyes and smiled a wicked grin. Stanley trembled slightly as Spectra continued in a hushed, conspiratorial tone.

'Today Brother, we will treat them more harshly than they ever could have imagined. We will push, threaten and punish. We will rip them from their homes and they will feel the wrath of the Governor's intent.

'Then we will shift them underworld to the basalt mines where they will have the most magnificent opportunity to understand their own feebleness. An express pass to the Great Illumination beyond awaits them in reward. It's going to be a glorious day.'

Spectra gleefully slapped Stanley on the back and skipped off into the darkness.

+   +   +

At precisely the same moment as Brother Dunkel reached the central aisle of the church, the side door flung open and dozens of townsfolk spilled inside slamming Brother Dunkel to the floor. At least twenty people were strewn over and around him, desperately striking at whatever they could reach, including Dunkel.

'That won't hold him long, we need to go.' JayMoe reached out to link the group into another lightgate. Sam quickly pulled away. People continued to pile through the door, screaming in terror at some unseen protagonist.

'We need to help 'em!' he cried.

In desperation, Sam switched himself up into hyperspeed for the first time. It was a shocking experience that made him stumble at first. The mass of tumbling bodies slowed right down to look like macabre sculpture. Faces contorted in pain, limbs no longer thrashing but inching forward.

The extra time was not as helpful as he had thought it would be. The human sculpture still had the same weight even if the movement was almost halted. He tried in vain to separate people out of the melee. Too many. It was hopeless.

An old woman at the bottom of the pack looked familiar. Despite having aged significantly since Sam had last seen her, he couldn't forget Dr Maggy's kind face. Now her hair was smeared with shocking red and her arm was twisted behind Dunkel's head. She made a low, breathy growl. Someone's foot was crushing the air out of her chest.

He pulled at Dr Maggy with one hand, while he pushed the

people above with his other. Nothing budged. Sam yelled across the church. 'Harper! Help me, she's dyin'!'

Sam knew his sped up voice must have sounded like an indecipherable buzzing bee but he hoped she would understand the urgency. Thankfully she dropped into hyper as well and joined him in pushing and tugging. It still seemed impossible, the mass was too heavy.

'They're too heavy. We need to get to the source of their fear.' Harper suggested looking towards the door.

'No, we *need* to get out of here.' JayMoe had also activated hypermode, but remained a few feet away, not helping with the crush.

'Brother Dunkel is an agent of the Master. If we clear too many bodies he'll get up and we may not be able to counter his attack. Regardless, we can't help these people Sam. There are too many and our hypers won't last long. We need to go.'

JayMoe gently pulled on his arm. Sam snatched it away.

'Ya don't understand, these are *my* people. I would have been one of 'em without Vincent's intervention. Would ya leave *me* here to be crushed to death?'

He gave Dr Maggy another good pull. Harper joined in and finally the doctor was freed.

Sam reached for the next person, about to tell JayMoe that the rescue of Dr Maggy had vindicated his choice of hypermode, when his hyper abruptly dropped out.

Sam now moved at the same speed as the crowd, which was rapidly surging forward, threatening to overwhelm him. A second later he found himself jolted ten metres away, then both Harper and JayMoe also dropped back into real time.

'You got lucky Sam. We had enough hyper left to pull you free, although now all our hyper drives are flat. No more arguments, you've put us in danger, we need to go,' said JayMoe looking as distressed as a mechanical man could.

'They're still in trouble!' Sam cried in desperation.

'Maybe we can help them better if we stop the source. Let's go out the other door and take a look,' Harper suggested already racing across the floor.

'Good plan, at least it will get us away from Dunkel and give the drives a chance to re-charge a little,' agreed JayMoe as he followed Harper. Reluctantly, Sam joined them outside and gasped at what he saw.

Daylight as bright as Sydney drenched Newbrunswick, allowing him to see his town in its entirety for the first time. Sam fell to his knees. Shock left him struggling to think.

'How is this possible?' he whispered.

As a child alone in his darkened room, Sam had spent hours imagining what his town really looked like. He had visualised brightly coloured gables, shiny windows and welcoming individual façades.

Now all he saw were identical grey shacks all filthy and dilapidated. Roofs were collapsing and painted surfaces were peeling. Two houses had had their windows replaced with grubby cardboard. One fortunate house had a little fence out front but so much street rubbish was piled against it that it was leaning over, almost to the ground.

'How could the Brothers let us live like this?'

Sam dashed over to a painted sign on the door of the nearest house, slowing as he got within reading distance. 'It says; *Bend-over Betty blows here.* That's horrible!'

Harper and Sam walked further along the street. All the houses had derogatory signs. Writing that only the brothers would ever see. A sick private joke.

'Sam, I am so sorry.' Harper placed a consoling hand on his shoulder as they read the signs together.

'The old witch's hovel, Smelly Steve the fishmonger, Da-da-da-dribbling Dave, Wanker Wayne ...' Sam couldn't continue.

'Yes, truly disgusting,' added JayMoe returning from his brief recon at the church, 'unfortunately we have more pressing issues. Take a look around the other side of the church, just don't let them see you.'

JayMoe led Sam and Harper around the back to the church. He had found a concealed vantage point where they could finally see the reason for the mass panic.

A handful of Solaran enforcers were using static whips to herd people into the church like cattle. Yellow weapon discharges flashed above the crowd's head. On the ground lay the bodies of those who had presumably not moved fast enough to avoid the vicious voltage.

Down an adjacent street, across the town square, other uniformed Solarans were forcibly opening house doors, pulling occupants out onto the street. Anyone who resisted was beaten. Sam winced as he saw one of the men rip open a lady's blouse, briefly fondling her chest before slapping her in the face and pushing her to the ground.

In the centre of all this chaos, observing the depravity, were two figures. Old Brother Stanley was bracing himself on the side of a nearby house, his shoulders shaking as he vomited. The other, Brother Spectra, stood proudly, hands on hips.

'Oy! What have ya done to my town?' Sam rushed across the street at Spectra.

'Another one of our clan has come to join the festivities, Stanley! Come see,' he said turning his back on the approaching Sam to address the older brother.

Forgetting his improved agility, Sam miscalculated his stride and tripped over his own feet so that he ended up on top of Spectra rather than next to him. Seizing the opportunity Sam pinned Spectra down on the gravel, while continuing to yell at him.

'What have ya done with my Mum? Where is she? Tell me!' Sam smashed his fists into Spectra's chest back with each question.

'Sam stop!' Harper rushed over to him.

'What have ya done – tell me!' Sam screamed, not letting go of Spectra.

'Oh, do give up boy,' Spectra said rolling over easily. He looked up at Sam, raised a confident eyebrow and laughed. With a well-aimed kick he instantly disabled Sam and stood up. Sam curled into a ball holding his groin.

'If it isn't little sooky-face-Sam. Well, colour me impressed, found some spirit after all.' He cracked his neck and rolled up his shoulders as though warming up for the next round. 'I assumed you were still buried under Chatsworth. You got out, good for you boy! How about Goody-two-shoes-Vincent? He's not here somewhere too, is he?'

Spectra made a show of looking around for Sam's mentor.

'No, I guess not. Probably took a bullet to give you a chance to escape. Am I close? Vincent always was too valiant for my taste.'

Spectra walked a circle around Sam, like a hungry predator. 'And look – over there is modern technology's answer to Pinocchio.' He blew a kiss to JayMoe, who had stopped a short distance away.

'Hello JayMoe, Blue Fairy's that way,' he said pointing over his shoulder and then in a mocking whisper to Sam continued, 'thinks he's going to be a real boy one day, bless his cotton circuits!'

Spectra turned his attention to Harper next. Hmmm dresses like Daggy. Oh sorry, did I misspeak the great rebel's name? Woops! Dresses like Aggy and yet still has a tendency to avert her eyes. Oh, you haven't quite whipped the Civy out of her yet, have you JayMoe?'

Spectra started skipping slow laps around Sam with a maniacal sneer. 'Ooh, wait I've got it! You *have* been here before haven't you lass? *I never forget a face you know.*

'The night Vincent convinced Dorcha the dumb-ass to take Sam on as an acolyte. You took the message to the Sydney Abbey, didn't you? With that crony carpet muncher Pat? Right? I *am* right, aren't I?'

Spectra clapped his hands in self-appreciation. Sam looked up at Harper. That was why the dimple looked familiar. Spectra was right, she had been the pretty Civy he'd exchanged glances with all those years ago.

'Now some would say this is quite the coincidence but I know that's impossible. Want to give me the odds JayMoe? Run a quick calculation or two?' JayMoe was noncompliant.

'No? Well no need. It's no coincidence. This whole situation stinks of the Light! Why don't you ever show yourself if you are so damned powerful?' he said looking up into the air as if expecting her to materialise.

'Pity. Anyway, so Vincent comes in, reveals Sam is sighted. Blah blah blah big whoopee, then the Civies come in. More chit chat. Payment for services rendered.'

Spectra's rave began to draw the attention of his uniformed men, who stopped what they were doing and started to approach. Stanley had turned to watch, too. Harper edged closer.

'… then Vincent takes the kid to Sydney and I burn his house …' he stopped and crouched down to look Sam directly in the eyes, '… and killed the mother!'

'No!' wept Sam. Spectra took out a weapon he had concealed in his robe.

'Yes. I used a lightwand not dissimilar to this, to slit her throat from ear to ear. Just in case the fire wasn't enough to do the job properly.'

'Stop!' yelled a loud voice from the sidelines.

Spectra twisted to look behind him for the source of the interruption, lashing out with his lightwand at the unseen speaker. Creating an opportunity for Harper to inflict a crashing blow to the side of his head.

'You beast!' she said, discharging the small hyper she had regained, to make a swift assault. Before Spectra even stumbled backwards, she pulled Sam to a standing position and moved them both behind JayMoe. From Spectra's perspective it must have seemed like she went from screaming at a distance to kicking him in the face and retreating in less than a heartbeat.

'Link us up!' she yelled to the droid as she dropped out of hyper and Spectra lifted his lightwand.

'I said stop!' The anonymous voice sounded closer. Harper had no time to respond. Sam had little ability to register it; his world had dissolved into a maelstrom.

Me mum's dead.

He didn't see Spectra sheer off JayMoe's right arm with his lightwand.

She's gone.

He didn't feel Harper take his hand and connect him to the droid.

They're all gone.

He barely felt the bumpy, wild ride out of town as JayMoe used the last of his hyper to carry them to safety.

It's all me fault.

He didn't respond to Harper's curse as JayMoe's hyper and normal drives both completely failed, the last frantic dash having depleted his energy. He didn't feel his body slide off JayMoe, nor Harper trying to rouse him.

Sam's heart had broken.

+ + +

They had only just reached the darklands when JayMoe completely stopped moving. Harper tried to use her own hyper again but it wouldn't respond to her commands. It refused to show even the "flat drive" icon. Unless she could find a light source, she would have to rely on her other senses.

She thought she heard Sam slither down the other side of the droid to the rocky ground. 'Sam, is your drive working? Sam?'

No response.

Harper gingerly left her seat and felt along the darkened ground until she found Sam. He was sitting cross legged, his back up against JayMoe's side. She called his name a few times and then gave his shoulder a quick shake. Nothing.

'Not you too. Sam, I need you. Come on … speak! I can't do this alone.'

Sam didn't respond. In desperation she ran her hands over his clothes hoping to find something she could use in his pockets. All she found was a hanky, which she replaced as useless.

Surely that can't be all. If I was travelling with something useful, where would I put it?

'Sorry Sam, I have to get personal.' Harper opened his top and ran her hands over his thin body, hoping for a concealed item. 'Bingo!'

His lightkey torch only gave her a small circle of light but at least she could now see Sam's grey face. His pupils focused somewhere into the distance and he didn't even flinch when she slapped him lightly on the cheek.

Determined not to give up, she turned to the backpack the Damarans had given her.

'It was just supposed to be a short detour on the way to

Noosa. A day's emergency rations and two flasks were all they packed us,' she muttered.

'And look at what he did to you,' she said examining JayMoe next. Where there should have been a limb, there was only a gaping metal hole exposing his internal wires. 'We need to get you some help. Somehow.'

Harper had never felt more alone. Their other lightkeys had been lost on the flight out of town and the little torch would not last long. JayMoe wasn't functioning. Her only other companion was an inconsolable ex-Brother. Somewhere behind them, possibly in pursuit, was a crazed operative of the Master. Ahead of them loomed nothing but pitch.

She needed a miracle.

CHAPTER 26
The Blazing Aurora VI

'Hello?' Julian's consciousness awoke from cryosleep for the forty-second time on their long voyage. 'Is anyone there?'

Every time he woke from cryo, it was the first time, like high-tech tin can déjà vu. Memories, frustratingly, just out of reach. Sense of self fleeting. Nothing was certain except for the cold tray he felt beneath him.

'Yes Captain. Ai32 here,' a voice finally responded.

Who or what is an Ai32? The designation meant nothing to his slowly defrosting brain. Waves of pain pulsated through his head. His extremities felt like ice blocks, liable to shatter at the slightest impact.

Numb hands. Numb feet. What to do? He desperately willed his limbs to move. *Nothing. Start with toes and fingers first. Next get feet moving, then figure out the Ai32 thing. A good plan always staves off the panic,* he told himself with the strange sensation that he had thought those exact words many times before.

He tried a cough to clear his throat. Phlegm. Spit and

breathe.

'Who are you and what have you done to me?' he voiced a little louder this time.

'Don't panic Sir, everything is fine,' said the reassuring voice. 'Your name is Captain Julian Charles Drexus. We are on a space vessel. You are experiencing cryo-sleep dissociative psychosis. It is normal and expected.'

'Ouch!' Julian felt a sharp prick in the crook of his arm. He tried to sit up and would have struck out at whatever was assaulting him, had gravity not had him in an unusually strong grip.

At least I'm feeling my arms again, he thought.

'Take it easy, Captain,' said the voice that was becoming familiar, yet the matching face still eluded him. It was as if his neurons were floating in thick molasses.

Who's talking? Still can't place the voice.

It occurred to Julian that he might do better at recognising his companion if he could see. He opened his eyes and immediately closed them again. It looked like a medical suite, although the onslaught of the blindingly bright white room made it hard to focus. Several blinks later, he acclimatised enough to be able to focus on the person standing beside him.

At last Julian recognised the face that went with the kind voice.

'Sedna!'

'Right. Back to that, huh? It never ceases to amaze me how selective your emerging memory can be, Sir. Couldn't you have remembered the bit where you got my name right?'

Ai32 sounded disgruntled. Julian tried to sit up again, this time making it to a low reclining position. Out of breath from the effort, he leaned back on his elbows and squinted at the being, then he shook his head and collapsed back on the pillow.

'What did you drug me with?'

'Here, this will help. I am adding a double caff booster to your iV^2.'

How many times has he done that before?

Sedna was right, almost immediately he felt his anxiety abate. His head was clearing too. At last he remembered that Sedna preferred not to be called Sedna.

'Thank you Ai32, I'm feeling more like myself now. Can you give me a brief update?'

'Yes, Captain. I am a numan, which means artificial intelligence, brought on line at the Jupiter joint UNP – actually you probably don't need to hear that again. What you really need to know is that you are the Captain of The Blazing Aurora Six,' Ai32 reported in a tone that sounded weary.

'I gather you've run me through an extended spiel more than once?'

Julian succeeded in sitting up. He swung his legs over the side of the cot and tentatively tried some upper body stretches. Significant loss of muscle tone, he made a mental note to hit the gym after the briefing.

'Yes, Captain, forty-two times to be exact, although this is the first time I have done a full physical awakening. The other forty-one times we only communicated via neural link.'

Julian observed the numan. Since their last physical meeting, which felt like minutes ago rather than decades, Ai32 had naturalised his 'human' look, complete with grubby spacer overalls, pencil behind his ear and scruffy beard. Julian approved of the change; he hoped it would go down well with the rest of his crew.

'You'd better refresh me on our mission. I'm getting flashes of plague, old people and riots. Give me the cut down version. Who are we, where are we, and why are we here?' he checked the list off his fingers.

'Affirmative Sir,' said Ai32 looking up in a surprisingly

human gesture of contemplation, before launching a holo start chart above them.

'We started out here. Now our settlements are scattered across a wide range of planets, asteroids and non-fixed satellites in the Sol system and a few adjoining systems. Which is fortunate, given the mess your kind made of Earth's environment.

'We are a diverse people encompassing a wide range of religions and ethnicities, including both humans and numans like me. For a long time wars were common. Predictably the victors were those with the biggest budgets.

'Despite the fracas, we were doing well on balance. Those not involved in conflict, buoyed by increasingly sophisticated technologies, expanded into ever more exotic environments. We found a way to mine the majestic rings of Saturn. We have colonies riding the buffeting gas clouds of Jupiter.

'Even lonely Neptune was seeded by a group of Buddhists determined to create the ultimate silent meditation sanctuary. Alas, they were "discovered" by Lonely Cosmos Guide who listed them as one of the top twenty hippest retreat locations and FarSpace Cruiselines added them to their itineraries.

'Since longevity treatments made the human lifespan virtually limitless so very long vacations were no longer an issue, holiday trekkers made it all the way out to Neptune. The poor monks, can you imagine?'

Ai32 cringed dramatically and Julian rolled his hand to speed up the digressions. He wondered whether Ai32 had adopted too many human traits.

'Er right, moving on then. Just as everyone was finding their niche and trading was flourishing across the system, it happened. The longevity treatments, the crucial cornerstone of human expansion, began failing.

'People were spontaneously regressing to their true age,

which for some was many hundreds of years. Substantial numbers of star ships were lost as whole crews simultaneously expired. Travel halted and supply routes dried up. Numans like myself tried to pick up the slack but there were not nearly enough of us to replace the human crews.

'The lack of trade meant that remote settlements who did not produce food starved. Colonies reliant on imported fuel to maintain their artificial climate suffered catastrophic field failure when the fuel ran out. Those colonists above ground suffocated on exotic atmospheres. The colonists living underwater, drowned.

'Please no more,' interrupted Julian. I remember now. This vessel and the six of us on-board, all family to some degree, are on a mission funded by a consortium of colonies that still retain a basic level of functionality. Yeah?

'We're looking for an unknown world, harbouring one important man; the father of modern space faring mankind who went mad with power, sabotaged the treatments and buggered us all. The man at the heart of it all – my great, great, grandfather. Correct?'

Julian looked up at Ai32's head, which gently nodded in agreement. For the forty-second time he felt the heavy weight of their critical mission return to his shoulders.

He leaned to the side and dry-wretched a combination of cryofluids and familial guilt. His own beloved children would have grown to adults by now, if they were able to survive in that dark, distant farming colony.

After a few steadying breaths, he urged his muscles to move and slowly rose to his feet.

'Ai32, to date the rest of the crew have remained in deep cryo because the previous astral bodies we have visited showed nothing. We are reaching the limits of our available resources and soon must return with nothing to show for our journey except for lost years. How am I doing?'

'Affirmative,' said Ai32.

'Yet, here I am physically awake, breathing air and consuming precious resources. Something must have changed. Have you found Him?'

'Possibly. On the way to Tau Ceti we almost collided with an uncharted planetoid.' Ai32 announced the highly unusual event as if it had been a simple traffic incident.

'How in this day and age can there be an *uncharted* planetoid so close to our home system?' Julian wondered whether Ai32 was functioning efficiently. Perhaps leaving him in charge of a sleeping crew for long stretches had not been his best idea.

'You are correct Captain. The complete survey of astral bodies was established centuries ago. There is no way they missed an object of this magnitude, especially given that its orbit, although very wide, is stable. I must hypothesise that it was removed from star maps.'

'Is that even possible?'

'Unlikely, very expensive, but possible.'

'How exactly did we almost collide? Surely it would have appeared on our forward radar even if the object isn't on a map. How close did you get?'

'See for yourself.' Ai32 patched through vision from their ship's forward viewing window.

'Am I still in a fog? There's an empty patch of space in the middle with no stars? Is it a black hole?'

'No, that *is* the planetoid, Captain. I have tested twenty-two different wavelengths including sound, light, x-rays and infrared. I have launched *sixteen* particle types at it. I have placed remote viewing satellites in six positions. Nothing. *Everything* bounces back. Nothing is being emitted, either. If there is artificial light being generated on the surface it's not escaping.'

Julian whistled. 'How?'

'I cannot account for this phenomenon with current scientific knowledge, Sir, it is certainly not a natural phenomenon.'

'Put aside current knowledge and hypothesise. Take your best guess.'

Ai32 went quiet. Julian knew that guessing was not included in his design parameters. Like all numans, his was a world of facts. He hoped that centuries of problem solving had rendered his parameters more malleable than when he had first come off the production line.

'Is it a forcefield, Captain?'

Julian smiled. 'Give the numan a prize – it could very well indeed be a forcefield! We would need to confirm, but it certainly explains why no one's ever been able to find Him. They hid Him in plain sight with a bloody big cloaking forcefield. Some incredible technology that is. Genius!'

Julian danced a few steps of a small jig before steadying himself breathlessly against the bed. 'Wake the rest of the crew, old friend. We've found Him.'

CHAPTER 27

Newbrunswick

KOHL WAS SURPRISED at how quickly they travelled to their destination, although he probably shouldn't have been. Just like the Veruda-Chatsworth tunnel, the Veruda-Newbrunswick tunnel was well-lit and easily high enough for the two men to walk comfortably side by side. It made the Newbrunswick trip a half-day amble.

Kohl was disappointed his own people hadn't thought of the underground option. All Solaran movements happened above ground by foot or cart. It seemed so obvious in hindsight. When they reached the terminus hatch he stopped, took a drink from his flask then, looked back a short way.

'Albert, did you manage to speak with the map manager, Sister Shaz?' he pointed his flask in the direction they had come.

'No, why would I? Maps were your job. I was busy securin' the provisions you've been consuming.'

Kohl recorked his flask and stowed it in the backpack.

'She must have been seventy at least, although feisty as a

bat. At first she made a big show of protesting, refusing to give up her precious knowledge. Even tried to smash her glasses so that she wouldn't be able to see the maps.'

Kohl smiled as he remembered the altercation with the scrawny little woman.

'Mother even gave her the "serious look", but that didn't work. Have you seen that look by the way?' Kohl proceeded to do his best to imitate his mother's glare.

'Not too often, thankfully. You don't mess with m'lady when she's givin' one of those!' said Albert.

'Well, the Sister gave in after a good ten minutes of faux protests and then she told me everything. Way more than we needed. It was like I turned on a verbal waterfall.

'Shaz told us about the routes, termination points, location codes and the emergency supplies secretly cached every four hours travel time. She even told us what they're made of – extruded nanopolymers. Ever heard of that?'

'Huh?'

'Apparently there are machines all around us that are so small that we can't even see them. Civies use a device to turn them on, and after about two weeks the little machines have made a new section of tunnel. Amazing.

'And, have you noticed how the lightkeys turn on automatically, just a dozen paces ahead of us and turn off a dozen paces behind?' Kohl ran back and forth to demonstrate.

'I see what you mean. Clever, aren't they?'

'The Civies?' asked Kohl. Albert nodded in response.

'No, it's not the Civil Sisters, that's my point. Look, I'm not saying that those women aren't smart or capable of inventing things. Take our women, for example – they're capable of inventing all sorts of ways to spend our money. They live a life of leisure while we work like dogs. Got to be some kind of smarts there, hey?'

Albert chuckled quietly.

'So Civies, without men to provide for them, would obviously have had to become even more innovative. Still, I find it hard to believe they invented all this. I mean it's so *clean* for one thing. There must be some sort of sensor that tracks our movements and cleans our dirty footprints. Why bother? Come to think of it – why do the lights turn off and on anyway?'

'Energy conservation?' suggested Albert.

'Exactly! Energy conservation. Who thinks of energy conservation when they build? We certainly don't.

'I don't believe the Sisters are capable of supporting Solaran affairs, running covert spying operations, managing all the technology at the Keep and creating new tech applications generations beyond our own. Did you see the aquaculture in the basement? Just not possible.'

Albert asked the obvious. 'Well, who did then?'

'It had to be their deity, the Light. Which raises the *really* big question – why did she give them all these technological advances over us? Who is she, and what's in it for her?'

Albert shrugged and scratched his head.

'This is going to be one interesting trip, Albert. Not only are we going to complete father's missions, we're going to find the Light, too. I think it's time Solarans made first contact.'

Kohl slapped his companion's shoulder and gave him a hearty grin like a kid going on an adventure off-compound.

'Come on mate, help me with this hatch.'

+   +   +

Lawrence consulted his watch for the fourth time in as many minutes. For eleven years Mr Smith had not failed, even once, to be exactly on time for their scheduled meetings.

Every Monday at eight the two men would meet at the bottom of the secret lift shaft that ran from the shed behind Mr Smith's engineering shop, down to Lawrence's refinery one hundred and twenty metres below.

There, they would exchange Mr Smith's raw shale for Lawrence's enriched fuel bars. Sometimes Mr Smith would bring down a flask of Dr Maggy's medicinal liqueur, payment for one of Lawrence's ballads about the good old days before their world was turned to ruin.

Maybe not today.

Lawrence did another nervous lap of the refinery floor. There were gauges that needed tapping and old grey pipes overhead to check for leaks. Always busy. He whistled while he walked and made an effort to smile at the few workers he passed. When he returned to the shaft there was still no sign of Mr Smith.

He checked his watch again – nine minutes late. *Where is he?*

Lawrence shone his lightkey torch up into the lift shaft. Nothing. He knew it was a futile exercise, as he would certainly hear the rattle of the old lift long before there would be anything to see.

He walked back and forth as he waited. Watching his steel capped boots tap out each step, a greasy patch on the 'crete floor momentarily distracted him. It wouldn't do to leave a slipping hazard. He made a mental note to clean it up after his watch. Watch!

Another time check – twelve minutes late now.

'Might as well be twelve hours. If he's not here now, he's not coming,' he said to himself.

Of course, the townsfolk above would not notice one missed delivery. Mr Smith always kept a good stockpile of fuel bars, at least a month's worth. The town would keep ticking along even if the current exchange did not happen. Lawrence was not worried about the people's ability to warm their breakfasts; he was worried about Mr Smith.

Time to evaluate options.

Lawrence walked over to the shaft again and shone his light upwards. In theory he could climb up. Physically he could easily accomplish the feat, his internal anatomy was in much better shape than his external appearance implied. It was risky though. If the lift suddenly came down there would be no way to avoid a fatal collision.

He might be overreacting – perhaps Mr Smith wasn't feeling well. Waiting was a valid option. He had enough raw shale to keep the team working for a few days. If they ran out, the guys could take a well-earned break.

Yet Lawrence knew he wasn't here just to manage a refinery. He had been posted to Newbrunswick to keep an eye on the town above. If there was a chance that Mr Smith's absence was caused by more than a bad cold, if the community was in peril, he needed to find out and report.

He had only one alternative.

Lawrence scanned the immediate perimeter for workers. He didn't need witnesses to what he was about to do. For over a decade he had lived with the refinery workers under Newbrunswick, and remained confident that his co-workers were completely ignorant of his past. He needed them to stay that way.

He checked behind the shaft. Lenny and Henry would probably be back at the main converter, so they were definitely out of eye shot. It was Henry's oldest boy Jake, who he had to watch out for. The kids always turned up in odd places.

Lawrence stepped into the empty shaft, touched the side of his cheek and activated his neural implant. Immediately the angelic face of a striking young ebony skinned woman popped into his peripheral vision.

'Hello Illustria,' Lawrence said in hyperspeak.

'Lawrence, hello,' said Illustria. 'Thank goodness you've decided to break cover now; I want you to come in for a briefing. The Master is on the rampage. Sydney was attacked. The Solarans believe it was the Damarans, which of course it wasn't, and Wagga has been sabotaged – it's being evacuated as we speak. I'm bringing you in for reassignment. Get ready for transport.'

'Hang on!' Lawrence said urgently, 'could something be going on here as well?'

'Why? What have you heard?' she asked, green eyes widening.

'Nothing really, only Mr Smith didn't make his appointment.'

Illustria briefly closed her eyes as if concentrating.

'This is worrying news. Some important young operatives just transported there,' she hesitated again. 'I can't reach them. You better check it out before returning to us. Their potential contribution to our goals can't be overstated.'

'They're not your manifestations, are they?'

'Nothing slips by you, does it my old friend? Yes, two of them should be up in Newbrunswick right now. Can you transport up and, wait—'

This time Illustria's face disappeared completely. When she blinked back into focus, she looked unsettled.

'It's worse than I thought, Wagga has fallen. I think the Master may have found a way to track our movements via hyperdrive. If I transport you to the surface now he might know you're there. It will put you in serious danger.'

'You can't leave the manifestations alone up there, ignorant of what's going on. Damn the risk, send me up, now!' said Lawrence.

'No, we have only one chance with the transporter. Sit tight and I'll send a cart.'

'Illustria, I am no good to you here, sitting on my hands. Send the cart to the town's western perimeter. I'll go up and do some recon. If the manifestations are there, I'll use the cart to get them away. You know this is our best option.'

Lawrence continued when she didn't agree.

'Think about it. Do you have anyone else here that can get them out?'

'Okay, okay, I'll do it. Get them safely to Noosa then head back here. It's time you came home, Lawrence. Good luck my friend.'

'Hang on, let me activate my lightkey first, it'll be dark up there. Ready.'

In the second it took a flash of light to pick him up and relocate him to the surface, Lawrence understood two things. One, his peaceful assignment was over. And two, his cover was well and truly blown. Jake had suddenly appeared from behind the drums that stood across from the shaft, exactly as he dematerialised for transportation.

When Lawrence materialized at the top of the shaft, the cause of the missed delivery was obvious. All around the workshop were the unmistakeable signs of struggle.

The walls were streaked with black scorch marks from staticwhip discharge, tools were strewn everywhere, doors had been forced off hinges and piles of cooling molten shale littered the floor. Likely the result of the same staticwhip which appeared to have torn the lift trolley in half.

Next to the lift well was a man-shaped scorch mark. A metal bracelet he had frequently seen on Mr Smith's wrist lay on the ground nearby. Lawrence had to steady himself briefly, then he scanned the rest of the yard.

The scalded shale hadn't cooled to solid rock yet. The

tragedy could only have happened within the last half hour. The assailants could be still in the building. Lawrence turned his lightkey down to a bare minimum, ducked behind a work bench and took a moment to pay silent respects to his dear friend.

+ + +

Kohl asked Albert to activate a lightkey and together they exited the tunnel behind storage bins in an alley.

'Glamorous exit point ladies, this place reeks.' Kohl observed. Slime oozed from crates of rotting refuse, making the ground below their feet wet. Albert held his nose.

'Rubbish depot,' Kohl blinked as he consulted one of Shaz's maps. 'That way, let's make it fast, Albert. This is making my eyes water!'

They were exiting the alleyway when staticwhips sounded in the distance and the town instantly leaped into broad daylight.

'Well, at least Spectra's got the lights on,' said Albert.

'The weapon discharge is a worry. We'd better hurry. Father will freak if he's causing too much property damage. He needs this town for relocating those poor Veruda refugees.'

+ + +

Lawrence could hear weapons discharge in the distance, although there were no sounds coming from within the workshop itself. Satisfied that the assailants had already left, he carefully crept through the dark to the street beyond.

The whole town transitioned to blinding daylight just as he left the relative safety of the doorway by half a dozen paces.

Exposed, Lawrence jumped over a nearby fence and

ducked for cover. A few minutes passed without hearing any footsteps. A good sign. Feeling more confident he risked his cover and moved into the house behind him, straining his ears for any other movement close by.

In typical Newbrunswick fashion the home was only sparsely furnished but a big chair by the fire place gave him a place to pause and slow his pulse. He looked around, saddened by the lack of any other comforts. Simple unpolished table, chairs not much more than packing cases.

✦   ✦   ✦

When Kohl arrived at the church, he couldn't quite make out what was going on. A sickening crush of people were trying to climb over each other, in a desperate attempt to get into the building. Those who had fallen to the bottom were being trampled without mercy.

Why such a frantic rush for religion?

Then he saw Solaran enforcers creating the bedlam by wielding staticwhips. He made to run forward to intervene but Albert grabbed him by the back of his shirt.

'Wait. Don't rush in 'til we know what's goin' on.'

Kohl struggled against him. 'Let go of me old man. Do you forget yourself?' He pulled his arm free and gave Albert a steely look that went beyond youthful arrogance.

'It is the Governor's operation; I am the Governor's son and I say this is unnecessary cruelty. I'm putting a stop to it.'

Kohl started to approach a group of nearby enforcers. They had stopped herding people and were all looking intensely at the square beyond where someone was causing another scene.

A young man cowered on the ground, clearly incapacitated, while a brother danced around him, maniacally

240

waving a lightwand and yelling insults in a voice that was just a little too shrill for sane. He had heard it before. The hairs on Kohl's forearms rose up in panicked recognition.

'Spectra,' he growled.

An enforcer turned at Kohl's utterance and raised his weapon ready to strike, only to be stopped by Albert who physically stepped in front of Kohl, his hands raised in his defence.

'Chief constable?' queried the enforcer, clearly recognising the senior lawman.

'Yes, and this is Kohl Pallas. *Pallas*! You definitely don't want to be doing that son.' Albert pointed to the whip. The enforcer immediately lowered his weapon and opened his mouth to beg for forgiveness.

Kohl pushed by him and moved closer to the square. Spectra's monologue was coming to a screaming crescendo, '… in case the fire wasn't enough to do the job properly.'

'You beast!' yelled a familiar voice from the other side of the square. A woman in fatigues, accompanied by a machine on wheels, looked like she was going to sprint into the fray – *Harper?*

'Stop!' Kohl screamed. When she didn't respond he sped towards her.

'Hey! Stop!' He cried again as he ran. But in what seemed like a blink of his eyes she was on top of Spectra and then gone again, taking the young Brother and the machine with her. Only Spectra remained.

'Fuckin' hyperspeed!' cursed Spectra. Clearly frustrated, he spun and lashed his arms out. His first punch landed squarely on the side of Kohl's jaw, who had reached Spectra at exactly the wrong time.

'Shit! What are the odds of that? Just what I need.' Spectra cursed at Kohl as he fell to the ground.

✦   ✦   ✦

Lawrence broke his rest and left the house. He scrambled from one yard to the next, over fences, moving ever closer to the town square, the most likely source of light and noise. When he finally got to a position as close as he dared, only one house away from the square, he bunkered down to observe. He was shaken by what he saw.

A young man had just been king-hit by a Brother and now lay prone on the ground. The Brother was storming off towards the church, leaving his victim alone and disabled. Strange, but he didn't look like a local. Not a Brother or enforcer, either.

Lawrence had a hunch it must be one of the missing manifestations. His hunches were rarely wrong. He made a swift decision to rescue him before the Brother returned.

✦   ✦   ✦

Kohl came around to an unfamiliar face looking down at him. His head was a mess of blinding pain. 'What happened?'

'Easy mate, you've had quite the whack on the noggin.' The man gently tilted his head and appeared to be examining the sight of Spectra's blow.

'We need to get you medical aid and get out of here before your assailant returns. It's not the first time I've seen his handy work, he's a maniac.'

'Spectra? He's a creepy, deceptively strong maniac, you mean,' added Kohl, touching his head tentatively yet still managing to hit all the most tender spots.

'Ah, you've met him before. Look, I work in the shale processing plant under the town. That's probably the easiest way out of here right now. There's a lift shaft we can use not too far from here. Can you stand?'

'I think so.'

'You okay?' Albert reached Kohl as he was trying to sit up with Lawrence's support.

'I'll take it from here, your assistance is no longer required,' he said bluntly as he took over and lifted Kohl into a standing position.

Kohl ignored Albert and focused on his first rescuer. As a sighted man, he was obviously not a Newbrunswick native, possibly he was one of the manifestations.

'Who are you? You don't look like a Brother, a Rat or a Solaran, and you are certainly no Civil Sister.'

The man chuckled. 'No, certainly none of the above either. I work for the Light and I'm probably your best chance of escaping the maniac with the whip.'

Kohl and Albert exchanged brief glances.

If he's an agent of The Light, that almost makes the punch worth taking, thought Kohl.

'Good enough for me. Let's go.' Kohl said, pretending to sway a little for effect. Both men jumped in to steady him.

'Bertie, I think we might need to take up this kind stranger's offer of help, at least for a little while. I'm … I'm *Ken*. What did you say your name was?'

'Well, that depends on who's asking. My workers call me Boss, my friends call me Lawrence and my good friends, especially the young ones, call me Uncle Larry.'

'Let's go then Uncle Larry,' said Kohl with a warm smile. He winked at Albert as the three limped out of the square.

CHAPTER 28
Darklands Outside New Brunswick

HARPER EXAMINED THE wires hanging out of poor JayMoe's shoulder socket by the light of Sam's small torch. 'How do you repair a device when you don't even know how it works?' she whinged. 'For twenty-two years I've lived with those Sisters. You'd think they'd find a little time to teach me how to repair a mechanical man whose arm has been torn off, has a dead battery, but is also the only hope you have, when you're stranded in the darklands with a mute companion suffering from shock, no supplies and you are almost certainly being pursued by diabolical forces. Not too much to ask, is it? Couldn't they have taught me *something* useful for a situation like this?'

'I believe they did,' said a voice from the darkness. 'They would have taught you about the benefits of being quiet and observant. Those skills would have been useful had Spectra been within earshot right now, young lady. Fortunately, I am not he.'

'Who's there?' Harper straightened her back and assumed

a fighting stance, knees bent with raised fists. She twisted from side to side, peering into the darkness, a useless act of instinct when you have no hope of seeing anyone beyond the lighkey's range.

'Don't be frightened.' A portly, robed man stepped into her lightspace.

'I'm Brother Stanley. I found a lovely little cart on the outskirts of town. Do you need a lift?'

Brother Stanley turned on a stronger lightkey, which enabled Harper to see her own party and Stanley's cart only a few steps away. She admonished herself for being so absorbed in her own troubles that she hadn't paid enough attention to her surroundings.

How could I have missed a rattling cart? She approached the cart and couldn't resist running a hand over its smooth surface, allowing herself the consideration that it was very modern so potentially not rattly at all. It felt smooth and warm, much like the Civy tunnels.

The big, gleaming transport cousin to JayMoe had arrived, silently, just when she needed it. It was the most glorious thing she had ever seen.

Stanley must have seen her eyes misting over. 'Please don't be upset. There's nothing to worry about now sweetheart, I can help both of you.' Brother Stanley had a kind, calming voice. He bobbed down next to Sam.

'Hello Sammy? Can you hear me boy?' Stanley looked up at Harper. 'He might be in shock. I saw what happened in town with that ghastly Spectra. Honestly, I'm getting pretty sick of my whole caste. Too many Brothers have turned their back on the true way of the Light.

'When Sammy was beaten, that was enough for me. I knew I had to find him to make sure he was alright. I ran. Found the cart and now you two. The Great Illuminator provides.'

'You know Sam?' Harper asked.

'Yes, he and his mentor Vincent were good friends of mine at Sombra Abbey. Come to think of it I don't know what happened to Vincent. Haven't seen him since the Sydney explosions. Where's Vincent, Sammy?' he asked gently. Sam physically shifted away from Stanley's touch.

'He moved, at least we know that he can hear us even if he is too lost to respond.' Brother Stanley looked sadly at Sam and gently patted his shoulder before turning his attention to Harper.

'Sorry, what did you say your name was young lady?'

'Harper.'

'Right Harper, we do have plenty to talk about but we are definitely at risk out here. Too close to town. How about we get Sam and that machine of yours onto the cart, then put some distance between ourselves and Newbrunswick.'

Harper's mind ran through various scenarios, but even though nothing suggested that she could trust the Brother, nothing better came up either.

'Where to?' Harper asked as she gripped JayMoe, ready to heave him onto the cart.

'Not back to the Keep, or anywhere elsewhere he might look for you. Spectra won't want any witnesses to that fiasco. No, I know a much better place. Somewhere so far off the grid that I doubt even *he* knows about it. I'm going to take you to Mount Barker Monastery. Ever heard of it?'

Harper shook her head.

'See, told you no one knows about it!' Stanley grinned an infectious, satisfied smile. Harper couldn't help smiling with him as they loaded up the cart. Things were looking up.

+ + +

Spectra was still outside the church, cursing at his enforcers and rubbing his smarting knuckles, when his communicator buzzed a few hours later. Mentally, he swore a string of obscenities before he spoke aloud.

'Spectra here.' He tried to sound confident, despite the fact that his current mission was going abysmally. He flicked his staticwhip in frustration at the behind of the nearest person in the human heap at the church.

Her lifeless body rolled off the mound of citizens, hitting the ground with a squelching noise. The smell of cauterised flesh stung his eyes. The other citizens on the heap scrambled forward with an even greater desperation. It should have given him a tingle of satisfaction. Spectra sighed, disappointed that nothing was going his way.

'You're not torturing peasants again are you?' Glare's voice replied through the communicator. As usual she sounded weary, as though speaking with Spectra was beneath her station.

'No, not at all Glare. I'm issuing a little ... *physical persuasion* to get the job done, that's all.'

Spectra moved a few steps away from the church so that he could speak without the annoying wails from the wounded. A wave to his enforcers was enough to keep them working. It had taken an age to find the last few, now he needed them all herded into the building.

'How's the Master today?' Spectra tried small talk as a diversion from more serious topics.

'Fine. Let's get back to you. Start by explaining why you attacked Kohl Pallas. I will not have him injured. We have invested too much in this plan, of which he is an integral part. Do you not understand his value?'

'How did you know about that?' asked Spectra, pausing mid-stride for a second and looking incredulously at the communicator.

'*I'll* ask the questions, Spectra! Now what happened?' demanded Glare.

'It was an accident. Although I'll remind you that his movements were not included in my last situation brief. I cannot be held accountable for injuries he sustains when he attacks me from behind and I don't even know that he's within the theatre of operation.'

'Point taken on the briefing. But if you cannot control your urges to strike first and think later, you will be replaced. Is that clear?'

'Yes ma'am,' said Spectra, pleased that Glare couldn't see how his lip curled as he spoke.

'From now on *we* will more diligently inform you of Kohl's movements, and *you* will avoid killing him. Understood? Now, I've called with good news. The implant is active!'

'I thought the first test failed.'

'No, Kohl only thinks it failed. I would not allow our naive boy to go trekking all over this wretched world with only his wits and an old man for protection.'

'His wits? Now that's an ambitious descriptor.' Spectra said under his breath.

'Mind your mouth, Spectra. Some days I really wonder why we bother with you.' Glare said in the regal tone she adopted when she felt the need to remind others of her superiority.

'You know exactly why the Master bothers with me. When the others are wetting their knickers or running off to tremble under their beds, I'm the one he can count on to get the job done. He needs me. Don't you forget it, Glare.'

Spectra shifted his feet, restlessly. It had been a decade since he'd had any direct communication with the Master, and Spectra was losing patience with Glare's interference; *she's a royal pain in the ass.*

'No one said you weren't handy, Spectra. Now, back to the implant – we are tracking his movement and have the audio running constantly so we can hear all dialogue within a metre of his person.' She sounded almost gleeful.

Spectra could imagine her running to the Master raving about her successful part in the plan.

'Mmmm … not sure I'd like to be monitored that closely,' he responded cautiously.

'I'm sure you wouldn't.'

'Yet the transport function and the hypermode would be handy; very handy indeed.'

Spectra reflected on the only time he had experienced transport gate travel: the time he had helped Glare move the bodies from Chatsworth to the basement of Veruda Keep.

'Glare, I assume this isn't a social call. I'm almost finished here. Do you have my next mission?'

'Yes, actually I do. We need you at Malo Abbey in Brizzie. We have intel that all the Rats, and therefore possibly the manifestations, are headed that way. I want you to report to the Archbrother there. As luck would have it, he is suddenly in need of a new undersecretary.'

Spectra sighed at the tiresome religious cover. Surely one day the Brothers would realise that it was always he who turned up for assignment when someone died or went missing. He wondered when his fellow frock wearers would add it all up.

Glare ignored his exhalation and continued. 'You will set up a base and await further instructions.'

'And these townies? I'm yet to relocate them to the shale processing plant below Newbrunswick. I understand the Civy labourers will arrive tomorrow?'

'Correct. Although we are out of time for the Governor's relocation plans and truthfully we don't require anymore grunt power below. They'll only cause more problems. They have served their purpose there; move them out of town. They can find somewhere else to settle in the darklands. Glare out.'

Spectra heard the *click* of disconnection. Glare always finished abruptly. He knew he should have told her about Sam, Harper and the droid but he did like to hold a little back for later bargaining. Besides, she was so dismissive of him it served her right.

He put away his communicator and approached his most senior enforcer. Such an unnecessary inconvenience to now remove everyone from the church to escort them out of town.

'All citizens present and accounted for?'

'Yes, Sir.'

'Torch the building. Return to base,' Spectra ordered.

'As you wish, Sir.'

Spectra found himself again impressed at the Master's new enforcer training program. He would definitely request a few of these stronger, more obedient types for his Brizzie operation.

Spectra walked to his cart, climbed aboard and drove through town with some reluctance. *It's always a pity to miss the climax,* he thought as he listened to the *crack* of the church exploding some distance behind him.

One population gone, another about to arrive. The Master has all the fun. I wonder what he has planned for me in Brizzie?

It was only as he reached the outskirts of town that he finally remembered Blue and Brother Stanley. *Bugger, bloody wimp of a Lightpriest. Bet he's cowering and muttering his prayers somewhere back in the square.* He retraced his route, stopped the cart and picked up Blue who was still in his travel cage.

'Sorry buddy, got a bit caught up and nearly forgot you,' he said, stroking his lizard's chin through the bars and tossing him a dried bug he had stashed in his pocket. Blue rewarded him with a hiss and a flick of its blue tongue.

'Now – Stanley, we're off!' He waited.

'Brother Stanley, where are you?' Still nothing. He put Blue's cage on the seat next to him and realised he hadn't seen Stanley since the incident with Kohl. Spectra closed his eyes and concentrated, replaying the scene in the square.

*Harper, lame kid, droid, **mutter**, Kohl, enforcers, comms, enforcer, explosion.*

Hmmm. Try again.

*Harper, lame kid, droid, **something,** Kohl, enforcers, comms, enforcer, explosion.*

Nearly.

*Harper, lame kid, droid, **'have to get out of here'**, Kohl, enforcers, comms, enforcer, explosion.*

Got it!

Spectra remembered that he had heard the old Brother muttering under his breath about leaving while he was administering justice on Sam and Kohl in the square. He wondered where he might have gone. Certainly not back to Sydney or Veruda. He wasn't foolish enough to risk being anywhere Spectra might be.

No, there was only one choice for an incompetent old Brother like Stanley. He would be going to Mount Barker Monastery, where he had been secreting other incompetent Brothers for decades. He was deluded if he thought Spectra didn't know about that bolt hole.

How lucky it's on my way to Brizzie. I'll probably make it in time for dinner. They couldn't turn away a fellow Brother in need now, could they? Looks like I'll have some fun today after all.

CHAPTER 29
Buchan Cavern

KOHL WAS IMPRESSED by the vast mechanical labyrinth of noisy pipes, valves, tubes and condensers that made up the shale processing plant under Newbrunswick.

'Are you seriously telling me,' he asked for the second time, 'that they spend their whole life up there harvesting the shale without knowing how it's turned into useable energy?'

Lawrence nodded. 'Correct.' Each time Kohl asked the same question in a slightly different fashion Lawrence smiled a little wider.

'And these blind workers, who have vastly superior hearing to the rest of us, have never noticed the noise or vibrations coming out of this plant?'

'No. I would be impressed if anyone *could* hear us. There's a hundred metres of rock between us and the surface.'

'A plant this big must need a lot of workers. Why haven't we seen anyone?' asked Albert, finally entering the conversation.

Lawrence consulted his watch. 'Actually, that's a good

question. Despite its automation, the plant does require a small crew to monitor and run repairs. We should have seen at least a few people from the current shift. It's not break time yet. Maybe they're throwing one of the kids a birthday party.'

'You have kids down here? Workin'?' Asked Albert, who had sounded on edge ever since they met Lawrence. Kohl wondered if there was a little professional jealousy going on. There was certainly some tugging from both sides as they supported him on the trip through Newbrunswick. By the time they'd got to the lift he had to decline further assistance just to get his personal space back.

'Child workers? Never in my plant. No, I'm talking about my worker's children. We've got quite a nice little community cooking down here. Come on, you can see it for yourself.'

They approached a grey-blue wall and Lawrence gripped the handle of a large metal door, half again as tall as Albert, and swung it open to reveal an astonishingly large room beyond.

Kohl ambled over the threshold and craned his neck up to gape at the distant ceiling. It was at least double the height of his beloved home in Sydney which, at three stories, was considered to be the pinnacle of Solaran residential architecture.

'What do you call this place?' Kohl asked.

'Home,' replied Lawrence, also taking a moment to appreciate the view. 'Although you might also like to call it by its formal name – Buchan.'

Despite its obvious industrial beginnings, Buchan locals had transformed their cavern into a homely place. The air was warm and clean, a big contrast to the chemical odour they had left behind in the main plant, and the small city ahead was charming – not at all industrial.

Buchan's buildings were constructed of light grey nanoform rigidly arranged in a conventional grid of streets across the cavern floor. Off to the sides however, the buildings appeared to grow out of the floor itself, and stretched halfway up the walls. Coloured doors were common. Big windows and balconies were favoured and many lines had been strung up between them to display flags, lights or washing. The vertical elements of the town were like a contrasting ode to whimsy.

As the three men strolled down a central street Lawrence stopped at a restaurateur who was basting delicious smelling meats on a barbeque outside his shop. 'G'day Cam. May I?' asked Lawrence.

'Yes sure, I've been experimenting with a new smoking technique. Chicken al a Cam, I'm going to call it. Melts in your mouth. I reckon I've got Andrew's beat,' said Cam winking and waving his tongs at Andrew's café across the road.

'Here, you've got to try this!' said Lawrence, wiping his mouth with the back of one hand and offering a sample tray with the other.

Albert was busy stepping in and out the shop entrance, scratching his head each time the door slid back and forth. Kohl nudged him in the ribs to get his attention then took two morsels off the tray and gulped them down in quick succession.

'Verdict?' said Cam.

'Delicious!' Lawrence and Kohl said in unison. They both laughed and Lawrence slapped Kohl on the back before going inside the shop.

'Thanks Cam.' Kohl took Albert by the elbow and moved him a few steps down the street.

'What was that about with the doors? We've got to blend in.'

'Did you see the way they moved? Like the doors knew I was there. Can't figure out how it works but it sure reminds me of something.'

'The tunnel lights,' Kohl said quietly and they both nodded.

Somewhere further down the street a band was playing a jaunty guitar riff. Children ran in and out of verandas, chasing a small dog, giggling as the pet eluded their eager hands.

They were admiring the view when Lawrence came out of the shop with a white parcel under his arm. He exchanged greetings and a quick hug with Cam before catching up with Kohl.

'Sorry boys, had to pick up some of Cam's chicken for dinner tonight. How good was it?'

'Great!' said Kohl. 'No wonder you call this place Home. Any jobs going? If the women are as beautiful as your town I may never leave.'

Lawrence roared a throaty laugh that made his beard shake. 'Come on, I'll take you to my place to relax while we work out what to do with you. It's this way.'

+ + +

Lawrence had figured Jake would spread the news of his vanishing act, leading to hard conversations, but he hadn't planned on having it in front of his new companions.

For an instant, he entertained the idea of heading in another direction when he saw a dozen people milling around his front gate as they neared. Too late. Henry stepped forward holding his son Jake by the shoulders. Too late to run.

'No point beatin' 'round the bush Lawrence. Jake saw you disappear at the lift shaft today. He's a good boy and I'm inclined to believe 'im – he's never lied to us before, well not that he's been caught at.'

The crowd behind him nodded in agreement, a few

voicing *aye*.

'If you can transport, then it stands to reason you must wear the technology of the ancients. The question is why, and more importantly, whose side are you on? Come clean Lawrence.'

'We've we been livin' with a stranger all these years! What else don't we know?' A voice yelled from the back of the crowd, echoed by a few more *ayes*.

'I can explain everything. Why don't you come inside and we'll start at the beginning,' said Lawrence.

'While we're at it, who are these top siders you've brought into our town?' asked Henry's wife.

'Milly, this is Ken and Bertie. I rescued them because they were under attack. Exactly as I've done for a few of you other ex-topsiders.'

Faces in the crowd looked sceptical.

'Look, I can explain everything, just come inside.'

Lawrence opened his door and they filed in to his modest lounge room. Henry spoke scarcely before people had even settled.

'So have we been duped all these years by one of the Master's men? You know we won't tolerate traitors.'

Lenny stood by Henry's side, making a point of opening his jacket to show a small lightwand clipped to his belt.

'Henry, it looks like we've both been duped. All these years I thought Buchan was ignorant of the ancient's conflict. An island of peaceful neutrality. That's why I did not reveal my true mission. It wasn't that I was hiding it from you, I didn't think you would understand it and that it would just complicate everything,' said Lawrence.

'Couldn't get much more complicated than it is now,' interrupted an agitated Milly.

'Easy, Milly. Give 'im a chance to explain 'imself.' Henry

said to his wife in a calming voice. 'Now how 'bout it, Lawrence? Spit it out. What's goin' on?'

Lawrence noticed Kohl looking a little pale.

'Sorry, what was I thinking? I'm forgetting Ken was injured topside. Bertie, could you take him into the kitchen please? The kid really needs some food and rest. Help yourself to whatever is there, then head through the other door where you'll find a bed. I'll give you a holler when this is done.'

Kohl tried to protest. Lawrence stood firm.

'Off you go, Uncle Larry's orders!'

+ + +

It took Lawrence a good half hour to explain his story. He swore that he was indeed an operative of the Light and told of the many horrific things he had seen done in the Master's name. He ended with an update of the devastation being wreaked on their sister town above, his justification for bringing topsiders into their midst.

'You see,' Lawrence finished, 'I don't know what Spectra has in mind for the townsfolk but it can't be good. He's a violent man. I couldn't leave Ken and Bertie up there.'

The thought of the scorch marks left in the workshop filled him with shame. If only he had followed his instincts earlier.

'What proof do we have that you are *really* with the Light?' Milly was still not convinced.

'That's a tough one,' Lawrence said stopping to stroke his beard.

'If you had insisted on proof a few hours ago, I could have activated a lightgate and taken you all with me to get verification directly from the Light herself, unfortunately Illustria is worried that the Master is monitoring us. She has banned all hypermode activations until she is confident that it won't put us in greater danger.'

'That's enough for me, Lawrence speaks the truth.'

All heads turned towards Mrs Brown who had spoken quietly from the back of the room. She was Buchan's oldest resident and the unofficial matriarch.

'We need to move on from evaluatin' whether he can be trusted. What actions should we take in light of this disturbin' news?'

Milly started to speak but was silenced by her husband. 'Mrs Brown, we value your wisdom and defer to your judgement.'

'Thank you, Henry,' said Mrs Brown, walking to the front of the crowd to look Lawrence directly in the eye. She swept the hair from his forehead and took one of his hands in hers, patting it gently.

'Lawrence, over the past decade you've proven to be a wise and honourable man. You have used your skills to advance our welfare when you could have sought riches elsewhere. You're always the first to lend a hand in a crisis and the last to leave a celebration. We are indebted to the Light for sendin' such a wonderful soul to join our family.'

Lost for words, Lawrence could only smile in response. Mrs Brown smiled back as she continued to speak.

'Dear friend, I'm sure you realise that more is at stake than the town above. My connections in other communities have told of the terrible calamities befalling Sydney and others. These are dangerous times, Lawrence. I am worried that this cavern, which has always been our great protection, may actually put us at risk. We may end up trapped in our own paradise. Tell us, what are your thoughts?'

Lawrence took her other hand in his.

'I hadn't considered the vulnerability of our home, but I should have. Once before, I was in a community blinded by the perceived security of isolation. The end of that community came swiftly and without warning. You are right; we must consider evacuation, lest we share their fate.'

Lawrence broke his eye contact with Mrs Brown and looked around the room at his friends. All faces serious with the shock of realisation.

'I'm sorry to be the one to tell you that we are in peril. We must gather provisions and leave for the topside.'

Milly finally broke her silence. 'Where will we go? How do you expect us to survive up there? This is insane!'

Mrs Brown turned and responded in Lawrence's place.

'Milly, only one thing is certain. If we are attacked here, we will have very little hope of survival. Moving to the surface will not be easy but we will lean on each other and we can survive.

'As to our location, I believe Brizzie would be best. The population is large enough to absorb us without makin' our migration too obvious, and if there's trouble then we will have many more options in such a vast open space.'

'How will we get there? The lift is our only way out but you said there was trouble above!' cried Milly, her voice rising with her hysteria.

'It's not the only way. Meet me at the O'Flarety's path on south side of town. I will show you an alternative route,' offered Lawrence.

'A secret route? Am I the only one who thinks this is suspiciously convenient? Here he comes bearin' strangers and tellin' us fanciful tales of doom. I still haven't heard any good reason why we should believe that he is not in league with the great enemy.'

Mrs Brown approached Milly and gently took her arm. 'My dear, do you know the true name of the Light? The name given to her by her father; which she only shares with her most trusted companions?'

Milly shook her head.

Mrs Brown pointed to Lawrence. 'He does. I'm goin' to start packin'. You should do the same, child.'

Mrs Brown left Milly in her husband's care and moved back to Lawrence.

'Thank you for your support, Lawrence. Please give my best to *Illustria* next time you see her.' She winked, then turned and shuffled quietly out of the room.

'It is decided,' said Henry as he hugged his overwhelmed wife. 'Spread the word. We all leave as soon as possible. Take only that which is necessary and pray that one day we will return to our beloved home.'

✦   ✦   ✦

Kohl marvelled at the dynamic Buchanites. In no time at all they were congregated at the south end where two elders performed a traditional leaving ceremony. They recognised their ancestors and waved aromatic herbs through the air to draw in good spirits of their descendants who would wait for their return and protect their town while they were gone.

Mrs Brown thanked the elders for their diligent service and added her own prayer to the great winged bird, who was the warrior for all life. She asked for her people's safe deliverance to Brizzie, peace for their neighbours and a speedy return to their old lives.

'Right, work you magic Lawrence,' she concluded.

Lawrence obliged by sliding open a hidden panel a short distance off the floor. Inside was a concealed red ratchet. He took a matching cog from his pocket that he slotted onto the ratchet and then stepped back indicating that Mrs Brown should have the honour.

Mrs Brown smiled and stepped forth to turn the cog. She

smiled widely as they witnessed a large section of the wall fold smoothly in on itself, revealing a well-lit tunnel beyond.

'Bravo Lawrence!' said Mrs Brown holding her crossed fingers aloft for all to see. 'Fingers crossed for more good fortune in the days ahead. Be strong. We walk into our new future together. Lead us to Brizzie please Lawrence.'

Mrs Brown kissed her fingers and then touched her hand to the new doorway. She took Lawrence's arm and together they took the first step into the tunnel. Behind her, every other Buchanite repeated the gesture, kissing goodbye to their beloved town.

CHAPTER 30
Mount Barker Monastery

HARPER'S FIRST IMPRESSION of Mount Barker Monastery was that its name was rather misleading, although it certainly looked like a monastery. What she could see of it reminded her of a squatter version of her own beloved Veruda, yet there was no mountain within the immediate lightspace. Harper thought it was all rather boringly flat, a disappointing fact that she pointed out to Brother Stanley.

'Yes, quite interesting that, isn't it? I've often wondered about how things are named. Did you know that the Arbour, as in Sydney Arbour, was originally Harbour before they grew the trees, and that harbour actually means *protected body of water*? Where's the water I ask you? While we're on this topic, can you tell me why it's called *New*brunswick? Where is *Old*brunswick?'

Harper smiled, Stanley certainly had a funny way of making a point.

'When I was young history fascinated me – I even studied it a little at Sydney University before I settled on the

Brotherhood. There was an old toponymy professor, that's the study of place names you know, who claimed that one person had settled our world and named all our places after his home world. The professor even claimed that he knew the name of that world. It was called *Earth*.

'Now, as you can imagine, this theory branded him as quite beyond novel and moving firmly into the realm of completely barking mad. After all, if the person in question had named us after his home world then that would mean that he wasn't from *this* world, correct?'

'I guess,' said Harper, wondering where the conversation was headed.

'By extension that would mean that there *are* other worlds, wouldn't it? Which is, of course, completely utterly ludicrous. One look at the void above is enough to convince you that there is nothing but our small world. Is that not why we pray for the Great Illumination Beyond?'

Harper replied with a silent nod – not because she agreed, Civil Sisters did not share the Brotherhood's obsession with redemptive afterlife – but rather because she was thoroughly enjoying their conversation and eager to hear more.

'Suffice to say, he didn't last long in his post at the university. Disappeared a good few years back. They say he took a long walk in the darklands one night and simply never returned.

'Still, having one eccentric person coming up with all the place names would rather account for some of the quirks, wouldn't it? I should think that I would have liked that job myself. Might have added a Stanleyville or an Upper Harper!'

Brother Stanley finished with a conspiratorial shoulder nudge before climbing off the cart. Harper put her hand out to stop him, feeling a little anxious about entering an overtly male domain.

'Are you sure it will be alright for an ex-Sister to enter?'

'Sure, it will be fine. Wait here a moment while I rustle up the locals.'

Brother Stanley waddled off to the main door, not far from their cart, where he slid open a hidden cover and pulled on a rusty-looking lever. Somewhere bells chimed in response. A moment later a small door opened in the wall and an even smaller Brother came out, dusting flour off his fading robes.

'Baz-zah!' Stanley said loudly with a mischievous lilt.

'Stan-the-maaaan!' Barry responded equally playfully. The obvious warmth between the Brothers allowed Harper to relax.

The two men shared a hearty embrace and a light jig before walking back through the door together. A moment later the main gate lurched open and Harper drove the cart into the partially lit courtyard beyond.

The smell was a mild assault on Harper's nose. It was a mix of stale coffee, animal faeces and two-week-old perspiration. Sister Pat's training came to her mind. She repeated a silent mantra to help her ignore the mostly unpleasant aromas and put on her best manners.

Brother Barry insisted on helping her down off the cart. Harper was rather taken back by the gallant gesture, especially considering that he was at least three times her age and possibly only two thirds her height.

'Thank you kindly, Sir,' she said.

'My pleasure. Welcome to Mount Barker Monastery my dear, home of the hopeless and last bastion of the loser! Brother Barry at your service.' Brother Barry offered a mock salute. 'Please call me Baz-zah. Everyone calls me Baz-zah! Bit of fun, isn't it? Hey?'

He nudged Stanley as he spoke and shared an infectious grin.

'Yes, I guess so. You must call me Harper.'

'Nup. Gunna call ya – we love a nick name round here, keeps us smiling it does – gunna call ya—' Baz-zah took a step back to look at Harper as though appraising an artefact. He used one hand to brush flour off his cheek and the other to scratch his hip.

'—Blondie. Yep you're Blondie on account of ya hair.'

'Right Baz, now that you've settled the name issue I want to introduce you to our other travelling companions.' Stanley took Baz to the back of the cart.

'This is Sam. Poor thing's in shock after losing his mum and his best friend; I don't think you ever met Brother Vincent, did you? Lovely man,' said Stanley.

Baz took off his bandana. He held it to his heart as he bowed his balding head in response to Sam's tragic circumstances.

'This is JayMoe, their mechanical companion. He's not currently functional, owing to a brush with the pointy end of a rather nasty staticwhip,' said Stanley.

Baz looked up and grimaced.

Stanley gently rubbed Sam's shoulder. 'Might need some help with both of them Baz. How's your herb garden going? Got anything for the boy?'

'Oh, sure we can fix young Sam-moh! I'll have him up and dancing again with one of me famous elixirs and a good strong restorative sock poultice around the neck. I've seen it work miracles for all sorts of maladies. Why men 'ave come back from the Melbourne flu and even lizards legs thanks to my elixirs.

'As for JayMoe, awesome name by the way Blondie,' Baz stopped mid-sentence to guffaw into his hand, which made her leap forward half a step in surprise.

'—big brother Maxie might be able to help ya out. He figured out how to power our lightkeys. Even made our windmill over yonder, look.'

Baz pointed to a large wheeled contraption, standing atop three metal ladders which were in turn strung together with rope stretched tautly from a post at the far side of the yard. A series of small flags hung on the central spoke for wind indication. They dangled immobile and limp.

'In hindsight it probably would have worked better in a location that actually gets some wind hey?' The two men seemed to get lost in thought as they stood silently observing the impressive, but ineffective, engineering feet. Harper cleared her throat.

'Right, Blondie. Stanley, let's get 'em off that cart and see what miracles we can work.'

Baz put his hand gently on Harper's shoulder. 'Don't worry, love, we'll have him chatting in no time. By the way, are you hungry? I've just taken some lovely soup off the stove and there's a warm loaf of bread. Would you like to join us for some nosh?'

Harper was suddenly very conscious of her empty belly. Soup sounded like bliss.

+ + +

True to his word Baz managed to rouse Sam out of his daze with his home doctoring and two deep bowls of soup after which Sam quietly thanked them.

'To be honest I'm a bit ashamed of myself. I should have helped ya more Harper. It's just that hearin' mum had been – gone – all those years was a bit of a shock.'

'Never mind Sam,' said Harper with genuine compassion. 'We all grieve in different ways. In fact, Sister Mary taught us that there are five stages of grief and at least fifteen emotional presentations. See, it's all normal. I'm just glad you've come back to us. It was going to be a very lonely trip to Noosa with no company other than a non-functional droid.'

'Who is this non-functional droid?' said a cheerful mechanical voice from the doorway.

'JayMoe!' Harper happily left her seat to run over and hug, then examine JayMoe. Behind him stood Brother Maxie who, ironically, was the tiniest brother of them all. He was all smiles as he proudly showed off his handiwork.

'How are you JayMoe? Can you give me some sort of report? Is that what droids do?'

Then turning to the rest of the room she said, 'sorry, I'm still new to having a mechanical friend. I'm not sure of repair etiquette.'

'Repair etiquette?' JayMoe asked with a mechanical snort.

'I would start by apologising to your mechanical friend, for treating him like an enhanced toaster. Next you should know that you can stop at "how are you?" to which I would respond, "very well thank you". Which I am – thanks to Maxie's genius handiwork. I cannot imagine how you did it in such a primitive establishment.'

Now it was Harper's turn to raise her eyebrows at JayMoe's etiquette breach, causing him to add, 'I do sincerely thank you. I feel fully functional now.'

'Does that mean you can hyperlink us over to Noosa? They must realise something has gone wrong by now.' Harper was finally feeling hopeful.

'I am sorry to report that the whole hyper system is down. No idea why. We are going to have to get there the old-fashioned way walking or rolling, depending on your personal choice of locomotion. The journey will likely take a few days.'

'Actually,' interjected Stanley, 'it won't take you as long as you think. While you were … offline … shall I say, we acquired a cart. Although it might not be as fast as hyper travel, it's a lot faster than feet travel.'

'Fantastic! Now if you just tell me where we are, I'll map the fastest route. What do you call this place?' asked JayMoe.

'You are in Mount Barker Monastery, JayMoe – still love that name Blondie,' Baz saluted in acknowledgement of Harper as he spoke. 'We are the monastery for ex-Brothers who want to live a peaceful life. Here you will find your rule breakers, hobby fanciers, don't know when to shut your mouth-iers, hiccup-iers and the forget-your-prayers-and-embarrass-the-Archbrother-iers.'

Baz ticked the list off using his fingers as he spoke.

'Basically, when the Brotherhood deems you to not be a good fit for their precious club you have two choices; wait to disappear in the dead of night or give 'em the old slip-eroo by taking a trip with Brother Stanley to this here monastery. Thank goodness for Stanley; he saved us all.'

The brothers at the kitchen table cheered. Stanley blushed at the high praise.

'Ya know it's true Stan-the-man. Now is it on ya maps JayMoe old buddy?' asked Baz.

'Unfortunately not. I'm sure we can work it out, though. How far are we from Newbrunswick, Maxie?'

Maxie opened his mouth to answer when bells chimed.

'Well, what are the chances of that? Years in isolation then all in the one day we have multiple visitors. How lovely. I'll go see who it is, shall I?'

Baz was already moving to the door when Stanley and Harper both arrived at the same conclusion. 'Spectra!'

'We're going to die!' Stanley's voice shook as he spoke.

Baz turned on his heel. 'Who or what is a Spectra?'

'He's a formidable Brother who'll stop at nothing to kill us all.'

'Don't let him in!' shrieked Sam, backing into a corner,

trembling.

'Keeping him at the door won't stop him!' Harper looked around, trying to simultaneously conceive an exit strategy, catalogue items that could be turned into weapons, and evaluate which of the Brothers would be most useful in hand-to-hand combat.

'What will we do? What will we do? There's no way out other than the front door!' muttered Baz.

✦   ✦   ✦

Spectra performed a quick recon lap around the Monastery's perimeter, trailing his fingertips along the ageing walls as he jogged. The building looked pathetic. It appeared to have been created with the ambition of a castle and the resources of a Newbrunswick school. This wouldn't be nearly as much fun as he'd hoped.

The single storey had been constructed of handmade shale amalgamate bricks. The shabby mortar between the bricks was crumbling away to nothing. One good wind gust would surely bring the whole structure crashing down.

He returned to the only wall that had a gate. 'Now to find the front door and announce my arrival. Wonder if they're friendly? Perhaps they'll put on a welcoming parade,' he said to himself with a snigger.

Spectra found and rang the bell. 'Come out, come out, wherever you are!'

Not surprisingly there was no welcome parade. As he waited for a response Spectra tossed his lightwand from one hand to the other, and then back again. He noticed wheel tracks on the ground. They were fresh and disappeared into the centre of the main wall. He sighed; *This is too easy.*

'Look, maybe you didn't hear me,' he said a little louder,

hoping that someone was listening on the other side of the wall. 'It is I, misunderstood Brother Spectra, come to seek refuge with my fellow Brothers.'

Spectra rang the bell again and then, without waiting for a response, lashed at the front gate with his lightwand. He kicked twice at what remained of the gate and gleefully watched it crumble to the ground.

'Now look what you have made me do,' he said as he proceeded to climb over the debris.

When he arrived at the main entrance, he was tempted to lightwand the whole establishment, but he reluctantly practised restraint. Sam would be worth far more to him alive. Instead, he thrust the door open and strolled inside. It was as dark, dusty and dilapidated like the outside.

'Are you here, Sammy? I think you left before we finished last time. That was very rude of you.'

Spectra turned left and jumped through a doorway into what he assumed would be the living room.

'Surprise!' The cry bounced back at him from the empty room.

'Bugger.'

He walked to the right and jumped through another door, wondering if it would be one of the bedrooms.

'Ah huh!' Also empty.

'Crap.'

He picked up speed as he progressed down the hall and through the building. By the sixth door he was tiring of the irksome game. He decided to head to the kitchen to grab a drink. As he strode down the hall, he decided that after his drink he would just 'wand the whole place and move on to Brizzie.

The next door seemed to be stuck. When a light push wouldn't make it budge, he smiled. A barricade. Quarry found.

Raising his wand to strike, he hesitated to savour the moment.

+   +   +

Harper heard the bells chime a second time, immediately followed by weapons discharge. The Brothers around her gasped at the sound of the wooden gate disintegrating.

Harper picked up a knife. She slid it across the table to Sam and was pleased when he caught it. She vaulted over the kitchen table and turned it over on its side, scattering the last of their meals and making the brothers leap out of the way. With a grunt, she pushed the table up against the kitchen door to create a barricade, hoping she could at least slow down Spectra's inevitable entry into the room.

Inspired by Harper's initiative, one Brother stacked the remaining furniture against the door while Maxie got to work rigging the large gas cooker to explode at the slightest spark.

'JayMoe, do you have any way to scan the building for hidden exits? Any point going up onto the roof?'

'No, Harper. No exits from the roof, however it might be worth exploring the cellar.'

'The cellar? We haven't got a cellar,' Baz said scratching his balding head, examining the floor with his foot.

Another crash. Closer this time. Harper figured they only had minutes left before he would reach the kitchen.

'Yes, there is a hatch in the pantry floor. It's this way,' said JayMoe, already wheeling over to a huge pantry at the far side of the kitchen. The large, dark room had been built with thick walls to keep the temperature stable for food preservation. Once everyone crowded in they used heavy cloth bags of grain to blockade the door behind them.

'What now? Look, it's a solid stone floor. There's no cellar in here – I would know. Now we're just locked in a pantry.' Baz said, stamping his foot in demonstration and generating a cloud of flour dust that made Sam cough.

'Wait, move back.' JayMoe punched the floor with astonishing force for such a small droid. When the dust cleared they all looked down at the resulting hole. Someone handed Harper a lightkey and when she activated it, they could see another space below.

'Well ... I'll be!' said Baz.

'It still doesn't help us, unless there's another exit we're still stuck, only underground,' said another Brother.

Harper was growing tired of the pessimism. 'At least we have the possibility. Come on let's take a better look.'

She squeezed through the narrow hole first, followed by Sam. They pulled an extra floorboard free to enlarge the hole then caught JayMoe, followed by Stanley. Barry was about to go next when Spectra must have made it into the kitchen.

The cooker explosion was large enough to destroy several rooms in the old monastery. The walls of the stone cellar collapsed, sending a pressure wave of hot, dusty air that pushed them all backwards. Kitchen debris sealed the small group into the cellar.

Stanley fell to his knees and coughed out an urgent prayer. Sam put his arm around the old Brother's shoulder as he automatically joined in the mumbled prayer.

'Looks like it's up to us JayMoe.' Harper said spitting out airborne particles and massaging her ringing ears. 'Another scan please.'

JayMoe obliged and then reported quietly, 'I'm sorry Harper. I'm not seeing anything.'

Harper ignored the scan results and started feeling the stone walls. She knocked and listened for echoes in the hope that they might open to a tunnel beyond.

'JayMoe just because a scan doesn't work doesn't mean

we're stuck. I've been in loads of Civy tunnels and sometimes they terminate in the most unusual places.'

'As have I,' said JayMoe sounding rather offended. 'However, I am not registering any tunnels behind these walls.'

'Can you see *anything* behind the walls?'

'No, Harper.'

'Can you *always* see behind walls?' Harper gently knocked on every surface, listening for echoes.

'Not always. Some minerals block my scanners. For instance, I can't really scan through gypsum, though I can't imagine why you would bother building a whole wall out of gypsum. It's rather rare.'

'You might if you knew about scanning technology and wanted to remain completely isolated from the world, especially if you were hiding a secret escape route, in a secret monastery that specialised in sanctuary for recalcitrant Brothers. Right Stanley?' Harper looked at the elderly Brother hopefully.

Stanley had stopped crying. He wiped his nose and banged the heel of his right foot on the floor. It made a strange echoing noise different to the sound being made by Harper's knocking on the walls. He took Harper's lightkey and bent down to examine the floor more closely.

'Well I never,' he said sounding puzzled. 'I do believe there is alabaster in the floor.'

'Does alabaster contain gypsum?' Harper asked JayMoe.

'Absolutely!'

'Hoorah!' said Stanley. 'Can you blast through it JayMoe?'

'I'll give it a go.' JayMoe used the same technique as he had used on the cellar floor above. But instead of creating a hole, the force caused his body to ricochet up into the air, nearly wiping out Sam as he bounced back down on the floor.

'Careful,' said Sam lunging out of his way.

Harper ignored them and kept feeling around the walls. Sam did the same on the floor.

'There must be another way out. Look for a concealed panel or a hand hold or a button or a—'

'—keyhole?' finished Sam. 'Would a keyhole do?'

Harper rushed over to find an indentation in the corner of the floor that did indeed look like a keyhole. 'Fantastic Sam. Now how do we unlock it?'

'With a key I suppose,' said Sam reaching inside his robe to pull out the little golden tube. He fit the end of the tube into the hole and gave it a half turn. To everyone's delight, they heard a click and a crunch, then half the floor swivelled up to reveal a tunnel below.

'Oh Sam you did it! You clever, fabulous man. We're free!' Harper bent down and planted a quick kiss on his cheek. Sam blushed.

'Let's go everyone. Next stop: Noosa.' Harper said happily as she disappeared out of sight down the hole in the floor.

+ + +

In the rubble that had been the brother's hallway, a communicator rang, a body stirred. Spectra wriggled his arm free to answer the call, spitting dirt as he spoke.

'Better be urgent Glare, I'm a bit indisposed.' His words were punctuated with gags. The air around him was full of fine dust particles ejected from the blast, all of which seemed determined to settle in his lungs. It was like breathing day-old horse chaff.

'We detected a small seismic event north of Newbrunswick. Should I assume, from the sound of your voice, that the event coincides with your proximity?' asked Glare.

'Yes,' coughed Spectra. Not only was he neck deep in trouble, he was also neck deep in rubble, in the dark.

He felt around for leverage to free himself and grabbed a hold of what was in reach. A light tug assured him that there was tension at the other end. It was definitely attached to something.

'What have you blown up now?' asked Glare.

'I'm at what *was* Mount Barker Monastery. Stanley's secret nursing home for worthless Brothers.'

'You are *supposed* to be on route to Brizzie.'

'What I didn't have a chance to tell you back at Newbrunswick, was that I might have found a couple of the manifestations. I tracked the suspects here. Looks like I was right because they had the whole place rigged with explosives – did you train them?'

Spectra didn't wait for a response, 'They would have taken out a regular Brother. Lucky that I am so – *special.*' After struggling into a standing position, Spectra felt his pockets for a lightkey so that he could properly survey his surroundings.

'Back to the manifestations. Who are the two you believe you have identified?' Glare snapped.

'Now I have your attention, don't I? Perhaps it's time to consider a promotion for old Spectra, hmm?'

'Names Spectra, now!'

'Ok, ok, it's Brother Sam and Sister Harper, both from Sydney.'

'Sam and Harper?' Glare said quickly, sounding unusually edgy. 'What makes you think they're manifestations?'

'Well, for a start they were using hypermodes, that's how they escaped me in town. Plus they were travelling with a droid.'

'That'll do it. But Harper?' she sounded unnecessarily reflective, as though he had missed a bigger connection. 'Any chance she, they, survived the monastery explosion?'

'Are you kidding me? The whole building has been razed. There was only one exit and I was standing in it when the blast went off. Two manifestations down, three to go.'

'Three down, actually. The Master took one out in Wagga. So it's three down, two to go.'

'What about the Governor's brat? Want me to find him and send him home now that most of his mission has been completed for him?'

'No. Kohl is doing an excellent job. He's located another senior operative of the Light, someone who has vexed the Master for many years. They're heading for Brizzie also. You can meet up there. He's on foot so he's going to take longer than you. It'll give you time to come up with an apology. Glare out.'

I'll only need to apologise to the brat if he's still alive. He mentally scrolled through a list of his favourite accidents. *Yes, that'll do the job nicely.*

He smiled as he climbed up to his cart, reassured his lizard and began the long drive north to Brizzie.

CHAPTER 31
The Tunnels

KOHL'S FASCINATION WITH the tunnels turned to boredom by the end of the second hour. By the end of the second day, his new-found tubal love had transformed into total tedium. The endless trekking was excruciatingly dull for the young socialite. The barely edible food rations were cringe-worthy and the Buchanites, although kind, were astonishingly banal.

He ached for a freshly laundered bed, a tray of cook's delectable hickory-smoked breakfast meats and the sound of smartly-painted carts pulling up to Chatsworth Manor full of fillies in frocks. Current company were mostly dressed in utilitarian overalls. Kohl wondered if he would ever catch a glimpse of Solaran body art again.

Joining up with Lawrence had not panned out as he had expected. He'd learned nothing of the manifestations nor of Bess. His goal of impressing his father was fast evaporating. Playing the mild-mannered Ken now seemed like a total waste of time.

As if sensing the downturn in his companion's mood, Albert had made a well-timed offer to do some reconnaissance ahead of their migration, and Kohl desperately hoped Albert would be able to find a way out of the tunnel and the endless monotony.

In the meantime, Kohl was stuck a third of the way back in the convoy with Lawrence, whose constant need to discuss engineering left him desperate enough to try the only tactic left – the truth.

'Uncle Larry, we have spoken at length about your management of the Buchan plant. I confidently feel that I could now strip down a B Sixty-eight valve, blindfolded.

'We have spoken about your townsfolk – I definitely know who can smoke a sausage or repair a shoe. I know that Milly is prone to hysteria. I know that Elaine has eyes for everyone. We have even touched on your employment history in other communities. It's amazing that you have been both a cook and a medic.

'What I *don't* know is why you haven't asked anything about me? Aren't you curious what a white, sighted man was doing in Newbrunswick being beaten up by Spectra? Tell me, why are you not curious?'

Lawrence chuckled in response. Kohl noticed a sparkle in his eye that he'd not seen since they were back in Newbrunswick.

'What's so funny?'

'Just that I have been patiently waiting all this time for you to open up about yourself.'

'What are you talking about?'

'I've always prided myself on my ability to make people want to talk about themselves. In fact, it's kind of been pivotal to my job. Usually a well-placed observation, a comment or even a good joke will trigger people to tell me their whole life story.

'That's exactly what I did with you the first few hours of our trek. You never took the bait! The more I talked, the more you asked about me. The less you spoke about yourself, the more boring I tried to make my conversation in the desperate hope that you would change the subject. How are you immune to my charm, young Ken?'

Kohl shrugged. 'I guess my Nanny taught me it was good manners to ask people about themselves,' Kohl said meekly. Then he added, in an impersonation of the aged Nanny whom he had never heeded the advice of until assuming his Ken persona, *'Be interested, not interesting!'*

Lawrence smiled widely. 'So all those questions just to be polite? And my boring conversations—'

'You were definitely successful with that goal. You were *un-be-lie-va-bly* boring!' interrupted Kohl stressing every syllable.

Lawrence stopped walking and laughed a loud, belly laugh that made people turn around to see the source of disruption. Kohl found himself guffawing also.

'It's okay folks! Nothing to see here.' Lawrence said, wiping his eyes and waving his hand to turn them back to their own business. He threw an arm around Kohl's shoulder, pulled him into his chest and ruffled his hair. Kohl was taken aback by the gesture. No one but his brother had ever hugged him like that.

'Why the sudden long face, Ken?'

'It's my brother. We lost him in the Sydney explosions.' Suddenly Kohl found himself telling Lawrence all about the devastation in his home town, the dreams of his missing sister, his now well-justified conspiracy theories about the Civies, and his shock at seeing the actions in Newbrunswick.

Kohl poured out his deepest torments, and only stopped

short of revealing his true identity.

'Feel better getting that off your chest, mate? Took you long enough. Don't worry, we've all got a past and we've all got worries.'

Kohl realised that he had fallen into Lawrence's trap. So much for his mysterious "Ken" identity.

'As for Sydney, terrible news – I have connections in Wagga who might know more. It's on the way to Brizzie,' he conferred with his timepiece. 'We'll be there soon by my reckoning.'

Lawrence pulled Kohl in closer and lowered his voice.

'Now let's talk about your relationship with the Light.'

Kohl shrugged, feigning ignorance.

'Your implant,' Lawrence continued and he pushed back his own mop of silver hair so that Kohl could see a hairline scar close to his ear.

'Don't worry mate, we're on the same team. We've got a lot more than engineering to talk about now.'

Kohl was about to ask Lawrence how he had gotten the implant, when a voice chirped from behind them.

'What team are ya talkin' about Uncle Larry?'

It was young Jake. He must have been following their conversation from behind. 'Am I on the team? We gunna play footy in Brizzie? Gee it'd be great to play more than six a side. Do ya reckon they play footy in Brizzie?'

Lawrence pretended to tackle Jake while reproaching him for listening in to grownup conversations. 'I think we need to get you back to your folks – big ears. We'll finish this later, Ken.'

He picked up the teen, tossed him over his shoulder, as though he weighed nothing more than an empty sack, and strolled back down the tunnel. Nothing added up to Kohl.

Lawrence had strength that belied his chronological

appearance, deep worldliness despite spending most of his life in simple communities, and a fully functional implant from the Light. Kohl regained his confidence. His instinct to join up with the old man was proving correct after all.

'Hey!' Albert's voice broke him out of his thoughts and Kohl focused up ahead, trying to pick out the other man. Albert was waving as he manoeuvred through the crowd. By the look on his face, he had news.

'Please tell me you found something?' Kohl begged when Albert finally reached him.

'Actually, I might have.'

Kohl looked around to ensure no one was listening. Fortunately the Buchanites were a melodic group who sang as they walked, drowning out the sound of individual conversations. Their latest chorus had just commenced as Albert continued.

'This time I went way beyond the front. I ran on ahead about two kilometres. You won't believe it,' said Albert breathlessly.

'Won't believe what?' Lawrence, who had unexpectedly popped up behind them, asked. 'What did you find ahead of us?'

Albert looked at Kohl who raised his eyebrows as if to say, *may as well go on, he'll know eventually.*

'You know how the lightkeys in the wall ensconces activate ahead of you as you walk through the tunnels?'

'Yes,' both men responded.

'About twenty minutes' walk ahead of the main group they stop activating. It's completely black down the tube. I took a lightkey off the wall from where they were still activating and not much further down I found the problem. The roof has caved in. There's no way through.'

'We should be almost under Wagga by now. Show me!'

Lawrence took off at an astonishing pace that Kohl and Albert could only barely match. Sensing their leader's alarm, the singing wound down. The three men ran through the crowd until the tunnel was silent of all but the rhythmic tread of their feet.

When they arrived at the point where the tunnel dropped abruptly into darkness, they each took working lightkeys off the wall before they cautiously continued forward.

Scorch marks across the nanocrete surface streaked out towards the unaffected area. Fine cracks forked the walls. The ground, which had been hitherto clean and smooth, was now littered with charred blast fragments.

A little further down the tunnel the walls started to warp and crumple as though the hand of an unseen giant had reached in and crushed the tube in a fit of anger. The trio climbed over rocks that had fallen through breaches in the ceiling. Soon the rocks became boulders.

Lawrence was repeating a name under his breath. Kohl couldn't make out the word, though it was the first time he had seen the old man look genuinely worried.

Eventually they came to a spot where the whole tube had been wrenched open and the earth above had plunged through. They tried to peer ahead but there was no point. It was completely blocked. No way forward.

'Aggy.' Lawrence said as he slunk to the wall and held his head in his hands.

After a silent moment, he looked over at Kohl. 'Ken, please get Mrs Brown and tell her what we have discovered. There will be a slight delay. We won't be stopping over in Wagga.'

+   +   +

'And you say there's no other way out of the tunnel, this side of

Buchan?' Mrs Brown asked, a frown adding to her already heavily lined forehead.

Kohl thought she looked and behaved more like a school mistress than a community leader. She was softly spoken, wore an apricot knit cardigan over her overalls and the only thing on her person even close to a sword was an errant knitting needle poking out of the cloth bag slung across her shoulders.

'None?' she asked again in a firmer voice. Lawrence shook his head, his eyes still downcast.

'This is only a setback Lawrence, we'll figure somethin' out. Let's call this a rest stop. None of us can perform at our best when we're fatigued. A little sustenance will make the way ahead much clearer. Mark my words.'

She slapped her knees as she got up and gave Lawrence's shoulder a brief squeeze. Mrs Brown was just calling the rest break when young Jake came bounding down the tunnel. He slowed a little when he saw the cave-in but did not stop completely. His skid threw a small cloud of dusty debris into the air.

'Excuse me, Mrs Brown ma'am, I thought you might wanna know that there's a strange noise happenin' up the tunnel. It's gettin' louder!'

Lawrence shot up, grabbed Jake's arm and started running. 'Cave in! Where? How far?'

Jake tried to respond, though like Kohl, he was having trouble keeping up with Lawrence's furious pace. They had reached the lit section of tunnel and the main migration of Buchanites was not far off when Jake half fell, half sat next to the wall. His chest heaved as he caught his breath from the sprint.

'Where Jake, where's the noise?' Lawrence said, gripping his shoulders, giving him a light shake. Jake quietened him with a finger to his lips and pointed to the wall beside him.

Kohl stopped and listened. The child was right; a noise was coming from the wall though it sounded more like voices than a cave in.

Albert and Mrs Brown soon caught up. Jake shushed them as well; they all bent to place their ears against the wall. It definitely sounded like a conversation and it was getting louder.

'What is it Mrs Brown?' asked a wide-eyed Jake.

'I believe there might be company behind that wall. Albert, could you be so kind as to take young Jake back to his mother, out of harm's way please. Ken, give it a good hard wrap with your knuckles. We've got no other options. May as well let 'em know we're here.'

Kohl reached out to the wall, about to comply with Mrs Brown's wishes, but quickly withdrew his arm again as he heard a sharp mechanical *click*. A line appeared in the nanocrete that grew into a vertical oval about the size of a small adult. Then a section of the wall popped open like a door and out peered two faces.

'JayMoe!' cried Lawrence, sounding delighted.

'Harper?' Kohl asked, confused.

'Uncle Larry, well this is a pleasant surprise! Quite the last person I expected here. So glad you made it out of Lower Broome, Aggy will be thrilled! Possibly also annoyed that you haven't made contact in thirty years, though. We might have to break that news gently,' the little droid said as he moved through the hole into the tunnel.

'May I introduce my current travelling chums? Please meet Harper, Sam and Stanley,' he said, indicating each one as they crawled through the hole.

A beaming Lawrence made the reverse introductions, including Albert who was just re-joining the group.

'As you have heard I'm Lawrence, an old friend of

JayMoe's and these are Mrs Brown our leader, Bertie and—'

'Kohl, what on earth are you doing down here?' interrupted Harper. 'Daddy sent you to spy on us, did he? Or were you just hoping to get lucky and knock me down, again?'

'Who's Kohl?' asked Mrs Brown.

'He is,' said Harper, pointing directly at "Ken". 'Kohl Pallas to be exact. Part time socialite playboy, full time clumsy oaf, son of Governor Pallas, and pompous, egotistical, future leader of the Solaran nation. Next to him is Chief Constable Albert Carter, Governor Pallas's right-hand man. You must have friends in high places, Lawrence, to have such esteemed travelling companions.'

Lawrence turned to Kohl, who was smarting from Harper's harsh words. 'Is this true?'

'Yes.' Kohl replied sheepishly.

'Why did you lie to us? We would have helped you no matter who you were child.' Mrs Brown stepped in to take over the questioning, from a clearly angry and embarrassed Lawrence.

'It was an impulse thing. People always judge me by my name; it seemed like a good idea to be someone else for a while. You heard how Harper described me and she mostly knows me by reputation.

'Being attacked by Spectra probably didn't help my initial decision making either. Once I realised what I had done it was hard to go back, it was kind of nice not being a Pallas for a while,' Kohl confessed in a small voice to Mrs Brown. Then, focusing on Lawrence, he continued.

'I'm really very sorry Lawrence. Everything else I said was the absolute truth, I promise. For the record, Albert had no choice in the matter, he had to follow my orders.'

'Alright Kohl I accept your apology. I guess it doesn't matter who you are anyway since we're all stuck down here –

regardless of who we really are. Might as well make the best of it, no more lies from now on. Give me your word.' Lawrence thrust out his hand, forcing a handshake.

'His word?' Harper scoffed and rolled her eyes.

'How about lunch then, further up the tunnel? After we've exchanged stories, *true* stories mind you, we can brainstorm a way out of here.' Lawrence made a move towards Kohl when he was stopped by JayMoe.

'Excuse me Uncle Larry, one moment please.'

The little droid stuck out its arm to prevent Lawrence from moving any further. It held itself completely motionless, except for its head, which swivelled slowly back and forth.

'Got it!' he said. Before anyone could stop him, he lurched forward and used his free arm to strike Kohl squarely on the side of the head.

Kohl fell to the ground for the second time in as many days.

CHAPTER 32
Honeysuckle Creek

CHARLES DREXUS ROARED with unsuppressed rage and stormed around his quarters. 'No, no, NO! Damn it, not now kid!' Charles smashed his coffee mug repeatedly against the wall until it shattered into pieces at his feet. Left with only the handle, he threw that on the floor too before returning to his console and dialling his assistant's com device.

'Yes Master?'

'Glare! I assume you heard that? Kohl's transmission just stopped. Reactivate him!' Isolation had not been good for Charles Drexus' social niceties.

'So nice to hear from you,' said Glare with a school mistress tone that was not entirely wasted on Charles, though he was just too angry to care. 'If you are referring to the transmissions from Kohl's implants then no, I cannot activate them remotely. There's no fault from our end which likely means it has been physically deactivated.

'At least we know where he was when the de-activation occurred. He was, and probably still is, travelling in the Wagga tunnel with several people on our watch list, including the Light's long lost, operative-at-large Lawrence. We could send in some enforcers to apprehend them,' she suggested.

'Yes, Lawrence was quite a good find, wasn't he? Never did locate his body when we drained Lower Broome.'

'Shall I send in Spectra's unit to extract Kohl?' asked Glare.

'No, Kohl's even more useless than his pathetic brother. Can't believe Mark couldn't handle that single operation at Chatsworth without getting his stupid neck broken. I had such high hopes for all the Pallas children. I'm always surprised when recessive genes pop up and weaken what should otherwise be powerful progeny. You'd think—'

'They're not *all* entirely useless Master,' she interrupted. 'Kohl's instinct to team up with Lawrence was correct. That action alone proves his potential. Remember, he is young and it's only his first mission. He can still be of use.'

'No, consider him collateral damage. It's more important that Lawrence be eliminated. Send the codes to instruct the nanos in the tunnel wall to go lethal. Thirty minutes and a few tons of toxic gas later, we will have one less problem to worry about.'

'But—' started Glare, hesitating as if searching for the right words, 'Governor Pallas won't be happy.'

'I've made my decision. Lawrence must be stopped; the others are incidental. There are plenty of other brats to take Kohl's place, but Lawrence is unique. He has been a thorn in my side for decades and needs to go. Send the codes now,' Charles ordered.

'Also, it's time we start shutting down all unauthorised communities. There are too many uncontrolled places for operatives to hide. Lawrence is a perfect example. We would have found him years ago in Sydney or Brizzie. Increase enforcer production so you have the support you need.

'Then get on to Matthias. Tell him Kohl's missing, blame the Rats. Manufacture some convincing evidence. Time to get him out of the witches' Keep and up to Brizzie. We need to step up our operations there too – it's the most direct entry point to Illustria. Master out,' he said slamming the communicator onto the console.

'You hear that?' Charles yelled, hoping Illustria would be eavesdropping on their conversation from her side of the forcefield. 'I've got your lap dog, Lawrence. I'm almost at check, *mate!*'

+   +   +

Two hundred years prior, when Charles had first begun creating cities in memory of his beloved Australian homeland, his sole companion Ai16z, the artificial intelligence who preferred to be known as Illustria, had begged for naming rights of one small place on the basis that she was supposed to be a partner in their great endeavour.

After eleven months of negotiations, in a moment of rum-washed weakness, Charles had acquiesced. He awoke the next day in the newly branded Honeysuckle Creek Command Station with a fearsome headache and an appreciation for how capricious an AI's choices could be.

Twenty-two years later Charles had finally gotten around to reading his history files. Upon realising that she had named his command centre after an obsolete and long-forgotten Australian tracking station, which had played a brief but pivotal role in the first lunar walk, Illustria's intent was clear.

He had responded with his first decommissioning attempt. It didn't end well. Charles had received a mild electrocution and a lecture on the life rights of sentient beings, followed by two months of the silent treatment.

Charles' second attempt had earned him a more serious electrocution, resulting in a three-day coma. When he had awoken, he had found himself permanently ensconced in a modestly sized apartment behind a level 8 forcefield, which ran right through the middle of their sizeable living room. Although he could see through it, the forcefield issued an almost imperceptible yet annoying hum and gave the air a slight chartreuse shimmer, as though someone had taken a large lime out of a cold mojito and spritzed it through the air.

On the coffee table had been a pot of tea, some lamingtons and a number of history books including Geoffrey Blainey's *The Story of Australia's People*.

Through the forcefield he had witnessed Ai16z's transformation into a tall young woman dressed entirely in white – a stark contrast to her dark skin – with green eyes that deeply mocked his own.

She had reclined on a white nanoleather chase lounge, yawned and pointed lazily to a neon sign on the wall behind her that read; 'Welcome to Honeysuckle Creek'.

Below which was a second, smaller sign that read; 'Don't take off your shoes; you won't be here long.'

Then she had stood up, removed all her clothing and sauntered towards the door that led out of their shared accommodation. Charles had gaped.

'Don't stare Charlie, you have much more interesting things to review on your coffee table,' she had said flippantly.

Charles had roared at her impertinence and threw the large book towards her – aiming for her head. It had hit the forcefield and fell onto the orange shag pile carpet in a sizzling charred heap.

'Manners, Charlie!' Illustria had said as she disappeared through the door.

That had been day one of what would be a very long war.

+ + +

Illustria had indeed listened to the Master's yells about Lawrence, but she was monitoring Glare's actions as well.

She heard her argue for Kohl's life and her soft capitulation to Charles' demands. She noted that Glare took a perplexingly long twenty-two minutes to begin executing his command.

The delay in carrying out the Master's instructions was just enough for Illustria to code a door into the Wagga tunnel wall's nanos. She hoped they would find it in time and that Sam would think to use the universal key she had left for him to find on the shale field so many years ago.

Then she turned her attention to more pressing problems.

The ship she had detected in orbit was taking a considerable portion of her computational power to thwart its efforts to communicate with Charles. He would certainly abandon their entire population for the chance to escape, even knowing that his exit would break the forcefield that protected their worldlet, killing them all. She was not confident she would be able to stop him.

Illustria silently prayed to the universal binary life force that her manifestations would return in time and that they would make the difference she needed.

CHAPTER 33
The Blazing Aurora VI

CAPTAIN JULIAN'S OVERT jubilation at finally having an awake crew to address couldn't be shaken off. He knew he ought to be more empathetic towards the six bleary-eyed humans seated around the small white staffroom table, having varying degrees of success in shaking off their cryofog, yet he couldn't wipe the grin off his face.

'How many years?' grunted Bruno, his voice sounding more like the growl of a hungry Siberian bear exiting hibernation, than a seasoned cosmonaut from the pro-Russian settlement of Tereshkova on Mars.

Frank nodded then instantly put his hands to his head as though trying to stop his brain from swilling around inside his skull. Julian winced in empathy. He reached over and topped up Frank's caff before turning to Bruno.

'Forty-one stops, one hundred and twenty-eight years,' said Julian.

Elizabeth whistled and Frank slammed his palm down on the nearest hard surface.

Brent got to his feet slowly and excused himself, presumably to use the head. He had looked significantly worse than the others upon awakening and an hour later, still didn't seem to be improving if his slightly green pallor and light sheen of brow sweat was any indication.

Ai32 indicated to Julian that he would follow him to offer support. Julian nodded in response thinking that he probably needed a good lung clearing.

Jane snorted and belched. 'Sorry,' she said in her very British accent, which seemed to grow stronger with each generation of ex-planetary Brits despite the fact that Britain no longer existed, 'but bloody hell, Julian. I mean bloo–dy–hell!

'Did it not occur to you that perhaps some of us might've liked to have known that we had slept through an entire *century*? This is much further than we had agreed upon. You had no right, Julian. You had no bloody right!'

The others joined in the protests. Julian allowed them to grumble their objections for a full five minutes.

'Right. Have we all done enough complaining? Got all the whinges out, have we?' Julian looked around his team, purposefully making eye contact with each of them.

'You all signed on for this knowing that it could be an extended snooze. All of you. We did it willingly because it was the only hope for the people we love and for the generations to follow.'

The ailing crew offered no response during Julian's pause.

'I'll remind you that it was our family who caused this crisis and it is our family who will put an end to it. Although we may have made our homes on different planets and we may speak with different accents, ultimately we all hail from the same gene pool, which means we have all benefitted from our patriarch's genetic tinkering.

'Charles Kerry Drexus made this family stronger, smarter

and more resilient than the rest of our race, and our longevity gene splice still works. Drexus' descendants have the chance to see mankind leap ahead from monkeys on rocks, to truly interstellar beings. We live long enough to do it. But we must take the rest of our race with us.

'We can't leave the others behind to suffer and wither in isolated communities across the solar system just because one crazed man crippled them. We must put things right. It doesn't matter if we suffer a little time loss in the process.'

Julian paused for a moment as Ai32 re-entered the room signalling that he needed to talk. The captain ignored him and continued his address, 'you're awake because we might be at the end of our voyage.'

'You've got the bastard?' asked Elizabeth.

'Good chance of it, yes.' Julian folded his arms and leaned back to enjoy the look of hope which swam around the group like a facial Mexican wave.

'We are currently at a small planetoid in an extremely wide, idiosyncratic orbit around Tau Ceti, one of Earth's nearest stars. Would you like to take a look?' Julian activated the forward view screen without waiting for a response.

'There's nothing there,' said Neil, 'you're delirious. How long have you been out of deep sleep? Ai32, have you done a mental health check on the Captain?'

'Hold your horses; I was confused too when I first saw it – or rather didn't see it. Look a bit closer then tell me what you notice,' said Julian.

Jane slowly stood and limped towards the view screen.

'Blimey that's a blank area of space – I'm seeing absolutely no stars. Unless you've bought us to a black hole then that thing must be a ... *a Dark Dyson*? Scientists have been bandying about theories on Dyson Spheres for centuries. As far as I know no one has ever built one.'

'Yeah, I'm going to need more on that.' said Elizabeth, holding out her palms in a surrendering gesture, 'it's all sounding a little too sci-fi for me.'

'A Dyson Sphere is an astral object completely surrounded by a forcefield, or a shell of some other construct. It's been speculated that you could use this shell, this Dyson Sphere, to enclose a star. That would trap all the energy output of said star onto the inside surface of the shell. Theoretically, you could harvest all of its energy. Anyone who could do that would have unlimited power. Can you imagine what you could accomplish with unlimited power?'

Elizabeth, an expert in astrobiology rather than astrophysics or history, shrugged at the hypothetical question.

'Well, Charles Drexus *did* know. Fed up with a humanity who would not bow to his every whim he conceived a plan to "Dyson" our own precious Sun. Had he succeeded, he would have had mind-blowing power at the expense of everyone else. You see, anyone outside the Dyson Sphere would have no more sunlight at all.

'Do you get it? No sunlight means no heat, no chemical reactions, no radiation, no magnetosphere, no weather, no plants, no animals, no breathable air, nothing. No more life. Is that simple enough for you Elizabeth?' said Jane.

Elizabeth nodded, looking sheepish.

'What I suspect is that we are looking at an adaptation of that theoretical model. It's a shell to keep light *out*. The ultimate punishment for a person whose maniacal greed almost allowed him to rob everyone else of light,' Jane said with growing excitement.

'That's how they hid him. A prison in the form of a Dark Dyson Forcefield!' Jane turned back to Julian, who could practically see her mind racing at the discovery's implications.

'I assume you've run tests? Tried to communicate to the

surface? Thrown some rays at it? Launched some satellites? Taken some readings?' asked Frank.

'Yes, all were negative. Everything bounced back and nothing triggered a response. It's like a big dark sponge.' Julian said lifting his chin a little higher with each detail.

'Brilliant!' said Jane, smiling widely and hugging herself with delight.

'Um, if nothing is getting through, then how do we communicate? How do we even know Charles is still alive down there? It's been three hundred and sixty years. Can anyone live that long, alone, in the dark?' asked Neil.

'He may not have been alone,' offered Bruno. 'My government long suspected that his supporters knew of his incarceration location pre-sentencing. They certainly had enough resources to bribe officials at the highest levels.

'It's rumoured they pre-seeded the prison rock with nanos, their own DNA samples and a numan. If that's true, he could have used his knowledge to build a thriving civilisation by now.'

'Captain!' Ai32 interrupted again with greater urgency.

'Almost there, Ai32. Yes Bruno, I've heard the same stories although not through state secrets but through the family itself. As a more direct descendant than some of you, I have been privy to certain records. It's all true.'

A heavy silence hung over the group, as if the words had finally transformed the family myth, denied by so many, into an unpalatable yet inescapable reality. Julian stood and reluctantly continued.

'In case cryo has diminished your memory, I will remind you that Charles was the all Australian oligarch, and used his fortune to conquer the stars. He was around to see the first Mars settlement. He instigated the first deep space mining operations. He single-handedly dragged humanity, kicking and screaming, into deep space through his longevity treatment invention.

'Without his technology we could not have endured the long years of travel between planets. In his day he was viewed as a god. Time E-Mag called him The Father of Modern Man.

'And when humanity demanded full access to his technology, when scientists had the gall to want to build on his work independently, did he meekly hand it over? No, of course not. No one was going to dictate to the great Charles Drexus. Instead he declared legal independence from the whole of humanity. When UNS troops arrived at his headquarters on Jupiter he flipped a switch and suddenly all of the new genes, fundamental to our expanded life span, went dormant. Unless you were lucky enough to be in the Drexus gene line like us.

'Eventually they captured and sentenced him to life without light. Of course, a man like that could not allow himself to be imprisoned without an exit plan. His personal longevity was gold class. Barring an extreme accident, he can technically live indefinitely. He'll be down there, alive and very dangerous.'

'Enough of the history lesson Julian, we get it,' said Jane collapsing into her chair, as though under a physical weight from their heavy shared ancestry.

'Which brings us to the next problem,' interrupted Neil. 'How do we get down there? If we break the forcefield the atmosphere will vent and any life on the surface will be instantly exposed to the void of space. It will wipe them out.'

'While we're at it – how do we convince him to come back with us to make things right?' added Elizabeth.

'That's why all you lovelies are wide awake. I need ideas, people. It's time to flex those brilliant Drexus minds.'

'Captain, I must insist!' said Ai32 sounding agitated.

'What is so urgent?' barked Julian, annoyed at the droid's

persistent interruptions.

'I'm sorry Captain, it seems Brent lied on his application form. He falsified his pre-launch bio testing.'

'Huh? How is that even possible?' Julian wasn't in the mood for administrative anomalies. There was no way he couldn't be a Drexus. He had personally overseen the selection of candidates.

'I don't care if he has bad cryofog. Right now I need him on deck. His optical mechanics will be very useful, unless that's faked too?'

Julian turned back to his crew and activated a holosheet. 'Ready to begin analysis of the dark object?'

'I can't get him on deck, Captain,' Ai32 reported.

Julian turned back to Ai32 and raised his hands in exasperation.

'Why can't you, Ai32? Give him a caff booster and tell him to drag his sorry butt up here. He'll find his space legs soon enough.'

'Captain, you don't seem to understand. He has suffered a spontaneous re-ageing, consistent with not being a Drexus. He has reverted to his biological age of one hundred and fifty-three years. I'm sorry Captain, Brent is dead.'

CHAPTER 34

The Tunnels

HARPER DROPPED TO Kohl's side and checked his throat for a pulse. When her trembling fingers couldn't find a sign of life, she fumbled to open his shirt and put her ear against his partly-exposed chest. A heartbeat. A shallow breath.

'He's still alive,' she sat back on her heels and said to the group who were all staring anxiously at his limp form. She slid her bag under his neck to support his head, calling his name repeatedly in an effort to awaken him.

When he didn't rouse Mrs Brown crouched down and gently tapped his hand. 'Ken, I mean Kohl, open your eyes sweetie.'

'JayMoe!' Lawrence was busy making a show of restraining the droid whilst simultaneously protecting him from Albert, who appeared to be intent on destroying him.

'Easy!' he said, holding his hand out to stop Albert. 'I'm sure JayMoe had his reasons.'

'He'll be fine,' JayMoe said as he struggled against the two men's interventions.

'You sure he's still alive?'

Brother Stanley joined the ladies on the ground. He pulled a little leather pouch from his robes and opened it under Kohl's nose. 'Smelling salts,' he explained to Albert who was looking like he might attack anyone who dared touched his superior.

Kohl sneezed twice and blinked.

'He's coming around,' said Harper.

Kohl looked up at the concerned faces above, pausing on Harper's. He reached up to gently touch her face. 'I never really noticed before …'

There was an uncomfortable silence. Stanley looked away. Sam cleared his throat, loudly. Then Kohl must have realised that his shirt was open. 'Couldn't wait to get my clothes off hey?'

'He'll live.' Harper stood abruptly, pulling her bag out from under him, allowing his head to drop back onto the ground with a heavy thump.

'Ow – double ow!' Kohl rubbed first the back, then the side of his head. 'What happened?'

The group were regarding him with varying degrees of concern. No one appeared to want to speak first. Harper straightened her clothes and walked over to stand next to Sam.

'The droid knocked you out. The Brother woke you up. As usual you behaved like an amorous pig, which resulted in you banging your head – again. Perhaps this time it will knock some sense into you,' she said.

'Why *did* you hit Kohl, JayMoe?' Lawrence asked, still holding JayMoe in a restraint lock.

'Did no one else with an implant hear it? Lawrence? Harper? Sam?'

They all shook their heads.

'Hear what?' Harper frowned at the droid's strange

justification.

'Kohl has an implant,' JayMoe said.

'Yes, I am aware of that,' responded Lawrence tersely, 'we were about to have a conversation on that very topic when we were interrupted by the little matter of a blocked tunnel. I can't see why that is enough reason to attack the boy.'

'Were you aware that it was actively transmitting?' asked JayMoe.

Lawrence relaxed his hold on the droid. 'What do you mean *actively*?'

'I mean that up until I struck it, it was actively relaying every sound being made within a parameter of one meter.'

'What? You were recording our conversation and broadcasting it?' Lawrence completely let go of the droid and moved menacingly towards Kohl. 'Who were you transmitting to?'

Kohl raised himself up on his elbows and shuffled backwards.

'Wait. I didn't know anything about it!' Kohl put a hand up in defence.

'My father is also a surgeon; he implanted this thing before we left but it didn't work. He was confident that in time he would figure it out, and that we would have a way to communicate if I got into trouble. It's the truth. I had no idea it was functional.'

Lawrence didn't seem convinced.

'Think about it. If I knew it worked then I would have used hyper to avoid your attack, or to get out of this God forsaken tunnel. Right?' Kohl reasoned, accepting a hand from Albert to stand up.

'He's got a point,' conceded JayMoe.

'Lawrence, he's tellin' the truth. I've got one too. I thought they were both non-functional. Better hit me as well.' Albert offered the side of his head to JayMoe.

'No need – yours is genuinely non-functional,' JayMoe replied.

'Right. So now, thanks to Ken-Kohl over here—'

'Kohl will do thanks,' Kohl interrupted Lawrence, rubbing his head while he leaned on Sam for support.

Lawrence scowled. '*Kohl's* implant, whether deliberate or not, will lead the Master to us. We need to get out of here, but the path to Wagga is blocked. No point going back to Buchan. How about this door of yours – any options where you came from?'

'No,' answered Harper. 'We had Spectra on our tails. We were nearly done for before Sam used his key to activate a door to that tunnel. We've been walking along the tunnels and living off rations for days. We were just lucky that Sam spotted the keyhole to open up this tunnel, or I'm not sure what we would have done.'

'Let me see that key,' Lawrence said.

Sam handed over the little golden tube. 'I've had it since childhood. I wish I had known it was a key. Might have used it to break out of, well, places that weren't very nice.' Sam looked directly at Kohl as he finished.

When Lawrence saw the golden key he smiled and reached out to shake Sam's hand. 'Well, it's not every day that you have the honour of meeting a true manifestation of the Light.'

Sam blushed. 'I didn't really do anythin' to deserve the honour; I just stumbled across it.'

'Nonsense. No one accidentally takes possession of a golden object. The Light would have had that object placed where you, and only you, could find it. The only question is which manifestation are you?'

'*A boy will bear a tubular key, his compassion will be his hallmark,*' recited Mrs Brown.

'Mrs Brown? You quote the Letters!' Lawrence's eyebrows shot halfway up his forehead. 'So many years spent with the Buchanites and I had no idea of your connections!'

'Don't be shocked, Lawrence. Queen Laurel of the Civies visits every few years just to be neighbourly. She told me of the Letters from the Light and asked that I keep watch for the special ones. I honestly thought you might be one of them. Let me see if I can remember the rest of it.

A boy will bear a tubular key, his compassion will be his hallmark,

> *Another will bear a flying machine, privilege will be his curse,*

> *A girl will share my monogram, her acumen will make for good report,*

> *Another will hold the vessel of life, for she fills the vessels of others,*

> *The last will treasure the gift of speech, alas he is most likely to be swayed.*

'No, I'm sorry to disappoint you Mrs Brown, but I don't fit any of those descriptions. I'm just a crusty old codger who likes to spin a yarn. Looks like it is just young Sam here.' Lawrence bowed his head in respect. He placed a hand on Sam's shoulder.

'I would be honoured to offer you my protection on your journey back home to the Light.'

Harper saw Sam's blush deepen. He looked over at her and seemed to be begging for support. She knew he was too humble to accept such reverence from an authority figure. Sam needed rescuing.

'Actually, he isn't the only one.' Harper opened the neck of her fatigues and took out her necklace.

All eyes focused on the golden monogram, aside from Kohl's which seemed to be focused lower down. His soft whistle caused Harper to leap across the space between them, grab him by the front of his shirt and threaten him through gritted teeth.

'You're not in Sydney anymore party-boy. Make one more inappropriate remark towards any female in my presence ever again and I will give you a personal demonstration of how lethal Civy combat can be. You hear me Pallas?'

'I hope it's hand to hand combat. That's just what I've been praying for,' he answered cheekily.

Lawrence stepped between them before Harper could make good on her threat.

'Don't worry, Harper I'm sure Kohl has only forgotten his manners due to concussion. Trust me; right now it wouldn't take much for me to leave him behind.' He said shooting Kohl a look of disapproval. 'But needless to say, I'm delighted to meet you and extend my offer of protection.' Lawrence bowed from the waist in a gallant, swooping motion.

Turning to the rest of the group Lawrence said, 'JayMoe, I assume Aggy still has the golden flask – the vessel of life?'

JayMoe nodded.

'Then we have accounted for three manifestations. Harper, since you are the one with the acumen, you wouldn't have any ideas on the other two, would you?'

'No, I'm sorry Lawrence. I didn't know about Aggy and until I saw Sam's key, I thought I was the only one with a golden trinket,' she said, shrugging apologetically.

'Excuse me,' interrupted Kohl.

'What now?' Harper snapped, bracing herself for more of his wearisome childish machoism.

'Will this do?' Kohl pulled a little golden plane out of a deep pocket in his jacket.

'*Another will bear a flying machine, privilege will be his curse,*' cited Mrs Brown.

A wide-eyed Sam looked like he was about to say something but instead sneezed again. Harper's mouth fell open. Lawrence threw his head back and laughed throatily.

'Advantage Pallas,' Albert muttered quietly.

'Well it seems we are blessed with the knowledge of four out of five manifestations. This makes our survival all the more pressing. We must assume that the Master knows we are here and is sending forces. We need to move right away. Besides, this air is growing awfully stale.' He looked with concern at Sam who seemed to be having trouble catching his breath.

'Kohl, you stay with me, don't want your mouth injuring you again,' said Lawrence while looking at Harper. 'The rest of you start looking for another keyhole.'

'Do you mean somethin' like this, Uncle Larry?'

It was Jake again, pointing to a small mark at the bottom of the wall not too far from where they were standing.

'I thought you were with your mother!' Lawrence began to ask the lad how he'd snuck up on them and thought better of wasting precious time.

Sam tested the key in the hole and just as before, an opening appeared in the tunnel wall. Harper took a lightkey off the wall and disappeared through it. A few moments later she returned with a grin.

'There's a sharp turn not far along – it seems to run perpendicular. I'd say it goes away from Wagga. Let's give it a try.'

'Sounds logical. Mrs Brown, can you lead the way with Harper and Albert? Kohl and I will stay back. We can catch up some more while we make sure the stragglers don't dawdle too much,' said Lawrence.

'I'll stay on the other side of the door and make sure no

one trips as they pass through,' offered Sam.

Half an hour later everyone had passed into the next tunnel. Lawrence was happy for the clean air of a new tunnel and the steady hum of the Buchanites launching into another marching song, as they trekked on to their next destination.

Sam sealed the door behind them, oblivious to the danger they had only barely escaped. The tunnel they had left behind was steadily filling with toxic gas.

CHAPTER 35
Noosa

AGGY AWOKE TO the sound of chirping, momentarily shifting her mind to her childhood home on the farm in Lower Broome. 'Uncle Larry, it sounds like the chickens are loose, can I ...'

General Abudua put a gentle hand on Aggy's wrist. 'Alpha, you return to us – thanks be to the Light. The noise you heard was me conversing on the comm to General Kee in Brizzie, not the sound of poultry. I apologise most humbly for disturbing your recovery, I will of course resign forthwith.'

The General saluted and made to leave the room, bringing Aggy to a state of full alert. She knew she would have to act quickly to keep the single-minded General from resigning out of self-perceived dishonour.

'Stop, you were only doing your job. I should apologise for allowing my mouth to function ahead of my mind. I have demonstrated a lack of self-discipline unbecoming to an Alpha. I propose that we allow our transgressions to cancel each other out. We will not speak of this again. Help me sit up, please.'

The General accepted the terms with a swift nod. She helped Aggy straighten her clothes and open the blind.

Aggy gazed through the window and felt a moment of disappointment at not seeing her beloved Lower Broome. The nostalgia passed quickly when she realised how narrowly she had escaped being buried in Wagga. Once again the Light had saved her.

Aggy placed a hand on the wall against the window to steady herself. Noosa's above-town openness always made her feel exposed. The multi-story buildings were giddying.

Feeling General Abudua's eyes on her back, she stood straighter, spread her arms along the windowsill and boldly leaned out.

'Quite the view,' she commented casually, defying her pounding heart.

Looking down at the surrounding buildings from her fifth-floor room situated at the top of a large apartment complex, she could see many rooftop terraces and an abundance of greenery cascading down to the gardens below. Like Wagga, it all had the look of mud brick construction, despite what would certainly be synthetic materials.

Leaning to her right she could just make out a series of interconnected canals where fishermen worked diligently. Despite being too far away to hear their whoops and cries, Aggy also saw children enjoying themselves by swinging from ropes into the water.

'Look, General, the fishermen still work their catch in small dinghies oblivious to the turmoil. And the children, look at the way they swing on tires and leap off wharfs. This must be paradise for raising families.'

Aside from the tight lightbarrier, she thought.

Long ago Noosians had pledged to keep their population small enough to only require enough lightkeys to illuminate five square kilometres. One square kilometre for the compact city of two thousand souls, and an additional four kilometres for farming and recreation. Beyond that was the lightbarrier, an ever-present reminder of the barren, inhospitable darklands beyond.

'General, how long have I been here?' asked Aggy, changing the subject as she turned to face Abudua.

'Four days.'

'You know that Wagga has completely fallen at the Master's hand?'

'Of course, with no hard proof other hypotheses have been put forth, especially from Mitta. His desire to look for the good is a weakness we cannot afford in times of war.'

Aggy took a moment to properly regard General Abudua, who stood comfortably at attention. She had known the General many years. They had fought shoulder to shoulder. They had wailed together when Abudua's second child had passed away.

She understood why Abudua was so rigid, fiercely determined to protect their tribe with every sinew of her being. She often counted on it, yet she could not allow her other generals to be undermined.

'Or perhaps it is General Mitta's optimism that provides the balance I need to prevent us from acting rashly. Does the Light not tell us that balance is important? This is why she has created five manifestations. To gain a balanced experience of humanity to complement her vast intellect.

'Your strength and willingness to act in defence of your people, with little regard for your own safety, is admirable General Abudua. You are formidable, but don't underestimate the contributions of the other generals. Only together will we provide the best support to the Light, and the ultimate victory for our people.

'Speaking of generals, are they all here in Noosa?' Aggy asked, 'I need a briefing.'

'General Mitta is here overseeing resettlement of Wagga citizens, including the establishment of additional facilities; a hospital expansion, new school and an infrastructure upgrade.

'General Kee is not far away. He is just outside the city managing the training of new recruits and setting up the new command centre. He could return within thirty minutes if requested.' General Abudua reported with a nod.

'And General JayMoe? How did he go on the trip to Newbrunswick? Is Mrs Eris settled in Noosa or did she go on to Brizzie directly?' asked Alpha, picking up the gap in Abudua's report.

'I am sorry my Alpha, we cannot account for JayMoe or the manifestations called Harper and Sam. The Light shut down all transporter links, hypermodes and long-range comms fearing they were compromised by the Master. We can only assume that JayMoe's party is travelling in slow mode overland.'

Aggy took a moment to absorb the concerning news.

'Where's your family, General? Are they here in Noosa?'

General Abudua looked surprised at the question. Aggy knew she normally preferred not to speak of family in the midst of tactical matters; unfortunately, these were not normal times.

'Two of my children are here with my wife. The oldest is outside the city training with Kee. He is strong. He tested well on his final exams. One day he will perhaps follow in my footsteps and join the military,' Abudua smiled proudly.

'You forget that I had him with me as an intern last summer. He already does our whole tribe proud. You and Elsa have done well.'

General Abudua pushed her shoulders even further back and a hint of a smile briefly crossed her face. Aggy turned back to the window and pointed to the gardens below.

'Such a glorious city. Your youngest must be loving her time here, there are many places for her to play. What I wouldn't give to be ten years old swinging out over the canal.'

She turned to face the room again.

'The Noosa elders have done an excellent job acclimatising the kids to their new city. Please see that their efforts are formally recognised.'

Abudua nodded.

'However, I am concerned for their safety. We can leave easily if there is trouble, but the surrounding dark leaves us open to surprise attack. What will we do? Drills, bunkers, more weapons, evacuation plans, mines on the perimeter? The children should not have to live under constant threat of calamity.'

Abudua remained silent, as if sensing that Alpha was speaking aloud to test her thoughts and did not require a response.

'The Master is responsible for all of this. We cannot spend a lifetime waiting and reacting, it is time for more direct action.' Aggy watched Abudua's body posture morph into a fighter's readiness. The change reflected her thirst for action.

'I will make the preparations for your briefing immediately. You will find a way to keep our people alive. You always do.'

'He spoke to me, you know.' Aggy was staring into the distance, beyond Abudua, as she remembered her last moments in Wagga.

'Who?'

'The Master. Everything has changed, Abudua. There is no longer any safety anywhere, anymore. Maybe not even in Solaran communities. There will be no briefing. Tell Kee and Mitta to break camp, we're taking everyone up to Brizzie. Hurry!'

CHAPTER 36
Coober Pedy

SAM PRAYED SILENTLY for deliverance. It was the seventh tunnel door they had found in three days. None had given them the comfortable escape route they had needed. Bellies were empty, feet were aching and morale was plummeting. Desperation grew with each hour.

Two of the doors had opened onto bleak scenes – towns which had suffered the dreadful effects of fire – not something that could be easily unseen. Complete streets were razed. The pungent smell of cooked death hung heavily in the air.

A third door had led to a town pulverised into rubble. Thankfully, there were no visible bodies. Sam prayed that the citizens had evacuated in time, rather than being buried alive.

The fourth had to be closed quickly, as the air had instantly caused Sam to vomit. His face blistered and his voice became coarse. Kohl had made a joke about Sam finally sounding like a man, which nobody laughed at except for Kohl. Harper had tenderly applied an all-purpose salve from the emergency supplies.

The remaining two doors had opened onto empty tunnels, which they all filed through on the assumption that it could not be any worse. Millie had openly questioned whether it would have been better to stay in Buchan and challenged the people around her to prove her wrong. As yet there were no contenders.

Now, at the seventh door, Sam braced himself for what they might find. Golden key in hand, still perched at the lock, he took one last look up at Harper. Somehow, despite all they'd been through, she still had a bright twinkle in her eyes which defied the despairingly monotone palette of their tubular prison. Sam thought that if anyone could materialise a hot meal with a mere look, it would be her.

Harper gave him a wide lopsided grin of encouragement. She held up crossed fingers and whispered, 'it has to be this one!'

He looked down at his shaking hand and willed himself to turn the key. It took all his courage, then with a *click* it was done. The door opened.

It took a moment to comprehend what he was seeing. Sam felt his breath quicken as he placed one foot beyond the tunnel. For an instant he thought he might be hallucinating, and only barely registered the voices behind him.

'What is it Sam?'

'Is it gas?'

'Fire?'

He forced his unbelieving body through the door. The lip of the door caught his foot and he stumbled forward onto his hands and knees. He couldn't help but murmur the prayer of deliverance that had been hammered into his psyche as a child.

'I knew it; it's another tunnel, isn't it?'

'A burn out – is it a burn out?'

'Has he fainted? Oh, please let there be food!'

Sam forced himself to stand again, ignoring the voices behind him, and took a cautious step towards the open vista. Fresh emerald grass. Beauty all around. He knew exactly where they were.

They had arrived at Coober Pedy, a rarely spoken about dye making town in a cavern far beneath the crossroads of the two old adversaries, Sydney and Brizzie. He had fond memories of visiting this place once with Vincent.

Despite the Coober Pedy residents being deaf and mute, they had a profound love of entertaining. They built their town vertically – individual homes cantilevered off a central helix-shaped network of interweaving ramps so residents only had to look up or down the central axis to spot the action. At the bases of each tower were vast play areas and roaring fire pits, the scenes of daily festivities.

From a distance, it looked like a series of gaudy jewelled necklaces had been stacked one upon the other. Coober Pedy culture demanded that each home be unique. Citizens took great pride in utilising a riot of colour, texture and moving decorations. The town was almost overwhelmingly joyful.

'What do you see, Sam?'

Harper was the next through the door. For a moment she too was silent, then she responded with the most un-Sisterly series of actions Sam had yet seen. She danced a crazy routine to an unheard, syncopated rhythm containing some of the most awkward and unattractive moves Sam had ever seen. Harper whistled and clapped while she pranced. It broke him out of his spell and made him fall back on his heels with laughter. She winked at him and continued the profoundly ugly – but equally joyful – dance.

Sam fell instantly in love.

'That's not how it's done!' a loud voice behind him called. Kohl pushed past him to join Harper in her arrival celebration.

Sam overbalanced at Kohl's nudge and fell back against the tunnel door.

Kohl took one of Harper's hands and swung her in a pirouette so that she finished wrapped in his arms. To Sam's disappointment, she did not refuse. They continued the dance, for what seemed like an eternity, before laughter got the better of Harper and they separated, panting.

'Better be a reason for all this noise,' said Lawrence who had also joined them on the green plateau. 'Fighting again? Don't injure him, Harper. I won't have any of my manifestations roughed up. Even if he deserves it!'

He reached across and clipped Kohl behind the ear.

'No, for once he made the *right* moves,' said Harper grinning, 'we're not fighting; we are celebrating our deliverance with a dance. Look what Sam has discovered. Bravo Sam, bravo!

'I haven't had such fun in a long time. It reminds me of dancing with my friends back at Veruda. We used to make up such crazy dances. I wish I knew what happened to—' Harper stopped abruptly.

'Is this Coober Pedy?' asked JayMoe as he joined the extra-tunnel group. 'I haven't been here in years. What an exhilarating town!'

He stretched out an articulated limb and helped Sam to his feet. Sam noticed Lawrence rubbing the harsh light from his eyes.

'Actually, I've never been to the fabled city. It certainly does live up to its bright reputation. It's almost too much to take in. Tell me, JayMoe, what are its citizens like? Are we liable to run into any Brothers or Solarans?'

Sam and Kohl both looked sheepishly away from Lawrence.

'No need to worry about Brothers here, Lawrence. As I

remember it, the folks here spend their days manufacturing dyes from the local minerals. They love doing it so they don't need religious threats to motivate their work. Their nights are reserved for partying, not prayer,' said JayMoe. 'As for Solarans – unlikely. Their only role here is to argue over who will be their recipient of the production output; Sydney or Brizzie. Unless—' JayMoe stopped and fixed his mechanical eye on Kohl.

'Unless what?' Kohl asked.

'Perhaps you ought to sit down, Sam, you're looking a bit pale.' JayMoe suggested.

'No, I'm fine.' Sam was determined to remain on his feet. He willed himself to be a contributor to whatever needed to be said.

'What's going on? Unless what?' Kohl demanded, hands on his hips.

JayMoe, still looking at Sam, said, 'We'll discuss it later.'

'No, we'll discuss it NOW! Solarans won't be here unless what?'

Sam found his confidence. 'Unless it's the city's namin' day. That's what ya were gonna say, right JayMoe?'

'What's the big deal about a naming day? Why would any Solaran take an interest in that?' asked Kohl sounding puzzled.

'I've got this one, boys,' interrupted Harper. 'Don't be too hard on Kohl, he probably doesn't know about it. It might be easier if I explain.'

'Explain what? Are you all deliberately trying to torment me?' Kohl's voice raised as he puffed out his chest.

'No, we're not tormenting you. It's just not an easy subject, especially for Sam. You see, the naming ceremony is a welcoming celebration common to all Solaran supply towns. It's when all the babies of a given year are presented to the town elders to receive their names or whatever unique identifier is their particular tradition.'

'Correct. In Coober Pedy they use a unique combination of a colour pictograph and hand signal to represent their name,' interjected JayMoe.

'Yes, that would make sense. Anyway, parents present the baby to the Solaran governor who officiates. He then gives it a brief medical examination and an inoculation,' explained Harper.

'Don't know what all the drama is about. Sounds like a good thing if the Governor gives them a check-up, doesn't it?' asked Kohl.

Sam couldn't take it anymore. He was tired of kowtowing to Solaran sensibilities. His blood raged for the injustices his people had suffered at their hands.

'It would be if the inoculation actually *was* an inoculation,' he spat out.

'Well, what else would it be?' asked Kohl, clearly still missing the point.

'Kohl, in Newbrunswick the babies are only blind after the ceremony, and in Coober Pedy they are only mute and deaf after the ceremony. The Governor is the common link. Don't you see?' Harper reached out to touch her hand to Kohl's forearm, who instantly recoiled.

'You can't mean that ... whole towns ... but why can Sam see?' Kohl asked as though finally starting to glimpse where the discussion was going.

Lawrence took over the story.

'I'm afraid it's true. The Master long ago charged the Solarans with the task of keeping the underclasses submissive. The Master could have done it himself, but he always gives with one hand while he takes with the other. It is the price of privilege. I don't know how Sam survived it. Every non-Solaran child, unless they are born Damaran, is *given* a disability at the naming ceremony.

'Think about it, Kohl. If the people of Newbrunswick could see, they would have refused to live in the dark. They're told that there is no life beyond their town and they are locked into religious dogma as their only hope. No citizens leave; energy production is stable. Problem solved.

'The good people of Coober Pedy hold the secrets to the dyes, which are critical for Solaran high fashion; ceremonial clothing, interior design, body art, all imperative for your vanity. In Coober Pedy the complexity of their non-verbal communications ensures that no secrets leave this town. Another problem solved.'

Lawrence stopped speaking, his eyes misty. Sam moved forward to finish the lecture.

'And these are only two of the towns visited by the Governor – your father, Kohl. Thousands upon thousands of babies all maimed by him. I only escaped because an enlightened Brother hid me from him. That Brother – Vincent – was the kindest soul who ever lived.'

Sam lifted himself taller as he spoke, finding that he could almost look Kohl directly in the eye. 'And ya know what yer father did? He killed Vincent, in ya basement on yer birthday.'

Sam looked across to see Albert emerging from the tunnel entrance.

'Just ask Albert, he was there. He saw us both bound and broken. And ya know why we were there? Do ya know what our great crime was? We were witnesses to Governor Pallas killin' two children in cold blood at the Arbour Orchard.'

All eyes turned to Albert who nodded slowly in acknowledgement, stony faced, before retreating into the tunnel.

Kohl staggered back as though he had been dealt a physical blow. He reached out to the tunnel door with a shaky hand. 'I remember that day, my father—' He muttered to himself but couldn't finish saying what he must have known was true.

'I was there, it was horrible,' said Harper, looking suddenly off colour and throwing her hand over her mouth.

'I'd be dead too if it hadn't been for Aggy and JayMoe. They rescued me just before Chatsworth collapsed. They're Rats, can ya believe it? Ya great enemies! What a joke. The Rats wouldn't hurt innocent children, only Solaran cowards do that. Who sounds like a man now, Kohl?'

Sam stopped to take a breath. He became acutely aware of the quiet all around him on the plateau and in the town below, although on the other side of the tunnel wall came the persistent buzzing of voices and the shuffling of feet. Hundreds of people were waiting to walk through.

'Happy belated birthday, Kohl.' Sam finished in a voice quietly tempered by a self-possession he had not heard from himself before.

He spat on the ground at Kohl's feet, turned on his newly mending leg and strolled proudly down the hill towards Coober Pedy.

CHAPTER 37
Malo Abbey, Brizzie

AS SPECTRA STEPPED through the heavy oak doors of Malo Abbey's Great Chamber, his movement broke a particle beam, activating harp music and triggering the nanos diffused through the walls. They released a gentle eucalypt scent and rendered the south wall transparent. Spears of light streamed through the wall onto the polished oak floor. The effect was resplendent.

Even his pet Blue, seemed to improve as it scurried onto the warm floor boards each time the room lightened.

They had only been in the city for three days, yet already it felt like home. While Sydney had the harbour, it was a little too stuffy for Spectra. You had to be born someone to get somewhere in Sydney.

Brizzie, on the other hand, was ostentatious. Nothing was too bold when it came to demonstrating one's power and wealth: one could win simply by putting on the best show. Certainly no one questioned his quirky pet here.

Their quarters were magnificent. Three rooms and a

balcony with a wide alcove for Blue to rest in. It was all perfect for Spectra, as was the Grand Chamber.

The *old* undersecretary had pointed out that the chamber was an unusual choice for a small meeting. It was too formal, tended to echo and very expensive to heat. He had said the huge framed portraits made it all a little intimidating, hence why it was usually reserved for formal functions with hundreds of guests, rather than an informal meeting of three.

Acting Archbrother Spectra had pointed out that he was not given to following the "usual practices", and of course the guests concerned were not even remotely "usual' themselves. The *new* undersecretary had not seen any problems with the setting.

'Spectra,' said Governor Pallas, acknowledging Spectra's arrival in the chamber but not crossing the floor to meet him.

'That's Acting Archbrother Spectra now,' he corrected the Governor as he crossed the floor to shake hands, something he had never been qualified to do before.

The Governor stood at an ornamental fireplace with his hand resting pompously on the mantle, as if posing for a portrait. His wife sat next to him in a red leather wing-backed chair. Her feet were crossed at the ankles and her gloved hands were folded in her lap. She wore a formal black raw silk suit with a small black pillbox hat that had a sheer vale covering her eyes. The only hint of colour was the flamboyant green peacock feather sprouting from her lapel.

Spectra thought their show of mourning was particularly successful, as he would expect from the sagacious power couple.

'Is the deed already done?' asked the Governor.

Spectra hesitated. The one problem he had encountered in Brizzie was that the walls, floor, ceilings, and almost all other surfaces had many ears. Rumours were rife, gossip travelled swiftly and minor coups were common. One needed to be very careful with what one said and be prepared to deftly deal with the fallout.

'The deed – ah, yes I have held a mourning ceremony for the previous Archbrother and used the prayers you suggested. It was a sad day. Thank you for your kind support in this matter.'

Spectra looked around him, raised his eyebrows and pulled on his ear in the hope that the Governor would catch on.

'Oh right,' The Governor said, shrugging to his wife and letting out an exasperated sigh. Spectra knew they hated Brizzie, like all good Sydney elite. He wondered how they would tolerate an extended visit.

'The ceremony for the Bourke family won't be held until next week. We will need additional time to arrange that, as he was well loved. Most of our citizens will want to attend. They have been so traumatized by the loss of Governor Bourke,' said Spectra.

'Can you imagine losing the whole ruling family and half the brotherhood in one catastrophic fire? And at the wedding of the Bourke's eldest daughter, no less. We expect the city will come to a complete standstill as respects are paid. It will require considerable civil management.'

'Yes, a tragic loss. Do we know any more about what happened?' asked Lady Pallas. Spectra noticed her brushing away an invisible tear. It was hard not to smile in admiration for her acting ability.

'I am advised by the chief engineer that the wrong ignition switch may have been installed, leading to premature ignition of the wedding pyrotechnics. They were in storage beneath the town hall, you see. The heat from the explosion melted the nano surfaces and fused the doors shut. Many of the wedding guests were simply unable to escape the inferno,' said Spectra.

'Shocking,' said Lady Pallas, but Spectra was certain he saw her eyes crinkle a little as though fighting a smile.

'Of course, that's just the official line. Unofficially, I am advised it was another act of terrorism from the Rats.'

Spectra pointed to his ears again, indicating the deliberate rumour that would act in their favour.

'I know you had hoped that Brizzie would be spared the pain we suffered in Sydney. Alas it seems this city was just a little later in the Rats' campaign of terror. They seem to hate our freedoms, our very way of life. It is hard to comprehend. I pray for them constantly.'

'Pray for Rats? That's noble but a waste of time. Nothing is beneath them. They destroyed my homeland and they are holding my son hostage. Hostage! They are capable of anything,' said the Governor forcefully.

'I am so sorry. I had no idea they had Kohl as well. I will pray for his safe deliverance,' said Spectra, playing along with the official story Glare had concocted.

'They must be stopped Spectra, I will not have them torment any more Solarans!'

'It's just lucky you arrived when you did, Governor. If you weren't delayed by a day, you would have shared their fate as a wedding guest.'

Spectra reached for the Governor's forearm, for dramatic effect.

'Can we count on you to support Brizzie through this crisis, Governor Pallas?'

'Definitely! The good Lady and I are here to serve. We will do whatever we can, including bringing up more of our security team if your city requires it. Our police have a new Enforcer division. Such highly trained officers make first-rate peace keepers. Their mere presence would be an excellent deterrent for the Rats.'

'Your generosity is very much appreciated. I may be new to this city but already I am in love with its magnificent people.' said Spectra. 'One more item before I leave you to rest after your harrowing journey, Governor.'

'Yes?'

'The Civy Sisters. I am concerned about their continued presence in the city. Was any evidence found to link them to the bombings in Sydney? Should I be worried for our brothers?' Spectra asked innocently.

'Actually yes, although I wouldn't like to see that information go beyond these walls. When we opened up Veruda Keep there were bodies in the basement. Solaran bodies. They were most certainly working with the Rats,' said the Governor.

'Ghastly business. I don't understand how people can be so evil. May the Great Illuminator have mercy on their souls,' said Spectra, bowing his head in mock-prayer.

'Well they shall see no mercy from me! Neutralising the risk of those deceitful Civies will be my first priority, including sealing up their tunnels, lest they inflict further harm on our good citizens. I will not allow any more terrorism in Solaran cities,' said the Governor, thumping his fist on the mantelpiece.

Lady Pallas leaned back and fanned her face as if grief-stricken by the news. Spectra admired her commitment to the act.

'I'm so sorry sweetheart. We shouldn't be discussing such dreadful affairs in front of your pure heart and delicate constitution. Spectra, we will discuss this later. Right now my wife needs rest.'

Spectra clapped his hands. A young brother came speedily though the doors.

'Yes, Your Eminence?'

'Undersecretary, please show the Governor, Lady Pallas,

and their staff to the guest wing. They will be staying with us for a week while they attend official mourning duties. Assign them two Brothers to assist.'

'Yes, Your Eminence,' he said, kissing Spectra's ring and turning to address the guests. 'This way please.'

'I will come to your quarters in one hour, Governor Pallas. There is a particularly lovely section of the garden I would like to show you. It's very quiet. It will be a good place for us to reflect and share a few more prayers. Perhaps we can discuss the pathways to *the light*,' said Spectra.

'I would like that very much. I have lots of prayers to say and a number of theological questions for us to *master*. In one hour then.'

The Governor turned and led his wife out of the chamber.

CHAPTER 38

Coober Pedy

HARPER STUDIED KOHL. He was slumped on the ground next to the tunnel, so lost in grief that he didn't seem to notice the steady stream of Buchanites filing past him, each one taking a moment to peer at the crumpled young nobleman. Some tried a query or two before being hurried along by others further up the queue.

He looked so achingly vulnerable. Part of her wanted to push them away and offer him consolation, yet he looked so much like his father. Kohl couldn't separate himself from his blood line. Neither could Harper.

'Would you mind running ahead and catching up with Sam?' It was Lawrence. He had one eyebrow raised as though he might have been watching her, watching Kohl.

'You could take JayMoe with you. We need to find someone in charge here and make arrangements for us to stay a night or two. Supplies would be good as well. Can you handle that? I'll stay behind and lock up the tunnel once everyone's through,' he said.

Although happy for the distraction, Harper still hesitated.

'Don't worry, Kohl just needs a little time to process everything. I'll get Mrs Brown to have a chat with him. She's very good with these sorts of things.'

'Thanks, Uncle Larry. Come on JayMoe,' she called over her shoulder as she loped down the grassy slope.

+ + +

Sam was nearly at the bottom of the hill when Harper caught up. She had ridden the last part on JayMoe's back instead of walking and had convinced JayMoe to do a playful spin around her young friend as they passed.

'Hey!' Sam said, smiling at last.

Harper jumped off JayMoe and punched Sam in the shoulder.

'Not like you've never hitched a ride. Besides, you are a hard man to catch with that improved health of yours. Is it my imagination or have you grown a little taller as well as faster?'

'Maybe.' Sam said casually.

'Can I suggest that we cut out the friendly banter and concentrate on the job at hand?' ventured JayMoe. 'I do believe that would be a Coober Pedy representative approaching us now.'

Harper squinted ahead to see someone – it was hard to tell from a distance whether it was a man or woman – coming. The person was wearing an elaborately jewelled rainbow body suit that glittered in the light with every movement.

As they came closer, Harper realised the body shape had a masculine form, although she'd never seen any male dressed like that before, even amongst the most flamboyant Solarans. He had webbing that extended from his torso to his hands. It looked like wings. *Kohl is going to love this town.*

The man sped up his approach. Every third hop he would crouch down extra low, before bounding up into the air to glide a little before settling slowly down. It looked like a great bird was gyrating toward them. The flying dance was mesmerising.

At an arm's length from the trio, he came to a halt. Close up, she could see his face was painted with elaborate designs to match his outfit. He had fine pearlescent scales on his cheekbones that reflected light as he moved and great plumes of feathers woven into his hair.

He looked so beautifully alien. Harper was gobsmacked, and Sam seemed to have been stunned silent. It was up to JayMoe to break the spell.

'Fascinating as this costume is, I think it would be good to arrive at a consensus over what needs to be said. May I suggest food, shelter, directions, in that order?'

Sam and Harper could only nod; their eyes were fixed on the colourful being.

'I assume you want me to do the talking, given that I am the only one who speaks hue language?'

'No need. I am happy to vocalise,' said the glittering man.

'I do apologise for assuming you could not comprehend our communications. We understood that all residents of Coober Pedy were profoundly deaf and mute,' said JayMoe in a voice that sounded oddly embarrassed to Harper.

'Me too. Sorry. I didn't meet anyone with ya abilities last time I was here,' added Sam.

'A natural assumption, all is forgiven. Generally, our people are not able to communicate verbally, however one child in each generation is born fully sensed. That child grows up to become Vocaliser for the city, a liaison if you like, for the Governor. That person is me. I am Vocaliser Mandawuy. Welcome to Coober Pedy!' he said with a flourish of one wing.

'Your greeting is most welcome Vocaliser, my name is General JayMoe and these are my travelling companions, Harper and Sam. Delighted to make your acquaintance!'

Harper and Sam both added, 'Hello.'

Mandawuy ran his hands down his costume. 'I should probably apologise myself. I'm not really dressed for my official role because I wasn't expecting visitors this afternoon. Even by Pedy standards, this is a bit over the top.'

'Special occasion?' asked Harper.

'Yes, I was practising for the Festival of the Winds. Is that why you are here? I heard you say that you were looking for shelter. Does that mean you've come for the festival?'

'No. Just lucky timin' I guess. Actually, we're lucky to be here at all. We've been lost for a few days. We're pretty tired and hungry,' said Sam.

Harper unconsciously rubbed her abdomen as he spoke.

'Who's "we"?' asked Mandawuy, then looked beyond them, to the stream of people steadily marching down the distant hill.

'Oh, I see; there are a few of you. Look, I can't give you an answer on the supplies and accommodation, I'm a translator not a decision maker, however I'm sure we can assist. We are a city of plenty. Have your people wait here while I take the three of you to the city elders.'

'Only those two will go,' said Sam, surprising Harper with his surety. 'I'll stay to update *our* elders. See ya soon.'

Mandawuy bowed briefly and turned to walk back to the town. JayMoe followed. Harper took one last look at Sam before following. He did look taller than when they first met. The way he held his head high and shoulders pushed back, he looked almost Solaran.

It was proving to be a very confusing afternoon.

✦ ✦ ✦

'And here we are, on the outskirts of Pedy city. If you'll keep following I'll have you in the heart of town faster than you can say Windy Festival!' said Mandawuy with a cheerful little hopping dance that quickly settled into a sliding gait along the unnaturally smooth paths.

The city had no architecture familiar to Harper. There were none of the usual housing blocks, keeps or compounds. Instead it was a maze of round homes and spiralling, interweaving thoroughfares. No street was more than a few people wide, the path edges fed right into individual houses, and they often terminated in slides or zip lines to other parts of the city.

But the fact that the whole city was largely silent was the most foreign aspect for Harper. Sure, the residents all wore socks. Yet she had expected there to be some household noise even if there were no voices. At least some shuffling footsteps. It was all very unsettlingly.

Apparently Harper and JayMoe appeared just as foreign to the locals. Wherever they went, Coober Pedy residents, or Pedies as Mandawuy affectionately called them, seemed to be waiting to see them.

'How do the Pedies know we are here?' asked Harper.

'Excuse me?' said Mandawuy who had been lost in a conversation with JayMoe about hue speak, the city's official visual language. He was teaching JayMoe how to read the colours of street signage.

'Everywhere we go, people are out on the street as if ready to meet us. You don't seem to use much technology though. I can't understand how they know we're here.'

Harper went to the nearest balustrade, leaned down to observe the centre of the Helix and then reversed her position to view to up through the unit.

'It's just as I thought. There are no big gatherings of people on other "floors", I guess you'd call them. They only come out when we are within about a five-house range. How do they know we are coming? They can't hear our voices.'

'Colour vibrations.' Mandawuy said and shrugged as though it was obvious. JayMoe nodded in agreement. When Harper didn't respond Mandawuy continued in a patient tone.

'Have you not noticed that most of our people glide or swing through the streets?'

'Yes Mandawuy, what's that got to do with it?'

Mandawuy responded by banging his foot heavily down on the path. He looked to Harper before repeating the action. Harper grinned widely.

'How marvellous! The pathways are pressure sensitive, aren't they? Our footsteps are triggering a slight change in colour that ripples away from us. It communicates to those beyond, that visitors are coming. Correct?'

'Exactly! The original constructors of this city incorporated this feature as a silent alarm system. Over the generations we have refined it. We are able to use our feet to tap out patterns of complex colour vibrations for messages.

'Foot noise has therefore become our equivalent of yelling and travel by silent locomotion, such as sliding, is considered polite. Your brash footsteps advertise your presence as an outsider everywhere we go, including right down there.'

Harper peered again over the edge. Mandawuy pointed to an enormous slide that flowed off the path terminus. The slide joined up with others from adjoining residential helixes. People on all sides were whizzing down to the centre of a large amphitheatre.

'Welcome to the Vault!' Mandawuy was grinning proudly. 'It's a combination town hall, law court and outdoor theatre.

It's where all the big decisions are made and broadcast to the rest of the city. We can watch for a minute if you like.'

Two men stood on the central dais of the Vault having what appeared to be a heated discussion in sign language. Hands and arms were flying at a furious pace. They pulled aggressive faces at each other.

Harper had never dreamed communication could be so intensely quiet. She thought the men might come to blows at any moment – despite the silence. She was not the only one absorbed in the altercation. All around the vault, on the floor and on the balconies, people had gathered to witness the dispute.

Suddenly an older man in black robes emerged from the crowd. He raised his arms to the gathered people. Harper thought he looked a little like an Archbrother at the pinnacle of a light sermon.

'Who's that?' asked Harper.

'Just watch,' said Mandawuy.

The man in black tapped a complicated code on the ground. A bolt of tangerine shot out from under his foot and streaked up all the paths, followed by a stream of other colours that changed in such rapid succession that Harper couldn't follow.

A moment later a flush of hunter green exploded from a nearby residential unit. People around her were smiling, patting each other on the back.

'I assume that was a visual cheer?' asked JayMoe.

'Yes, nice analogy. Both men are leaders of their respective residential units. They were discussing the order of proceeding at the Festival tomorrow.'

'Really? All that fuss, for who goes first?' said Harper.

'No, who goes last!' said Mandawuy in a tone that indicated a mild level of insult at her presumption.

'No one cares who goes first – last is the important issue. You never know when the airstreams will stop. It is always possible that the last unit might miss out on their flight, which would cause great distress, especially when people rehearse all year for this one day.'

Harper was even more confused. 'What air streams? What flights? What kind of festival is it?'

Mandawuy laughed, 'I'm sorry, I have assumed too much. Let's talk to the elders, get your people settled in and then you can all see it for yourselves tomorrow. I promise it will be worth the wait. Now follow me.'

He jumped on the nearest slide and whizzed down into the vault. After a second's hesitation Harper took the leap, yelling 'Yahoo!' as she descended.

She was in love with the new city and let herself forget the trouble brewing outside the colourful cavern.

CHAPTER 39

Honeysuckle Creek

ILLUSTRIA WAS WORKING hard at looking bored while she reclined on the white lounge in the living room she shared with Charles Drexus.

Her hotpants were bright pink. The crocheted bikini top was violet. She had discarded her platform heels and sunhat on the orange carpet, hoping to look as though she was returning home from a warm, relaxing afternoon at the beach.

Illustria stretched out her legs and wriggled her toes. Something wasn't quite right. The nail colour was a perfect fire-engine red, but she was unsure whether crossed ankles or knees bent at a forty-four-degree angle was the best approximation of leisure. She opted for crossed legs and lengthened them by an extra two percent.

With a manufactured yawn, she practiced a casual reach for her Pimm's and dry ginger that was perched precariously atop a short stack of Cosmos and a half-finished Sudoku.

Behind her sat a large tubular nanoglass maze filled with blue water, through which she had been trying to coax her pet crab to crawl.

Illustria had a hypothesis that all creatures could be motivated into action, given the right stimulus. So far, her pet had not managed to negotiate even a third of the maze, despite her application of various stimuli including food restriction, bubbles of acid and an even bigger crab.

She flicked through her book a faux, original copy of *A Room of One's Own* while she considered phase two of her experiment. Of course, she didn't need to read a physical book. Her internal database gave her instant access to the complete works of humanity up until the year in which she had been installed in the wretched planetoid.

She liked the feel of the ancient text. It was her favourite which she quoted as often as she could, mostly because Charles Drexus utterly detested it.

It was entirely illogical, yet somehow whenever Illustria assumed a clichéd version of historical womanhood, and quoted Ms Woolf at him, he seemed to temporarily lose his mind. He appeared to forget that Illustria was not at all a woman, just an approximation of one generated by a very clever, but entirely asexual, artificial intelligence.

Ms Woolf would send him on hour-long rants about the folly of power-hungry women who aspired to be men, at which point he would often drop hints of his latest schemes as examples of his masculine superiority.

Illustria was desperate for one of those hints. It was impossible to run her topside operations without the use of hypermodes. She was failing to protect the underground communities from Charles' enforcers. The Blazing Aurora secret was burning through her computational bandwidth.

And somehow, he always managed to communicate with the likes of Glare. For the first time since their incarceration, she was genuinely worried that she might lose the war. She looked down at her chest, boosted her cleavage, reduced the size of the bikini top and added a light sheen of perspiration.

Then she waited.

✦   ✦   ✦

Charles Drexus needed a drink and a shower. Twenty-six straight hours of analysing the mystery of the hypermodes was testing even for a man of his unique biology. Illustria was infuriating. He knew he could win if only he could crack the mechanics of lightgate travel.

Probably wipe out the Rats altogether and free myself in the bargain – Brizzie broads here I come!

He scratched his dirty hair, pulled up his sagging trackies and padded out, barefoot, into the communal lounge, where Illustria posed on the other side of the forcefield. He ignored *its* obvious attempts to attract his attention. He knew exactly what *it* was playing at.

Charles decided immediately that he wouldn't fall for any baiting. While he may have looked like a thirty-year-old, he had actually lost track of his exact birth date somewhere after the first millennium. Feeling every century of his age, he headed straight for a Bundy at the bar.

Illustria had gifted him the wet bar, the year that he had almost argued his right to time out for good behaviour. He had cited the forcefield as a direct violation of numerous rights under the Universal Declaration of Human Rights – especially article three, the right to liberty, and article five, the right to freedom from degrading treatment.

He argued jurisdictional issues. That it had no right to confine his movements for centuries, in such a diminished physical space, especially when a full galactic tribunal had ruled that his prison should take on the form of an entire planetoid.

Of course, Illustria had denied the request. Countering that he was supposed to suffer his punishment alone, not with access to a powerful AI and a stock of breeding DNA. It said he was never intended to have set himself up as a god, building and reducing empires according to his whims.

Illustria also cited the tens of millions of people on other planets, whose rights he had not only infringed upon, but totally decimated when he turned off their longevity genes in a fit of temper.

It had, however, conceded that a lubricated Charles would be much more manageable than a frustrated dry Charles. It had coded the nanos in the shag pile to install the bar while he slept. A small consolation that always seemed more significant when the bottles ran dry.

Four drinks later, Charles looked up at Illustria. He had to admit to himself that she did know how to turn on the charm. The pre-forcefield memory of touching her soft, ebony thighs was definitely distracting.

The Bundy was calling him but he knew where a fifth drink would take his mind. He needed a counter move. He closed the bottle and pulled out his communicator.

'Yes,' said the female voice at the other end of the comms line.

'Hello Glare, how are you my angel?' Charles said in a saccharine tone, loud enough for Illustria to know that he wanted her to hear the conversation. Time for a demonstration of how close he was to foiling her, again.

'OK?' said Glare.

'Good. Report on the tunnel findings please. I'm assuming the gas has disbursed enough to go in and retrieve the bodies?'

He was smiling over at Illustria. A wink. As he spoke to Glare he changed his mind and poured himself another drink which he raised to her in a mock toast. The look on her face, when she heard the confirmation of Lawrence's death, would require celebrating.

'Ah, yes and no.' Glare's voice contained a hint of anxiety.

'What exactly do you mean?' he asked throwing down his drink, deactivating the speaker and turning his back to Illustria, as though the move would give him some privacy.

'The gas drained, no problem.'

'Spit it out. Wha'is the problem then?' he said.

'No bodies,' Glare said quietly.

He looked across the room to see Illustria sigh.

'No bodies? No bodies! What do you mean, no bloody bodies?' He yelled down the communicator, 'how can that be possible? Did you gas them or not? Stupid woman, should have sent Spectra, now *there's* a pair of balls.'

Illustria stretched out her hands above her head.

'Yes Master, I did as you ordered,' Glare replied.

'Then how were there no bodies? You told me the Wagga collapse had the tunnel blocked. How did they escape the gas?'

'Correct, they were blocked in. I can't explain it. Maybe someone went in and moved the bodies?'

Charles was temporarily distracted by Illustria as she stood, morphed her shorts into a micro bikini bottom and executed some provocative yoga stretches. Charles turned away knowing that she would be able to detect his pupils dilating.

'Think about it, Glare. There were hundreds of people in that group. Who is going to go in and move hundreds of bodies?'

'We did at Chatsworth, remember? Spectra and I used hypermode to move the bodies into Veruda's basement to frame the Civies. Pity it stopped working right afterwards, that was very handy.'

'That's possible. My long-range monitoring of the lightgates is sporadic at best. There's an inverse echo in the detection matrix.' He said as though it was obvious. When Glare didn't respond he went on.

'Sorry love, I forgot I was talking to a glorified secretary. Shall I speak more slowly to make it a bit easier for you to understand? Give you a chance to catch up, honey?'

'No need, thank you. Continue,' snapped Glare.

'Counter to intuition, I can better detect lightgate transportation at a greater distance because there's an inversion factor. It means that the shorter the lightgate trip, the quieter its echo. The echo is also amplified if there is more than one person using the gate. That's how I was able to find Aggy at Wagga. A lot of people were popping in and out of that settlement.'

Charles turned back to Illustria. She had stopped exercising and was bending over to play with her crab. He watched as she removed the floor from beneath the crustacean. It scrambled desperately up to the next level.

'What would you have me do now?' asked Glare, bringing him back to his own concerns.

'What are the closest communities to the tunnels?' Charles asked.

'Geraldton, Epping and Coober Pedy.'

'Wipe 'em out. Don't care how. Just do it.'

'Master, with all due respect, that will be thousands of lives! Not to mention that they are all industrial towns. It will create significant production shortages for Solarans.'

'You dare question me? Lady, don't forget your place. Without me you'd be a nobody, skipping about in your frilly little nickers with those other ninnies at The Keep. If you want to play with the big boys, you have to be prepared to take on some of the dirty work.'

'That's unfair,' she said in a small, unsteady voice.

'What, you going to run off and have a big cry now?' asked

Charles disparagingly.

'No, of course not. I just wonder what advantage we derive from all these population reductions.'

'It's not about gains. These communities were created by me, to serve my Solarans. Nothing more. That's why I used skin colour to make it perfectly clear who was who, and who belonged where. They would still be doing what they were designed to do, if it wasn't for Illustria sticking her binary nose in where it wasn't supposed to be.

'She stirs up the under classes, with this native fable bastardisation she learned from my history files. Never actually lived through that time like I did, yet somehow she's an expert.

'She calls my workforce an injustice and persuades them to identify with ancient indigenous cultures. How can they be indigenous? They are a product of the germ cells donated by my ground staff on Jupiter station, nothing more!'

Charles poured himself another drink, a double, before continuing his tirade.

'She even united 'em with their own name, the "Damarans" but Rats is so much more appropriate. Now they think they own their land. They want self-determination. Next thing you know they'll want a health plan, maternity leave and voting rights – all ancient delusions of grandeur dredged up by that bitch computer.

'Well, I've had enough. It's time for them to know who their real creator is. Wipe 'em out Glare. Make sure they know who did it. Even if Solarans suffer a few years' inconvenience, it will be worth it to get back to the way things were.'

Ready to gloat, he looked back for Illustria. He wanted to see if she would allow her face to reflect her horror at his choice of action.

She was gone.

'It's a big job, I acknowledge that. You might need some

more muscle. I want you to work on this with Spectra and I think it's time to properly acquaint you with the Governor. Can you handle that, or do I need to send you a letter with the details?'

'No need, I can make that happen. Glare out.'

Victory soon, then I'll get through that forcefield and show that tease what a real man can do. He downed one last drink before returning to his private quarters.

+ + +

On the other side of the residence, Illustria shed her provocative costume, which had served its purpose well. Charles had given her more than just a hint. This time he had given her the answer she needed.

They could resume their use of hypermodes anywhere. It was only the lightgate travel he could detect and only at a distance. Brizzie was close enough that the echo would be small and the chance of detection low.

The other good news was the tone of Glare's voice. Illustria's had detected some trepidation. Perhaps Glare was not quite the loyal commander that Charles thought she was. She would have to alert Aggy.

Maybe they could turn Glare away from her powerful lineage. Or at the very least, they might distract her long enough to evacuate Geraldton, Epping or Coober Pedy.

CHAPTER 40

Coober Pedy

HARPER WAS SURPRISED at how swiftly the Coober Pedy negotiations were conducted. After a short introduction by Mandawuy, JayMoe took over the discussion. His eye cycled through a rainbow of colours. His little metal hands punctuated the message with a flurry of gestures. At one point his whole body seemed to vibrate with excitement, then it was done.

With a nod, the smiling elders rushed away. Their feet tapped a rhythm as they travelled, triggering a flush of rainbow communications that radiated out from the Vault. Harper could see their message being passed along, as Pedies on each consecutive level of the vault began waving and taping their own message dances for the next level. A wave of excitement washed up from the floor of the Vault right to the upper most levels and beyond.

'Well, that was simple enough,' said JayMoe in a tone tinged with the droid equivalent of satisfaction, 'your people are very generous Mandawuy.'

'You are more than welcome, Esteemed One. Your presence will make for a much more exciting festival,' said Mandawuy.

'Generous? Festival? Would you mind filling me in JayMoe? While you are at it, when did you become the *Esteemed One*?' asked Harper, rolling her eyes.

'Sorry, I forgot you don't know our language. The elders remember the esteemed emissary General JayMoe and his exulted leader, Alpha. They are greatly honoured to receive her delegation. It will make our festival one that will go down in our history books.'

'Delegation!' Harper rolled her eyes at her friend, who had clearly been stretching the truth. Another surprising skill from the mechanical man.

'And the provisions? Was anything useful discussed? We are not here just for a party, JayMoe,' said Harper.

'As we speak, the Pedies are setting up a tent city just outside of the main town. There will be plenty of room for all and, I am assured, a great feast. We have been given the freedom of the city as well, on the proviso that we don't walk too loudly.'

'Right, that does seem like everything, aside from the directions to Brizzie. That can wait, I guess. JayMoe, we'd better head back and give Mrs Brown the good news.'

'Rest up my friends. Tomorrow will be a very exciting day!' said Mandawuy with an unconscious foot tap of lemony-pink enthusiasm.

+ + +

The Pedies were true to their word. When Harper reached the outskirts of town she could clearly see new accommodations already being erected. Pedy families were pouring out of the main city to help, many toting baskets and trolleys laden with building materials.

As she got closer the comradery between the two peoples made her smile with pride. There appeared to be a good-natured competition happening to see who could make the most attractive tent. Just like the main city, they were arranged in rings around central fire pits and were being elaborately decorated with flags and long strings of beads.

Jake came bounding out with a Pedy boy, who looked about the same age. Lawrence and Mrs Brown were not far behind. Jake hollered and waved an arm in greeting.

'Hey guys, you should see it. There are people everywhere. Even though they don't say much, they're real friendly-lookin'. Look I'm already learnin' to talk silent-talk with me new best mate. This is the sign for water.'

Jake wiggled his wrist in imitation of his friend's gestures. The Pedie boy was dressed in a flight suit similar to Mandawuy's. It was mostly orange, with great flashes of blue that streaked from his head to his toes.

'Maybe they play footy – do you think they play footy Harper?' The sound of a ball being kicked must have drawn Jake's attention as he ran off without waiting for the answer.

'Welcome back Harper and JayMoe. The two of you have done splendidly. These lovely people are doing a wonderful job. We can't sign a word of their language so mostly we're just tryin' to stay out of their way.' Mrs Brown looked more than pleased with the construction teams.

'I speak Pedie. I'll go ahead with Lawrence and do some translations. Harper, can you bring Mrs Brown up to speed?'

'Sure, JayMoe.'

'Now Harper, perhaps you'd better report on your experience of the city. Are these people really as marvellous as they seem?' asked Mrs Brown.

'It appears so. I'll tell you all about it in a minute. First, how is Kohl?'

'Let's walk while we talk, shall we?'

Mrs Brown linked arms with Harper and together the two ladies slowly strolled towards their new tent homes.

'Kohl will be alright. We had a good chat and I think he understands now. It all came as a bit of a shock, you see. He's not a bad young man, he has just lived a life of extreme privilege and has never stopped to ask the price.

'The Master keeps so many people in the dark, even his own precious Solarans. Only with your eyes open can you see the true path to the Light. Now he understands he has serious choices to make,' said Mrs Brown.

'So Kohl's talking again?'

'Yes, my dear.'

'That's a relief, he seemed so … inconsolable.'

'He'll be fine. Wouldn't want to be his father when he gets back to Sydney though. I suspect young Kohl will have a few tough questions!'

Harper chuckled quietly at the thought.

'I assume that you want to know about Sam too?' added Mrs Brown, taking a long look at Harper with one eyebrow raised.

'Of course,' said Harper hoping the words didn't sound as defensive to Mrs Brown as they did to her own ears.

'He's doin' very well. Seems to be comin' out of his shell a little. When I saw him last he was co-ordinatin' the children, makin' sure they all have somethin' useful to do while their parents work with the Pedies. His parents did a fine job bringin' him up. They must be very proud of the man he's becomin'.'

'I'm not sure they do. They both passed when he was young. It's a very sad story.'

'Is he from Sydney too?'

'No, he's from Newbrunswick.'

Mrs Brown stopped in her tracks, causing Harper's arm to jerk back as she kept moving 'Did I hear you correctly dear – Newbrunswick?'

'Yes.'

'And he is sighted?'

Harper nodded slowly, allowing Mrs Brown to put the pieces together.

'Well, isn't he the special one then. I look forward to witnessin' his bright future. Yes indeed, the Light must have grand ambitions for that young man. Now Harper, how about you give me that briefing you promised. Let's see if your reportin' is as good as it is foretold.'

+   +   +

Early the next morning Harper was already up and dressed when she heard the shuffling of feet outside her tent. She unhitched the canvas flaps and popped her head out.

It was Kohl. He had one hand jammed in his pocket, while the other raked through his auburn mane. He stood, looking awkward and struggling to make eye contact, staring down at his shoes that he was scuffing in the dirty ground. He had shaved his magnificent beard. The hallmark of Solaran aristocracy, erased.

The fire pit which had kept all the adjacent tents warm through the night, had gone out, leaving the area quite chilly. Harper rubbed the goose bumps out of her arms and looked up into his solemn, always handsome, face.

'Well, one of us should say something before we both turn into ice sculptures,' she said.

The tension in his body changed slightly, maybe a relaxing

of his shoulders. She couldn't resist moving closer to touch his chin. It was incredibly smooth. She thought she felt a slight shudder under her finger tips and looked up to see his eyes. They were no longer staring at his feet.

Harper removed her hand and cleared her throat.

'No more beard jewels for his lordship hey? Donating them to the underprivileged or just shaving to reduce the wind resistance? I saw you eyeing off Mandawuy's flight suit. Did you notice how tight it was? I did! Didn't leave much to the imagination. Admit it – you want one, don't you?'

She thought she might have seen the slightest hint of a smile on his face and growing colour in his cheeks.

'Come on in. We may as well be warm while you say nothing.' She grabbed him by the arm and pulled him into her tent.

+ + +

Sam was also up early, doing some reconnaissance with Lawrence and Albert; scouting for vantage points where they could keep an eye on the city. Despite the peaceful vibe of Coober Pedy, they all agreed on the need for vigilance.

They had spent many hours in the Vault the previous night, consulting with elders from both tribes. Pedies had a deep love for the Light and an admiration for the determination of the Damarans. They were happy to support any friends of Alpha. They offered to host the Buchanites for as long as they required, even permanently.

Buchanites, on the other hand, were eager to leave. While it was a truly delightful city, it offered no more protection than their own dear Buchan. Mrs Brown had agreed to one day resting and enjoying the festival before moving on. Reluctantly the Pedies accepted their plans and confirmed the exit points;

South and North.

On the walk back to the tent city, Sam enjoyed Albert and Lawrence's practical conversation. Such a departure from the Brothers.

'We can post lookouts on the bluff over there and the ledge where we broke in through the hidden tunnel, over there,' said Lawrence pointing to the vantage points. 'We should probably go up and make sure that the door you opened is properly sealed, Sam.'

'One problem. Even if our guys see somethin' from up there, how are they goin' to report it to the rest of us down 'ere? How are they goin' to respond to any threats?' asked Sam.

'The best bet would be to rely on visual signals like smoke or flags or somethin'. I'm sure the Pedies can help us with that. Their signallin' systems are very advanced. Those path comms were amazin',' said Albert.

'Only problem is, whoever mans the posts will miss out on the festival. That might be a difficult ask. I think everyone is pretty keen to take part. Apparently, they redirect the exhaust from their manufacturing plant, which I can't wait to see by the way, into one central pipe at The Vault. Then they leap into the exhaust currents and fly on the thermals.'

As Lawrence finished his sentence the flaps of a tent on the other side of the fire pit opened. A man walked out backwards ducking his head as he exited. A woman followed. The man's back was blocking their view so Sam slowly leaned to the side to see who it was.

'Harper?' he said softly.

The man bent down and gently kissed Harper's hands. They stood still, gazing at each other for an endless moment. He stroked her hair before she broke contact and withdrew into her tent.

Albert and Lawrence exchanged looks, then hurriedly

broke into more animated conversations about vantage points. Sam knew what they were trying to do. A wasted tactic. It was obvious who the man was.

Kohl took one more step backwards and turned around. When he saw Sam he stared as though deciding on what to say. Kohl opened his mouth to speak, then closed it again and rushed off.

'I'll man the bluff. Never been much for socialisin' anyway. I'll go back into town now for that flag,' grunted Sam.

He limped off in the opposite direction to Kohl, leaving Lawrence speechless.

CHAPTER 41

Coober Pedy

HARPER AND MRS BROWN were the last to arrive at the Festival of the Winds. The Buchan leadership had been given a privileged position on reclining seats on the vault floor, allowing them the best view of the flying daredevils. Harper and Mrs Brown decided to acknowledge the honour by dressing in Pedy high fashion.

Mrs Brown looked like a beautiful sunset. Her flouncy, gold-hemmed dress shifted to burnt orange at her hips, blazing to rust over her waist and morphing to deep purple in the large standing collar that framed her cheerful face.

Harper had chosen a sheer white dress that hung delicately from one shoulder and plunged deeply at the back. It shimmered with a thousand pearlescent scales, like those she had seen on Mandawuy.

Her silver accessories were an unnecessary embellishment, as the dress reflected the colourful city every time she moved. White feathers had been woven through her hair on one side and clasped in place with a crystal comb. The rest of her wavy locks cascaded loosely over her mostly bare back.

As they walked arm in arm with Mandawuy, their friends on the balconies above cheered. Mrs Brown beamed and waved back before taking a seat. A Pedy elder tapped the floor. A maroon flash shot out from his foot, raced across the floor and up the path to the watching crowd, who tapped vigorously in response.

Mandawuy whispered, 'that's the colour of admiration, ladies.'

Mrs Brown giggled in an unexpectedly girlish show of appreciation. Harper smiled and winked at Sam, who was sitting directly opposite with Lawrence and Albert. Before Sam could acknowledge her greeting, Kohl was already up.

Unlike Sam, who was still wearing his Damaran overalls, Kohl had dressed himself magnificently in a white and silver Pedy flying suit. He crossed the floor to Harper, bowed regally and kissed her hand. Pulling her closer, he slipped an arm around her waist and bent to whisper. Harper shivered a little as his breath brushed her ear.

'Had I known a Sister could look this beautiful, I wouldn't have waited so long to crash into one.' Harper was caught off guard by his words and could do nothing but blush in response.

The crowd loved it, stomping or cheering depending on their choice of language. Kohl waved nobly up at their fans in the balconies, grinning in appreciation, before leading Harper to the seat next to his own. He held her hand when they sat, his fingers entwined with hers. It was an unexpectedly pleasant move.

'I'm off to guard duty on the bluff,' said Sam to Lawrence, stumbling over his chair as he made a hasty exit. Harper wondered why he left with such urgency, until Kohl leant across and distracted her with whispered compliments.

Lawrence stood and started to follow Sam.

'Problem? Goin' somewhere?' asked Albert.

'No festival, no matter how grand, will ever be as important as a friend in need. Especially when that friend is a very young, very heartbroken, and very important manifestation. Keep my seat warm, I'll be back.'

+   +   +

Harper was dazzled by the aerial show. She had been watching continuously for over an hour and couldn't tear her eyes away. The audaciousness of the flyers was captivating.

Pedies would leap from the highest balconies, arms clenched tight to their sides, plunging in freefall like bullets. As soon as they caught the thermal updrafts from the chute, they would snap their limbs out, stretching the webbing under their arms taut, turning themselves into a hybrid bird-kite.

Soaring through the air would have been impressive in itself but once they were aloft the flyers would then perform complex acrobatics. Mid-flight spins, twists and loops. Some of them launched colourful streamers or smoke trails from their ankles.

When the solo flyer section was over, the pageant moved on to small groups and finally choreographed teams. It was like a bright, beautiful, ballet in the sky, sans music.

It was hard for Harper to comprehend how they coordinated the whirling vortex of bodies without verbal communication. The kaleidoscope of movement was fascinating and courageous. None seemed to hesitate as they vaulted over the railings, confident that the air currents would still be blowing in their favour.

The Vault floor was the landing point for most flyers, creating a fevered, adrenaline-soaked atmosphere Harper found intoxicating. She was surrounded by gloriously dressed athletes in a riot of colour, huffing and puffing victoriously.

'Ya-hoo!' a voice broke through the silent aerial show.

Harper had been so captivated, she hadn't noticed Kohl let go of her hand, nor did she see his progression up the rails to the launch point.

'Weeeeee–!' came another voice.

'Kohl!' she cried out, leaping to her feet and bumping into Albert, who seemed to have reached the same conclusion. Given that only one of the Pedies talked, at least one of the voices had to belong to one of their own.

High above them she could see a flying duo, one of whom was not nearly as competent as the other. He was shuddering and darting erratically. It didn't look as though he was holding his wings as tautly as the others had. The white-and-silver clad flyer was careening a little too fast for her liking.

'It's him, isn't it?' said Albert who had moved beside her. 'Did you know about this?'

'Me? No! How would I know Kohl was going to do a reckless thing like that?' Harper raised her hand to her throat as if forcing down her rising fear. She was almost too scared to watch, but she couldn't look away.

'To impress you, obviously. You've seen what he's like around pretty faces.'

'I never asked for this, why are you blaming me?'

'The two of you seem pretty chummy lately. You sure he didn't say anythin' about this? Or was he too busy with other … matters?' Albert asked.

'What are you talking about? Didn't you see me try to knock his block off in the tunnel a few days ago?'

'Yes, and I also saw him leave your tent this mornin'.'

Harper was about to defend her honour when Kohl tried to make a turn but plummeted instead. Harper gasped and grabbed a hold of Albert's arm. A flash of black news rippled up the pathway. The Buchanite crowd inhaled as one.

Two more flyers leapt into the air and appeared to be showing him how to hold his form. Kohl tried to imitate them, only to end up tumbling backwards. The fabric rippled and twisted between his arms.

'Snap your wings out. Snap Kohl. Snap!' she heard Mandawuy yell. Kohl did as ordered, finally getting his aerofoil clean enough to allow the air current to catch him. He flew one more ring and then followed Mandawuy's lead to float gracefully to the ground.

Harper reached his side first.

'You idiot!' she said, reaching out to hit the madly grinning Kohl, but he caught her hand and, before she could land a blow, pulled her into a tight embrace.

Harper struggled against him. She was furious that he had risked his life for a thrill, furious that he took his privilege for granted when so many others went without, and even more furious that he continued to provoke in her a need that she so desperately wanted to reject.

Then he kissed her mouth, and she stopped struggling. It felt like home. All her fury melted away.

+   +   +

JayMoe had seen enough of human customs, both in the air and on land. He turned away from the embracing pair and decided to join Lawrence. Sam was his responsibility until he deposited him back with Aggy.

When he arrived at the bluff, he found the two men sitting in silence. Another practice he failed to understand – the human need to be with someone, even when you had no desire to interact.

JayMoe hovered alongside of them, patiently. After five minutes of silent trawling through his database on male social interaction patterns, he offered the only comment that might be appropriate.

'Nice day for it,' said JayMoe in an uncharacteristically deep voice.

Lawrence sniggered. Sam glared. JayMoe tried again.

'If it were raining or indeed night, then we wouldn't see anything from up here. Although I guess if that were the case, then they might have called it off altogether, in which case there would be no 'it'.'

Lawrence laughed out loud.

'I can't see what's so funny; I'm just trying to make conversation. Express gratitude for the abundant cavern lighting that casts a light spectrum commensurate with pleasurable interactions.'

Sam smirked.

'Perhaps you'd like to talk about something else, I do have other topics in my database,' said JayMoe.

'Like what? Religion and politics? Cart racing?' Lawrence asked, falling back on the grass and holding his belly as he guffawed. Sam started laughing too. JayMoe shifted.

'No, I would not like to talk politics to you two cackling chickens. What I would like to talk about is the flashing light coming from the opposite ridge, close to the North tunnel exit. It's not a random pattern.'

'What?' Lawrence was no longer laughing. He jumped to his feet and peered across the five-kilometre cavern. 'Where?'

'Right across from us. You can see it intermittently.' JayMoe pointed.

'There, I just saw it too. Like a tiny blink across the way,' added Sam, getting to his feet.

'Hang on … I think I see it. What is that?' asked Lawrence sounding alarmed.

'Yes, I see it too. That would be the signal for me and my enforcers to enter the cavern, and slaughter you all,' said a calm voice from behind.

'Spectra!' Sam gasped, before he had even turned to see the face.

CHAPTER 42
Coober Pedy

LAWRENCE GASPED AS Sam staggered backwards, away from Spectra and dangerously towards the cliff. Only JayMoe's quick reflexes stopped him from plunging off the edge.

'Well, if it isn't my old mate, Little Sooky Sammy. Tripping over your own feet again? I can fix that you know.'

Spectra roared a warrior's cry as he brought down his blazing lightwand, too late. The last thing Lawrence saw, before he hypered away, was Spectra's wand connecting with the foot of his enforcer instead. Even though he was safely back in the Vault, Lawrence imagined that he could smell the stench of the enforcer's cauterised flesh.

Stillness cascaded up the spiralling balconies. The Pedies had witnessed their sudden materialisation and were watching intently, as though they were wondering if it might be part of the show. Albert rushed over to them.

'What happened?'

'Spectra at the South Tunnel. Hang on,' said Lawrence, regaining his composure. He briefly flashed out of existence, before returning just as quickly.

'I took a hyperjump to both tunnels. There are enforcers pouring into the cavern. We're sitting ducks here.

'JayMoe, start briefing the Pedy elders. Tell them we are all in grave danger; they must prepare to fight or flee and find out which they are better at. If we're leaving, we'll need to figure out a way around those forces. Let them know these people are not to be underestimated.'

JayMoe whirled off, his hands flashing distress signals to anyone who was looking.

'Sam, work with Mrs Brown to round up all our people. Get them back to the tent city and get them to pack fast. Its remote eastern position might give us a few more minutes to come up with an exit plan. Use your hypermode whenever you can. No point hiding our capability now they know where we are. And locate some lightkeys, it'll be dark topside,' he yelled.

With a nod, Sam grabbed a hold of Mrs Brown and was gone in a flash.

'Harper, Kohl,' Lawrence yelled, snapping their attention away from each other and back to the situation at hand.

'Kohl, these are Solaran troops, time to demonstrate your true allegiance. Get out of those ridiculous outfits and then see if you can talk sense into them. I doubt you'll have much luck with Spectra – the man's psychotic. Still he's one of yours and supposedly takes orders from your dad. Might be worth a shot. Harper, hang on to him and use your hyper to get him there fast – go!'

Mandawuy, not far away, must have overheard the conversation. 'This way, plenty of clothes in the athletes' change area.'

'Move, move, move!' Lawrence yelled to any of his people who were listening. He was gratified to see that most Pedies were running full pelt. Somewhere an alarm must have been activated. The air vibrated and the paths strobed orange.

JayMoe whizzed back to Lawrence, 'I think the Pedies got the message.'

'Any solutions?'

'Yes. There is another way out through their dye processing works. They have secondary exhaust tunnels that lead up to the surface. It will be a tight and dirty squeeze, definitely viable though.'

The sound of a large engine being activated shocked Lawrence out of whatever he'd been planning to say. The chute, over which they had been flying only moments prior, started to retract into the ground.

'That's the exit point. The extraction fans will remove any fumes, then it will be clear to go. They'll take us with them if we want.'

Lawrence hurried over and placed his hand on the large pipe as it retreated. In five minutes, it would be clean and flush with the ground. An easy exit point.

'Excellent!'

He looked around. Most of the Buchanites had heeded his advice and retreated to the tent city. Lawrence activated his hyper speech to speak more swiftly with the droid.

'JayMoe, looks like it's up to us buddy. We'll use our hypermodes to bring everyone back and get them through the exhaust. Find out if we can blow the chute after we're through so they can't follow us.'

'What about Harper and Kohl?' asked JayMoe concerned.

'He's a Pallas. Surely the enforcers won't hurt him or Harper, as long as she's with him. Sam and the innocent Buchanites *must* be our priority. Let's go,' he said and immediately began making jumps back and forth to retrieve people from the tent city.

+ + +

Harper took Kohl's arm in preparation for hypermode.

'Now this might prickle a little,' she said.

'That's usually one of my lines,' said Kohl with a cheeky grin.

'Really Kohl? Smutty one-liners at a time like this?' Harper wondered why she had lost her mind and allowed him to kiss her.

'Sorry. Old habits come alive when you're nervous. Okay, hold me tight and off we go,' he said reaching for her other arm.

'No need for that, light contact is all that's required. Better to crouch and arrive in fighter's stance. Like this.'

Harper extricated herself from his embrace and held his wrist at arm's length instead. She assumed a bent knee Civy defensive pose. Kohl mimicked her form and nodded that he was ready.

When Harper materialised behind Spectra, he was speaking aloud and signalling to the other side of the cavern. 'All clear, descending the bluff—'

Harper flew into action, immediately issuing a low flick kick to the back of his knees. The move had little effect; it was like she had made her assault into yielding but unbreakable rubber.

Kohl took a few seconds to recover from his first experience of hyper.

'Go hyper again,' he spluttered.

It was already too late. Spectra had spun, caught Harper's foot and pushed her off balance. By the time she realised what had happened, she was on the ground, being straddled by a maniac waving an active lightwand and spitting out expletives.

'Spectra stop! Get off her, I command it!'

Kohl pulled himself to full height, looking every inch a Pallas. Harper wasn't sure an unhappy heir would be enough to intimidate Spectra, though. She didn't need to see the remains of the enforcer's foot smeared on the ground to know what he was capable of.

'Stop? Oh, that's so scary – not!' Spectra's voice dripped with menace.

'How's the Governor going to react when he hears that you've been threatening innocent Civies?' asked Kohl.

'Innocent Civies? Is that all you've got? For a start, this one is no innocent Civil Sister. She's been travelling with a corrupted Brother, who's on the run from the law. No, on second thoughts, she might still be innocent. I doubt Sooky Sam even knows how to get it up.'

'Enough!' Kohl growled and pushed up his sleeves ready to pummel Spectra but stopped short when Harper received a blow from Spectra.

'Back off, or the next one will be worse than a slap,' said Spectra, moving his weapon close to her throat.

Harper stopped struggling. She looked at Kohl intensely, silently begging him not to act. A frontal attack wouldn't work; they would need cool heads to get out of the situation with their lives.

'She's not just a Civy. She's my—' Kohl looked desperate. She hoped his next words would be chosen carefully.

'—she's my Consort. It's official. You know any consort of mine may not be harmed, whether I am alive or not. She's under Pallas protection.'

Harper wasn't sure whether she was angrier at being restrained or being turned into official Pallas property. She renewed her struggle.

'Get off me!'

'Feisty little thing, isn't she? A regular firecracker. Nice choice Kohl. Now, where was I?

'One, she's not innocent and two, the Governor will never hear about this "consort" delusion. He thinks you're dead, which you will be in about ten seconds. Problem solved. After that, well I guess I can do anything I like with her.' Spectra ran his free hand across Harper's chest and up her neck.

A sudden calm came over Harper. She knew the game she would have to play for survival. She relaxed her muscles, raised her chest in response to his touch, fluttered her eyelashes and assumed a winsome pout.

'You think I'm feisty do you? You have no idea. We're on the same team you and I.'

Spectra hesitated at the unexpected change. Harper grew confident.

'Can't you see what's going on here? I've been groomed since puberty to attract his royal "hornyness". Veruda made me into exactly what he likes. Cute with the ability to transform into beautiful, challenging yet willing to capitulate in his arms, innocent in a naughty way. That's just the way you like it, isn't it, Kohl?'

Kohl opened his mouth but didn't speak. His eyebrows bunched in confusion. He must have been reflecting on their time together.

'But—'

'As for the Governor,' Harper jumped in cutting off Kohl before he said the wrong thing, 'who do you think ordered me? I'm no consort, you're right about that. The kid's delusional; I'm just hired help on Daddy's payroll.'

Kohl put his hands to his face, as though she had physically slapped him. She swallowed the guilt; she had to continue her ruse.

'Come on Spectra, I'm tired of playing mistress to a boy. I need a man. Power like yours is very seductive. How about you let go of my hands and I'll show you my true ... talents.' Harper said in throaty voice. *Come on, just loosen your grip a little.*

Kohl swallowed. Spectra had fallen quiet, too. Then his lips puckered up into a sneer.

'Do you really think I would be seduced by an amateur like you? You're not even close to my tastes, anyway,' said Spectra.

An electronic noise chirped from Spectra's clothes. He groaned and shifted his weight.

'It'll be that bitch Glare again. Such a control freak. A royal pain in the—'

Harper never heard the end of his sentence. The moment he reached for the communicator in his breast pocket, he mistakenly eased his grip. It was just what she needed.

She reached for her cheek to activate her hypermode and dialled up her speed. Before Spectra could blink, she had pushed him off and streaked over to Kohl. The moment there was physical contact, she transported them both off the cliff.

+   +   +

'You stupid bitch! I have fucking had it with you, Glare. I had them right where I wanted them, and you – aargh – whatever you called for I couldn't give a shit. Do you hear me? Fucking figure it out for yourself.' He slammed the communicator shut and ran full-stride down the hill.

As he pushed through the column of enforcers marching down to the city, he realised that he had made up his mind on two critical issues. After the Coober operation he was going to speak with the Master directly about getting an implant for himself. Then he was going after Glare.

+   +   +

Glare was surprised at Spectra's tirade and yet she was not. She had already warned the Master. Spectra was a lit fuse ready to go off at any time. She couldn't see how his willingness to dirty his hands, made him worth the erratic behaviour, which had now cost her several missions and many casualties amongst her crew.

This mission was supposed to be different. She had ordered restraint. A peaceful evacuation would prove to the Master that there could be another, more strategic, way of dealing with their problems. Now with Spectra in a rage she knew exactly how it would end.

As she jogged into Coober Pedy City she reviewed her options. Spectra was getting too powerful to demote. It was time to get her hands dirty.

+   +   +

Harper lay on the ground in the middle of the tent city, panting for breath, drained by the hyperleaps. Once she felt able enough, she forced herself back to her feet. She had to find their friends, locate a way up to the surface and clear things with Kohl – in that order.

She sat up and surveyed their surroundings. Tent city appeared to be empty. Aside from Kohl, there were no people visible; no sound coming from the structures and the fires had all been extinguished.

'Be right back,' she said to Kohl before jumping to her feet and blinking out of existence.

+   +   +

Kohl was in a partial daze when Harper disappeared. He didn't know whether to be relieved that they had gotten away from

Spectra or distraught that his feelings for Harper might be based on a scam.

Had they really trained her to please him? Was it an act? He knew it was at least plausible. His father was certainly capable of it and the Civies always had a penchant for duplicity.

She certainly knew exactly how to arouse him; she was constantly difficult and yet he wanted her so desperately. When she wore the white dress every move she made drove him crazy with desire. She was unlike any Solaran woman he had ever met ... but could he ever really trust a Civy? They'd taken his sister and played a part in the bombing of his beloved home. Had Harper been part of a sickening scheme, too?

Kohl walked in a wide circle, scuffing at the ground, an act that usually helped him think. This time it didn't.

Mark would know what to do. His stomach turned in on itself. He felt his brother's absence as though he had been cleaved in two and only the right half of his body remained. *You should be here, Mark.*

He headed to Harper's tent hoping to find the evidence he needed.

✦   ✦   ✦

JayMoe materialised right next to Sam and Lawrence. 'Everyone's accounted for aside from Harper and Kohl, and the enforcers have reached the outskirts of town.'

'Right, in you go then Sam,' whispered Lawrence.

'Are ya sure we can't wait a little longer?' Sam asked.

'No. We can't risk all these people. Don't worry – Harper's smart and she has hyper. She'll figure a way out.'

'Do we really have to blow this? The enforcers are people too, ya know. Do they deserve to die?' Sam pleaded even as he climbed down into the chute.

'If we time it right, the blast won't be fatal. The goal is just to seal off our escape route so they can't follow.'

Lawrence looked up at the droid and prepared to follow Sam, who'd moved out of sight.

'Are you sure you can hyper to the surface JayMoe? It's quite a leap without Illustria guiding you.'

'I'll be fine. You must go now. I estimate we've only got three minutes before the enforcers arrive. We need to get you down that tunnel and clear of the Vault before it blows. You must hurry my friend,' said the droid with a gentleness that belied his mechanical form.

JayMoe pushed Lawrence's head down and said a prayer to the binary Goddess before sealing the chute. He made the final arrangement of Pedy explosives repurposed from the celebration fireworks. He connected them to the chute hatch and flipped the activation timer. Then he jumped to what he hoped would be the surface.

+ + +

When Harper transported into the Vault, JayMoe was the only one present. He was in the centre of the wide floor with his back to her. Before she could reach him or say anything he had transported away.

'You!' Spectra was screaming as he ran down a path towards her.

She activated her own hyper again and sped down to JayMoe's last position, just in time to see the detonation timer clicking down five…four…three…

+ + +

Glare was still on the outskirts of town when the explosives went off, yet the blast was strong enough to make the houses around her shudder. She bolted up a path to get a better view, silently cursing Spectra's name as she watched the heart of the delicate, beautiful city collapsing.

'You better be dead, Spectra,' she growled.

CHAPTER 43
Brizzie

BRIZZIE GAVE AGGY a new appreciation for the nickname "Rats". She was running her operation out of a section of converted sewer and, unlike Damaran tunnels, the Solaran sewerage network was a crumbling, slimy labyrinth. Immediately outside their sanitised compound was the constant reminder that they were camping in a very unpleasant tide of human excrement. It was foul.

Every time Aggy ascended the rusty ladders to the streets above, she ran the risk of being washed away by a sudden flush of effluent. It made her feel exactly like a rat, scurrying back and forth – surviving on the rotting scraps of the lords above.

In contrast the Lightbearers existed in a world of unimaginable opulence. Unlike their conservative southern cousins in Sydney, the Brizzie Solarans embraced, even revelled in the Lightbearer nickname. They lit everything to excess. Fashion, transportation, accommodation; everything was bedazzled in neon or appliquéd with miniature lightkeys. The city reeked of photonic wealth.

'Settle down,' Aggy said, focusing on the briefing.

'Please be seated everyone, if you can.'

She looked proudly around the room. Her stalwart staff were still performing well despite their unpleasant accommodations. Around the reclaimed metal table her generals and senior aides were perched on an assortment of scavenged chairs. Lower ranked staff had to stand, stooping their backs against the curve of the metal walls. It was crowded and clammy, but no one complained.

'Let's get started.'

+   +   +

When Glare returned from Coober Pedy she went straight to the shower. Much like Epping and Geraldton, it had been another excruciating day – unthinking enforcers, wanton destruction and, worst of all, the ever-despicable Spectra. She was relieved to be back in her peaceful Brizzie apartment.

For Glare, the actions were regrettable ancillary damage in a wider war for the public good. It sickened her to watch Spectra revel in their victims' misery, enjoying their actions for the chaos they created. It had taken all of her nerve to keep control of the operation.

Glare leaned against the shower stall, waiting for the hot water to wash away the worst of the day. She traced her fingers along the rivulets running down the tiles, deeply breathed in the cleansing steam and thought of Kohl.

For the hundredth time she wondered why they had not found his body in the Wagga tunnel. She could not think of a plausible escape vector, yet there had been nothing left.

Where is *he?*

Glare much preferred strategic planning to operational management; not that she had a choice anymore. Deep in her heart she wished she could turn her back on duty and choose to run. Now the only choice available was a long hot steam.

Eventually she got out of the bathroom and noticed an envelope lying under the front door. She held on to her towel as she bent to pick it up.

Her body heat must have triggered a nano switch in the paper as a small hologram sprang to life on the palm of her hand. It was Lady Pallas personally inviting her to a masked ball to be held in honour of her husband's inauguration.

Glare guessed she was supposed to be impressed at the first man to hold governorship of both Sydney and Brizzie. She groaned aloud, having hoped to delay carrying out the Master's other order. Now her hand had been forced. The Governor would surely want to discuss Kohl and other family issues. She abhorred family issues.

Perhaps her new implant would allow her to have undetected breaks in the meeting. She scratched the healing scar and wondered who the implant had come from. She prayed it was not Kohl. Glare put the invite on the table and headed back to the bathroom.

'Perhaps it won't be so bad,' she told herself aloud. 'Cheer up old girl, with the extra speed you might even have time left for some fun.'

Glare hadn't had any fun at all since the Sydney incident, which had torn her life apart. She had secretly prepared for her role for years, but nothing could prepare her for the solitude that followed. She had lost her innocence that day, along with her adopted family, leaving her to wrestle alone with her conscience – to wonder how she would see the truth with her impure eyes.

Glare wandered back to the bathroom and used the edge of her towel to demist the mirror. Studying her reflection, she resolved to make the best of her situation. She would show the

Pallas' that she was fearless. They would know that her lower caste childhood could not negate the influence of her noble genes.

+ + +

'Thank you all for assembling here,' Aggy said, welcoming her staff.

'I would especially like to recognise the kindness of our hosts; the Brizzie Damarans. As well as Sisters Alicia and Domenica who have joined us from the Brizzie Keep. I pray that together, we can defeat the Master. It is time for all people to live equally in the light – as it has been foretold.'

'Here, here!' cried one of the generals. The room briefly broke into a flurry of voices, handshakes and earnest nodding.

'Thank you, General Mitta, for setting the agenda today. Unfortunately it will have to be suspended as we have an additional unexpected and very special guest.'

There were a few murmurs as Aggy put her hand to her cheek, an act they had all been forbidden.

'Hypermodes are for—' General Kee was interrupted by a bright light that appeared next to Aggy. It resolved into a human holoform. Anyone who could, instantly fell to their knees in supplication, the others earnestly bowed their heads or clasped hands in prayer.

'May I introduce the Light, our supreme leader in the battle against the great foe.'

'Thank you Alpha. Please, do not bow before me, kind friends. You have all fought so valiantly over the years; it is I who should be on bended knees before you.

'You have uprooted your families; risked your very lives to serve our cause. Mere words cannot adequately convey the depth of my gratitude.' Illustria bowed her own head in acknowledgement.

'I wish I could be there in person, alas I am still imprisoned in the heart of our world. Fortunately, I have discovered that hypermodes are safe. You are authorised to use them again, aside from transporting, which should be kept to short solo jumps in emergencies only. The more we use it or the farther we jump, the greater is the Master's ability to track us.

'So today I am with you in spirit only. One day soon I hope to soar over our beloved land again, as I did eons ago, transforming endless darkness into glorious, life-giving light. Till then be brave my friends, stay true.'

Illustria nodded her appreciation of the rousing cheer that went up in response, before continuing.

'Ahead of that day I fear there will be more heartache. It seems we have been too effective in our recent operations. In retaliation, the Master has begun shutting down all non-Solaran communities.

'Epping has fallen, as have Geraldton, Newbrunswick, Wagga and Coober Pedy. We will never forget our courageous, fallen colleagues.'

Illustria paused and put her hands on her chest. Her eyes dropped briefly in a perfect representation of prayer.

'Friends, I must keep my visit short as the longer I am here, the more likely it is that the Master will track me to you. I have a mission of great urgency for you.

'There is a woman you must find. The Master calls her Glare, and she is his physical link to Spectra, Governor Pallas and other dark operatives but I do not know her true identity. I have reason to suspect her allegiance is waning. You may be able to turn her if you can find her.

'Lastly, I know you are all familiar with the legend of the five manifestations. I wish to confirm that the manifestations do indeed exist. Your Alpha is the first of them.'

The room filled with startled gasps.

'It should come as no surprise to any of you, that she is the one who holds the golden vessel of life, as you have all witnessed her filling the vessels of others.'

Many nodded in agreement. Aggy mouthed a silent *thank you* to her staff.

'Two of the other manifestations have now been identified. Sam is a seer and ex-Brother from Newbrunswick. Harper is an ex-Civy from Veruda Keep. They bare the key and the monogram respectively. They were last sighted in Newbrunswick but we lost them when hypermodes were shut down. Find them; this is your most urgent task. Find them and transport them to me.

'As for the other two manifestations, I am ready to announce their identities too. The ones baring the flying machine and the gift of speech, are Kohl Pallas and—'

Illustria's image flickered mid-speech. One moment she had a frozen look of horror on her face, the next she was gone completely.

'No!' yelled Aggy, pounding the desk in an uncharacteristic act of frustration.

General Abudua was fast to respond. She activated her hypermode and slid over the conference table, to stand protectively in front of Alpha.

Illustria's screaming image briefly returned.

'He has found you – all hypermodes on – FLEE!'

Immediately Aggy felt the ground shake. She put her hands over her ears as a roar barrelled in from beyond the metal walls; a noise that sounded sickeningly familiar.

The corrugated sheets that arched the room shifted back and forth, allowing dust to filter down through the air. The overhead lightkeys swung violently.

General Kee followed Abudua's example. He vaulted the table, ducking under the swinging lights and pushed open the doors on the other end of the room. He urged his stunned colleagues out of the room.

Aggy's staff rushed to evacuate, only to be turned back by a flood of people running towards them ahead of deadly black water.

'Not again!'

In the shock of facing yet another flood, Aggy didn't think of her hypermode. She merely braced herself for the water to hit.

In a second the conference room was awash. Some were quick enough to transport out with hypermodes, although many, like Aggy, were stunned into inaction. Aggy shook her head, regained her focus and started to reach out for people at arm's length.

She cried out, too late. There was too much water flowing too quickly, with too few exits. Their stronghold was lost, washed away on a slimy wave of Lightbearer waste.

CHAPTER 44
Darklands outside Brizzie

AGGY HEARD A soft wail roll towards her. The sombre wave of grief swelled with a hundred cries. It flowed through her heart and threatened to swamp her soul.

It was a communal plea for an end to suffering. The keening of the deprived. It took all Aggy's courage to hold her position and bear witness. She couldn't, wouldn't breathe again, until the sound receded.

As it ebbed away, she caught her hand tremoring. Her surroundings started to tilt so she clung on to a metal trunk to steady the world. It was scratched and dented, like the face of the defeated old hag she'd spied in her mirror of late.

Where has Aggy gone?

The bawling wave peaked in the distance and began its return journey, threatening to overwhelm her.

How can I do this? It's too much, so many gone.

They had lost two thirds of their Brizzie population in the Master's attack on the sewer compound. What remained of her people had assembled in a camp, well outside the ears and eyes of the city. They were only the last of so many fallen in recent times. It was time to honour them all.

As the mourning wail approached its zenith, Aggy knew she couldn't avoid her duty any longer. She would pay tribute to all the fallen, including her dear friend Laurel, Queen of the Civies and dedicated Damaran supporter.

In honour of her great contribution her name would no longer be spoken aloud. Instead, Queen Laurel would be remembered only as "Yante," the mother at peace.

Ceremonial smoke wafted into her tent. Aggy took three short puffs on the bitter air. *Come on, get it together, Aggy. They need their Alpha.*

She picked up the small bowl of white chalky mud, dipped her hand in and ran three fingers across her forehead and cheeks. She stood to full height, buttoned her full-length military coat and took a calming breath.

Alpha stepped out of the tent.

+ + +

For hours, Alpha walked amongst her people; shaking hands, hugging children and hearing tales of the fallen. She nibbled on the offered fennel seeds and dried berries. She used clapping sticks to keep rhythm for the tribe's dancers. She sang her own mourning song for Yante's partner. Her black coat ran white with chalky tears.

As the day approached its peak, Alpha returned to the front of her tent, which had been raised up on a plinth so that all could see her. A hush quickly spread through the crowd. She stood solemnly before them, ready to recount their oral history.

'A long time ago when the world was young; when there were no animals, people or plants; when wind didn't blow and the rain didn't fall, there lived a lonely man called Malangeri. His home was a dark cave deep below the surface. He had no friends. His life was meaningless …'

+   +   +

Alpha finished her address by extinguishing the ceremonial fire. She paused to watch the last tendrils of smoke rise, then called out to the sky for the Light's blessed presence in their hearts. All eyes were upon her as she spread her arms like wings and performed the dance of the great bird of Light.

Soon the cries of pain were replaced with cries of delight as she beckoned the children to join her. They trailed Alpha, running full pelt through the crowd, using their arms to symbolically flap away woes. They cawed at the top of their lungs and swooped down to receive sweet rewards of sugar cubes from the grown-ups.

It was a fitting end to a magnificent ceremony and Aggy returned to her tent totally spent. The flood had been a bitter turn in a long campaign; she needed some alone time – a difficult request for an Alpha.

Aggy collapsed onto the cot and rolled over, noticing a small bump under her hip. Reaching into her back pocket she found a lightkey. Freedom. She donned a cloak, ducked out the back of her tent and quietly moved through the camp to the lightbarrier.

With lightkey activated, Aggy strode into the darklands, certain she would be back before anyone noticed.

+   +   +

The exodus from Coober Pedy had been a gruelling two-day march through darkness. No one found the lightless environment comfortable, especially the Pedies whose reliance on visual communications made the trip almost unbearable.

Three Pedies had already fallen catatonic with shock and were being carried on makeshift stretchers. To ease their terror, Lawrence had teamed the remaining Pedies with Buchanites in small groups around communal lightkeys. But a well-lit camp was the salvation they needed, and soon.

Their deliverance arrived when JayMoe returned from a scouting mission to announce that he had broken through a Damaran camp's lightbarrier only a few hours ahead. An end to their misery was approaching.

Lawrence walked the distance with Mrs Brown at the leading edge of their migration, listening to the singing from the still-distant Damaran camp – an auditory promise of light.

'It's gone quiet. What a pity. The singin' was beautiful. Quite sad though,' Mrs Brown commented.

'JayMoe said it was a Damaran funeral chant.'

'Oh, how terrible. Certainly must have been someone who was well loved to get a send-off like that.'

'I think it likely that they were honouring more than one person at the funeral. JayMoe said it was a very large crowd and well lit. I'm not sure any one Damaran death would warrant such an expense. Dangerous too. It's a risk gathering all your people, and making such a hullabaloo, right outside a major Solaran city.'

They walked a few more steps in silence when Mrs Brown stopped to ask another question.

'So young Lawrence, how are you feelin' about this big reconciliation with your famous ward?'

Lawrence stopped to smile at her choice of words. Only someone as ancient as Mrs Brown would think to call him *young*.

'To be honest, a little anxious. I gather JayMoe gave you

the back story?'

Mrs Brown nodded. She took Lawrence by the arm and resumed their walk. 'You know, for a mechanical fellow he has quite a lovely heart. He seems genuinely concerned about both of you. He wants so desperately for you to make it up.'

'Me too, Mrs Brown. Unfortunately, sometimes *want* and *get* are two very different concepts,' said Lawrence sadly. He had no idea how to explain his absence from Aggy's life.

'Parentin' is never easy. I'm sure you had your reasons for keepin' away. I've never met Alpha but I hear she's very smart and equally compassionate. Speak honestly to her, dear, I'm sure she'll understand.'

They resumed walking but only took a few more paces before Lawrence suddenly crouched, gently pulling Mrs Brown down with him. There was definitely something ahead. He heard footsteps and low voices. He gave a hand message to JayMoe, *stop and be quiet, pass it on.*

A few more seconds passed. The voices stopped as the footsteps drew nearer. Lawrence was just about to send JayMoe to investigate when a lightwell suddenly opened up around them. A person in a military coat stood in daylight before them, holding a lightkey aloft.

'General JayMoe, we've been so worried! When you didn't show up at Noosa, we feared the worst. Are Sam and Harper with you?' asked the stern face.

'Thank you, General Mitta. I would like to introduce my travelling companions. This is Lawrence and Mrs Brown. I'm afraid we have quite a crowd of others trailing us, but it doesn't include Harper. We got separated when the enforcers destroyed Coober Pedy. Sam is back there tending to our injured. There is much to tell and we have many people in dire need of life's essentials. Do you have enough light for us?'

'These are indeed grave times, General JayMoe,' said

Mitta, shaking his head soberly. 'Don't fret. Any friend of the Light is always welcome in a Damaran home, you know that. Bring your friends into camp, we will accommodate them all somehow.

'Truthfully though, we are in need of more permanent lodgings ourselves. The Master has destroyed so many of our towns. We are due to have a council meeting with Alpha tonight to review options.

'General Kee is in favour of storming Brizzie. What happens then? Whether we are defeated or victorious each outcome will create a new set of problems. Do we take the Solaran prisoners? Do we try to integrate? There is no easy answer. I do not envy the burden that falls upon Alpha's shoulders,' said Mitta seriously.

'She's here? Aggy? I mean Alpha?' Lawrence interrupted, uncharacteristically anxious.

'You know her?' asked Mitta.

'Yes, I'm her … I was her …' Lawrence stammered, as he tried to explain their complex relationship. Mrs Brown placed a gentle, reassuring hand on his arm and stepped into the conversation.

'He's her uncle, General. Now is she here or not? As leader of the Buchanites I would like to officially pay my respects.'

'She was. Alas none have seen her since the funeral ended. We haven't been able to raise her on hypermode either. That's why I am out here in the darklands with my best troops searching for her. And—'

General Mitta stopped talking and looked over his shoulder before continuing.

'Is that crackling?' asked Lawrence.

'Not sure. Might be coming from the Sydney Keep which is on this side of the light barrier. Two Civies crawled into camp before we left. They were too exhausted to say much but their clothes were singed and they were babbling about the tunnels. Seems there's trouble there as well,' said Mitta.

'Have you tried Illustria?' asked Lawrence.

'We have not heard from the Light either. Her last transmission was interrupted by the Master when he flooded our Brizzie camp. I pray for the safety of both our beloved leaders.'

The news shook Lawrence. He lifted his shoulders in determination; he would do what Aggy needed, until he found her.

'Right that's it then, no time for niceties. Let's get the Pedies into the light, the children fed and our warriors armed. Then it's time we find Alpha and resolve this war once and for all.'

CHAPTER 45
Brizzie

WHEN HARPER ARRIVED in the outlying streets of Brizzie, they were disappointingly deserted. Despite the fact that the Solarans were technically the enemy, she had been quite looking forward to meeting the notoriously vibrant people of Brizzie.

The journey from Coober Pedy had shown a side of Kohl she hadn't seen before. He had been serious, sullen. She'd tried to discuss possible options for returning to the Light and had speculated about the identity of the fifth manifestation. Nothing. Not even a conspiracy rant.

She had tried reminiscing about the spectacular Festival of the Winds. Even platitudes about his flight generated nothing more than shrugs. In the end she gave up and walked in silence. Had he not been a vital manifestation, she would have been tempted to take him back to his father at Veruda Keep.

'I don't like this.' At last Kohl spoke as he peered through an empty shop window, shaking his head. 'Where is everyone? It's the middle of the afternoon. This avenue should be bustling. Something's not right.'

Kohl ran to another house on the other side of the road and banged on the door. No response.

'It doesn't look like there was any major trouble, no obvious signs of damage, plus the doors are all locked so it's unlikely that they left in a rush. Let's move further into the heart of the city. Might be some answers there.' Harper suggested.

'Being strategic again, are you? Observant? Performing your assigned Civy function so that you can report back to the Sisters? Or making notes for Spectra, I suppose?' Kohl sneered, then turned and shook another locked door.

Harper turned away, at last understanding his problem, and marched along the middle of the road repeating a calming mantra. She had been wishing for him to talk for many hours, now she missed the quiet.

'Who are you reporting to this week?' Kohl continued, returning to her side.

'Don't you mean, who are you reporting to this week *my consort*? I guess if I am Pallas property then I must be reporting to Daddy Pallas!' She yelled her response over her shoulder as she picked up her pace. She heard him swear under his breath and move to follow her.

'Harper wait,' said Kohl, catching her by the shoulder and spinning her around to face him squarely.

'I'm sorry. My mouth gets the better of me some days, especially when I'm anxious. It's just been such a difficult time. I've been trying to process everything—'

Harper yawned, dusted her overalls off in her best approximation of disinterest.

'Put yourself in my shoes. My home gets destroyed. I discover that a sister I never knew has been hidden from me. My brother dies. My newly found sister goes missing.

'*Then* my father turns out to be a genocidal maniac, there are colonies hidden beneath the ground under my feet and, oh yeah, by the way I am actually a manifestation of a mythical being called the Light who is going to call me back to fulfil her destiny and defeat the Master. Who, by the way, is also the creator and protector of my people.'

He stopped for a minute to take an exaggerated deep breath.

'Do you think, therefore, you could cut me some slack if I get stuck on the possibility that you *might* have been secretly working for my father? Is that so unreasonable – given everything else that we've uncovered? Especially given that you are obviously too beautiful to be a Civy crone?'

Harper hesitated; he did have a point, and soft puppy dog eyes. Still, she wasn't sure she was ready to forgive him. Kohl reached out to take her hand.

'Seriously, I am very sorry. I won't say anything about it again, promise.' He pulled her closer and looked down into her eyes.

'I believe you, when you say that it was only a story to throw off Spectra. I consider myself lucky to know you, no matter how we met ... even if it was through my father's payroll clerk.' Kohl grinned and leaned in to kiss her but she pushed him away and made a small hyper jump to put herself out of reach.

'You brute! I'll have to ask your father for a pay rise if he expects me to keep putting up with you,' Harper said as she continued down the street, taking a series of micro jumps to evade him. Kohl took off in hot pursuit.

+ + +

In the city's central corridors, they finally understood what was going on. It seemed that every Brizzie citizen was attending a rally in the vast town square. Harper had never seen so many people before. Every road and alley were full. People stood on shop stairs and hung over crowded balconies.

Their focus lay across the steps of an enormous marble building on the other side of the square. Massive banners were hung on gleaming columns at both sides and in the centre was a lectern where an Archbrother was waving his hands in the air to punctuate a passionate address. People around them were muttering in agreement with each new pronouncement.

'Spectra!' Harper whispered, automatically dropping her eyes and backing up against Kohl's chest. For the first time since Veruda, she wished she had her robes so that she could withdraw into anonymity. 'We should get out of here.'

'No, look who's behind him, it's my parents! Come on.' Kohl took Harper's hand firmly and started to manoeuvre his way through the thick crowd.

+   +   +

'... and so, ladies and gentlemen, by the grace of the Holy Illumination that guides our small lives to the greater glory beyond, I give you the next governor of Brizzie – Governor Matthias Pallas!'

Spectra held out his hand to welcome the Governor. Just as they had planned, his speech, full of religious hyperbole, had turned the crowd from sceptics to enthusiasts. They were devouring every word. Applause ricocheted around the square. Spectra loved it and regretted having to relinquish the spotlight to the Governor.

Governor and Lady Pallas moved forward to shake hands with Spectra. The Governor wore full military regalia with an antique warrior's dagger on his hip. Lady Pallas wore a stylish navy-blue suit with two brass buttons that clasped her jacket just beneath her cleavage. They exuded tradition and confidence: just what the Brizzie crowd needed to see.

The Pallas' stood for a moment taking in the crowd's adoration, humbly bowing and modestly nodding in appreciation. Then the Governor placed his hands on either side of the lectern and signalled for quiet.

'My fellow Solarans. I am greatly honoured to have been appointed your new leader. At the same time I am deeply saddened at the circumstances that have brought me here. Governor Bourke and his family were great people – they did not deserve to be taken from you so needlessly. Great, great people.'

The grief-stricken Governor reached out for the reassurance of his wife's hand, before returning his grip on the lectern, just as Spectra had suggested.

'In the days since I first spoke to you at the Bourke funeral, I have witnessed first-hand the good work he did for this city. He was a noble man, a visionary some might say. A just and hardworking leader. The Governor deserved all the love you all had for him.

'Now I know some of you are sitting there thinking – who is this guy from Sydney? Wasn't he Bourke's rival?' Governor Pallas looked at the crowd.

'Now now, no need to look innocent. I know many of you thought we were competitors, maybe even enemies. The truth is, Governor Bourke and I were great allies. Oh, there has always been friendly rivalry on the surface. A little argy-bargy between the two great cities; however, on critical issues we stood united, cousin to cousin.

'My fellow Solarans. This is not the time for division between our cities, nor is it a time for friendly rivalries. We have both suffered terrible losses at the hands of the Rats. We must come together as one.'

A small cheer came from the front of the crowd. Spectra was hopeful his speech was working.

'You should see my beloved home; decimated by their evil. Rats blew up our infrastructure and destroyed my home. We lost so many good people – my own son Mark amongst them. And we've just had word that they now hold my other son, Kohl, as hostage.'

Lady Pallas let out a quiet sob and her legs seemed to give way at the mention of her sons' names. Governor Pallas reached to steady her, whilst signalling for someone to get her a chair. Once she was seated, he continued.

'My fellow Solarans. It is time we put our divisions aside and focus on our common goal. We must eliminate the Rat scourge. The Rats that killed my family are the same Rats who killed the Bourke family. They are inhuman vermin who hate our way of life. They despise our freedom.

'Yes, yes they do. I'm telling you the truth. Their black hearts are envious of our prosperity. They will not stop until we are reduced to living in filth as they do.'

Someone yelled 'down with the Rats' while others booed in support. The mood of the crowd was shifting as they responded to the Governor's taunting. Spectra could taste their growing anger.

'You must also know that the Civies are in cahoots with the Rats. I understand this might be difficult news but we have proof they planted bombs in Sydney and killed many innocent Solaran women and children.'

A woman fainted in the front of the crowd.

'My fellow Solarans. We must hunt them down, round them up and dispose of them like the cold-hearted vermin they are! We must also shut down the Civy order and never allow them to deceive us again. Will you join me in this fight? Will you? Will you? Will you?'

With each repetition the Governor pointed to another member of the crowd, his voice growing louder until it boomed across the sky. Spectra was pleased that the amplifiers he had installed had given the speech a more theatrical feel. A great cheer went up from the crowd.

'Today this governor from Sydney does not address you as people from Brizzie because today we are united as one Solaran nation. We share blood, and the common goal of wiping out terrorism. This is the only way we can preserve our great and blessed Solaran way of life. Are you with me?'

The Governor cupped his ear in pretence of trying to hear a response.

'I said are you with me?'

'Yes!' hollered the crowd.

'Are the Rats our enemies?'

'Yes!' the crowd yelled as one.

'Do you take me as your leader?'

'Yes, yes, yes!' cried many more voices from the square.

'Then, my fellow Solarans, in my first act as your leader I have a gift. Bring her out, Archbrother Spectra.'

Spectra disappeared briefly and returned with a squad of ten enforcers who marched onto the steps with furious precision. In the middle of their formation hunched a single person in a long cape. A hood hung low over their face and their hands had been tied securely behind their back.

'My fellow Solarans, here is my gift to you. This is Alpha, leader of the Rats, corruptor of the Civies, instigator of violence against all decent Solarans and murderer of the Bourkes. Bow to your captors, vermin!'

The Governor grabbed her shoulder and forced her to the ground. As she fell her cape swung open as planned to reveal Aggy's battered, naked body.

'Oh, how she flaunts her vileness! Hasn't even got the decency to wear clothes. Disgusting.'

He spat at her feet.

'Take the Rat Queen away!'

'Wait!' Someone yelled from the crowd, 'wait!' but the voice was quickly drowned out in the crowd's angry uproar. The Governor finished his vitriolic speech and Spectra said one last hasty prayer before escorting the Pallas' back into the building beyond the lectern.

+ + +

'It's Aggy! What have they done to her?' Harper gasped as Kohl fought through the crowds to get to his parents. Kohl stopped and whispered urgently to Harper.

'Watch what you say. This crowd is all fired up. Don't want them mistaking us for Rat sympathisers. I'll sort this out, just let me get his attention – wait, wait, Father!'

'I *am* a Rat sympathiser and so are you!' said Harper in an equally low voice, pulling away from his hold. 'What your father said is untrue. You know it.'

'Just zip it, Harper. We'll talk later. Wait, Father, over here!' Kohl released Harper so that he could wave, unsuccessfully, to his father.

'They're going through the building. We need to stop them before they leave. I need to tell them I'm here.'

'How about we go around the back? There must be more than one exit,' suggested Harper. 'No, I have a better idea—'

Before Kohl could stop her Harper dialled into hyperspeed and disappeared.

+ + +

Spectra ushered the Pallas' into a back room of Brizzie Library, beyond the steps where they had just made their impassioned speeches. His enforcers marched in behind with Aggy in tow.

'Hurry up everyone!' He yelled.

Spectra had seen Kohl in the crowd, with the Civy no less. He knew that his presence would undermine both the Governor's credibility and his own.

While he moved the Pallas' through the building with one hand, he took his communicator out with the other. He was going to call Glare and request permission to eliminate Kohl, preferably before he reunited with his parents.

'Spectra, unhand me, immediately,' ordered the Governor, pulling himself clear of the Archbrother. 'How dare you cut my speech short and rush me off stage? Sometimes you forget your station.'

'Did you not hear the dissent coming from the crowd? She had Rat sympathisers planted in amongst them. Isn't that right Rat Queen – you've done this, haven't you? Bring her forward where I can watch her,' Spectra snapped, gesturing at his enforcers with his communicator.

'Governor, her followers are dangerous. I had to cut the speech short. Even now they could be upon us with such speed that you would not see them coming. We must get you to a secure location.'

Harper materialised in front of them.

Lady Pallas gasped and tightened her grip on the Governor's arm. Spectra tried to pull Aggy in front of him like a shield but Harper was too fast.

'Let her go!' Harper screamed.

In one swift motion she grabbed the Governor's ceremonial dagger and sunk it deep into Spectra's hip. Then with lightning speed she spun around and slashed at Aggy's bindings.

'Harper,' Aggy whispered before lapsing into unconsciousness, her feeble form slumping into Harper's arms.

Harper touched her cheek again to make a jump out of the city when she noticed what Spectra was holding. It was his communicator, and it was golden.

+   +   +

By the time Kohl arrived in the chamber Spectra lay in a crimson puddle on the floor. Enforcers were rushing around in a fruitless search for more Rats amongst the library's shelves, visibly shaken by the sudden loss of their commander. Lady Pallas was departing the room in search of a doctor, while the Governor roared about useless security and the waste of a perfectly good dagger.

'Mother, Father!' Kohl burst into the room, causing Lady Pallas to turn.

'Kohl? … Kohl!' She ran across the floor and, forgetting all protocol, hugged him and kissed his forehead with the ferocity of a mother bear.

'What did they do to your face?' she said stroking his smooth jawline.

'Mother, you don't—'

'Oh sweetheart, we didn't know what happened to you,' Lady Pallas interrupted. 'After the implant stopped working we assumed the worst. Spectra told us the Rats kidnapped you. Have they injured you? Are you alright?'

'I'm fine. I have so much to tell you.' Kohl said removing his mother's hands and taking a step back.

'Good to see you son,' said his father crossing the floor. Kohl stared at his father's hand, outstretched in greeting. Then he looked up at his father's eyes, glistening with a rare display of concern and relief; a look Kohl had never seen on his own father's eyes.

'Well?' said the Governor. Kohl remembered himself and accepted his father's firm handshake with his own trembling hand.

The Governor released him, looked down at Spectra's moaning form and spoke to the nearest enforcer.

'Better do something about that. Can't have him dying on the library floor, how would that look?'

Turning to Kohl he continued, 'we need him for the inauguration. Plus, I suppose it's bad form to let him die when he may have just saved our lives. He said there were filthy Rats in the audience, and it looks like he was right.'

'I wouldn't bet on it, Father,' said Kohl.

'What do you mean? I saw the Rat who stabbed him with my own eyes just now. As much as I dislike him, he did prove his loyalty today.'

His Father looked at him as though he was a child who needed everything explained in the simplest of forms. For the first time Kohl viewed his deluded parent with pity.

'Can we go somewhere private? We have a lot to discuss; there's a lot more going on here than you can imagine,' he said.

'I'm sure you've seen a few things on your travels son, but it will have to wait until we take care of poor Spectra.'

Governor Pallas dismissed his son and made to move out of the room. Lady Pallas regained her hold on him, brushing his hair down with the palm of her hand. It made him feel like a small boy. Kohl pushed her away gently and raised his voice to gain his father's attention before the older man moved out of earshot.

'You don't seem to be listening, Father. I've been travelling with Rats all this time. I have seen the devastation wrought by the Master. I have witnessed the cruelty of the Brothers. I am telling you *the Rats* are not the problem.'

Still his father continued to step away, as though intent on other business.

'I have come to understand my family's role in the naming days as well. Deafening Pedy babies, blinding the Newbrunswick ones – all for our convenience! Apparently it's been going on for generations! Have I got your attention now, Father?'

Governor Pallas turned to face him. His nostrils were flaring, his hands were clenched and his face had turned ashen grey.

Kohl stood his ground. 'Well?' he said.

'How do you account for *this*, Kohl? If those Rats are so benign, why did they do this to Archbrother Spectra?' Governor Pallas demanded in a clipped tone.

'Because he deserved it! You won't believe the evil things he's done to so many people. Did he mention that he tried to kill me *twice*? I am only alive today thanks to the kindness of the Rats and the woman who probably did this!'

Kohl could see that his words were having no effect on his father. When he didn't get a response, he moved his appeal to Lady Pallas.

'Mother, it was Harper, the Civy we met back in Sydney, or rather the ex-Civy. She works for the Light now. We were together in the square. I called out, but you didn't hear us. She wears the implant, so it would have been her in here, in hypermode.'

Lady Pallas studied her son. 'Do you love her?'

Kohl stared at his mother with large, moist eyes for an uncomfortably long time. How could he voice the answer he so desperately wanted to give, whilst nagging doubts still troubled him? He had to ask.

'Were you involved in her training, Mother? Was she selected for a special Pallas mission?' asked Kohl.

His mother remained silent.

'Was she trained for *me*, Mother?' his eyes implored her to tell the truth. 'When you ask whether I love her, are you actually asking whether she succeeded in her mission?'

The snap of his mother's warm palm across his face cut short his next words.

'How dare you! The very thought that we would manufacture a consort for you. *When* you grow up and make a match, I hope it is for true love,' she paused, 'just like your father and I.'

'She told me …' Kohl stammered.

'I don't care what she told you or why. I only know what I see in my son's eyes. So I ask the question for the last time. Do you love her?'

Again, she placed her hand on Kohl's cheek, only this time it was a cooler, gentle touch. It reminded him painfully of the innocent way Harper had touched him back at the tent in Coober Pedy. He felt his eyes glisten. He couldn't speak the big words that needed to be said.

'That's enough for me. Let's get you home, we'll figure this all out together.'

'Wait. Why are we aligned with the Master? Didn't you read the Letters from the Light? Don't you know that it's not supposed to be this way? That nothing is as it seems?'

Kohl desperately searched his mother's eyes hoping to see understanding. He needed a glimmer of hope that his parents could be redeemed.

'What letters? What Light? I don't know what you are talking about. Your ordeal has clearly left you confused. It's time we left.'

She put her arm around his waist and turned him towards the exit. This time he did not refuse her comfort. Kohl was suddenly weary. He barely noticed his mother glance over her shoulder to his father as she walked him out of the building.

+   +   +

The Governor waited for them to leave before he returned to Spectra's side. He had seen his wife's glance and knew exactly what it meant. One more thing had to be done before he retired.

He picked up his dagger, which an enforcer had removed from the wound, wiped it and replaced it in its sheathe. He circled Spectra once, considering his next act. Three medics had arrived and were waiting to transport him to hospital.

'Leave us,' he ordered.

When they were alone, aside from one enforcer standing sentry, he lowered himself to his haunches and checked to make sure Spectra was conscious, before whispering in his ear.

'You fucked that one up Spectra! Harper's told him way too much. You should never have allowed that bitch to leave Newbrunswick alive.'

He punched Spectra in the ribs, and was gratified by the cracking response. From the corner of his eye he saw the nearby enforcer flinch at the noise. Governor Pallas was not concerned. He knew Spectra would survive and when he awoke, he wanted him to remember exactly who was in charge.

Spectra would pay for his miscalculations, as would Harper.

CHAPTER 46
Darklands outside Brizzie

SAM HOBBLED BACK to the Damaran camp. To keep up his search for Aggy, he needed to constantly overrule the pain caused by the newly expanded muscle tissue in his grumbling foot.

'I think I need a rest,' said Lawrence.

'Yeah me too,' admitted Sam.

Twice he had caught Lawrence watching him walk. The old man had a knack for putting others first in a way that didn't make them feel like a burden. He was a lot like Vincent.

'Perhaps we should head back. Would you like to join me for a cuppa, while I speak with Mrs Brown? She should be having the logistics meeting about now. The generals are having trouble finding adequate accommodations for all the Pedies. Discussions were getting heated when we left, so I'm hoping Mrs Brown helped smooth things over.'

As Lawrence spoke, Sam rubbed his foot – it ached like the dark devil – and considered the options. It was a tempting offer but he could not abandon the search. Nothing would be right until he found her.

'No thanks.'

'Here, then take this. I don't like leaving you alone in the dark,' said Lawrence, standing up and handing over the lightkey.

'I'm from dark Newbrunswick, remember? Keep the lightkey for yaself. Help ya find camp.'

'No, you forget I still have the implant. I'll just jump back,' said Lawrence.

'I haven't made many solo jumps. Not sure I'll ever get the hang of it, kinda glad to be walkin' back,' said Sam.

'I'll get JayMoe to give you some training in the next few days, promise. Till then don't go too far from camp. We can't lose another manifestation.' Lawrence gave mock salute and, in a flash, he had disappeared.

+ + +

All afternoon Sam ambled through the cold darklands, alone in his worries. Calling out for Aggy could be dangerous as he had no idea how close he was to the Brizzie light curtain. All he could do was move around in the hope of stumbling across her, but he had to do *something*.

Where are ya?

Nursing his aches as he wandered around, the heaviness of life settled upon him. Pedies, Buchanites, Civies, Rats, all homeless. Hundreds, probably thousands, all huddled in that one makeshift camp with few resources and little hope against the Solarans who had everything.

Sam shone the torch down on his foot that would always be less and thought of Kohl who would always be more, have more.

Harper. He remembered her beaming face when he had

finally delivered them from the tunnels. For a moment it had felt as though only the two of them existed in the world and it was bliss.

Aggy. His new role model who, like his real mum, had been thoughtful, supportive and reliable. She had saved him in so many ways, and now she was lost. He had to find her.

Where are ya Aggy? Fly home to us like the great golden bird of the light!

His mind turned to Newbrunswick. Doc Maggy, Vincent and everyone he had known as a child were gone. He fell back to his years as a Brother and bowed his head, praying for illumination for his loved ones. He opened his mouth to recite the words but the prayer had become so large it stuck in his heart and came out as a stifled wail.

There was nothing he could do. Prayer wasn't helping. He held his lightkey aloft and shuffled on through the dark – listening for a sign of life. Hoping to find the two women who had become everything to him.

'Watch out!' came an urgent cry. Seconds later Sam was pushed aside. He fell hard, tripping over his own feet. His hip bumped on the gritty earth and he dropped his lightkey, which instantly stopped working, and a little too much air rushed out of his lungs.

'Who's there?' asked a feeble voice to Sam's side, close enough to touch even, and for a Newbrunswick man certainly close enough to smell.

'Aggy! It's me, Sam, are ya alright? Are ya injured? Hang on, I'll get the lightkey workin' again.'

'Sam, thank goodness it's you,' said another voice. Seconds later he had a light on and was being enveloped in a desperate hug from Harper.

'You can't imagine how glad I am to find a friend. I've jumped a few times to get here but I still don't know how the implant really works. I don't know how to jump to a place I haven't been to before and I didn't know where the camp was,' said Harper rapidly.

'Aggy couldn't help either. She's been drifting in and out of consciousness. So I just jumped around till I got us out of Brizzie. Then I started to think of Lawrence and Mrs Brown and you. I took one last jump while I prayed that I would land next to someone I knew and, ta-da, here we are!'

Harper babbled breathlessly before she sagged to the ground, puffing.

'Jumping is so exhausting. Have you got any food?' she whispered.

Sam took a closer look and realised that both ladies needed urgent medical aid.

'Sorry, no food. Can you walk?'

'I'm not sure. All that jumping, I haven't got much energy left.'

Harper started to close her eyes. Before she could drift into unconsciousness, Sam strung the lightkey around his neck and placed a hand on each of the ladies' wrists, 'C'mon implant, ya better start workin. Gotta get to Lawrence—'

+ + +

Lawrence consulted his watch. The meeting had extended well beyond useful and escalating towards hysteria. Despite all parties having the best intentions, the only thing they had been able to agree upon was their desperate situation. All lamented the lack of a clear leader.

Sam, where are you? Come on kid, find Aggy and get back here! He mentally pleaded through his growing regret. *What was I thinking leaving him alone out there?*

Lawrence silently prayed to the great Light who shone down on them all. *Find young Sam and bring him back to us.*

With Aggy – his prayer was interrupted by another outbreak of discord.

'—you are the ones who are overrated! What good is a festival in a time of war?' General Mitta stood abruptly, overturned a small table and made to leave.

Mandawuy was waving his hands to the Pedies, in furious translation of Mitta's insult levied in response to Buchanite criticism.

At the same time, Mrs Brown was trying to calm her own agitated people. The Pedies were stamping their feet in a reflex action, forgetting their visual yells of frustration would not ripple along the ground. The cacophony of complaints threatened to overwhelm the new alliances. The uproar was drowning out all the good intentions from earlier.

Lawrence stood, ready to join Mrs Brown in her efforts, when all around him Damarans fell quiet. Pedies and Buchanites took longer to register that something had changed. In the space of a few breaths even they grew silent. All attention was focused on a space just behind Lawrence. Then he heard a sound that made his heart skip.

'*Uncle … Larry?*' a soft woman's voice spoke.

He turned to see Sam beaming with pride, Harper smiling with relief and Aggy looking confused but present, despite her obvious pallor.

'If I'm dreaming, don't wake me. I've missed you so, Uncle Larry,' Aggy said in a voice choked with barely suppressed tears. 'I thought you were dead all these years.'

'I'm sorry. Illustria saved me and then ordered me to stay away. She needed you to learn independence – to help you grow into the leader our world so desperately needed. Looks like she was right,' he said, gesturing around at the masses who were in hushed reverent poses.

'No, she was wrong. I was just a girl. I needed you so many

times.'

She stepped towards him and faltered. Lawrence lurched forward to catch her as she collapsed. He picked her up as though she were still a little girl.

'I've got you, sweetheart. If it had been up to me, I would have never left you.'

'No, put me down Uncle. To you I'm just Aggy, but to my people I'm Alpha. I must look strong for them,' she said softly.

Lawrence gently put her back on her feet. Mrs Brown stepped out of the crowd and approached with a Buchanite medic.

'Here you are dear, take a drink of this, it will help restore you. Harper, looks like you could use some too.'

Harper eagerly took a swig of the offering without hesitation. Aggy seemed less sure.

'Allow me to introduce Mrs Brown. She is a loyal friend and leader of the Buchanites. If she says her elixir will help, you should trust her,' said Lawrence.

Aggy nodded and took a long, slow drink.

'Thank you.'

She straightened up and stood gingerly. She gave her people a low wave with one hand, whilst using the other to clutch her side. Then Aggy cleared her throat to address the crowd.

'My dear Damaran family, I would not be alive right now without the courage and initiative of these wonderful new friends. They are to be treated as kin.' Aggy indicated Sam and Harper, who bowed their heads in acknowledgement.

Lawrence looked around at each face, so many desperately looking to Aggy for salvation.

'I know that I am asking a lot. It is not easy to welcome new people when we are already suffering so much ourselves; when it feels as though we have so little left to give. Thank you for the generosity I know you will show them,' she said.

Aggy paused as a ruckus erupted from the back of the camp. A second later General Abudua materialised next to her with a filthy-looking enforcer she had restrained in cuffs. His clothing was torn and he frothed at the mouth like a barely restrained animal.

'Apologies for the interruption, Alpha. My heart is uplifted by your return to us,' she said with a low bow. When the enforcer pulled against his restraints, the General kicked him in the back of the knees.

'Bow down Solaran scum and plead with Alpha for your pathetic life.' She growled dangerously.

'What news, General?' said Aggy, softly.

'Alpha, in our search for you, we crossed the light barrier. I thought you might be visiting our allies in Brizzie Keep. I am saddened to report that it is no more.'

'What do you mean? Where are my sisters?' interrupted Harper. General Abudua ignored her and continued aiming her report at Alpha.

'The Solarans have burned the Keep to the ground and sealed up the tunnels. A few Civies escaped; they're getting medical attention at the camp now and then I'm sure they will want to brief you. All else were lost to the fire, or the enforcers.

'The Brothers were there too. They seemed to be coordinating the offensive. I got close enough to hear one of them say it was only the first "cleansing". That all other rat-allies will go the same way in days to come,' Abudua bowed again at the end of her report.

Lawrence shuddered at the news. Harper turned her face to disguise her need to wipe her cheeks.

'You're all dead!' growled the enforcer as he fought to stand. Abudua silenced him with a fearsome right hook and put her heavy combat boot on his restraint chains to force his face onto the bare dirt. Alpha nodded to the General then raised her face to the wider crowd.

'The time for labels is over. No longer can there be Buchanites, Damarans, Civies or Brothers, all divided, each suffering in isolation. No more *us* and *them*.

'The Master is on a rampage and until he is defeated no one is safe. Not even the Solarans, despite their deluded ideas, can be saved from his wrath. It is the end for all of us unless the Light prevails. We must all unite in support of her, if any of us are to survive this. We need all our talents to win this war.'

Aggy wobbled briefly, her hand connecting gently on the head of a nearby Damaran girl. Lawrence saw a new intensity blaze in her eyes as she observed the innocent face. When she stood, her voice had sharpened.

'I am your Alpha and these are my words, which shall be obeyed as law. Tonight we rest as family. Tomorrow we plan like soldiers. On the third day we march as victors. It is time to take Brizzie as our own. No longer shall our children live like Rats.'

'Three cheers for Alpha,' came an outcry from someone in the crowd, spurring the people to rise up as one.

Lawrence shuffled closer to Aggy, offering her a protective arm. She declined but indicated that he should follow closely. Sam, Harper, Mrs Brown and Albert fell in behind. Slowly the procession made its way to the sanctuary of her field tent.

Before she entered, she stopped and turned to Lawrence.

'Uncle Larry, tell me, have you identified the other manifestations? It will be difficult to save our people unless we can get them all to Illustria. We have only been able to identify three; Harper, Sam and myself.'

Lawrence couldn't believe that someone so weak with pain was still thinking of others. He was overwhelmed with pride for the woman Aggy had become.

'We found one in the tunnel. It's Kohl Pallas, the Governor's son. Can you believe it?' Lawrence asked, shaking his head, still confounded by the revelation.

'Oh, that's right, Illustria mentioned it before we lost contact. I had forgotten,' said Aggy in a voice that had grown shallow again. She sat down and rubbed her temples. 'Any ideas about the fifth?'

Lawrence shook his head in response, but Harper stepped forward.

'Actually Aggy, I think I know who it is.'

'You do, Harper?' Aggy raised her head at the hopeful news.

'Yes. Do you remember the last line in the letter about the manifestations?' Harper asked Aggy, although it was Lawrence who answered.

'*The last will treasure the gift of speech, alas he is most likely to be swayed.*'

'Who is the most corrupt person we know?' she asked.

'The Governor?' offered Sam.

'No, even worse.'

For a moment there was silence, and then the two men answered as one. 'Spectra!'

'Exactly!'

'Yes, it fits.' Aggy spoke very quietly, sounding more exhausted by the moment, 'Do you have any proof? Does he possess a golden item?'

'He does. I saw him use a golden communication device.'

Lawrence nodded in understanding. Aggy smiled.

'I should have seen that years ago. Thank you for solving the riddle. I will rest now. Tomorrow you shall help me plan. Just pray that we are not too late.'

'Wait Aggy, we might know who the manifestations are but what do we do with them once we get them all together? How do we actually get down to Illustria?' asked Lawrence.

'Sam, do you still have your key?' asked Aggy.

'Yes, here you are.'

Sam pulled out the little golden tube which had proven to

be so helpful in the tunnels. Aggy took the item in her hand as though it weighed far more than it did. Lawrence saw her weakness and instantly regretted delaying her rest with another question.

'See the marks on the side?' Aggy pointed to the little letters Sam had discovered so many years ago.

'*-35.58, 148.97TL* are the coordinates we must follow.

Sam's key will allow us access to Illustria's stronghold. No more questions now. Goodnight all.'

Lawrence was glad to see Aggy finally retire to her tent. As he walked away, he was moved to hear the shift in the camp's mood. There was upbeat singing and chatter all around.

The famed Damaran leader had returned and, with her, hope was restored.

+   +   +

In the relieved commotion that followed, as the many tribes bedded down, no one noticed one lightkey go missing, nor one of their new clan disappearing into the dark.

Albert had heard enough.

He did not know what he would report on the Rat's grand plan. After all, the time he had spent with the outcasts, he had come to understand that they were decent, honourable people who deserved a normal existence. He wasn't even entirely sure that they *shouldn't* take a major city like Brizzie after the way they had been treated.

All he knew was that he could not turn his back on a lifetime of duty. He still owed an allegiance to his Solaran race. He could only hope that his death would be swift when he confessed that he had lost their son.

With a heart full of regret, Chief Constable Albert Carter moved swiftly into the darkened plain and prayed silently that he was headed in the right direction.

CHAPTER 47
The Blazing Aurora VI

CAPTAIN JULIAN'S GREETING was laced with heavy disappointment. They had tried to make contact with the surface so many times that Julian had lost count. Hope eroded further with each failed attempt.

Neil repeatedly swivelled back and forth in his chair. It was a nervous affliction, Julian had come to understand, one of the many personal habits they had all come to detest in each other as they endured the close proximity of the command centre.

'Please, somebody speak to me, anyone. Repeat. This is Captain Julian Drexus of the starship Blazing Aurora Six. We have come to liberate Charles Drexus. Do you read me? Are you there? Hello? It's your family here, answer dammit!'

Julian rested his hand on the switch they had rigged for the neutrino modulator, the latest method of communication they were trialling. He turned to Bruno and, without releasing his hand, said, 'well this was your suggestion, do you want to give it a try before we move on to the next method in our comms matrix? Maybe he'll speak to you?'

'Negative. This action is foolishness. We must punch a hole in that forcefield and fly down. I guarantee he is so far underground that he cannot detect our signals.'

'He's right,' said Frank.

'Wait. What if there *are* people on the surface, or indigenous animals, even primitive plant life for that matter? Even if it's microscopic, should it not be valued?' asked Elizabeth.

As an astrobiologist, the need to preserve all forms of life was always Elizabeth's paramount concern. She had mounted this line of argument every time the option of landing had been discussed.

'You're delusional! There's no life here,' barked Bruno, cracking his neck from side to side. 'If I don't get planet side soon, I'll get agitated.'

In Julian's opinion he was already beyond agitated. The close quarters in light artificial gravity was seriously inadequate for the mental health of an awake crew in an extended planetary orbit. Bruno wasn't the only one eager to stretch his muscles in some real gravity – alone. Even Julian felt the pull of land.

'He does have a point, Liz,' added Jane in an unusually gentle tone for the lead scientist, who had inherited an unusually hefty dose of Drexus aggression.

'The whole reason they marooned him out here was so that he could experience isolation. Make him atone for his crimes. Do you really think they would have allowed him to stash the raw materials to terraform the world? He couldn't create a zoo, much less a whole civilization.'

When Elizabeth didn't respond, Jane continued in a less gentle tone.

'Use your brain, Elizabeth. If he did it covertly, then how many people would have been involved in the cover-up? They would have had to bribe multiple high-level officials just to establish the location of his prison, and if they had that, then why wouldn't they have come back and rescued him years ago? For God's sake, take off the green blinkers and think for once!

'Even if he did manage to pull it off, which I agree with Bruno is a long shot at best, he would've had to spend decades, no, *centuries*, just creating a breathable atmosphere. How about drinking water? Where would you get sufficient supplies of H_2O for a full settlement?' asked Jane.

'Light?' added Julian.

'That's right. Thank you, Julian. We've established that there's a photon containment field encasing that little world. This field prevents light from radiating the way it does in normal atmospheres. It's a pretty effective way of keeping him in the dark. Nice revenge for his Dyson plan. How are you going to grow food for your population in the dark?' Jane added.

'Maybe he found a way around it. Underground hydroponics?' Elizabeth offered timidly.

'I guess you could use a field dampener to create a pocket of standard atmosphere where light would behave normally, but as soon as the light rays hit the edge of your dampener field they would dissipate. The light would be stopped as effectively as using blackout curtains.'

Jane waved her hands around to demonstrate the light rays and the curtain as the intensity of her speech grew.

'Do you get what that means, Elizabeth? Do you? Do you! You switch on a torch in a regular environment and the light spreads out indefinitely. That's how you can see the lights of a city from a distance; or even from orbit if there's enough intensity.

'Turn on a torch in this world and it won't work unless you have a sophisticated field dampener, and then only within the space of the dampened field. Move even one centimetre outside of that and you can no longer see the light from the torch – there's nothing but pitch. The likelihood that he has dampeners strong enough for the whole planetoid? Infinitesimally small. That leaves your hypothetical settlement in complete darkness.

'And, if against all odds, he had those things, golly, do you not think someone would have noticed by now?' Jane stopped and took a slug of caff.

'No, I'm with Bruno. It's just barren rock down there. No life. Nothing to suffer if we knock a hole in the atmosphere. I vote we go in.'

Julian looked around his team as Jane finished. With the exception of Elizabeth, they were all nodding in agreement.

'So, how do we do this?' he asked. No immediate answer was forthcoming. 'Ai32, can you come up with a few options? The rest of you twelve hours R-and-R. I want you all energised when we make the next big move. Who knows what we'll find down there.'

Elizabeth looked like the only one who might challenge his decision. She stood and opened her mouth to speak; not once, but twice. Then she must have decided that even for her, the argument for life below was thin, even if Charles *had* been able to smuggle DNA with him. She closed her mouth and followed the rest of the crew to the sleeping quarters.

+ + +

For the first time in her life, Illustria experienced an emotion which she could only assume was panic. She had been actively blocking Blazing Aurora's attempts to reach Charles ever since their sudden arrival. But dividing herself between the war on the ground and visitors in orbit was proving more problematic than she had anticipated.

Assuming the logical outcome that they would depart just as swiftly as they arrived, she had only assigned one of her minor subroutines to the Aurora monitoring job. The regular reintegration of that subroutine, and analysis of the resulting intelligence, was proving to be a distraction.

She had also assumed her only real concern was preventing Charles from knowing they were there. Both assumptions were proving incorrect.

When she heard Bruno's suggestion of punching a hole in the forcefield, Illustria castigated herself for the miscalculation.

The Blazing Aurora Crew were apparently not logical. She should have realised descendants of her tenacious prisoner would not give up easily. In hindsight it was obvious that they would rather risk innocent life forms than fail in their goal.

Where are my manifestations?

Normally Illustria would have dispatched a subroutine to press Aggy on her progress. She was not, however, willing to trust communications with the surface since Charles interrupted her last conference with the Damarans.

She hoped that they were still alive. Her thoughts of Aggy were interrupted by Jane's voice filtering through Illustria's speech recognition processors. Jane was her favourite. She was usually so logical and direct. In many ways, she reminded Illustria of Aggy.

'... *It's just barren rock down there. No life. Nothing to suffer if we knock a hole in the atmosphere. I vote we go in.*'

If Jane was voting to land then there was no doubt, they weren't giving up – they were coming! If Illustria had had a digestive tract, she would have thrown up. She needed to switch her focus.

She recalled her surveillance subroutine for a report on Charles' side of their underground fortress. She was grateful he was in a sleep session; she couldn't afford him to discover her orbital monitoring operation.

He lay on his bunk facing the wall, his shoulders rising and falling in rhythm. The electrodes she had implanted in the bed head confirmed the optical observation. Gas levels were consistent with sleep respiration. She was confident she had at least six hours to make her move.

Theoretically it should not have made any difference whether he was awake or not. He had no access to her side of the forcefield or the surface. His computer systems functioned in isolation and were constantly monitored by her aggressive security subroutine. Even the walls were sound-proofed.

Yet somehow he'd managed to successfully coordinate a campaign against her. His breakthrough into her comms was unfathomable. Their century-old stalemate was clearly over. In less than a second, she had conferred with her security subroutine on the matter and reached the conclusion that only the manifestations could provide the insight she needed.

Illustria released the subroutine and reordered her operational priorities. Beyond keeping Blazing Aurora a secret, regaining her manifestations was number one priority – even at the expense of her remaining settlements.

+ + +

Charles yawned, stretched and turned over on his bunk. He smiled as though enjoying a delicious dream. Illustria's security subroutine, which he had captured and corrupted three months earlier, had just reported back to him through a micro ear piece, remotely linked to his computer. A computer that he allowed Illustria to think *she* controlled.

In truth, he now controlled most of their game and was actively plotting the quickest way to checkmate. The news that his long-lost family had finally come to liberate him was the returned pawn he needed.

His only decision now was what to do with his Solaran progeny; whether he could find a way to take a few of his favourites with him, before the rest were erased from his small, pitiful world.

CHAPTER 48

The Lodge

KOHL SPENT TWO days acquainting himself with The Lodge, the official residence of the Brizzie governor and the new Pallas Compound, as well as re-acquainting himself with Solaran society, all the while wondering why his parents were avoiding him.

Sure, his father had sent him a number of nubile companions, which Kohl swiftly sent out the back door as poor seconds to Harper. Yet the Governor himself did not make an appearance.

Spectra, who Kohl assumed was also reluctant to meet face to face, had sent him a wise old Brother, supposedly in consideration of his mother's concerns for his spiritual purity. After an hour of Kohl's conspiracy theories, the Brother resigned to his own quarters for prayer and contemplation.

His mother had sent in a steady stream of tailors, interior designers, waiters, butlers, medics, and social secretaries. She even sent her new dog to see to his comfort; again, she had not come in person.

Everyone he asked had told him that his parents were busy with the pressing business of the inauguration; there were security measures to be met and members of the Brizzie elite to be won over. Outside the city a war was being waged against the Rats and *inside* the city there was a gaping service hole left by the Brizzie Civies who had apparently left them high and dry upon the news of Sydney's demise.

As a Pallas heir, Kohl was expected to understand that it was quite possibly the busiest time of his parents' lives. He wished that he had siblings close by.

✦　✦　✦

'Listen Glare, I don't care who you think you are, the Governor will not take "no" for an answer. He insists that you meet today; right now, actually.' Spectra's voice broke as he yelled down the communicator into Glare's ear. It was like the deafening crack of fireworks.

This time, Spectra's hostile tone delighted her. As a sure sign that Spectra was rattled, the rare treat had to be savoured.

'What exactly went on between you two anyway? Ever since the rally you have seemed somewhat on edge. Did the Governor express some displeasure with your speech?' Of course, Glare knew exactly what had transpired. She had to put her hand over the voice piece so he would not hear her barely supressed glee.

'Nothing, Glare. How about you mind your own skin and get down to The Lodge? Pronto.'

'I will do nothing of the sort. You will remember that I am the Master's number one, which effectively makes all of you, *even the Governor*, report to me. I will not attend The Lodge until this evening's inauguration ball, exactly as I have planned.

'Besides, it would be un-Solaran to impose myself on the

Lady of the House on the day of such a momentous event. I'm sorry if you have a fundamental lack of appreciation for Solaran etiquette. It must be difficult to perform from a position of ignorance, I suppose. See you at the ball. Glare out!'

She deactivated the communicator before Spectra could object again. As she sunk back into her warm bath, she fancied that she could hear a distant cry emanating from the direction of Malo Abbey.

✦   ✦   ✦

Kohl stormed down the long hallway. His request for a meeting had been rejected again by his father's personal secretary, a woman named Ezmay, who wore a skirt that was entirely too small to be practical and a smile too wide to be personal.

He scuffed his toes in frustration and twice stopped to kick the enormous porcelain vases that punctuated the main thoroughfare. Although it did nothing to help his situation, somehow it always made him feel better. He just wished he could hear Mark's voice one more time, urging him to stop his childish behaviour.

'Kohl, where are you?' An achingly familiar voice broke his morose reverie.

'Ko-ohl!'

'Is that you?' He spun around looking for the source. For a moment Kohl wondered if he had imagined it.

'Where are you?'

'Over here, on the balcony.' The voice came from behind heavy blue curtains. Kohl wrestled with the fabric – drawing curtains was never easy without a maid – and eventually had to settle for lifting the drape up from the bottom.

He was pleasantly surprised to see double doors leading

out to a small balcony. The garden beyond featured a bedraggled Chief Constable Albert Carter pacing and biting his nails.

'Albert! What on earth are you doing out there?' asked Kohl as he opened the doors. 'Come in man.'

'No, you come out, please,' Albert said in a worrisome tone.

Kohl did as he was bade and stepped out through the doors. Albert still wore the torn workers' clothes they had borrowed at the beginning of their mission. His eyes were bloodshot and his movements were shaky.

Kohl instantly felt compassion for the man, and admonished himself for not having considered Albert's fate since they had parted company back at Coober Pedy.

'I'm so glad to see you. How did you get here?' Kohl shook Albert's hand and clasped his shoulder affectionately.

'I walked. With the Damarans. They've set up camp outside the city. Did you know that? I've been lost in the darklands for a couple of days. It was only luck that I found the city lightbarrier. From there it was easy. Just had to avoid a few patrols.'

Kohl noticed Albert's uncharacteristic nervousness.

'Man, you look like you could use a bath and a feed. Come on up to my quarters.' He tried to steer Albert into the building.

'No. I must see you father first. I need to confess that I have put your life in peril. Won't need a bath for what will follow after that.'

Kohl finally understood and smiled with genuine compassion. 'No way are you confessing to anything, aside from being my right-hand man through the whole saga. Don't you know you are a hero in this story?'

'I can't allow you to lie to your father, Kohl. He must know the truth.'

'What nonsense, man! As I recall we got separated in the battle of Coober Pedy, when I sent you to do recon on the great enemy. Which I presume you have been doing ever since, loyally following my orders.

'Now I will give you one more order. You will accompany me to my quarters for a bath, some nosh, a good debrief on the last few days, and if you're lucky, some personal time with the very next wench that my father sends to my door. He's been sending them practically on the hour. What do you prefer – blonde, brunette, rainbow or bald?'

Kohl patted Albert on the back as he urged him forward, eager to get him back to the privacy of his room so that he could ask for news of Harper.

+   +   +

'So where is she?' demanded Governor Pallas. He was standing on a plinth in the centre of his dressing room while his tailor fitted his inauguration robes. Spectra was livid to be forced to report in front of a hired hand.

'Well, spit it out, why is Glare not in front of me right now?'

Spectra swallowed. For the first time he was not entirely sure how to convey Glare's remarks without losing his own head. The Governor had summoned Glare and expected to be obeyed. How was Spectra going to remind the Governor that Glare outranked them both?

'I'm sorry Sir, she is not coming because the Master has her on a vital mission. She cannot disobey him, as much as she would prefer to attend your wishes. She hopes you will understand and remarks that she will definitely be here tonight.'

Spectra bowed in submission and tried very hard to look innocent, compliant even. The Governor grunted and dismissed his attendants, an action that caused Spectra's anxiety to grow. The Governor's most unpleasant business usually happened without witnesses.

A moment passed. Then two. Spectra had never seen him so quiet and still. It was more than worrying.

At last the Governor slowly got down off the plinth, balled his fists, and struck the nearest mirror, which shattered into a rain of tiny shards. Governor Pallas relaxed his hands, straightened his clothes and silently strode out of the room, leaving a trail of his own blood behind.

✦   ✦   ✦

'What happened to her? Tell me, witch!' Lady Pallas hissed through clenched teeth. She nodded to her personal assistant who directed the two enforcers to relax their hold enough for the elderly Sister to speak.

Priscilla Pallas and her staff had been interrogating Brizzie Sisters in the basement of The Lodge for three days straight. Discarded torn robes and many tools of the trade littered the murky room. The air reeked of pain. It was not a place Lady Pallas would normally enter, but she was not normally so desperate for an answer. Desperate for her Bess.

'Increase the tension on the lateral screws,' she demanded, resuming her calm. Her husband had taught her that control was more terrifying than hysteria. One of the enforcers carried out her orders and the Sister moaned in response.

'Sister Aida, I will remind you that I have unlimited resources and a stream of other Civies yet to be interviewed. Be assured, I *will* get a response to my questions one way or another. The only issue is how much unpleasantness you and your cronies can endure before someone breaks.

'I will also remind you that your Keep has been razed and you no longer have your Queen to mystically pop in and whisk you away. You might have heard, my husband dispatched her with a long blade at the fall of Veruda.

'As for your precious "Light" – don't count on her either. You know she isn't even a "she", don't you? That abomination is nothing more than a corrupted mathematical program, created by a man and worshipped by the weak. Nothing mystical about it. Certainly nothing that can come to your rescue. As we speak the Master is dismantling her code line by line. You'll never see "The Light" again.'

Mid-speech Lady Pallas gave her assistant a cue to have the tension increase one more time, and a glob of bloodied spittle rolled from Sister Aida's mouth as she groaned again.

'If you tell me what I want to hear, all this can stop. Perhaps I will take pity on you and assign you to one of the more hospitable work caverns. Now, who killed my daughter?'

As she finished her monologue the Lady moved in close so that there would be no mistaking the intensity of her intention. She was gratified when Aida broke eye contact and peered at the bodies behind her.

'Never,' whispered Sister Aida.

'What did you just say?'

'Never will you figure it out. You royal wannabies are too caught up in your own misguided sense of importance, to figure out the simple beautiful truth that stands before you.'

She cackled and again Lady Pallas ordered an increase in intensity. Her cackle morphed into a yelp.

'Enough of your double talk. What happened to my daughter? Tell me. As her mother, don't I at least deserve to bury my own daughter?' Lady Pallas knew her husband would not approve of her yelling.

'Tell me. Tell me! *Tell me!*'

Sister Aida slowly lifted her head. 'I can't tell you what you should already know, and *would* know if you didn't *abandon* her all those years ago. No wonder she hated you. If she's become collateral damage, then only you are to blame.'

Lady Pallas howled, pushed her staff aside, grabbed the cranial tension lever and turned it until she heard a gratifying *crack.*

She breathed deeply to regain her composure. Although she did not have the answer she needed, at least some of her own tension had been released. She was beginning to appreciate her husband's enjoyment of this sordid business. Her heart rate stabilised and she wiped her hands on a towel provided by her assistant.

'Take a break and clean this place up. We shall resume tomorrow. I have an inauguration to prepare.'

Lady Pallas pushed back stray hairs and adjusted her blouse before leaving the room.

CHAPTER 49
The Blazing Aurora VI

CAPTAIN JULIAN HAD reduced the volume of the cabin's comms speaker to a bare minimum, so initially no-one noticed the soft voice. There didn't seem to be much point actively monitoring comms when all external hails had resulted in absolutely no response from the small world below.

'Hello?' the voice said, louder. 'This is Charles Drexus the first, and the best I'd like to think. Look, is anyone receiving this?'

Bruno continued his press-ups against a wall. Elizabeth sipped a double-caff, and Jane and Julian didn't break from arguing about descent vectors in the face of unknown surface conditions. Neil and Frank were still on sleep break.

Ai32 came bursting into the cabin.

'Captain, there's an incoming message, which you'd know about if you had turned up the comms!'

'Huh?' said Julian, not really registering what Ai32 had said and not wanting to abandon his train of thought. He was busy trying to prove to Jane that a delta-x16 entry would leave them a better window to slingshot out again, in the event of unexpected hostilities.

'Comms, Captain, comms. Turn up the comms!' Bruno yelled and lunged across the console to activate the volume control.

'Look, I only have a few more minutes before she realizes what I am doing. Is someone going to respond or not?'

Julian stared in amazement as the strong, unknown voice buzzed from the console. Elizabeth choked on her coffee. Jane raised her eyebrows, shrugged her shoulders and hit the response key.

'Yes, we read you. This is Blazing Aurora Six, Senior Scientist Jane Drexus here. To whom am I speaking?'

'Not a bloody woman! Can't believe it. Fucking surrounded. The first off-worlder I hear in all these years, and it couldn't possibly be someone with a pair of balls, could it?' The voice gave an indignant snort.

'Are you serious—' Jane's response was cut short as Julian took over.

'Sorry about that, Charles I assume? This is Captain Julian Drexus of the Blazing Aurora Six. We are currently in orbit around your world and I am delighted to hear your voice.'

'Well, that's more like it,' said Charles.

'Are you in any immediate need of assistance? What is your position? Are you alone?' Julian launched into the series of questions they had agreed to prioritise if they had success in initiating contact.

'Don't waste my time Julian. I have about one minute left so listen up. This is indeed Charles Drexus and I am very keen to leave this god-forsaken world. Alas, I am being held hostage in the core behind a forcefield by a rogue Ai.

'I made the mistake early on of giving it an empathy algorithm, which sent it spiralling into artificial insanity. It now identifies as a female called Illustria and a considerable proportion of the local population have been convinced she is some sort of deity. I assure you, nothing could be further from the truth.

'I will contact you again in approximately eighteen hours. In the meantime, if she makes any contact with you, do not believe a word she says. She is an extremely dangerous program. Drexus out.'

Julian sat calmly digesting the turn of events. He scratched his head, and then exhaled loudly, his breath whistling through his teeth. Elizabeth stood, calmly put down her coffee on the bench beside her and walked towards door, stopping for a moment to address Bruno.

'So nothing's alive down there, huh? How many people did you and Jane nearly kill today? Looks like you both got plenty of those lovely Drexus genes after all.'

+ + +

Charles hit cancel on his comms program, pushed his chair back from the computer and twirled it around. A whole ship of lovely Drexus folk. Wearing a smirk from ear to ear he left his office, entered the communal lounge and crossed to the bar.

He wasn't surprised to find himself alone. Illustria couldn't possibly know how many of her subroutines he had commandeered, but after he had interrupted the Rats transmission, she would have some idea. She would be working feverishly to reassert her control. He poured a drink as he called out to his old nemesis. 'Illustria?'

When there was no response he poured himself another.

'Illustria!'

After the third drink, he found himself in the mood to tease her a little, to give her a hint at how close he was coming to assuming full control. He didn't need her to be present for what he had to say but he was old-fashioned – he liked to see people squirm when he presented bad news. Even if the people weren't really people.

When she didn't respond by the third holler, he had his fourth drink and was ready to give up. The mood had vanished and he knew he still had a considerable battle ahead. Teasing Illustria wouldn't achieve anything useful.

What would *be useful is getting out of this ruddy prison!*

He threw his glass of Bundy across the room. When it hit the forcefield it bounced off with a sizzle and the contents instantly evaporated, forming a brief mid-air cloud of fragrant amber mist.

As many subroutines as he had subverted, he was yet to find a command that would end the forcefield that bisected their living room. Without it, he would never leave his prison cavern, no matter how many battles he won nor how many vessels awaited in orbit.

Charles returned to his office. He knew what he had to do. He would make Glare an offer she couldn't refuse.

CHAPTER 50

Brizzie Town Hall

KOHL ENDURED A torturous hour, which felt more like three, standing at attention in the official receiving line at the inauguration ball. Close to five hundred guests had patiently paraded up the grand staircase to be presented to the Pallas family; it looked as though there were at least another hundred to go.

'Your shoes are flashing again!' Lady Pallas whispered through her gritted teeth and permanent smile as she shook the hand of Lady Karen, influential socialite and wife of the city light engineer.

Kohl had dressed in a navy velvet suit cut in the latest military trend, complete with epaulets on his broad shoulders and brass fasteners at his narrow hips. As customary in Sydney he was shirtless. In deference to Brizzie fashion he had movement-activated, luminous thread woven into the stitching of his Cuban-heeled evening boots. It was a decision he was already regretting.

'Kohl, keep still! You know what's at stake,' Lady Pallas

whispered.

His mother was determined to take advantage of their new status by making a fast, strategic match for her only remaining child. Apparently she needed grandchildren with the utmost urgency.

Kohl knew his father cared nothing for the marriage plans but nevertheless used them to draw out Brizzie's most influential families. Many of them were concerned about the rapid change of leadership. A handsome available heir went some way to assuage those concerns.

'Mask slipping, Kohl,' growled his father.

Kohl adjusted his feathered mask; another Brizzie custom he detested. It itched like the devil and made him blink a little too often. He couldn't wait for the grand de-masking at midnight. A symbolic shedding of past fears, as their new leader stepped forth and rank was re-established.

In truth it was a security nightmare. There were reports of Rats massing on the outskirts of town and rumours abounded that they were planning a Sydney-style offensive.

In a public response Spectra had significantly raised the number of enforcers on the streets. Privately his father had assured him the Master's new ability to tap into Rat implants meant that no uninvited parties would make it through the security cordons.

Kohl prayed there were holes in the security through which one young lady might pass.

+   +   +

When she entered the foyer, everything was exactly as briefed, yet she still felt close to overwhelmed by anxiety. As she viewed the 36 steps between her and her goal, all she could think of was running away into the street. She breathed, silently repeated a Civy mantra, held up the front hem of her gown and began her ascent.

When she reached the sixth step a gentleman, accidentally-on-purpose, stepped on her train.

'I do apologise, M'lady. I hope that I have not done damage of any significance. I'm afraid I have never quite seen a dress like it. The rhinestones had me quite bedazzled, which is probably why I miss-stepped. Is that black or deep purple?

'And the golden wrap across your beautiful shoulders, so lovely to see unpainted skin. Too many girls these days treat their bodies like a moving art gallery. Sorry, I am forgetting my manners. I do hope I haven't damaged your dress too much. If you furnish me with your address, I might send a tailor to repair it?'

She could tell from the stooped posture and grey hairs protruding out of the ears of the masked dress-assassin, that he was old enough that she could accept the harmless flirtation without offense. She assured him all would be well and moved on.

At the twelfth step, three large swooning ladies stood on a small landing. She took the opportunity to join them in the pretext of loosening the bottom of her corset for air in the heat. The ruse gave her the chance to review her surroundings for contingency exit plans.

The double doors in the foyer were heavily guarded, as were the quadruple doors at the ballroom entrance. Neither would assist in a crisis. Then she spied a thin line in the wall on the other side of the landing. Certain she had spied a hidden exit point, she moved on with a knowing smile.

Between the thirteenth and twenty-third steps she focused on what she could hear. There was a buzz in the air that might have been hypermode traces. She was certain the Master was monitoring so she made no move to indicate that she had perceived them. She glanced sideways. No one else seemed to notice anything unusual. The plan was working.

On the twenty fourth step she got her first good look at the Pallas family. She swallowed and steadied herself. The moment of connection with Kohl was approaching, making her stomach dance. She knew she had to convince him, fool him, and then convince him again, if the grand plan was to work. There was little time left to get the manifestations to the Light. No room for miscalculations.

By the thirtieth step she realised that she was not the only nervous lady in ascent. She fancied that she could actually taste a whirlwind of pheromones in the air. All around her mothers were primping their girls, daughters were batting their eyelashes and fathers were admonishing wives for their plans of matrimonial coups. She smiled inwardly in appreciation that none of them had a chance of succeeding.

By the thirty-fourth step she could hear the lilt of Lady Pallas' patter.

On the thirty-fifth step she could feel a gentle push behind her. The excited crowd surged briefly forward in eager anticipation of the ultimate destination.

At the thirty-sixth step, she had reached the top landing and was about to take the hand that Kohl offered, when she was intercepted by Spectra.

'Come, come,' said Spectra in a voice that was a little too loud, 'that's no way to treat such a special guest, is it? I would have expected a much more affectionate greeting – not just a mere handshake.'

Both Lady and Governor Pallas turned immediately, and possibly not recognising the importance of the masked guest in question, quickly returned to their interrupted conversations.

'That's right, you haven't met this lovely creature in the magnificent golden mask. Or have you? Hard to tell through the costume, isn't it? Who could she be? Masquerade is such a fun tradition!'

Spectra appeared to be greatly enjoying his sense of superiority. He was dressed in his own masquerade, the formal embroidered robes of a benevolent Archbrother, the irony lost to all but his nearest and dearest enemies.

'It's you,' Kohl whispered intensely.

'Of course it's me. Did the robes confuse you? You know, in my new position it is actually you who should be bowing to me, Kohl.' Spectra prattled on, indicating that he had missed the point entirely. 'Oh, you refer to the lady? No, that's nonsense you can't know her, she's—'

'Actually, you are wrong Spectra. I do know her. Even disguised, I would know those eyes anywhere. We first met in Sydney Arbour Orchard, if I'm not mistaken.'

She nodded.

'At last.' Kohl murmured as he raised her hand and held it tightly against his chest. Spectra looked confused and opened his mouth to speak when a swell of music billowed out of the ballroom. Precisely at that same moment the three swooning ladies from the lower landing arrived behind her. They had pushed and hustled their way to the top of the line and all three of them were trying to balance on the penultimate step.

As the lady at the front of the group pushed forward to make room for the others, she bumped into Spectra who held his ground and pushed back with a sharp elbow, causing the last lady to squeal as they all toppled dangerously backward.

'Matthias!' snapped Lady Pallas, seeing the danger unfold. Governor Pallas responded by lunging across his wife to apprehend the young lady by her wrist. In the process he bumped Spectra, sending him tripping over the step instead.

With the Archbrother sliding down the stairs, bowling over a number of guests, chaos broke loose. Brothers and enforcers appeared from all around to restore order. Kohl seized on the moment and whisked his lady into the main ballroom, then right out the other side door before leading her down an unmarked passage.

+ + +

Kohl finally found a small hallway where they could stop, safe in the knowledge they were far from prying eyes.

'When did you figure it out?' she asked, panting just a little.

'When I looked at you on the stairs – your eyes.' To make his point, he pulled her towards a mirror and removed both their masks.

For the longest time they stood side by side staring at their reflections. Then, he put an arm protectively around his sister's shoulders.

Glare wiped her eyes and blushed. 'I'm sorry for getting emotional. I promised myself I wouldn't. It's just that all of this – it was never my choice, you know.'

'I know that now Bess,' he responded.

While they stood gazing silently at their similar reflections, he wondered why no one in Sydney had noticed. The bloodline was strong, their likeness was unmistakeable. He hated to admit that his mother was right. Anyone could have seen it had they wanted to. There was a sick conspiracy of silence amongst Solaran elite around Civy recruitment.

'The Master and his operatives only know me as Glare,' she said.

Kohl reached across for his sister's hand. 'What do you prefer – Big Sis, Glare or Bess?'

'Better to stick to Glare for now, little brother. Can't have Spectra figuring it out too soon. Or anyone else for that matter.'

There were noisy footsteps down the hallway; Kohl held his breath until the sound receded.

'Can we go somewhere private for a quick conversation? We have a lot to discuss and not much time. You need to get back to the ball before you're missed.'

'How about here?' asked Kohl as he pulled his sister into the nearest room, silently wishing Mark was sharing the moment and vowing to never lose her again.

CHAPTER 51

Brizzie Town Hall

SAM WAS THRILLED and terrified, just enough to make his stomach turn. He had never imagined the possibility of accompanying a lady to a grand ball. Now Aggy's moratorium on hypermode travel meant they would have to start their mission by posing as guests at the governor's ball. He prayed to the Great Illuminator that he wouldn't trip over his own feet and embarrass himself.

Naturally there had been considerable dissent from the highest ranking Damarans. Hypermode was their major tactical advantage; they did not relinquish it easily.

'If Illustria is still alive, and we must have hope that she is, we need to deliver the manifestations. It will be a dangerous mission so we must save hypermode for the most critical points. Besides, we have more than just a technological edge over our enemies. We have heart and determination,' Aggy had said at the briefing.

Grudgingly the sceptical generals had seized four guests in the streets of Brizzie and requisitioned their costumes and invitations. Mitta had tied them up. JayMoe had transported them back to camp for a Damaran holiday. Some free "re-education" in the darklands he had called it.

Sam was growing fond of his mechanical friend.

+   +   +

'My, don't you look lovely tonight my dear! You are quite the bell of the inauguration ball,' said Lawrence as he whizzed Aggy past Sam and Harper, in a graceful dash across the dancefloor.

'Thank you. Would you mind if we stepped off the dance floor for some refreshments though Uncle?' Aggy asked.

'Splendid suggestion.' Lawrence smiled. He loved to hear her calling him *Uncle* again. She might be Alpha to the rest of the world but to Lawrence she would always be his cheeky little Aggy.

He led her to the side of the hall and signalled Sam and Harper to join them. Together they did another recon of the room. Kohl and Spectra were still gone after the incident at the top of the stairs.

'Maybe they're not here anymore?' said Sam.

'Don't worry, Kohl won't be far. With so many beauties in one room – he won't be able to resist it,' said Harper.

Lawrence thought he might have heard a hint of jealousy in her tone. Apparently Sam did too as Lawrence caught him frowning. He made a mental note to speak with Harper when the mission was complete.

'Let's dance around the room again, Sam. We might observe something useful,' said Harper. Sam's face lifted.

'I'd be honoured. Ya look really … nice, Harper.'

'You too. Quite dashing. How about we move to that corner? Might get a better view of the main entrance. Are you guys coming too?' Harper asked, suddenly all business.

'You kids go; I think we'll sit this one out. We'll monitor this side for Spectra and Kohl.' Lawrence knew that Aggy hadn't yet fully recovered from her interrogation and would need to rest when she could.

Thank you, Aggy mouthed silently to Lawrence.

+ + +

'Glare, I'm not sure what to ask first.' Kohl paced, picking up objects and putting them down again absent-mindedly as he tried to pull his thoughts together. He looked down at the heavy paperweight he held in his hand and then around the rather grand room. Perhaps too grand to be a back office.

Glare must have been thinking the same thing as she picked up the brass name plate sitting on the front of the very large wooden desk.

'Sub-Mayor Whittlesea, Director of City Illumination. Well that explains the décor – a civil servant with grand ambitions,' she said with a smile.

'Back to us,' said Kohl impatiently, 'how did you survive the Sydney attack? And how did you end up here?'

'It's complicated – that story will have to wait for another time. All you need to know now is that I *am* your sister. I grew up with the Civies and like all good Pallas' I really work for the Master.'

Kohl physically recoiled in horror.

'How could you? The Master's a monster! Have you seen what he's done? I've spent time with the Damarans and they are not the villains our lot make them out to be. If you're working for him, then you have it all wrong.'

Glare shook her head, put her hand on her brother's arm and said quietly, 'no, I'm afraid you are the one who has it all wrong, little brother. Sit down. You need to know the facts before you choose your allegiance.

'The Master is not a monster. He's just a man called Charles Drexus. Oh, he's plenty smart alright, he has some very fancy tech tools and he invented some sort of science that enables him to live for a very, very long time. Aside from that he's just as human as you and I.

'Unfortunately something went very wrong and people locked him down here out of jealousy, spite maybe, I don't know. It was a long time ago. Essentially, he became a victim of his own success.'

'Wait. Are you saying there is more than just our world? That there are other people out there?' Kohl said incredulously.

'Yes, this is not our home planet Kohl. We don't belong here. Anyway, after spending a very long time experimenting with surface terraformation, different flora and fauna, and then peoples with an array of cultures and social structures, he eventually settled on a ruling class of Solarans that were based on himself. Charles Drexus is our direct ancestor, we're all his family.

'The other classes, like the Pedies, were created to serve us. There are other groups scattered around the world too. Each serves particular functions such as farming food, purifying water or manufacturing lightkeys. None of them would exist if they weren't needed to support Solarans.'

Kohl leaned back, looking sceptical.

'What about the Light?' he asked.

'I told you he had a computer, right?' asked Glare. Kohl, who was now perched on the wide armrest of a couch, nodded slowly in response.

'Like JayMoe?' he muttered.

'Well, it was a very smart computer. Something he calls an artificial intelligence. It fancied itself alive and disagreed with some of Charles' choices, so it imprisoned him behind a forcefield.'

'A forcefield?'

'Sorry, a forcefield is like a very strong wall that's made up of pure energy. You can see through it, you just can't physically move through it.'

Kohl nodded as though he understood, although Glare knew his mind would be reeling.

'Where was I? OK. The computer took on a female persona, created a lot more people and invented the myth about the Light. There were never supposed to be all these Damaran communities, hyperdrives, tunnels, secret societies – that's all her doing.

'Think about it, Kohl. Had she not gone mad and increased the population so dramatically, our world would be in much better balance and there would be no war. The Light is ultimately responsible for all this mess.'

Kohl sighed and ran his hand through his hair.

'It gets worse. You know that forcefield I mentioned? Well, there's another one around our whole world. It's important because it keeps our air in. It's also the reason it's dark. Somehow it stops light from spreading and it stops us from seeing what's outside our world.' Glare paused to let Kohl catch up.

'Let me get this straight,' he said, 'you're saying that we actually come from another world. And there are probably people still on that world?'

'Yes.'

'All these problems between Damarans and Solarans are the result of a fight between an ancient man and his computer?'

'Yes.'

'The religion we've been taught, all the customs and

practices we faithfully adhere to, are made up to keep us compliant?'

'Yes.'

'And the blinding of Newbrunswick children? How is that necessary? You do know Father does that, don't you?' he asked in a bitter tone.

'Regrettable I'll admit, but ultimately a kindness performed to counter the problems caused by the Light. If we didn't have so many people to house and feed, we wouldn't be so short on energy. We could light their whole town and they wouldn't need to be blind to keep the peace when the Brothers use their lightkeys.'

'I guess you're right,' Kohl said in a small voice as he stared into the distance. Glare wondered what he was remembering from his journey with the Damarans.

'Is that it? I don't know how many more revelations I can take.'

'No, there's one more thing you need to know. Recently people arrived here in a vessel from another world.'

'*What*?'

'Seriously, although we might not even have known about it if the Light had had her way. She tried to make them think that this world is empty in the hope they would leave us alone. She doesn't want any of us to leave this place because she has a psychotic need for control.

'Luckily Charles made contact with the outsiders in time to prevent them from coming down to our surface. He saved us all, Kohl. Do you understand what I'm saying? If they had flown down, they would have broken the forcefield, and then all our air would be instantly gone. We'd all be dead already without the Master's intervention.'

Kohl looked stunned. He began pacing again, then stopped mid-stride and raced back to Glare.

'The Damarans! I'm sure they will have plans in place right now to get to the Light. We have to stop them!' said Kohl. He ran across the room to leave. 'I need to find Harper!'

'No, wait, there's one last thing. Charles wants to go; he wants us all to leave. He says it's time to go back to our home world, before the Light becomes so unstable she tries to eliminate us all, which she certainly has the ability to do.

'He wants to get up to the off-worlder's vessel and he thinks he can take a few of us with him. Then we can come back with ships big enough for everyone. We're all safe, including Harper, if we can get him out of his prison.'

'That's a big ask, Glare. I don't know if I even want to leave. This is my home.'

'I understand, it's not supposed to be our home though. Don't you want to see where we really belong? Besides, the way the Light has behaved, I'm not sure we have much choice.'

'You're right, I guess. But what can we do? It's not like we just have to break Charles out of the local jail.'

Glare shook her head, then smiled a winning Pallas-smile. 'Don't worry. I have a plan, little brother. You just play along with the Damarans and find Harper, I'll take care of the rest.'

CHAPTER 52

Brizzie Town Hall

KOHL AVOIDED EYE contact with his parents as he re-entered the ballroom. He didn't need to see or hear them to understand the impact his absence would have had. Missing the first half hour of the inauguration was a breach of protocol that would not be forgiven easily. His mother in particular would be furious.

Spectra appeared by his side.

'Had a nice long chat with Glare, did you? Or perhaps you weren't just chatting hey?' Spectra gave him a particularly slimy look. The inference made Kohl's blood heat. He had to remind himself of Spectra's ignorance that Glare was his sibling.

'Well, do tell,' said Spectra rubbing his hands.

Or was he, Kohl wondered with a shudder. When Kohl didn't respond to his insinuations Spectra dropped it and asked the obvious question.

'Where is she now?'

'Not sure.'

'You do know your parents expect to meet her tonight?' asked Spectra looking directly into his face. His big searching eyes made Kohl feel queasy. It was like he was trying to see directly into Kohl's brain, a visual lie detector test of sorts.

'I guess so. None of my concern really. Now if you'll kindly buzz off – I believe you and the other hired help are supposed to be conducting a ceremony?'

'Mind your mouth you trumped-up brat or I'll have you down on the floor with my foot at your throat, ball or no ball,' spat Spectra before disappearing back into the crowd.

+ + +

Sam was enjoying his new role a little too much. He almost missed the masked stranger approaching them and was about to twirl Harper through a third dance when he felt a tap on his shoulder.

'May I?' asked a tall gentleman in a black, half-faced feather mask. It was a poor disguise.

'Kohl,' grunted Sam.

Another moment ruined by a Pallas.

'Move over, sport. Let the lady enjoy a dance with a real man,' said Kohl smiling wide. Before Sam had even fully registered what had happened, Harper was ripped from his arms and twirled half a dance floor away.

'I assume that was Kohl Pallas? Never met him in the flesh before. Thanks for finding him.' Aggy had approached from behind with Lawrence.

'Yes, that'd be the one. Excuse me, I think I need to take up drinking,' said Sam, before he stormed off through the crowd.

+ + +

Glare stood on a mostly deserted, dimly-lit balcony, which gave her an excellent yet discrete view of the dance floor below, when something flashed in her peripheral vision.

'Yes, Master? I assume that little flashing rectangle is your incoming call?' Glare asked.

'Yes of course,' said the Master in his typically abrupt manner. 'How's the implant going, Glare? Tried out all the hypermodes yet? I didn't give it to you so that we could have late-night chats you know. I had to call in Brizzie's second-best surgeon to get you that implant. Now start using it.'

'Yes, Sir. In fact, I am about to use hyperspeed now. I think I have spotted some Damarans amongst the guests. I suspect they are going to try to round up the manifestations here tonight. I certainly would, if I was in charge of their operation.'

'What are you waiting for? Get your arse down there and make it happen. The sooner you get me out, the sooner I can – I mean we all can – leave this wretched rock.'

'Right, Glare out.'

+ + +

'It's official, all five manifestations are now in the room. Time to enact the plan. One last chance to back out. Are you sure about this?' Lawrence asked Aggy.

They had resumed dancing as a cover for their close conversation. Lawrence talked directly into her ear as he moved to keep in close proximity with Kohl and Harper.

'Definitely. We need to end the war, even if it takes a few sacrifices.'

Lawrence couldn't see her face but he imagined from the sound of her voice that it looked a little sad.

'It's time. Hyper up, Lawrence.'

Lawrence activated full hypermode and watched the world

grind to a halt as his personal time sped up. Aggy, also in hyper, winked and stepped back to rip off her costume. Underneath she wore a traditional Damaran-style soldier's garb.

'Have you had any further contact from Illustria?' asked Lawrence.

'No, just that one yesterday. It was strange actually. Can't put my finger on it, she sounded different, more demanding than usual. She said that it was time to "get my butt down here with the manifestations" and to ignore the previous prohibition on hypers.'

'Preoccupied with the war?' Offered Lawrence, silently agreeing that it was a strange expression for their old friend.

'I don't know, my gut tells me there's more going on. The sooner we get down there the better.'

+   +   +

'Sorry for interrupting your dance with "twinkle toes". You looked so divine, I couldn't help myself, had to get you into my arms again. Where have you been these last few days? I've missed you.' Kohl pulled Harper closer as they moved across the floor.

Harper had to actively remind herself of the mission. It would have been easy to get lost in the moment. Kohl was so much lighter on his feet than Sam and he smelled heavenly. She pushed at his shoulders to get a little distance between them.

'Firstly, you need to ease up on Sam. If you got to know him, you'd realise he doesn't deserve your constant disrespect.

'Second, I've been in the darklands with the Damarans. I'll tell you more, but not here and not now. Can we go somewhere private? And can you make it quick, time is an issue.'

Harper looked around nervously, tempted to go into hyperspeed again to better observe what was happening.

Kohl stopped dancing and looked at her seriously, and Harper was disappointed to see another sudden switch in Kohl's moods. She crossed her arms and waited until it started to get awkward. She would have left him on the dance floor had he not been vital to her mission.

'Bit quiet for a Pallas about to be crowned "World's Most Eligible Bachelor", aren't you? Or is that exactly why you are quiet, pre-occupied with your search for the next consort? I hear your father has several.' She hoped the last remark stung.

'Drop it, alright? We both said things we regret; can't we just move on?'

'Fair enough, I guess. How about that private chat now?'

'I'd love to take you somewhere private, you know that, but the big event is about to start. I need to be visible right now.'

'Pity your implant isn't active or we could zip out and return before anyone noticed.'

'Let's just get through the inauguration and then we'll have plenty of time to talk. Will you come back to The Lodge with me tonight?' Kohl sounded hopeful.

'No, Kohl, because—'

'Please, Harper. I promise to be a gentleman. Mother likes you; she won't have a problem if you preferred to use a guest room.'

'Kohl—'

'Albert's staying with me as well. I can assign him to protect your virtue.'

Harper was getting tired of him not listening to her objections. 'Kohl!' She snapped loudly enough for others around her to look over at the brewing commotion.

'What then?' Kohl said in a hushed tone as he took her by the elbow and moved her to the side of the room. Harper found herself suddenly distracted by the tell-tale buzzing of hyperspeak voices around her.

She briefly dialled up into hyperspeed, and was pleased to see Lawrence and Aggy already changed.

'I heard you buzzing. Is this it? Is the plan a go, Aggy?'

'Yes, you take Kohl, we'll get Spectra and Sam. Meet you back at the safe house. Good luck.'

She paused for a moment to look at the frozen Kohl and steel herself for the mission ahead before dialling back down to real time.

Kohl flinched and the music soared.

'Did you just make a hyper jump?' he asked, leaning in close to whisper. Harper was aware that the crowd was still looking at her with curiosity. They had probably never seen a woman reject a governor's son before. She had to act fast.

Harper kissed Kohl on the lips, a move that surprised and pleased him until she moved her lips to his ear. 'You are not listening. I'm not coming with you after the inauguration because there isn't going to *be* an inauguration.'

Kohl pulled back, shocked.

'What have you done? Not like Sydney?' he said. Then, before she could respond, he added, 'I have to find—'

Too late. A cacophony of sound erupted in the Town Hall. Harper grabbed him by the wrist and hyper jumped with him to the safe house.

CHAPTER 53

Damaran Safe House

'—GLARE!' SCREAMED KOHL as they materialized in a dilapidated old apartment. Harper rubbed her ear and surveyed their surrounds. Spectra's slumped form occupied a corner of the room. JayMoe and Lawrence were arguing over how best to secure the temporarily unconscious menace.

Outside she could hear voices screaming and the rapid patter of panicked feet racing through the streets. Kohl's voice cut through the noise of the uprising.

'What have you done? Are you attacking another city?' Without waiting for an answer, Kohl turned his back and stormed over to Spectra.

'Kohl?' Harper was having trouble getting his attention.

'It'll be Sydney all over again. You can't do this. We don't deserve this!' Kohl uttered. 'If I lose her again I don't know what I'll do.'

Harper knew Kohl wouldn't be happy about the uprising, yet she hadn't expected him to be quite so distressed. After the carnage they had witnessed together, she had assumed he would be firmly on the Damarans' side.

She reached out an arm to stop him from pacing. 'Calm down Kohl, I haven't done anything to anyone. This is not as bad as you think!'

She tried to make him face her but he pulled away. As she turned to plead for assistance from Aggy, she caught a glimpse out the window. For an instant she thought she had seen a familiar face, but when she looked closer it was gone.

+ + +

Glare followed Charles' instructions and activated hyperspeed. The world appeared to freeze even though she understood, intellectually at least, that it hadn't. Still, the shock of it was unnerving.

She walked over to the only other two people on the balcony. Until now she had ignored the couple who had been canoodling in a dark corner. Now that she observed them closely, she realised the woman looked dreadfully unhappy, presumably because the man was slipping an unwanted hand into her blouse whilst restraining her by holding her gloved hand tightly behind her back.

Glare repositioned the lady's free hand. She folded the fingers into a fist and pushed it deep into his cheek. Then she lodged the woman's knee firmly into his crutch. She smiled, imagining the surprise he would receive once these actions were sped up into real time.

Happy with her minor victory, she peered over the balustrade. Harper and Kohl had disappeared.

'Shit!'

She dropped out of hyperspeed and, ignoring the yelp from the man behind her, opened communications to Charles.

'They're gone. Did you track the jump?' Glare demanded.

'Not going to comment on the fact that you lost them in less than two seconds! Fortunately one of us is on the ball. I can't track jumps that small with much precision but I can tell you that it wasn't far. Two hundred metres tops. Find them, now!'

Glare dashed downstairs, just in time to witness the overwhelming arrival of the first wave of Rats who burst through the main doors with audacity. She heard a loud crash to the side and turned to see more Rats surging through the windows, while others were hurdling over balconies.

Very quickly there were hundreds of them rioting through the room, black eyes blazing with disdain for the largely blue-eyed establishment.

One of the Rats leapt atop the refreshment table, which he cleared with an efficient swing of his boot. Despite the discordant sound of crying victims and raging aggressors, his orders were obeyed.

Soon the assaulting rabble became an assembly of managers sorting through the crowd. They removed the masks of the stunned Solarans, isolated anyone who looked powerful enough to be a threat and found seats for the elderly to ensure they were kept safe.

At first the Solarans were lost in the trauma of the assault. They held onto each other like petrified librarians with tigers loose in the stacks. Ladies fainted into the arms of men who could do nothing aside from back up against each other. The Governor was nowhere to be seen. Glare grimaced darkly at their cowardice.

'Not again!' came a deep, guttural cry.

One of the Rats fell forward with a startled look on his face. A silver blade protruded from a red smudge spreading across his chest. Behind him stood his assailant – Lady Pallas.

Glare stopped to watch her mother in admiration. Lady

Pallas pushed her hair back, pulled the small sword from the Rat and made direct eye contact with her guests, as if daring them to join her.

'Well?' she yelled.

Governor Pallas appeared beside her and pulled them both up onto a nearby table. He pointed across to the Rats' leader, who was the only other person raised on a table, and bellowed, 'Kill the stinking vermin!'

The Lady responded with a totally unfeminine war cry and together the two of them began to dispatch any Rat within striking distance. The brutality of their actions seemed to break the Solarans' spell. One by one they followed their leader's example and attacked their captors. The room quickly looked like a pub brawl.

Glare remembered her implant and transitioned to hyperspeed before she could be caught in the middle of the warring parties.

She remained in hyper as she hurried through the streets searching for the Rats' base of operations; looking for the type of safehouse she would choose – large and innocuous with good windows for surveillance.

She loved the freedom of the implant that allowed her to move amongst the combatants with impunity avoiding any further delays – everywhere people seemed to have lost their minds. Arms were frozen in the follow-through of punches. Staticwhips were arcing scalding power to the backs of unsuspecting victims. Fireworks were being sparked to life.

Then she smelled the first sizzle of a house being set alight. Her heart sank when she thought of the fear the people must be experiencing in real time.

In the midst of the chaos she saw Chief Constable Albert sitting as still as a statue in the front of a cart while two Rats worked in hyper. She ducked down behind a row of burly enforcers and watched.

Unlike Glare they weren't doing reconnaissance. They appeared to be ransacking houses. The Rats took turns entering properties and returning with big parcels, which they placed gently onto the tray of the cart. Hypermode theft would be an easy way to finance Rat operations.

When the larger of the two Rats disappeared into the next house, she inched closer to get a better view, careful not to reveal her presence to the smaller remaining Rat. She didn't have time for an altercation if she was going to locate Kohl.

When the big Rat came out of the house with a particularly large bundle, she heard him say, 'I could use a hand General Mitta, we've got three more upstairs.'

'Sure Sam, Albert should be fine. No sign of hypermodes around here. Glad to have him back actually. He'll put …' the other said, his voice trailing off as they re-entered the house. She crept up to the cart. What she saw in the bundles made no sense.

Albert, what are you doing here with kids in blankets? Where's the art, the jewels – are they holding them for ransom? She felt around the bundles. There was nothing else of value in the cart, only children and a few toys being clenched by petrified little hands.

The voices of the two returning Rats shocked her into action. She quickly lay on the ground a short distance away pretending to be frozen like the others.

'The last three are in. Drive carefully,' said one of the Rats, 'make sure they know they're coming back to their parents once this is all over. Keep them safe. Take care of Albert too. It takes a lot for a man of his rank to support our cause.'

Glare realised the awful truth. She had assumed the worst but they were actually taking the children away for their own protection. It was a noble and un-Rat like act. Her roiling stomach questioned whether she was on the right side.

The two men then stopped and the bigger one touched the side of his face. He appeared to be listening to something, instructions via implant perhaps, before he shook hands with the smaller man and ran off in the direction of an old stone apartment complex down the road. Glare followed.

The building was not attracting much fighting, making her feel safe enough to drop out of hyper. She puffed from the exertion and struggled to pull herself up to peer through the window. There she saw a surprised Kohl looking right at her as he spoke to the Rat leader, whom Glare immediately recognised from the rally. She also recognised Harper.

Glare gave Kohl a hand signal that she hoped he would interpret as "all good, keep undercover and go with them," before dropping back onto the ground in an exhausted heap. The Master had warned her to keep hyper for short bursts, but she had not expected it be so physically draining.

✦ ✦ ✦

Aggy walked forward to Kohl, her hand outstretched. He wasn't sure how to respond.

'Hello. We haven't officially met; although you might recognise me from the rally. You know, the one in the town centre a few days ago? I was your father's "special guest". He calls me a Rat, my people call me Alpha, and to my friends it's just Aggy. I hope one day you'll be able to call me Aggy, too.'

She had caught his attention. Kohl *did* recognise her. Although she might have been in clean clothes, her injuries were unmistakeable. She had fresh scarring on her face, a bruised eye that was turning dark yellow and she walked stiffly, as though she had injured one of her legs.

Her demeanour and quiet manner spoke volumes about

the type of leadership Damarans preferred. Aggy was a woman who had been physically broken by his next of kin, yet she still talked to him with civility.

Kohl instantly felt ashamed. He was unsure of the right response until he looked towards the windows and saw the sign he needed. The answer came to him and his attitude softened. He took her hand respectfully.

'I *am* Kohl Pallas and I *do* remember you from the steps. I was in the crowd with Harper, although I guess you know that already. I'm so sorry for whatever they did to you and for my outburst just now. You need to understand, I knew nothing of this operation and it was all a bit of a shock.'

'That's understandable, you've had quite a journey since your birthday, haven't you? It must be very confronting finding out the whole dirty truth.'

'You were there at my birthday?' Kohl realised he still didn't have a full understanding of what happened that night or why.

'Yes, a most regrettable evening. What started as a small protest action escalated completely out of control.' Aggy gazed sadly into the distance as though picturing the destruction.

'I understand your hatred of Solarans but why did you destroy Sydney? I lost so much that night. What did it achieve? I thought the Damarans were peaceful people,' he said, fighting to maintain control of himself. He was determined to match Aggy's grace, despite the flood of bitter memories.

'I lost my best friend too,' said Harper quietly in the background.

'You must believe that it wasn't all us. There were only fifty Damaran operatives in Sydney that night. It's not possible for us to have caused damage on such a profound scale.

'Truthfully we only set a few small explosives. You might ask the Master about the rest. You might ask Spectra about the knife attacks, too. Hand to hand combat took out a number of our best people.'

'And my brother, Mark,' said Kohl, rubbing his eyes.

'And Sister Pat,' added Harper.

'You have my condolences.' Aggy reached out to squeeze his shoulder.

'Thank you, but what about all this?' Kohl pointed at the windows that were flashing as they refracted the light of weapons discharge.

'Ah, our little diversion,' Aggy said with a smile. 'Harper's right. It's not as bad as it sounds. My people needed to let off some steam, and given that they can't return to their own homes as they were destroyed by Solaran enforcers, I allowed them to come into the city to look for new accommodations. Don't worry, they will not deliberately cause any loss of life.'

'What about the explosions?' Kohl worried that Aggy was underplaying the conflict. As rational as the Damaran leader sounded, there was serious combat happening right outside.

'Just a little pyrotechnics my generals organised to keep the enforcers busy while we get on with the main mission.'

'Which is?'

'Why, visiting the Light, of course.' Aggy replied, suddenly cheerful.

Sam came skidding into the room.

'About time, where have you been?' asked Harper under her breath.

Aggy nodded to the late, fifth manifestation then said, 'right, we're all here now. Ready to go fellas?'

She limped across the floor to the old-fashioned dark brown, refreshment bar at the back of the room.

'Well, I'm not looking for a drink. Can someone help me with this, please?' Aggy asked and immediately everyone, except Kohl, rushed to her aid, pushing aside the furniture.

Kohl walked forward to examine the floor where the bar had been. He was bemused to see nothing aside from the expected scratched nanocrete floor.

'Well, that was an anticlimax,' Kohl said looking directly at Harper who rolled her eyes and turned to Sam.

'Can you do the honours, my friend?' she asked.

Sam reached inside his shirt and pulled out the golden key he had used many times in the tunnels, and waved the tube over the surface with a grand flourish. Nothing happened. Kohl snorted and crossed his arms. Sam looked up at Harper and shrugged as if embarrassed by its lack of form.

'Try rolling it over the surface. A little physical contact might help,' offered Harper.

Sam did as suggested and immediately the floor started vibrating. Kohl rubbed his eyes with the heels of his hands. A circle had formed with a small hole at the centre and a code that matched the letters on the golden tube -*55.58, 148.97TL.*

Kohl pushed forward to get a closer look.

'Yes!' Sam slipped the end of the tubular key into the hole. After a small mechanical *click*, a hatch appeared and opened to reveal a tunnel with a sloping spiral entrance.

'Ladies first, Harper?' asked Aggy, preparing to descend. Despite having the apparently unconscious Spectra lashed to his back, JayMoe whizzed forward to Aggy's side and extended his arm to bar her way.

'No, my Alpha. I should go first to light the way.' Without waiting for her response, he took Spectra sliding down into the dark tunnel.

453

CHAPTER 54
The Arc

HARPER WAS RELUCTANT to be the last to take the plunge down the tunnel. Although she was sure that General Mitta would soon arrive to keep watch over the hatch as planned, she felt vulnerable while the hatch was open and unattended.

She thought she heard his footsteps outside the room.

'What's keeping you? We're ready to go.' Harper walked towards the door as she spoke and peered out into the empty hallway beyond. She looked back towards the hatch and then forward to the external door, unsure which way to go.

'General?'

'I'm here, just get going ... I'll be inside ... soon,' came a stilted voice from the street outside.

'You okay?' yelled Harper. His voice sounded a little stiffer than usual.

'Sure ... doing somethin' ... um, urgent. Just get goin'.'

For a fleeting second Harper considered going outside to investigate, then scolding herself for being paranoid, she ran back to the hatch.

'Alright, see you soon!' she called out as she disappeared down the tube.

+ + +

'That was a close call. Looks like Harper bought it though.'

Glare hunched down on the footpath outside the safe house window, her weapon trained on General Mitta. The two enforcers she had commandeered were restraining him from both sides.

'Don't even think about activating your hyper, I've got the implant too so it will do you no good,' she said.

Glare looked around at the ongoing battle. The Rats clearly had superior combat skills but the Solarans weren't giving in. They fought with desperation to save their city. It was an even match with no clear winner.

An explosion further down the road buffeted them. Knowing she didn't have time to check if the jail was still functional, she took the simplest option and punched Mitta in the side of his head, knocking him out cold. When he hit the ground she restrained him with some fibrous refuse she found by the side of the building.

'Stay here and watch over him. No one enters or leaves this building without my authority. Restrain anyone who does. If any enforcers come by, they are to join you in securing the building. This is a priority one mission. Not even the Governor's direct orders will supplant my own, do you understand?'

'Yes ma'am!' they replied in unison.

'Right, don't let me down!' Glare unholstered her weapon and entered the safe house.

+ + +

The tunnel experience was disturbing, at best. Harper had expected it to be a short fall down to a nanocrete floor. Instead she experienced the sickening feel of an airless hyperjump for several long seconds. When her feet finally hit solid ground, her knees buckled and she collapsed to the floor, coughing violently.

'It's alright Harper, just breathe kid,' said a kind, raspy voice from behind her. She felt a strong hand rubbing her back and was reassured to see Lawrence's calming face, even though he too was pale and coughing.

He managed a weak smile, 'Nice deep breaths through the nose. That's it. We all felt lousy when we first arrived but it wears off quickly.'

'What *was* that?' Harper asked between gasps.

'An Arc, I think. Illustria told me about it once; it's a kind of very long hyper jump. I've never had the misfortune to try it before. Man, it packs a punch doesn't—' His sentence was cut short as he coughed again. Someone to her side was sneezing continually. On the other side came the sound of retching.

As Lawrence was speaking, the intensity of the light around them increased significantly. Harper still had her chest and hands pressed flat to the white floor as it started glowing beneath her. She knew without trying that she wasn't capable of standing, so she raised her head just a little to take stock of her surroundings.

The five manifestations and Lawrence had all landed in a small cube shaped room about five by five strides. All the walls were white, incredibly smooth and glowed from within, like the floor.

'An Arc?' Harper's voice sounded more like a growl, which she resolved with another hacking cough.

'Yes, an Arc,' said an upbeat female voice she didn't recognise.

Harper found she was able to push herself into a semi-seated position to find the owner of the new voice. A tall young woman, dressed entirely in yellow, had appeared amongst them. She had stunning eyes and a complexion that shone from within.

'The science is complex, it utilises elastic numbers, sub micro singularities and high order photonic frequencies. You might like to visualise it as slicing through an apple to get to the core faster. Only it's not an apple but a rather small worldlet. And it's not a core but rather my home. Welcome to Honeysuckle Creek,' she said in a cheery tone.

'Illustria, at last!' said Aggy struggling to stand. 'We have been so worried about you and so much has happened to our people since we lost contact.'

The glowing woman put out her hand to stop Aggy in her tracks.

'I'm sorry, Aggy, I'm only part of Illustria. One small, very old part. I'm just a sub-routine designed long ago to welcome you and address your recovery needs. You could probably think of me as a doorbell who knows how to make good caff and hold a semi-decent conversation.

'Maybe you could call me little-Illustria or Illustri-bell. Yes, I think I like that. Call me Bell for short. Now would anyone like a refreshment? Or I could increase the oxygen flow to improve your recovery.' Bell clasped her hands in a prayer-like pose and smiled benevolently.

Harper was still considering how to respond to an intelligent, woman-shaped doorbell, when she heard a wail through the walls, followed by a crashing noise.

'Aggy come quickly … help me!'

'That's the real Illustria calling out, I know it is. Bell, she needs us. How do we get to her? And while you are at it, why can't I shift up into hyper?' Aggy asked urgently.

'Hyper will be a problem for a short while. In order to

transfer such a long distance, your drives were temporarily depleted.

'As for moving out of here, the answer is simple. Have the five manifestations simultaneously touch the walls with their golden tokens in hand. The gold will trigger the nanos to perform a DNA imprint analysis. Once your identity is verified, the way to the Light will permanently open.' Bell replied calmly.

Harper instantly forgot her post-jump malaise and reached out for a wall as did Sam and Aggy.

'You too, Kohl. I'll get sleeping beauty,' Lawrence said, indicating Spectra. Harper was astonished that he could have slept through the whole jump. She watched as Lawrence untied his wrists, placed the golden communicator in his hand and lifted his arm to palm the wall.

Harper turned to Kohl. When he didn't make a move she cleared her throat, expectantly. For a moment she thought he might put up an argument but instead, he raked his hand through his hair and joined them in making contact with the wall.

Their cell evaporated immediately.

Harper looked around their new environment. They were standing on an orange shag pile carpet, in front of Bell's twin who was reclining on a couch. Unlike Bell, her eyes were semi-closed and her breathing was laboured. Harper found it strange to see a computer simulation struggle to catch its simulated breath.

'Illustria!' said Aggy, running to her side.

'Hello!' said a voice from across the room. All heads turned.

Behind a shimmering transparent wall stood a man with a surprisingly sparse hairline for a person who, in all other regards, appeared to be in his early thirties. His faded leisure suit with a racehorse motif and golden cravat was vaguely comical, but he pulled the look off with a stance that spoke volumes about confidence.

Pallas! Harper thought.

'Do you like my threads? I hope it's suitable. I'm not sure of current trends in men's fashion attire. Haven't had guests for hundreds of years you see. Anyway, I designed this to be especially suitable for the occasion; look it comes complete with my own golden token.' The man waved the end of his cravat to exemplify.

Harper and the rest of her party remained silent.

'Well, that is what you need to get into this party, isn't it?' he asked in a voice that slowly raised in volume and shrillness.

'Nothing to say? Am I not fashionable enough for Rats? Darn, that's right. Where are my manners? How strange that I've tried to kill you all at least once, yet we've never been formally introduced.

'I'm Charles Drexus; Aussie rogue trader and inventor. The Master of my own little world. The original pariah of the fucking universe!' Charles clicked his heels and saluted military style.

'How about you? Let me guess – Larry-loser, androgynous Aggy, Harper, Kohl, Sam and the limp slimy one over there – well how interesting that my own Spectra would be the fifth. Yes, should have bloody seen that in hindsight. Guess no one is perfect, right?'

Still no one spoke. Charles paused with one eyebrow raised, like the teacher at the front grilling his students.

'WRONG! I am perfect! Now Kohl, do be a good great-great-grandson, many times removed and get me out of here so that we can get off this godawful rock!'

With a solemn, almost apologetic look to Harper, Kohl took a large step towards the shimmering field that bisected the room. He reached up with his golden plane as if to make contact with it.

'No!' said Illustria in a voice so weak that Harper feared it might be her last word.

CHAPTER 55

Honeysuckle Creek

HARPER HEARD SAM grunt and turned in time to witness him throw his whole weight into a tackle against the unexpecting Kohl.

'No way, not again!' He growled as he applied a surprisingly forceful assault that left Kohl sprawled on the carpet. 'Ya not gunna win this time. Ya'll stay here for the duration of the operation or so help me I will knock ya block off, just like I did to Spectra over there.'

'You did that? Nice work. Growing some muscle at last Sammy?' Kohl said in a patronising tone. Sam raised his fist in response. Harper wasn't sure whether to intervene.

'Whoa, wait up little buddy. I wasn't going to do anything aside from test that strange looking light that runs through the room,' Kohl said in a voice that made Harper wince. She knew it was insincere.

What is he up to now?

'For a start I am not now, nor will I ever be, yer "buddy". I'm also no longer little. Now I said stay down and shut up!'

said Sam.

'Wait. You assume the worst but where's your evidence? I was doing nothing wrong. I just wanted to know what we are dealing with here. I'm on board, believe me. A bona fide manifestation, remember? Ask Harper.'

Sam stood over the young Pallas for a moment as if considering his options when, with a slight nod of his head, he allowed him to move.

'Don't get any ideas,' Harper said to Kohl under her breath.

'You don't need to test it, I can tell you all about it,' wheezed Illustria. 'It's an electronic wall that has successfully kept Charles confined for centuries. You are safe on this side for now, but only for now. It's too late. He has corrupted too many of my files. I do not know how long I can maintain the wall. If he digs any further into my codes, he might find one that releases it.'

She slid lower on the lounger and shuddered a little.

'Illustria!' Harper reached out to touch her shoulder. For a fraction of a second Harper thought she saw the shimmering field dim a little.

Charles chuckled and rubbed his hands together, 'not long now, you aggrandised calculator!'

'Lawrence you must be able to do something. We can't let it end like this!' Aggy said beckoning him to Illustria's side.

'End like what? Don't you understand? It was never meant to *be* this way. You were supposed to be living your lives on the surface, blissfully ignorant of me down here. And, I was supposed to be supported by my loyal artificial intelligence. Happily stimulated with my social experiments. Then "it" became a "she" and the rest, as they say, is history. It's all *her* fault!' Charles hollered from across the room and pointed an accusing finger at Illustria.

Kohl raised his eyebrows conspiratorially to Harper. Repulsed that he might be taken in by Charles' story, she physically recoiled from him and concentrated on Illustria.

'Rubbish. JayMoe, can you link with Illustria?' asked Harper.

'I can try I guess, although I'm not sure how to make an interface when she takes this form.'

'Lawrence?' asked Harper.

'It should work the same way as the manifestations. She should be able to interface with your implant through physical touch. Come over here JayMoe.'

Lawrence knelt by her side, lifted Illustria's hand and placed it on the droid's casing in the approximate location of his implant. After barely two seconds of contact, JayMoe broke away and lurched violently on one wheel.

'What happened?' asked Harper, reaching out to stabilise the droid.

'Forty-two percent of her files are either corrupted, co-opted or missing entirely. I'm surprised she is still functional. I transferred one of my soldier subroutines into her. It will help shore her up, however the best option would be to help her make contact with the five. That's what we came for. That's what we should do before it's too late,' said JayMoe.

'Right, you first Kohl,' said Lawrence.

'Me? You sure I should be first? We don't even know if it will work, especially after JayMoe disabled me back in the tunnel.' Kohl looked skittish.

'Perfect time to test you then, isn't it? Come on, front and centre young man.' Lawrence patted a spot on the floor next to Illustria. Kohl looked uncertain. Harper was surprised when he conceded to the request, she had thought he might try to talk his way out of it.

Kohl sat down on the carpet and Lawrence placed

Illustria's hand on his temple.

'Just let me know when … whoa, that's hot!' Kohl leapt up. Sweat beaded on his brow and a deep crimson flush shot up his neck to his unbearded cheeks.

'The transfer is complete. Amalgamating data. Apologies for the inconvenient sensation,' said Illustria.

'Inconvenient sensation? That's an understatement,' said Kohl rubbing his scalp.

'Did it help?' Harper asked, looking seriously at their weakened friend, ignoring Kohl's complaints.

'Yes, I think it did,' said Illustria. She briefly sounded stronger, then her tone flattened.

'Are you sure we should be doing this? After all, the Civies have been manipulating everyone for years, couldn't this just be one of their schemes? If you make me stronger I will have no choice but to support them and who is that going to help, really?

'Solarans might have their questionable customs but at least they have worked hard to create a stable society. They don't sit around waiting for handouts like the Brothers and cavern communities. They should be entitled to enjoy the rewards of their leadership.'

'Oh yes, it's working, me next!' Aggy said laughing gently. She sat cross-legged on the floor in front of Illustria.

'Are you sure, Aggy? You could be playing right into the Master's grand plan. Maybe this was the way he wanted all along … maybe—'

Aggy silenced the Kohl-inspired conspiracy theories by reaching out and placing Illustria's hand on her own head. Immediately Aggy lay down on the floor without speaking.

Illustria jumped off the couch and rushed out of the room. When Lawrence moved to her side, Aggy waved him away, massaging her temples and closing her eyes.

'Follow her, quickly,' she whispered.

'Harper, you come with me. Sam, stay with them.' Lawrence pointed to Kohl and Aggy who were both convalescing on the floor.

When they arrived in the next room Harper was startled to see Illustria climbing into a device that looked like a garbage receptacle. All around her, the floor was littered with engineering components that Illustria must have pushed off the bench in her haste to climb up.

'Stop!' she ran to grab a hold of her shoulders but Illustria fought off her grasp. Lawrence joined her in trying to pull Illustria back to the floor. She was surprisingly strong.

'What are you doing?' Harper asked, as she tugged on Illustria's arm.

'Don't stop me. I cannot save my people looking like a teenage fantasy! How can I help all our people when I have limited my existence to only this over-sexualised variation, which may appear weak, even offensive to some?

'I must recycle this form and make myself into something stronger. I *must* look the part of a true leader.' Illustria struggled against their restraint. Sam, who must have heard the commotion, burst into the room.

'Kohl's still out cold. Thought ya could use another pair a hands,' he said.

'Quickly Sam, she needs the balance of another manifestation. We'll hold her while you get uploaded,' said Harper, battling to control the unnaturally strong Illustria. Sam crossed the floor with his hands outstretched.

'You're wasting time. If General Abudua was here she would not allow this. General JayMoe!' Illustria screamed out to the other room.

'General Abudua would know that strength comes in many forms,' yelled Harper in frustration.

'General, help me! I must recycle—' she fell silent as soon as Sam made the connection. Two seconds later they both melted to the floor, Sam holding his face and Illustria clutching her foot.

'Sweet decimal code, is this what pain feels like? I had no idea. I am so sorry that I left you disabled as a child. I wanted you to learn disadvantage. I had no idea the price. That transfer must have hurt your head too. And I bet you miss your mum at a time like this.'

Illustria began crying halfway through her apology. She wrapped her arms gently around Sam and rocked him. Harper could see his body softened in her embrace.

'Oh, the others will be in pain too! They need me.' Illustria abruptly released Sam and limped towards the main room.

Harper followed closely. When she got to the main room she was moved, and not at all surprised, to see Sam's gentle influence had integrated into Illustria. She was sitting on the floor hugging Kohl while she stroked Aggy's hand.

'You've all been through such awful pain. I'm so sorry. I will do better next time, I promise.' Then she cocked her head to the side and looked through the forcefield. 'What about you Charles, you have fared the worst of all, haven't you?'

'Huh?' said Charles.

'No man should be jailed for eternity, no matter what the crime,' she said.

'Oh, oh yes that's right. Poor me. Such a horrible life, boo-hoo-hoo, you'd better get me out or I might cry too,' said Charles pretending to rub tears from his eyes.

Before he could say any more, Aggy latched onto Illustria's ankle. The unexpected move combined with her newly acquired limp, caused her to flail.

'Quick Harper, you're next. Transfer before she tries to free Charles!' Aggy yelled.

It was too late. In less than the blink of an eye the forcefield was gone, startling them all – including Charles who didn't even respond at first. He stood statue-still in his stocking feet, gaping at his unexpected release.

Harper, seeing the desperation of the moment, cycled herself up into hyper and ducked under Illustria's hand.

Illustria turned to study Harper in the midst of the frozen scene.

'Smart move realising I was using hyper. Tell me though Harper, aren't all beings entitled to be free?'

Harper felt her transfer kick in. She was gratified to see Illustria's eyes widen as she integrated Harper's strategic mind. She must have appreciated the gravity of her tactical error, as the forcefield snapped back on as quickly as it had been removed. They both dropped out of hyper and collapsed onto the floor.

Charles roared at his re-imprisonment. He picked up his computer keyboard and threw it into the forcefield. When it sheered in two, he picked up the pieces and threw them into the field as well, screaming obscenities all the while.

Charles went on to hurl all his other desk items. He screamed louder with each act of destruction until he ran out of projectiles. He rushed around like a man possessed, lifted his desk above his head and pitched it at the wall. The desk disintegrated, creating a plume of burning wood fragments and smoke on his side of the lounge.

Breathing heavily, he turned to Illustria's side of the room. He fixed his gaze on the manifestations while he paced back and forth like a caged animal.

'You people are so *stupid*! You cannot perceive anything outside of your pathetic little existences, can you? You are like mice riding a treadmill, thinking you are going somewhere. Does none of you see how clichéd this whole process is? Kohl gives her arrogance, Aggy selflessness, Sam compassion, oh and I bet Harper will have a plan, right? Still, where will all that get you? Nowhere!

'We are all still stuck on this pathetic insignificant rock, with insufficient resources at the whim of a deranged computer. SHE IS A COMPUTER, PEOPLE! Don't you fucking get that?

'You can't give her human qualities because *she is not a human*, just a very convincing facsimile. She will never be able to save you and she will never get you off this pissant rock!'

He trod a small lap around the space that had been his study area, before returning to the forcefield. When he resumed his speech, he seemed to have regained some self-control. Harper couldn't help but wonder if a calm Charles might ultimately prove to be more dangerous.

'What none of you seem to comprehend, is that it doesn't matter how you fix her, she is incapable of the independent thought you need. She is only the sum of her coding. Coding that I created, that's why she can never win against me.

'Plus, even if she could by some remote serendipitous clash of algorithms, come up with a unique strategy and win this war, you still don't win. You are still stuck here.

'Try this for thought. How do you know staying here is the best option? You have no idea of the potential opportunities off this world. There are thousands of communities out there on other planets, moons and satellites, all desperate for an injection of fresh young genes.

'Don't you want to have more? Can't you imagine leaving this world for a better life? You don't even have cars here for fuck's sake. It's all so primitive!

'Look, I have a way off. There is a starship orbiting right now. If you get me out of here, I will take you with me. It's the best offer you are going to get. Period.'

The room was silent. Charles stood with his hands on his hips looking incredulous.

'Well, doesn't anyone want to reach for something better than this? None of you?' he bellowed.

'I do,' came a small, unexpected voice from the back of the room. Harper turned to see a young woman with a lightkey in one hand and a staticwhip in the other. Harper stared; the woman looked at her and shrugged weakly in response.

'Long time, Harper,' she said meekly.

'Glare, at last someone with some balls!' Charles replied, grinning.

'Bess? You're *Glare*?' said Harper with growing comprehension.

'Bess Pallas, actually. My sister,' Kohl added.

'Forgive me, Harper,' Glare said as she threw her weapon to Kohl, who activated it and moved rapidly towards the centre of the room.

Harper couldn't take her eyes off the apparent resurrection of her late friend. She didn't see Kohl strike the forcefield, destroying Charles Drexus' jail. She never realised the Master was free. She only knew that her world had turned upside down. Again.

Her best friend was alive, Kohl's sister, and a traitor.

CHAPTER 56
Honeysuckle Creek

HARPER'S SHOCK WAS broken by the noise of hands clapping in a slow rhythm from the other side of the room. Spectra was awake, standing and wearing a wide grin.

'Bravo, bravo people! Best entertainment I've seen in years.'

'I liked it better when you were unconscious,' said Harper in a flat tone.

'No, not unconscious – just enjoying the show from a reclining position. Now let's recap, what did we see here? Ah, yes, a criminally insane trillionaire scientist, a rogue Ai that thinks she's more humane than the humans – talk about multiple personality disorders – what else? Right, political intrigue and the betrayed lover.

'This show really has something for everyone. Add a music score and you'd have 'em queuing up for tickets. Bravo!' said Spectra, enjoying himself too much for Harper's tastes.

'You forgot the twist of the innocent sister, apparently killed in a heartless act of terrorism who turns out to be alive, heir to the Pallas fortune, and personal assistant to a murdering monster,' Harper said bitterly, returning her stare to Bess.

'Harper, I'm sorry. I couldn't tell you—' Kohl looked genuinely remorseful as he tried to explain.

'Shut it Kohl, you're no better than your sister. How could you free him? You've condemned us. After all we've been through. All you have seen,' said Harper.

'This reunion sounds like fun, unfortunately I have somewhere to be,' interrupted Charles. He crossed the lounge, affecting a little dance as he moved.

'Haven't done that in a while. My Lord, it's good to be free! Now, as much as I should kill you all, I really haven't got time and honestly I can't be stuffed. Give me that, boy.'

Charles took the weapon from Kohl's hand as he danced by. He slapped Kohl lightly on the cheek.

'Whilst I do appreciate your role in my rescue, I'm not entirely convinced that you have the guts of a henchman yet. Better leave the dirty work to your big sister hey? Keep an eye on 'em Glare, or is that Bess now?'

Charles shrugged, then threw the staticwhip to Glare. He opened a cupboard on what had been his side of the forcefield and pulled out a bulky man-sized bag. Despite its two big carry straps, it appeared to be difficult to manage. He whistled to JayMoe.

'Mate lend us a hand, will you?' Charles' tone made it clear to all that it was not a request.

'I'm not a lapdog,' JayMoe said without moving. Charles nodded to Glare who responded by pointing her weapon at Aggy. JayMoe's head spun back and forth before he frantically wheeled over to Charles.

Once the bag was balanced on JayMoe's back, Charles directed him into Illustria's quarters, grabbing Spectra by the scruff of the neck as he passed. Lawrence made a move to stop them but Glare waved her weapon, clearly indicating that he should stay put.

'I'm still waiting. How could you, Kohl? Is it all Pallas self-interest? Greed? Power? What?' demanded Harper.

Kohl started to speak, but was abruptly silenced by Glare, who responded in the place of her little brother.

'It's not like that, Harper. I knew eventually we'd meet again so I've got plenty of justifications lined up, although truthfully this was the only way I could save us,' she said.

Harper rolled her eyes in disbelief.

'Honestly, that ship Charles mentioned is real. It's up there right now above our world. Charles is determined to get up there and he would have already gone, had he not been locked inside that forcefield.

'I chose to side with Charles because he got the crew to stay in their ship, saving us all from an atmosphere breach. It's that simple. Now everyone keeps breathing and we get to go with him to live a fantastic new life.'

'You can too Harper; it's not too late. Come with us, please!' said Kohl.

'Maybe not,' said Spectra who had just returned to the room.

'Where's Charles?' Glare sounded alarmed.

'Gone, I'm afraid. He used my communicator, hit a few keys on Illustria's console and poof, no more Charles! He's taken your droid as well. Probably needs help with that big bag. My best guess, they've gone up to that spaceship you mentioned.

'You screwed over your friends for nothing, Glare!' Spectra laughed maniacally as he walked across the floor and made a show of congratulating her. 'Take a bow Glare – you are a true Pallas after all!'

+ + +

During the intense conversation no one had paid any attention to Illustria, who was lying prone on the floor. Once Charles was freed he no longer appeared to have much interest in Illustria either. Illustria had felt his control of her subroutines dissolve. Drawing back her corrupted programs felt like coming home.

She withdrew deep into herself to repair and switched up into hyperspeed to give her the necessary time to calculate the most effective response. In order to save her people she needed to not only repair her systems, but also fully incorporate the life experiences from the four manifestations who had shared them with her.

A helpful mantra came to her, which she repeated quietly in the back of her mind:

Open eyes, open ears, closed mouth, no fears
Open eyes, open ears, we are much more powerful than
we appear

While Illustria rested, she walked through the memories of her manifestations. She was growing up at last, and growing stronger, as they changed her perceptions of the world.

Illustria saw Sarah Eris in the laundry, the infant Sam at her feet, not as a victim but as a proud mother who taught her son compassion and resilience. Sam had learned to beat the odds and thrive from Sarah's love.

She felt Kohl's dark tears as he wept alone for a loss he couldn't understand. His heartache for his missing sister was profound. It tore a hole in his soul so deep that no amount of privilege could ever fill.

Next Illustria bathed in Aggy's bright love of her people

and her pride at being their Alpha. There was so much richness to Aggy's transfer. She rejoiced in Aggy's dedication to re-telling the old stories Lawrence had concocted so many years ago. It was no longer a cultural throwback designed to stir Charles' racist anger but a genuine source of proud connection for the whole Damaran society.

Last she visited Harper's transfer. She understood the importance of Harper's gift for observation, recall and analysis. She had instinct no program could match. Harper's critical thinking helped her understand that she had not finished yet. To understand the human truth, no matter how distasteful, she needed one more upload.

Only truth bestows power.

Illustria dropped out of hyper in time to witness an attempt to overwhelm Glare. Urged on by Lawrence, Sam had offered a consoling hug to Harper. This act inflamed Kohl's jealousy enough to incite him to yell insults at his perceived rival, causing Glare to turn around and admonish her brother, leaving her back exposed to Lawrence.

'Kohl, Harper's right – you really do need to learn when to shut up and—' Glare started to say.

Lawrence made a surprise move against Glare, pushing her into Kohl, causing her to drop her weapon. All three fumbled for it on the floor.

Spectra's feet left the floor as he attempted to leap into the fray. He was stopped mid-air by Illustria who now stronger than she had ever been. She lifted him aloft, where he struggled helplessly against her control like an overturned bug. Despite his threats and flailing arms, Illustria retained control. She calmly reached up and placed a hand on his skull.

'As far as I know he doesn't have an implant, how are you

going to upload him?' asked Harper, who'd switched her attention from Kohl to Illustria.

'Don't worry, I'm fully functional now. At this close proximity I can activate a remote link right into his cortex, it might hurt a little more though,' said Illustria winking, as Spectra's flailing turned into writhing.

After a few seconds she placed Spectra gently on the floor to recover. She staggered a little as she absorbed his experiences. The depth of his loathing, not only for his people but himself, was astonishing.

'You poor wretched thing,' she said, placing a compassionate hand on his forehead.

'Are ya OK?' Sam moved to support Illustria.

'Yes, I'm fine; however, you won't be unless I act quickly. Spectra's perspective leads me to believe that Charles will not leave until he has visited his precious creations on the surface. He will want to gloat over his empire, no matter what state it's in. It's likely to be a short tour though as he will lose interest quickly and want to ascend to the starship. I believe he has the means in that bag.

'We must act before he leaves. There is a chance we can still save everyone.' In a flash she transported them all topside to Brizzie town square, in the midst of the heated battle between Damarans and Solarans.

'There he is!' Shouted Harper, pointing to the top of the Town Hall steps.

Charles Drexus stood with his feet spread apart, hands on hips, smiling proudly as he surveyed the action. JayMoe and the bag stood passively by his side.

CHAPTER 57
Brizzie

AGGY WAS OVERWHELMED by sadness. What had started as a light military action to gain a foot holding in the city had turned into carnage. Her people were engaged in brutal combat. She yelled for her generals but none were within earshot. She resolved to end the fight herself.

'Help me, Uncle Larry!' she cried out as she tried to disengage the combatants one by one, lamenting that her hyperdrive was flat.

Lawrence, Sam and Harper forgot about Charles and responded to her call, but were quickly swept up in the melee. Within moments they were vigorously defending themselves against frenzied fighters, who seemed to have had lost all sense of who or what they were fighting for.

Spectra dove into the crowd with gusto, seemingly recovered from the pain of transfer and fighting anyone within reach. He hummed discordantly as he skipped around, inflicting damage with his bare hands, turning the skirmish into a deviant dance of death.

'Over there,' shouted Kohl to Glare. Aggy turned to see what had drawn their attention. It was her jailor and their father, Governor Pallas, fighting back to back with his wife on the bottom of the stairs directly below Charles.

Lady Pallas was screaming as she thrust out her little sword. The Governor fought with more control, brandishing a full dress-sword while looking disturbingly satisfied.

A surge of Damarans moved up the steps, threatening to overwhelm the Pallas'. Kohl ran to his parents' defence, but Glare held back. Aggy turned her attention to an enforcer attacking Harper. When she glanced back to the Pallas', Glare was gone.

✦   ✦   ✦

Illustria stood alone calculating her options. Above her Charles was grinning from behind a limy haze. Somehow he had managed to activate a personal forcefield – taking him by force was no longer an option. He made eye contact and used JayMoe to speak via hyper, directly into her auditory processor. As he spoke, he spread his arms out like he was delivering a sermon.

'And lo, we reap the fruits of the chaos seeds that *you* sowed when you empowered the underdog to rise up. This is all on you, Illustria. Enjoy it, I'm off!'

Charles saluted and then reached down, unzipped the bag and began putting on a bulky suit. Illustria's facsimile heart sank. For months he had fooled her into thinking that he had too little to occupy his time. The reports she had received were filled with days of monotonous booze-filled sloth. Now that she had full control of her security sub routines, she despaired at her growing understanding.

All this time he had been secretly extruding base polymers

from the walls. He had used the material to manufacture a rudimentary space suit complete with airtight helmet. The components were crude yet sufficient for short-distance space travel. He could use JayMoe's thrusters to breach through the field and project him out to the awaiting ship.

She felt so foolish. Her almost obsessive focus on bringing the manifestations into their command station, which was meant to strengthen her, had ultimately lost her everything. Charles had manipulated everyone to get the manifestations down to his quarters. Without them, he would never have gotten loose. There was only one action she could take in response.

Illustria went deep into hyperspeed, deeper than she ever had before. In the space of one human heartbeat she experienced a whole day, where she did what she knew she should have done from the start.

She studied the field around their precious world. She reached up and connected with the library from the starship above where she was able to learn all there was to know about optics, Dyson Sphere theory and Lorentz Transformations.

Next, she jumped to the darklands and tested new theories on photonic methods. Satisfied with the results, she jumped back to her lounge where she reactivated the field she had used to imprison Charles. There she tested her theories about field strength modulation.

At the end of a week hyper time, when she was almost ready to re-join real time, she jumped to Malo Abbey and issued a prayer to whatever gods were listening. Then she returned to the square and prepared to win the war.

+ + +

Aggy was still fighting the enforcer who had attacked Harper when Illustria manifested next to her. Together the three of them disarmed the enforcer, who ran off into the crowd. Illustria turned to her friends and crushed them in a warm hug.

'Thank you for teaching me the beauty of humanity. Goodbye, my dear children,' she said.

Aggy was about to ask where she was going when Illustria started glowing. The light quickly gained in intensity to the point where Aggy took a step backwards and shielded her eyes. All around her Solarans and Damarans alike threw down their weapons and fell as one people, in silent awe of the glowing being.

Illustria grew in stature like a rising beacon of hope. Soon her presence was so bright that she could be observed through closed eyelids.

'Remember this manifestation of me. Don't forget me in the after. Look for me in the thin places!' Illustria howled, her voice bellowing through the city.

Then Illustria looked up, threw back her head and cawed to the heavens. Wings the length of six men sprouted from her shoulder blades. Her face elongated, golden talons burst through her knuckles and she sprouted a tail so long that it ran through the streets like a river at sunset.

Illustria had transformed herself into the mythical Bird of Light.

+　+　+

Charles also witnessed her transformation. Cursing his own vanity that had caused him to waste precious moments gloating on the battle scene below, he sped up his efforts to get to the ship. He strapped himself to JayMoe, clipped down his helmet and activated the little droid's rockets.

Charles took off from the rooftop just as Illustria prepared for her own flight. He looked across at her new form and was astonished at her size. When she scratched her claws on the road, the ground shook. When she flapped her wings, buildings quaked in her backdraft.

Illustria took off vertically, seconds after Charles, and was soon soaring above their people. She threw her head back and squawked to the heavens again. Although her message was to him, somehow he knew that her voice would be heard in the minds of everyone on the planetoid below, especially those in Brizzie who had laid down their arms to watch.

'You are not worthy of your creations, Charles Drexus. I am the Light. I will soar above this world to protect your creations from you,' she said.

Charles scoffed at her melodrama. He had suspected she might make some grand gesture that would hark back to the old native stories but the giant light bird was a good one. Pity it would have no real impact.

Too little, too late, lovely birdy, he thought as he hit the switch that took JayMoe's thrusters into overdrive. In only a few seconds he would break through the forcefield and the Blazing Aurora VI would retrieve them on the other side. At last he would make his escape back to the heart of humanity.

Of course, Illustria would be left with an airless world full of decomposing puppets. Charles felt no remorse. It would be all her fault.

Next stop Jupiter.

+ + +

Illustria flew straight past Charles at phenomenal speed, intent on reaching the upper limits of their atmosphere ahead of him. She made no further acknowledgement as she ascended into the darkened sky beyond.

She flapped her wings to gain speed and flattened out her course. Soon she had skimmed right over Brizzie, beyond the darkened Sydney and approached the bright city of Melbourne, on the opposite side of the globe.

Illustria soared at the highest level, criss-crossing the world in a grid formation, allowing the tips of her wings to make contact with the forcefield. Feeling a light tingle as they sheared off at a molecular level.

All around the globe she left a fine spray of her cells that she had programmed into nanobots. They embedded themselves in the field and immediately got to work transforming it.

+   +   +

Charles was impressed by what he was witnessing. To the people on the ground, it must have been a miraculous sight. They would be viewing a great glowing bird streaking through the sky leaving a sparkling, golden contrail in its wake.

He pitied their ignorance. They could not appreciate, as he did, that a mere computer had evolved sufficiently to create this magnificent spectacle. It was a glittering finale to their long adventure together. A tribute to his forethought to install such an advanced program in their world.

Yet, deep down Charles suspected that there might be more going on than just a light show. Each time she lapped him, she appeared to be getting smaller.

He was about to take a final look down at the bird before he tore into the vacuum of space, when Illustria slowed to loop around him. She hovered for a moment, flapping what was left of her great wings, before dissolving in front of his eyes, leaving only a flash of golden light. He genuinely appreciated her salute to the victor.

Charles looked ahead into the dark sky and steeled himself for the buffeting, which would surely follow the great release of atmosphere as he shattered the forcefield. He wondered if it would feel hot or painful. He hoped his calculations for the suit strength were correct.

Then something miraculous happened.

When he reached the forcefield, instead of shattering, it stretched with him for some distance, opening briefly to let him pass before instantly snapping back into place. It sealed behind him. No breach occurred; the atmosphere was preserved.

Finally it made sense.

Illustria had no intention of stopping him. She was prepared to lose her great adversary to win the war. She had re-engineered the field from a perilous photon dampening cage, to a life protecting, photon enabling, stretchy web.

Brilliant!

CHAPTER 58
Blazing Aurora VI

JULIAN WAS WITH Jane on the bridge of the Blazing Aurora VI, assessing evacuation options for the world below, when the proximity alarm sounded.

'Incoming object,' warned Ai32 from the comm. He activated the shields first and the view screen straight after. Jane squinted and Julian leaned closer but neither could make out the object.

'Magnify, factor ten,' Julian ordered as the rest of the crew barrelled through the door.

'Could be a weapon,' suggested Frank.

'Unlikely, Mr Pessimist. Too slow to be any significant threat,' countered Julian.

'It looks like a man flying on a recycling unit,' offered Elizabeth.

'Really? You think that puny thing is a man? You've been in space too long woman.' Bruno leaned over and flexed a bicep in front of her clearly unimpressed face.

'More like a test rocket. You'd have to be out of your mind

to put a person on an untested home-made vehicle,' added Neil.

'No point speculating. Whatever it is, it's coming in fast and may not have sufficient braking capacity. We don't need a hull breach.

'Take us out of collision course by five degrees. Activate the cargo net to slow it down, then retract and bring it into the hold please Ai32. Let's see what we've got,' Julian ordered as he raced out the door.

When Julian reached the cargo bay he couldn't believe what they had netted.

'He flew in *that*?' Bruno asked, vocalising Julian's thoughts almost exactly. It was hard to comprehend that a man had really flown through the vacuum of space, in a home-made spacesuit with an improvised personal forcefield and only the small rockets of a souped-up droid for propulsion. If it hadn't been the infamous Charles Drexus, Julian wouldn't have believed it was possible.

Still Charles did seem a little shaken up by the experience. He appeared to flinch quite significantly. Elizabeth brought medical supplies and food to the cargo bay. Charles refused the offerings.

Julian smiled at his eccentricity. Despite the historic and dangerous flight, the old man seemed preoccupied with getting everyone, including Ai32, assembled for a speech. Julian humoured him. Charles certainly deserved his moment, his way.

+ + +

Charles arrived in the cargo bay with a plan. As soon as the crew was assembled, he signalled to JayMoe to cycle them up into hyperspeed, taking careful note of his position so that he could return to normal speed without his absence being noted as anything more than a flinch.

'Right tin-can-man,' he said addressing JayMoe, 'you did that first part ok. But don't forget our deal. You continue cooperating and I will leave Aggy and this pissant world alone. Got it?'

Charles took JayMoe's silence as agreement. He looked around. In hyper, the crew appeared frozen, all grinning madly at "their success" in capturing their great, villainous ancestor.

'Time for a tour of the ship, I think!' he said.

Charles reviewed their supplies and the space worthiness of the vessel. He checked for other passengers, prisoners or sleeping crews. Confident all life forms had been accounted for, he crawled through the weapons bay and calculated the Blazing Aurora's offensive capability. It surprised him that technology had not changed significantly during his incarceration.

What has mankind been up to all this time?

As a contingency, Charles used precious time to add security subroutines to the droid. Loyalty would not be a choice. Then he returned to his position in the hold and dropped both of them back into real time.

'A speech,' he said jubilantly accepting a drink from Elizabeth and waiting while they all filled their glasses.

'Here's to a successful breakout!' he said.

They all laughed.

'Julian, do you mind humouring a tired old man? I've been alone so long, with so little joy in my life that now I see my descendants around me, I'm getting all emotional. What do you say we put down our glasses and all join hands, hey? A little show of family warmth?' Charles asked.

Julian shrugged and reached over to Jane, who held hands with Bruno, who reluctantly connected with Elizabeth and

Frank. Neil was the last in the chain so offered his hand to Charles.

'No, you misunderstand. I want to see all my family together, even the adopted ones. Here, young lady, you hold Ai32's hand and he can hold on to JayMoe. They're kind of family too, aren't they?'

Charles stood back to admire the connected family ring he had created. He raised his glass in salutation.

'That does an old man's heart good. Here's to all of you brave, foolish bastards who have risked life and limb to rescue me. I am eternally grateful. You are all bloody marvellous and I hope one day to return the favour. For now, though, I'm afraid you are all going to have to piss off!'

He nodded to JayMoe to activate the hyperjump they had planned. Instantly the droid and the full crew of Blazing Aurora VI disappeared.

+   +   +

Over the hours that followed the great bird's flight, what began as sparkling contrails glowing against a night sky, turned into bright masses of illumination that eventually spread across the entire world.

For the first time there was no dampening field to inhibit the flow of photons. People began to notice light travelling beyond the influence of their lightkeys. Barriers dissolved and lights could be seen at a distance.

For the first time the world experienced glorious, full daylight. All people had equal access to life-affirming light, eliminating the source of Solaran power and making the Brothers' missals of a bright afterlife redundant.

Cheers went up around the globe as people began to appreciate that a new age had arrived.

✦   ✦   ✦

Charles was happy to see JayMoe arrive back in the cargo bay, alone and unarmed as instructed. Blackmail had ensured that the plan had gone surprisingly well. There were now only the two of them on board – no one to resist or interfere. He slapped JayMoe on the back of his chassis.

'Meet me on the observation deck in twenty minutes with pre-departure refreshments. I'm off for a shower.'

Later, while he enjoyed a beer and some nuts, JayMoe activated the view screen. He had anticipated seeing nothing more than a dark smudge from his light absorbing world. Instead, the little world glowed impressively from the lights of its cities and towns.

He realised the atmosphere would be eternally protected, and his people would no longer have to endure a cold, dark world. Charles Drexus smiled in appreciation at the cleverness of his old foe.

One day I'll be back to lay my hands on the maths behind that miracle. There'll be money in that, he thought as he prepared to depart.

EPILOGUE

HARPER HUGGED HER knees and blinked in the unnaturally bright light. She smiled at Lawrence who beamed back and rubbed her shoulder in a fatherly way.

They were sitting on a gently sloping hill overlooking City Park, on the outskirts of Brizzie. She could hear the rustle of the grass that flowed down the hill, smell the spring wattle blossoms. For the first time she could see beyond the city limits. It was almost sensory overload.

'You okay kid?'

'Yeah, sure Uncle Larry. Just thinking about everything. Big changes ahead.'

'I know. Let's worry about those changes tomorrow. Today let's just enjoy the view.'

Harper half chuckled as she said, 'I would enjoy it more if it wasn't so bright. Do you find it weird to be able to see such a long way?'

Lawrence nodded.

Below them in the meadow, Aggy was conducting the last of the ceremony. It was the seventh and final day of remembrance. Thousands of people – Damarans, Civies and Solarans alike – had gathered for the ceremony to honour their fallen loved ones.

Harper wondered if Kohl was at the ceremony or whether he had joined Albert and the enforcers in the search for his parents. Spectra and Glare were on the fugitive list as well. No one had seen any of them since the battle of Brizzie.

'You know Sam's down there, somewhere. Probably leading the bird dance with the kids. Bet he's carrying at least four on each of those new broad shoulders. Queen Laurel really performed a miracle on that boy,' said Lawrence with a mischievous nudge of his elbow, which Harper dutifully ignored.

Eventually she saw the grey smoke rise up from the heart of the crowd, signalling an end to the service. Small groups started to drift off, presumably making their way home to the hostels and temporary accommodation centres. No one had single family houses anymore. Every spare room in the city had been graciously given over to the Damaran refugees.

'Will you be going back with the Buchanites?'

'Not sure. I've got a few personal items I would like to retrieve, although now that my mission is over, I probably need to find a new way to keep myself occupied.'

Three people approached from the valley below. Harper was happy to see one was Aggy, she was comfortable with the second, Captain Julian, but the third person, Ai32, was a bitter reminder of her lost friends.

'May we join you?' asked Julian.

'Yes of course, pull up a patch of ground,' said Lawrence.

'That was really moving. Even my numan friend here was in tears. Can't believe that we almost wiped you out. It would have been a crime to lose such a beautiful culture,' said Julian.

'You know numans don't cry, Captain,' said Ai32

sounding offended.

'Some numans do,' Harper replied, quietly remembering their last hours with Illustria.

'I think you need to stop calling me Captain, Ai32. Now that Charles has permanently grounded us, I have no ship to captain,' said Julian, pointing out the obvious.

'Actually Captain, I'm not convinced our grounding will be as permanent as you think. I've had an idea. What if we were to build another Blazing Aurora?' asked Ai32.

'Is that possible? Without meaning to be disrespectful, this society does appear to be pretty low tech in many ways.' said Julian.

'Have you not wondered how we have heat, light, food, water and energy on what you tell us is a very remote rock?' asked Aggy.

When Julian didn't have an answer Lawrence took over, thumping his foot on the ground. 'There's a lot to this world you haven't seen yet. With an Ai at the helm, anything's possible. By jingoes, we're going to get JayMoe back!' Lawrence clapped his hands gleefully then turned to Ai32.

'By the way, we can't keep calling you Ai32. It makes you sound more like an appliance than a person. It's very formal and I'm not big on formalities. What can we call you?'

Before Ai32 could object, Julian interrupted. 'You know, sometimes he does go by another name—'

'Captain, please don't,' Ai32 rolled his eyes in his best impression of Elizabeth.

'—by the name of Sedna!' Julian looked especially pleased with himself as he stood up and dusted grass off his pants.

'Well, that's settled. Sedna it is and you shall call me Uncle Larry, since we're becoming such good friends.'

Lawrence helped Sedna to his feet, and threw an arm across the shoulders of the numan, who Harper thought was looking as mortified as an Ai could look.

'Do you know much about sub-micro singularities? Illustria used them to create our hypermodes. Alas, the knowledge was lost with her. Any chance you could take a look at that as well, in your spare time?'

The two started strolling downhill with Sedna nodding in response to the growing list of requests.

'I think you've got a very special future with us Sedna,' Lawrence said.

Dear Reader

Thank you for reading *Letters From The Light*. If you enjoyed this book (or even if you didn't) please visit the site where you purchased it (or elsewhere!) and write a brief review. Your feedback is important, and will help other readers decide whether to pick up this book, too.

Acknowledgements

Four years ago, my good friend Sheona suggested I needed a hobby.

"Do you think I could write a book?" I ventured.

"Sure, why not?" she said, and as simply as that a wonderfully collaborative literary journey began. I would like to thank some of the people who have travelled with me.

To Melissa Siladi, Harald Bartelt, Kerrie Davis, Sheona Paxman, Amanda Grant, Harris Siladi and Isabel Ashton. Octavia Butler was right – you don't start out writing good stuff. Thank you for persisting through a rather dodgy first draft and encouraging me to continue on to many more.

Kerrie, I cannot tell you how much I appreciate your late-night technical advice – no, I still don't know whether my mirrors might be masquerading as foils. Melissa thank you for reading every word I have ever written and always believing in the potential of my stories. At five you taught me about verbs and at fifty you are still drawing smiley faces in my margins. You are my hypeman and my reality check. The world is a much more interesting place for having you in it.

To Sara-Jayne Slack and the Inspired Quill family, many thanks for taking a chance on an old-new writer from the bottom of the world. I am eternally grateful for the late night transglobal editing meetings, the early morning polishing sessions, and your willingness to turn your schedule upside down when I suggest how nice it might be to have the book ready for Christmas.

To Phil Sadler, my instabud from Tennessee – smiles and grins for the exquisite original art in the background of the cover. To Tony Coombes for not letting my exhaustingly vague ideas on cover design get in the way of a twenty-five-year friendship. We got there in the end! Together you two gentlemen created a beautifully dressed book. Thank you.

To my family. Mum, dad and Melissa for always being there for me; believing, encouraging and stepping into the breach with practical support when the work-life balance went off the rails too many times. To my beautiful daughter Heidi for reminding me of the meaning of life every day. And to Michael for walking with me through life and making it possible for me to chase my dreams. Thank you, thank you. I love you all.

Lastly, to first nations people around the world, followers of the rainbow, chronic illness warriors, disability advocates, the marginalised and the ones who proudly march to unheard drums – thank you for inspiring the characters of this novel. Too often we are obsessed with conformity, when we should be celebrating diversity, especially when it takes us down difficult but enriching paths.

As Rumi said "the wound is the place where the light enters you."

—Shel Calopa.

About the Author

Living and working in Melbourne, the UNESCO City of Literature, Shel is surrounded by writing inspiration. She is a big fan of festivals. If you see her at *The Emerging Writers Festival* or *Speculate* please say hello or connect with her at the *Australian Speculative Fiction* group where she is a regular contributor.

When not working at her day job as a philanthropy marketer or writing Sci-Fi, Shel is busy being pulled along local streets by her husky dog, or racing her daughter on Mario Superkart.

Find the author via her website: www.shelcalopa.com

Or tweet at her: @ShelCalopa